"I'm surprised Admiral Schreiber didn't contact me about this while I was on Drakar."

Bingo.

The cracks in Admiral Payne's composure turned into fissures as the comment pushed on a fault line. "He's...away...at the moment. Personal leave."

Aurora pretended surprise. "Oh. I hadn't heard. Do you know when he'll be back?"

"I couldn't say."

Uh-huh. But her emotions were saying plenty. Aurora shrugged as if Payne's reaction was perfectly normal. "It's not important. I was just hoping to see him." She headed for the door. "I'll be in touch."

On the way to the address Cade had given her, she analyzed the bizarre conversation. She'd been in too many mission briefings to accept the Admiral's behavior as normal. It had to be a setup. But for what?

The location for their proposed mission seemed odd, too. Studying a binary system in Teeli space? That was unprecedented. The Teeli had always been cordial in their dealings with the Fleet, but to her knowledge they'd never invited cooperation on matters of science.

The Council was deliberately maneuvering her crew out of Fleet space. She could think of several reasons why, none of them good.

THE HONOR OF DECEIT

Starhawke Rising Book Three

Audrey Sharpe

Ocean Dance Press

THE HONOR OF DECEIT
© 2018 Audrey Sharpe

ISBN: 978-1-946759-05-4

Ocean Dance Press, LLC
PO Box 69901
Oro Valley AZ 85737

Cover art by Significant Cover

Visit the author's website at:
AudreySharpe.com

One

The soft mewl of a muffled sob jerked Aurora Hawke out of dreamland and dropped her onto her bed with a thump.

Her small fists clutched her pillow in a death grip, her neck and shoulders bunched by her ears. Her breath hitched in and out of her raw throat and her tummy filled with rocks.

Turning her head, she stared into the gloom of her bedroom. A breeze blew in through the open window, brushing her wet cheeks. She shivered.

Letting go of the pillow, she curled into a ball, wrapped her arms around her legs and summoned the warmth. The warmth would make the bad feelings go away. It always did.

But her throat and tummy didn't get better. They got worse.

She let go, sliding to the edge of the bed and dropping to the floor with a thud-thud. Her nightgown brushed her legs as she crept over to My-a's bed.

My-a would know what to do. My-a would help her.

But the bed was empty. My-a wasn't there.

Her heart skipped. She glanced around the dark room, the rocks in her tummy getting heavier. Where was My-a? Why wasn't My-a here?

Her breath caught in her throat. She had to find My-a.

Stumbling to the door she grabbed the handle and pulled. Light flooded in from the hallway and voices drifted up from downstairs. Mommy and Daddy's voices. Maybe My-a was with them? But she couldn't see them. The wall was too high.

She ran to the stairs and scrambled down, stopping on the first landing when she saw Mommy and Daddy standing in the center of the main room. But something was wrong. Mommy was crying. Why was Mommy crying?

Daddy turned toward the stairs, and Aurora spotted My-a beside him.

"My-a!" Aurora started down the stairs.

"Aurora. No!" Mommy's words shot at her like arrows.

Aurora stopped. She hadn't done anything bad, had she? She shuffled her feet. "Mommy?"

"Stay there, Aurora." Mommy's face was twisted up and her eyes were wet.

What was wrong with Mommy? And why wasn't Daddy helping? He always knew how to make her laugh when she was sad. Instead, he looked very serious. Why wasn't he making her laugh? "Daddy?"

"Listen to your mother, Aurora."

Daddy's eyes looked wet, too. And his voice was wrong—like a frog.

Daddy put his arm around Mommy and squeezed her tight. So tight.

The rocks in Aurora's tummy got bigger. She started to shake. "My-a?"

My-a peered at her around Daddy.

Aurora wanted to go to My-a. My-a would make her tummy and throat feel better. But Mommy and Daddy had told her to stay put.

Daddy let go of Mommy and took My-a's hand in his. After a long look at Aurora, he turned away from the stairs and walked to the front door, taking My-a with him.

A rushing sound filled Aurora's ears. Daddy and My-a were leaving! She forgot about Mommy and Daddy's words. She forgot about the ache in her throat and tummy. She forgot about everything except getting to My-a.

"My-a!" She raced down the stairs. She didn't care if she fell. The warmth would protect her.

But when her feet touched the floor, strong arms came around her from behind, holding her back.

"No, Aurora." A familiar voice. A soothing voice.

But she didn't listen. She struggled to get free. "My-a! My-a!"

"Ror!" My-a fought too, pulling against Daddy's arm. But Daddy scooped up My-a and kept walking.

Aurora kicked and punched, but the arms holding her didn't let go.

My-a twisted toward her as Daddy opened the door. "Ror!" But Daddy didn't stop. Didn't even look back. The door closed behind them. They were gone.

Heat burned through her like the sun, surrounding her, making her strong. She shoved outward with a screech, clawing her way to freedom.

But a wave of cold blocked the heat, breaking it apart like tissue paper.

She swung around, ready to launch another attack. And met Mya's brown-eyed gaze.

"It's okay, Aurora." Mya stroked Aurora's hair, her touch soothing, calming. "It's going to be okay."

Aurora's head swam as she dragged her gaze away from Mya and stared at the closed door.

"It's okay, Aurora," Mya repeated, pulling her close. Her voice was changing, growing deeper as she repeated the phrase over and over.

Aurora barely heard her. If Mya was the one holding her, then who had walked through the door?

Aurora opened her eyes. Every muscle in her body was clenched, from her curled toes to her tight jaw. Her hands were latched onto the strong arms that held her close.

She blinked and focused. Not feminine arms. Masculine arms, corded with muscle and sprinkled with blonde hair.

"It's okay, Aurora," a male voice said.

She came into the present with a rush. *Cade.*

She wasn't a child anymore. She was on the *Starhawke.* Her ship. In her cabin. With Cade. She looked over her shoulder.

His green eyes clouded with worry. "Hey, there." He brushed her hair back from her face. "You okay?"

She closed her eyes and drew in a shuddering breath. "Only a dream." But even as she said the words, she didn't believe it. It hadn't felt like a dream. It felt like a memory.

"Must have been a bad dream." Cade continued the soothing caress. "Why did you call out Mya's name?"

She cracked open one eye and peered at him. "I said that out loud?"

The low light from the bedside lamp created a halo around his tousled blond hair. He must have turned the lamp on when he'd realized she was having a nightmare. "Yes, you did. A couple times." His brows drew together. "I was afraid to wake you, though. I didn't want to startle you."

No worries, there. The dream had already wound her up. She relaxed her death grip on his arms. "Thanks for watching out for me."

The corner of his lip turned up. "You're welcome."

The tension in her muscles eased as he gathered her close. She'd never met anyone whose presence comforted her the way Cade's did.

His voice rumbled next to her ear. "What were you dreaming about?"

"My family. My mom and dad. And Mya."

"Your dad? Really? I didn't think you even remembered him."

"I don't. At least, not consciously. I was still a toddler when he died." She paused as the significance of what she'd said sank in. "I think that's about how old I was in the dream."

"Huh." He twined his fingers through hers. "What happened in this dream?"

"I was at home. It was nighttime. I saw my parents standing in the main room, hugging. They were acting like they were saying goodbye to each other. But when I tried to reach them, they both told me to stay put."

"Why?"

"I don't know. And then my dad left, taking Mya with him."

"He took her away from you? That *would* be scary. No wonder you were calling out for her."

"Yeah. But that's where it got weird." She tilted her face so she could see his expression. "Someone was holding me back, keeping me from reaching my dad or Mya. But when I looked up, it *was* Mya."

His brows lifted. "That's a twist. So she was both the one being taken away and the one holding you back?"

Aurora nodded.

"Interesting paradox." He traced the curve of her cheek with his finger. "Although it's not surprising that your subconscious would be popping out some strange connections, after all you've been through."

He didn't need to elaborate. They'd both been leaping over hurdles left and right for months.

"I suppose. The part about my dad leaving I certainly get. It's how a two-year-old would interpret the death of a parent—that he left and never came back. And my mom not wanting me to go to him makes sense, too." She mentally worked her way through the dream. "She never wanted to talk about my dad or what happened to him. So, her stopping me from getting close to him fits."

"But what about the paradox with Mya? She's never left you, has she? Or held you back, either."

Aurora sifted through the contradictions, looking for clues. "The part where she was holding me back might have been in response to you, actually."

"Because you think I'm holding you back?"

He said it in a teasing tone, but she detected the current of unease that came with it. Their relationship was still new. He wasn't the only one with doubts about where they stood.

She turned in his arms and placed her hands on his chest. His very warm, very sculpted chest. "Never."

He trailed his fingertips down her neck. "Good."

"But you were holding me here, in the present, and my brain must have integrated that into the dream. That felt very real."

"Makes sense."

"So that just leaves the part about my dad taking Mya away." She chewed on her lower lip. In the dream, she hadn't been able to picture either of them distinctly. Her dad had been a shadowy figure. She'd felt him more than she'd seen him. And while she could replay Mya's actions like she was watching a movie, she couldn't describe what Mya had looked like. Except for one strange detail. "Mya was too young."

"Too young? How so?"

"In the dream, my dad picked her up and carried her. She couldn't have been more than four or five. But I never knew her when she was that age. She was six when I was born."

"What about when she was the one holding you back? How old did she look then?"

Aurora closed her eyes and concentrated, trying to pull up the fragments that were scattering like leaves on the breeze. "Older. At least eight or nine. She looked the way I remember her. Her face was framed by the..." She trailed off as a missing piece settled into place.

"By what?"

She met his gaze. "Her energy field was engaged. And so was mine."

"In the dream? Why?"

"I was angry. Furious, really. And she was trying to calm me down. When I was a kid, Mya always got called in whenever I threw a tantrum. My mom and I would butt heads all the time, but Mya was my rock."

"Which explains why she was the one trying to soothe you in the dream." He nestled her head under his chin, his hands stroking her back. "Sounds like you're feeling vulnerable. The prospect of confronting your mom about your past may be triggering some deep fears."

"It's definitely given me things to think about." Like how she was going to convince her mom to tell her the real story of what had happened to their homeworld forty years ago.

"Are you worried?"

"A little. She's never wanted to talk about it. Stonewalled me every time. And I haven't figured out a new plan, other than showing up unannounced to catch her off guard."

"You'll find a way. Remember, you're not a little girl anymore. You're a strong, capable woman. The captain of a starship. And the guardian of the Suulh." He was silent for a moment. "Are you sure you don't want me to go with you?"

"I'm sure." She sighed. "Explaining how we ended up back together would only complicate things."

He grunted. "I'm not exactly your mom's favorite person."

"True." She placed a kiss on his neck. "But you're one of mine."

"Thank you."

She followed the kiss with a nip, eliciting a rumble that was somewhere between a purr and a moan. "And I'll have Mya with me." As well as Kire and Jonarel. But she wasn't about to bring Jonarel's name into the discussion.

Cade tilted her chin up and brushed his lips across hers, sending shivers of sensation racing along her nerve endings. "What happens if you need to blow off steam afterward? I won't be there to help you." The heat building in his eyes left no doubt as to what kind of help he was referring to.

The last time she'd needed that kind of assistance, Cade had been happy to supply it—in a panoply of pleasurable ways. That night had changed everything.

She cradled his face in her palms. "You'll only be a call away. And I'll see you when we return." She traced the curve of his bottom lip with her thumb, and his eyes darkened. "You'll be busy at Council HQ tracking down leads on the Admiral's disappearance. He needs your help too, you know." And that thought made a different kind of tension curl in her belly.

His hands settled on her hips and upper back, pulling her flush against his chest. "Hey. Don't you start worrying about the Admiral. You have enough on your plate. Locating the Admiral is my job."

"I know. But—"

"Uh-uh." He tightened his grip. "No arguments."

"But—"

He silenced her with a kiss, coaxing her lips apart with a deft touch that turned her inside out.

She was breathing hard by the time he released her. She gazed into his eyes. "Cocky man. You think you can make me forget about the Admiral, don't you?"

His smile was pure sin as he rolled her to her back, pinning her to the mattress. "Rory, before I'm done, I'm going to make you forget your own name."

He was right.

Two

The noisy bar looked like a million other hole-in-the-wall establishments of its kind, hunkered down in a section of a former mining tunnel at the center of a barren moon. It sat cheek-to-jowl with the grimy storefronts of businesses of questionable repute, most shuttered for the night cycle.

The transient clientele passing through the bar's doors was a hodgepodge of humanity drawn from freighters, passenger transports, and ships that didn't broadcast their primary function. Locals were an endangered species on the small moon, but a few had remained after the mines had closed, working the hard labor jobs that kept the outpost running, and living in the cell-like dormitories that served as housing for the underprivileged.

For those in positions of power, money still poured through the former mining outpost like water. *Might makes right* was the local code enforced by those who made a living from illegal and unsavory practices. On Gallows Edge, anything could be purchased for a price. And a steady stream of visiting ships insured an abundant supply.

The bar was no different. It wasn't a fancy place. It wasn't even a cheerful place. But the liquor flowed and the gaming tables provided temporary distraction from the troubles of life beyond the front door.

A man walked along the hard concrete path that followed the carved rock wall of the tunnel on one side and the block masonry of the buildings on the other. The pale yellow glow from the overhead lights cast shadows on his lined face as he made his way to the bar's entrance. The heavy metal door swung open with a groan. He paused in the doorway, scanning the collection of dark booths and scattered tables to the left and the gaming tables to the right, before claiming a vacant stool at the L-shaped bar along the back wall.

The bartender approached, exchanging a few words and taking payment before placing a thick mug of something pungent and amber-colored in front of the stranger.

The man sipped his drink, his gaze on the row of garish and grandiose liquor bottles displayed behind the bar, though anyone paying close attention would have spotted the sidelong glances he gave each customer who passed through the front door.

The stranger ran his hand over his bald head in an unconscious gesture he'd made a thousand times. He set the empty mug on the stone-topped bar and summoned the bartender, sliding a few thin disks across the expanse, which quickly disappeared into the bartender's hand.

The bartender took his time pouring the stranger another drink. He rested his arms on the bar after he delivered it, his voice too low to carry over the murmur of conversation and the clicks and clatters from the gaming tables. A curt nod from the stranger was the only confirmation that a deal had been made.

A flow of customers came and went, but the stranger remained at the bar, apparently lost in his own thoughts. No one paid him any mind, including the young woman who entered the room through an archway along the back wall.

She approached the bar, drawing glances from the other customers as she passed. A dark brown duster concealed her figure, but couldn't disguise her petite stature. The haphazard cut of her dark hair didn't improve on the scowl that marred her delicate features. She settled onto an

"Good call." Aurora murmured. Her mom had a passion for decorating, especially with lights. The plants in her mom's greenhouse and outdoor nursery were always decked out, but at home she strung lights everywhere, including places that required an extension ladder and two sets of hands to access, thanks to the two-story domed ceiling. Since Gryphon, Mya's dad, was a head taller and had a longer reach, she usually cajoled him into helping her.

"She's already putting up holiday decorations?" Kire's thin brows lifted as his gaze met Aurora's. "But we're barely into November."

"In my mom's world, it's never too early to decorate for the holidays." And Aurora loved that about her. When her mom was in the throes of whatever decorating scheme she had in mind, she let go of her obsessive fear and worry, if only for a little while. "If she and Gryphon are working on the main room, then she's already finished the Hawke wing."

"And she was threatening to start on my family's side." Mya glanced out the window and smiled. "You'll see soon enough. We're here."

The irregular curve of the cove and the rocky bluff that shouldered the small town to their left came into view as the monorail slid into the station.

Jonarel was out of his seat before the train stopped. He grabbed Aurora's overnight bag off the rack and handed it to her.

"Thank you." She slipped it onto her back with a slight shrug. Her years in the Fleet had taught her how to pack light.

None of the other passengers, male or female, dared to push past Jonarel as he blocked the aisle, making room so Aurora could lead the way to the exit, with Mya and Kire close behind.

Now that she knew how much he was suffering, every act of kindness he showed her pricked like a needle. She also couldn't shake the feeling that he was biding his time to see if her relationship with Cade would take a bad turn. Hopefully it wouldn't. For many reasons.

She joined the stream of passengers as they disembarked and made their way down the stairs to the transport center.

A squeal from Mya announced that she'd spotted Marina. Moving with uncharacteristic exuberance, her friend darted through the crowd and launched herself into her mom's arms, almost taking Marina down in the process.

Aurora slowed her steps, not wanting to interrupt, but a lump lodged in her throat as she watched them. She'd always yearned for the kind of openness that Mya and Marina shared. They were so relaxed together, so comfortable. And the older they got, the more they acted like best friends rather than mother and daughter.

Aurora had never felt that way around her mom. They had fun together, but her mom never treated her like a friend. There was always a parental line Aurora was not allowed to cross. After the revelations on Gaia and Azaana, Aurora had a better understanding of why her mom kept barriers around her emotions, barriers that were as impenetrable as her energy shield. But that didn't make the situation any easier.

Marina had a knowing look in her brown eyes as she released Mya and pulled Aurora into a hug. "Welcome home, Sahzade."

She sank into the comfort Marina offered. "Thank you, Marina. It's good to be home."

"And it's good to have you here." Marina's smile widened as her gaze shifted to Jonarel. "My, my, Jonarel. Is it

my imagination, or have you gotten bigger since the last
time I saw you?"

Jonarel's golden eyes glowed with amusement.
"Perhaps. I have to work hard to keep up with your daughter
and Aurora."

Marina laughed. "Now that, I believe." She turned to
Kire. "And how are you, Kire? Happy you left the Fleet to
join Aurora's crew?"

He grinned. "Absolutely. Life on the *Starhawke* is
never boring."

Marina's smile faded as her gaze returned to Aurora.
"You won't have to worry about boredom while you're here,
either." Marina wrapped her arm around Aurora's waist and
squeezed. "Don't worry, Sahzade. You can do this."

The lump in her throat turned into a boulder. "I hope
you're right."

Marina kept everyone busy answering questions
about the *Starhawke* during the drive, but it did little to
distract Aurora from the upcoming confrontation. The
drizzling rain and grey clouds covering the sky matched her
mood perfectly.

Marina made the turn off the main road and they
twined down the driveway, their path lit by box lanterns that
guided them through the redwoods. At the end of the lane
the trees parted to reveal the stone foundation and domed
wooden roofline of the house her mom had christened
Stoneycroft.

The structure had been built before Aurora was
born, and like the settlement on Azaana, it was based on a
classic Suulh design, with a half-moon wing for Aurora's
family on one side, and a matching one for Mya's family on
the other. The main room joined the two in the center,
providing communal living and dining space.

Marina pulled into the detached garage that connected to the main house through a vine-covered portico. The greenery grew so lush along the trellis that the path was almost weatherproof.

As Aurora walked through the archway into the central room of the house, a feeling of unreality washed over her. Images from her dream overlaid the scene like ghosts of the past. Her gaze traveled from the wide foyer near the front door to the curving staircase that led to the upstairs gallery. Had it only been a dream? Or part of a memory?

Her mom stood at the base of a tall ladder, feeding a light strand up to Gryphon, who was attaching the lights to the archway of the east wing.

"Look who I found wandering the streets!" Marina called out.

Aurora's mom turned, her grey-blue eyes widening in shock. "Aurora!" Dropping the lights like they were on fire, she covered the distance between them in several long strides and yanked Aurora into her arms, crushing her ribcage in a fierce grip.

"Hi, Mom," Aurora wheezed.

"Oh, my baby girl." Her mom's eyes glistened as she stepped back, keeping a grasp on Aurora's upper arms like she was afraid to let go. "Why didn't you tell me you were coming?"

"I wanted it to be a surprise." Which was certainly true.

Her mom glanced at Marina. "But you knew?"

"Uh-huh."

Her mom's eyes narrowed. "For how long?"

Marina was the picture of innocence. "A few days. But I didn't want to ruin the surprise, just in case their plans changed."

"I see." Aurora's mom pulled her into another hug, this one less likely to break any ribs. "I've missed you."

"I've missed you, too."

She released Aurora, her gaze moving to where Jonarel stood with Kire. Her smile widened. "Jonarel! You came, too?"

"I go where Aurora goes."

Aurora stifled a groan. Her mom would read meaning into that comment that wasn't accurate.

"Of course you do." Her mom gave Jonarel a hug, her petite frame dwarfed in his arms. "And Kire. Good to see you, too. Welcome to our home."

"Thank you, Ms. Hawke. I'm honored to be here."

"And we're delighted to have you. As you can see, we're gearing up for the holidays." Her mom clapped her hands together. "This is my favorite time of year."

"The plethora of lights are a good clue." Gryphon winked at Aurora as he pulled her and Mya against his sides in a three-person hug. "Welcome home, you two." He ruffled Mya's hair like he used to when she was a kid.

She gave him a playful shove. "Dad."

He chuckled, his lean face creased in a smile as he shook hands with Kire and Jonarel. Unlike Aurora's mom, Gryphon stood shoulder-to-shoulder with Jonarel, although Jonarel's muscular frame made Gryphon look thin by comparison. "I think you've grown since the last time I saw you."

"That's what I said." Marina glanced at Mya. "Don't you agree?"

A slight blush tinged Mya's cheeks as her gaze darted from her parents to Jonarel. "Uh. I guess so. I haven't really noticed."

Aurora studied her friend. Mya did not blush easily, but for some reason she seemed embarrassed by her parents' comments. And she was avoiding Aurora's gaze. Interesting.

"Is that your famous zucchini bread I smell?" Mya asked her dad, turning toward the open kitchen.

He nodded. "Baked it this morning. Is anyone hungry? I made a big batch of vegetable stew for dinner. And brownies for dessert."

Now that Mya had mentioned it, Aurora caught the tantalizing aromas wafting from the kitchen. She'd grown up enjoying Gryphon's culinary creations, which were always hearty, nourishing, and delicious. She had a particular weakness for his fudge brownies.

"If you're offering, I'll take you up on it," Kire said. "The food we had on the monorail tasted like cardboard."

Gryphon made a face. "That isn't food. Let's get you boys settled in and I'll serve you a meal you'll never forget." He motioned to Kire and Jonarel to follow him through the archway of the west wing to the guest quarters.

Jonarel shot Aurora a look that made her lips twitch. Gryphon was probably the first person in more than a decade who had referred to Jonarel as a boy.

"Your rooms are ready, too." Marina picked up Mya's pack as the men left the room. "I made them up this morning while Libra was on her walk."

Aurora's mom pursed her lips. "If you had told me they were coming, I could have helped."

"And ruin the surprise? Never."

Aurora and Mya followed their moms up the stairs. When they reached the first landing, Aurora paused, glancing over her shoulder at the foyer. Yep. Exactly as it had appeared in her dream. A shiver of unease trickled down her spine.

"Something wrong?" her mom asked.

They'd all stopped, waiting for her. Aurora shook her head. "Just taking it all in."

"How long are you staying?" her mom asked as they reached the second landing. Mya and Marina took the stairs to the west side of the house, while Aurora and her mom turned right, to the east wing.

That all depends on you. But she certainly wasn't going to say that. "We don't have a set timetable. I left Celia in charge of the *Starhawke.*" Her mom and Celia had never met, but Aurora and Mya had shared plenty of photos and stories about Celia with their parents over the past two years.

"You must have a lot of faith in her."

"I trust her with my life. I can certainly trust her with my ship."

Her mom was silent as they walked through the archway that led to Aurora's childhood room. As Aurora pushed open the door, more images from her dream drifted back like déjà vu.

She glanced toward the spot where Mya's bed had sat. Of course, it wasn't there now. Mya had moved into her own room on the other side of the house when Aurora was five. The twin beds had been replaced with an adult-sized sleigh bed and a decorating scheme that her mom had tried to talk her out of for months, although Aurora had prevailed.

Hundreds of celestial objects hung from the ceiling— stars, planets, even miniature comets, most of which glowed in the dark. The curtains were made of a velvety material in midnight blue with small gold stars stamped over it. The deep blue matched the sheets and comforter on the bed that depicted a starscape. Aurora hadn't spent much time in this room after she'd left for the Academy at thirteen, but it was still her favorite spot in the house. And her mom hadn't changed a thing.

"Still looks the same." Aurora dropped her bag on the desk beneath the window. For a moment, she pictured curtains fluttering in the breeze of a warm summer night, even though the window was shut tight against the winter chill. She shivered.

"Aurora?"

She turned, and found her mom standing in the doorway, watching her.

"Yes?"

"When are you going to tell me why you're really here?"

Busted. "What do you mean?"

Her mom rested her hands on her hips. "I'm not a simpleton. You have your own ship now. And while I'm happy to see you, I find it hard to believe that you just happened to be in the area with nothing to do."

Aurora swallowed. "I needed to check in with Admiral Schreiber." *True.* "I haven't talked to him in a while." *Also true.* "It seemed like a good excuse to come visit you." *Liar, liar, pants on fire.* "I didn't get a chance to see you before we left in August."

Her mom's expression tightened. "I'm sorry about that. I know how much you wanted me to see your ship."

Aurora shrugged. "It's okay. Space travel has never appealed to you. I get that." *Now more than ever.*

"So, you're not mad at me?"

such despair punched her in the gut. She'd been hoping her mom would give her hope. "I know it won't be easy. But we must convince Libra to tell Aurora the truth. So much depends on it."

"She'll never do it." Her mom shook her head, her gaze straying to the hallway outside the partially closed door. "Never."

Mya stiffened. Not the response she'd wanted. And not the response Aurora needed. "Aurora's not going to give her a choice." *And I'm not giving you one, either.*

She didn't say the words out loud, but her tone must have conveyed the idea, because her mom pinned her with a look.

"We have to succeed, Mom. Those refugees are only the beginning. If Aurora and I are right, there are thousands more who need our help."

Five

Cade's comband pinged as he exited the transport he and his number one. Justin Byrnes, had hired to take them to Admiral Schreiber's beach house. He glanced down, his pulse quickening, but the message wasn't from Aurora. Just an automated alert notifying him that payment for his fare had been accepted.

He sighed as the vehicle pulled away and continued down the street. His team spent so much time on starships or far-flung planets that day-to-day suburban life on Earth seemed alien by comparison. The place that felt most like home nowadays was the *Starhawke*. With Aurora.

But she was dealing with her own problems right now. Going home wouldn't be a picnic for her. He understood why she hadn't wanted him along, but it still rankled. Especially since Clarek had received an invitation.

Pushing away the unwelcome thought, he shifted his attention to the curving driveway that led to the sprawling house overlooking the Pacific.

Justin stood a little way up the drive, surveying the surrounding hills.

"See anything unusual?" Cade asked as he joined him.

"Not yet."

"Alert me if that changes." Cade continued up the driveway, with Justin close behind.

The house was modest compared to most in the area, but the location was primo. While not an extravagant man by nature, the Admiral loved the sea almost as much as he loved space. A well-worn path to the left led to a set of stairs and a private beach at the bottom of the bluff.

Cade had spent quite a few evenings on that beach with his team and the Admiral, discussing upcoming missions and enjoying the view of the setting sun on the water. Hopefully they'd have that opportunity again. But first they needed to find the Admiral and bring him back safe and sound. Cade refused to even consider the alternative.

The wind off the water had a bite this time of year, making the air feel a lot colder than his comband indicated. He pulled the collar of his jacket tighter and quickened his pace. Keeping one hand within reach of his pistol, he strode up the stone walkway to the front door. Justin watched his back as Cade stepped in front of the security scanner.

"Welcome, Cade Ellis," an electronic male voice greeted him. "I regret to inform you that no one is available to see you at this time. Would you like to leave a message?"

Exactly the response he'd expected. Slipping a hand into his pocket, he retrieved one of Bella Drew's tech gadgets and attached it to the security scanner. The Admiral wouldn't mind if he bypassed the system. There was a reason he'd selected Cade to lead the Elite Unit.

The system emitted a bell tone and the front door swung open on well-oiled hinges.

Cade stepped inside and did a quick visual scan of the foyer. Siginal Clarek had stated that he hadn't heard from the Admiral in a few weeks. The condition of the house confirmed the Admiral's absence. The inside air smelled stale and a thin coating of dust covered the console table in the entryway.

Justin closed and locked the door, his gaze sweeping their surroundings. "I'd hoped we were wrong."

"Me, too." Cade motioned in the direction of the Admiral's study. "I'll secure the rest of the house while you tap into the Admiral's personal files."

"On it." Justin crossed the planked floor while Cade turned right toward the kitchen.

Searching the house only took a few minutes. He didn't find any sign of forced entry, and all the furnishings were where they belonged. But the house had an abandoned feeling to it. He and Justin were probably the first people to set foot inside in more than a month.

Where had the Admiral gone? And why hadn't he left word with Siginal Clarek? Cade didn't like the pompous Kraed, but right now he was their best link to the Admiral's movements. If they didn't turn up anything here or at Council HQ, he'd have to ask Aurora to reach out to the Admiral's son, Knox. That would involve going through Fleet channels, which would leave a trail, something he'd prefer to avoid. The Admiral had indicated he didn't know who at the Council they could trust. But Knox was Aurora's former captain, so she might be able to contact him without drawing undue attention to their search.

He hadn't talked to the Admiral since Gaia. He and Aurora had followed their orders to maintain comm silence until the Suulh were safely transported to their new home. It had seemed like a wise move at the time. They hadn't anticipated that the Admiral would disappear in the interim.

As commander for the Elite Unit, Cade had sworn an oath to serve and protect the Admiral and the Fleet. But his commitment went way beyond the bounds of his job. If anything happened to the Admiral on his watch, he'd never forgive himself.

"What have you learned?" he asked Justin as he joined him in the study.

Justin swept his fingers across the surface of the Admiral's desk, pulling up multiple files. "Nothing that would indicate where he is. According to his calendar, he left five weeks ago for a two-week inspection tour aboard the *Cassini.* He never returned. I cross-referenced a note from his Council data file that indicates the Fleet has placed him on medical leave."

"Medical leave?" Cade's stomach twisted. "Do they say what for? Or where he's being treated?"

"The medical files are locked. It looks like the *Cassini* was at Hydra One when he was admitted, but I can't find anything that confirms that he's still there." Justin met Cade's gaze. "Big red flag."

"Agreed. We need to keep digging." And they wouldn't find any more answers here.

He sent a request for another transport as they stepped out onto the front porch. "Ping Williams and see if he can pull any information from the medical files." Since Tam Williams was the Admiral's personal physician, he had a legitimate reason to access the Admiral's private medical records.

Justin sent the message from his comband. "Bella and I can track the digital trail—Fleet communications and reports. See what we can learn."

Cade refastened the front of his jacket while they waited for their ride. "Good. Have Reynolds and Gonzo reach out to their contacts and see if anyone has noticed unusual activity at Council HQ in the last couple months."

"What are you going to do?"

"Check in with Lieutenant Magee at HQ. Hopefully she'll have information for us." Magee had been the Admiral's aide for years, and was a loyal friend of the family. She wasn't aware of the Elite Unit's true function, but if the

Admiral had entrusted someone with a message for Cade, she would have been the logical choice.

"And if she doesn't?"

"Then I'll be shaking a few trees. I'll also contact Reanne Beck and find out the last time she heard from the Admiral. We'll need her to arrange for off-planet transportation for the unit in a few days, anyway." Talking to Reanne was one of his least favorite activities, but he wasn't about to quibble while the Admiral was AWOL.

They caught the transport back into the city, parting ways outside Council HQ. Justin left to meet Drew while Cade headed inside the high rise.

He bypassed the elevator in favor of the stairs. He could use a little exercise to calm his agitation. He exited on the tenth floor and passed through security, using his Fleet Commander credentials to insure no one would ask questions about why he was there. The Admiral had provided his unit with several sets of security passes which could be switched out depending on the mission they were asked to complete. The one he used the most identified him as a Rescue Corps pilot.

The Admiral's office suite was located at the back of the building. The outer door to the suite was closed, but the glass insets on either side showed the lights were on inside.

Cade pushed the door open. A man he'd never seen before sat behind Magee's desk to his left.

The man glanced up when Cade entered. "Can I help you?"

Cade paused as warning lights flashed. *Where was Magee?* "I'm looking for Lieutenant Magee. I was told she worked in this office." He'd play dumb until he figured out who he was dealing with.

"She used to." The corners of the man's eyes narrowed a fraction, his expression growing more intense. Analyzing. Evaluating.

Alarm bells joined the warning lights. "Used to?"

"She's been reassigned. Maybe I can help you. What did you need to talk to her about?"

No way was he giving this joker any information. He ignored the question. "Do you happen to know where she was reassigned?"

"I'm not at liberty to say. But I'd be happy to forward a message. What's your name?" The man sounded like he was trying to be helpful, but his eagerness had little to do with providing assistance. He looked like a cat waiting to pounce on a mouse.

Cade's heart rate accelerated. This was worse than he'd anticipated. The Council wouldn't have reassigned Magee unless they believed the Admiral wasn't coming back.

The man behind the desk had informant written all over him. He'd been planted here by someone. But who?

Cade wanted answers, answers he wouldn't find here. He needed to disengage without drawing attention from this troll. "Don't worry about it." He flicked his hand and summoned a cocky grin. "This was personal business. Met her in a bar last month. Guess I waited too long to follow through. But I was otherwise...occupied. You know how it is." He tossed in a conspiratorial *it's tough when you're in high demand* look for good measure.

The troll swallowed the lie in one gulp. His smile made Cade's skin crawl. "Her loss."

Cade shrugged nonchalantly. "A lot more fish in the sea. Thanks, anyway." He was out the door before the other man could reply.

He wiped his palms on his pants as he walked down the hallway. He needed a shower after that encounter. The aftertaste of the offensive words he'd spoken didn't help, either. If Aurora ever heard him talking like that, he'd be lucky to keep his knees intact.

He made his way back to the stairwell. After checking to make sure he was alone, he opened a comm channel to Justin. "Magee has been reassigned."

"*What?* Why?" Justin sounded as dumbfounded as Cade had been.

"The troll who took her place wasn't offering information. I need you and Drew to track her down. And find out when the orders came through and who authorized them."

"We're on it. And Cade?"

"Yeah?"

"This is bad."

"I know. I'll check in after I've talked to Reanne." He closed the channel and headed down seven flights to the Rescue Corps offices. Flashing his pilot ID at the security station, he proceeded to the Director's office. Pilots held a privileged position in the RC, and Reanne had made a point of getting to know all of them. That had made it easier for him to visit her office without drawing attention whenever he needed to coordinate mission details for the Elite Unit.

The Admiral had been in close contact with Reanne while they'd been on Gaia, and he'd still been working with her when Cade had left the planet with the Suulh refugees. He was hoping she'd be able to fill in some of the gaps about the Admiral's movements since then. She might not be in her office, but he could leave a message with her assistant, Sarah, if necessary.

A dagger twisted in his gut, but he had to be realistic. To find the Admiral, they needed money. And a ship. Right now, they were zero for two.

His team...no, his *friends*...exchanged glances, but it was Justin who fixed Cade with a pointed look. "If you think any of us are bailing just because we're against a wall, then you're an idiot. We're in. All of us. We'll find the Admiral. Whatever it takes."

He swallowed past the tightness in his throat. "Then we need a plan."

Six

The muscles around Aurora's mouth ached from the effort of keeping her smile in place. All through dinner she'd forced herself to join in the good-natured banter as Gryphon regaled Kire and Jonarel with stories or embarrassing anecdotes from hers and Mya's childhoods. Her mom and Marina had chimed it with a few as well, but Gryphon was in his element. He loved having guests, and his vibrant presence kept the lively discussion going.

She welcomed the distraction. Her chest felt like it was caught in a vise. And sitting next to her mom wasn't helping.

Gryphon rubbed his hands together and stood. "Who's ready for brownies?"

Aurora jumped up like her chair was on fire. "I am." She grabbed her empty bowl and reached for her mom's.

"I can do that." Her mom moved to stop her, but Aurora waved her back into her chair.

"I've got it." She needed some space, even if it was just the short distance to the kitchen counter.

Jonarel and Kire followed her lead, gathering bowls and plates while Mya helped Gryphon serve the dessert and coffee.

Aurora took her time clearing the table and organizing the dishes for cleaning. What she really wanted to do was go for a run to release the nervous tension winding her up like a clock.

Marina shot her a sympathetic look as she returned to the table.

"Will you have time to stop by Hawke's Nest while you're here?" Aurora's mom asked, taking a sip from her coffee mug.

The question caught her off guard. "Uh, I suppose so. Maybe tomorrow?" Unless her mom wasn't speaking to her by tomorrow.

Her mom smiled. "Wonderful. I've hired two additional part-time staff to help with the holiday requests for wreaths, poinsettias, and live trees."

Over the years, her mom's nursery had developed a reputation for the finest plants and holiday decorations in the northwest, drawing loyal customers from San Francisco to Seattle. "Do you still decorate all the wreaths yourself?"

Her mom's grey-blue eyes twinkled. "That's half the fun."

It used to be fun for her, too. She'd always loved helping her mom assemble the wreaths she gave to loyal customers as gifts. Coming home for the holidays was one of the things she'd missed since joining the Fleet. Seasonal celebrations were quite different when you lived on a starship.

Her mom slipped her hand over Aurora's and squeezed. "But I miss having you here. It's just not the same without you and Mya around."

"I know." Her mom wasn't trying to make her feel guilty. But her words had that effect anyway.

"But at least you're here, now."

Oh, yeah. That made her feel *much* better. She expected her spine to crack from the weight pressing down on her shoulders. She glanced across the table to keep her mom from reading her expression, and discovered Marina watching her.

Marina gave Gryphon a subtle nudge with her elbow as he sat down.

He glanced at her, then his gaze focused on Aurora, picking up his cue. "So, Sahzade, tell us what you've been up to on that impressive ship of yours." He leaned back in his chair in a casual pose that contradicted the line of emotional gunpowder he'd just poured across the table.

Aurora wet her lips. Showtime. "We've been busy." She clenched her hands in her lap to keep them from shaking. "For our first mission, the Council sent us to investigate mysterious plant destruction on Gaia."

Her mom jerked in her chair. "Gaia?"

"You were on Gaia?" Marina echoed. A flare of anxiety flowed from both women, tension visible on their faces.

"Yes." Aurora shot a look at Mya, who shrugged, apparently as confused by their moms' reactions as she was.

And here she'd expected the beginning of the story to be the easy part. "Entire farms had been laid to waste by an unknown force. The structures were fine, but all the plant life had been destroyed, with no clear cause."

"Was anyone hurt?" Marina asked.

"No, thankfully. The attacks occurred at night while the residents were sleeping."

"Attacks? So this was planned?" Gryphon asked.

"Yes." They just didn't know by whom.

"Were you able to figure out the cause?"

Aurora's gaze shifted to Mya, drawing strength from her calm presence. "Yes, we did. The plants' cellular structure was destroyed using energy fields."

Her mom's sharp intake of air matched the spike in her anxiety. "Energy fields?"

"Yes." *Breathe, Aurora. In. Out. You can do this.* She faced her mom. "Exactly like the ones we generate."

Her mom gaped at her, her gaze darting to Jonarel and Kire. "What are you talking about?"

Aurora continued before her courage could fail her. "Jonarel and Kire already know what Mya and I can do. It's not a secret anymore."

Her mom's eyes widened. "*What are you saying?* You didn't—"

"I did. Jonarel's known since I met him. And Kire found out during the mission."

Her mom trembled like a leaf, her hands gripping the edge of the table.

"But it's okay. They would never betray us. You can trust them."

Kire spoke up. "Jon and I would never say or do anything to hurt Roe or Mya, Ms. Hawke. We're here to help."

"Help?" The word came out on a puff of air. "Help with what?"

Aurora braced for impact. "With rescuing the Suulh."

"*Suulh?*" Her mom's gasp sounded like the scrape of a match.

"Yes, Suulh. We rescued three hundred of them from the ship that attacked Gaia."

Her mom stared at her. "You *saw* them?"

"Yes. And they recognized us by our energy fields." She held her mom's gaze, willing her to hear her words. "Mom, we're not the last of our race."

Her mom's mouth sagged open. She tried to speak, but nothing came out. At least, nothing audible.

Aurora took advantage of the silence to make her plea. "The Suulh need our help."

Anger replaced the fear in her mom's eyes, turning them into twin storm clouds. "That's why you're here?"

"Yes. I need your help. Please." She reached for her mom's hand but grasped only air.

Her mom shoved away from the table. "I can't help."

Aurora stood. "Yes, you can. We're the Sahzade. The Guardians. It's our job to protect them."

"*Protect* them?" Her mom's mouth twisted into a snarl as she turned her anger on Mya. "You promised you would never tell her!"

Mya didn't flinch. "I didn't."

"Then how—"

"The Suulh called her Sahzade when they saw her energy field."

Her mom crossed her arms, her glare sweeping between Mya and Aurora like a laser beam.

Marina left her chair and moved around the table to Aurora's side. "Please, Libra. Be reasonable. We have a responsibility. We ne—"

"Not anymore."

Marina's dark eyes flashed fire. "So you're going to turn your back? Ignore the fact that our race survived after we left forty years—"

"We can't change the past!" Her mom's voice shook. "You know what they did! What they *will* do! We saw—" She slapped her hand over her mouth and stared at Aurora in shock.

"It's okay, Mom." The jumble of emotions rolling off her mom in waves made it difficult to focus, but it made it easier to understand her mom's stance. "You want to keep me safe. And I appreciate that. But you can't protect me anymore. I know the truth."

"No, you don't."

Not what she'd expected. "What do you mean?"

Her mom just shook her head and backed away.

Marina moved with her. "Libra, stop. It's time to end this. You've kept her in the dark long enough. Too long, actually."

Her mom rounded on Marina. "Who are *you* to tell *me* how to protect *my* child? Just because you don't care about yours—"

"That's enough!" Marina stalked forward until they were centimeters apart. "You think you're *protecting* her? Because that's not what I see. She's not a child anymore. And all of us have a responsibility to..."

"No, we don't!" Her mom's shriek echoed through the room. "The only responsibility I have is to Aurora! And I will protect her to my last breath!"

Her mom's pain burned Aurora like a brand. She wanted to ease her suffering, not make it worse. But she couldn't turn her back on the horrors the Suulh had endured as Necri, either. Hundreds, maybe thousands, of Suulh were still trapped in that unspeakable existence. She'd felt their pain, too.

She took a cautious step toward her mom, hands out in supplication. "I know you don't want me to get hurt, Mom. I don't want you to hurt, either. But it's not just about us anymore. This is so much bigger. The ones we found? They're only the beginning. There are more out there. I've felt them. And they're in pain."

"Pain." Her mom spit out the word. "What do you know about pain?"

Aurora reeled like her mom had slapped her. *What did she know about pain? Was she serious?* Her temper flared, but she tamped it down. Her mom was trying to goad her, get her off track. She couldn't allow that to happen. "Please, Mom. Help me."

Her mom stared at her for an eternity. "What do you want from me?"

Aurora spread her arms. "The truth. To know what you know about the past. To hear the story of what really happened when our homeworld was attacked and you fled."

"Why? Because you think you can save them?"

"Yes, I do."

"Then you're a fool."

The words tore a hole in her patience. "Then help me to understand! Tell me who attacked the homeworld."

"No."

"*No?*" The hole turned into a canyon. Aurora threw her hands up. "They're keeping the Suulh in *cages*, Mom! And using their own children as blackmail. They almost captured *me*!"

Her mom fell back a step, placing a hand over her heart like she'd been stabbed. "Captured you?" Her gaze shifted to Jonarel and she jabbed an accusing finger at him. "You *promised* me! You swore that you would protect her."

Jonarel flinched as the accusation hit its mark. "I failed."

Aurora wasn't about to let her mom launch an attack on Jonarel. "It's not his job to protect me. It's *my* job. Just as it's my job to protect the Suulh."

"No, it's not." Her mom's eyes took on the haunted look Aurora had seen since she was a child. "You can't win."

The hopelessness in those words ripped Aurora apart.

Gryphon appeared by her side. He rested his hands on her shoulders, offering his support. "We don't know that,

Libra. We were all so young when we fled. You were just a child."

"And Aurora's *my* child. I won't risk her safety."

"Aurora's not you. Or me. Or Marina. She's older than we were, she's stronger, and she's well-trained. At least by the Fleet. And you could teach her—"

"I have nothing to teach her."

"Liar," Marina snapped.

Her mom's lips flattened but she didn't respond.

Aurora blew out a breath. "Fine." She turned to Marina and Gryphon. "What can you tell us about the attack?"

Her mom moved like a striking snake, placing herself physically between Aurora and Mya's parents. "No!" The command echoed like thunder as she stared down Marina and Gryphon. "If you say *anything* to them about our past, you will be dead to me."

Marina locked gazes with Aurora's mom, their emotions clashing like sabers.

But it wouldn't matter. Even before Marina spoke, Aurora knew what the answer would be. It was the only answer Marina had ever given.

"We won't tell them anything."

Seven

Mya was livid.

It wasn't an emotion she had much experience with, and she wasn't handling it particularly well. She just couldn't believe what her parents were saying. "You won't tell me *anything* about the attack on the homeworld?"

Following the tsunami downstairs, and the resulting arctic freeze that had settled over the household, the cozy reading room adjoining her parents' bedroom had seemed like the best place to make her case. There was zero chance Libra or anyone else would overhear them.

Her mom's dark brows drew together. "I'm sorry, Lelindia. I can't."

"Can't? Or won't?"

Her mom's gaze didn't flicker. "I can't."

Mya wanted to scream. "Fine! Then Dad can tell me." She turned to her dad, who was seated in the wingback chair across from her.

Lines creased his forehead, his blue eyes filled with misery. "You know I want to help, sweetheart. But we can't go against Libra's wishes. Not when it comes to Aurora."

Mya shoved to her feet. "This is ludicrous! Do you hear what you're saying? You're willing to let hundreds, maybe thousands—hell, *hundreds* of thousands—Suulh suffer because Libra doesn't have the guts to help Aurora do what she was born to do?" She'd expected Libra to stonewall them. It was Libra's default setting. But her parents' unwillingness to challenge her was making Mya's blood boil. "Libra's supposed to be the Sahzade! How can she turn her back on the Suulh? Doesn't she care?"

"Of course she cares." Her mom's calm voice grated on her nerves. "But she's terrified of losing Aurora. It would destroy her."

"Destroy *her?*" Mya snapped. "What do you think it would do to *me?* If something happened to Aurora, I'd..." Her throat closed. She couldn't even finish the sentence. She'd faced that possibility too many times over the past few months. That fear was driving her now.

She drew in a shuddering breath. She had to make them understand. "If you think Aurora's going to give up just because Libra won't talk, you're delusional. The only thing Libra's accomplishing is making Aurora fight blind."

Her parents exchanged a worried look. "You think Aurora would try to locate the Suulh on her own?" her dad asked.

Mya snorted. Didn't they know Aurora at all? "Of course she will. The Suulh are in trouble. She can't walk away. Not after what we've seen." Unlike Libra, Aurora would never turn her back on their people. Ever.

Her mom's face paled. "And you would follow her?"

She answered without hesitation. "Yes."

Her dad shifted in his chair, resting his elbows on his knees. "What about the rest of the crew?"

"I can't speak for Cade's team, but our crew is all in."

Her mom's eyes widened. "Cade? Do you mean Cade Ellis?"

"Yes." She'd forgotten her parents didn't know about that development. "His team joined ours on Gaia. He and Aurora are back together. At least, for now."

Her dad's eyes narrowed. "And what about Jonarel? How is he handling that?"

Mya flinched. She really didn't want to think about Jonarel and Aurora's relationship right now. "He's hurting. But I think he's accepted that it's Aurora's decision to make."

Another look passed between her parents, this one much more difficult to read. Her mom folded her hands in her lap. "I hope that's true. Aurora will need his support if she continues on this path. And so will you."

The finality in her mom's voice made her heart sink. "You're really not going to help us, are you?"

"By going against Libra's wishes? No." Mya started to protest, but her mom held up a hand. "Stop, Lelindia. You won't change my mind. Libra has a right to protect her daughter." Her mom's chin lifted. "But I have a right to protect mine, too. And I will do everything in my power to support you on *your* path."

Not the response she'd been hoping for, but better than nothing. Especially if she read between the lines. "Thank you."

Her dad stood and drew her into his arms. "We love you. You know that, don't you?"

She pushed back the tears that threatened to spill onto her cheeks. "I know." That's what made this so hard. "I love you, too."

He released her and her mom stepped forward, cupping Mya's face in her hands. "Aurora's lucky to have you by her side."

And just like that, a light dawned.

For some reason, she'd never considered that her mom felt the same way about Libra that Mya felt about Aurora. That bond ran through their cores, joining them together. Her mom couldn't knowingly sever that connection any more than she could cut off one of her own limbs. And

Mya needed to stop asking her to. "Libra's lucky to have you, too."

Her mom's sad smile acknowledged the understanding that had passed between them.

After saying their goodnights, she retreated to her old bedroom. And found Aurora waiting for her.

"Hey." Aurora looked like death warmed over.

Mya didn't feel much better. "Hey." She sat beside her on the bed. "Want to talk about it?" Aurora had avoided her earlier. After Libra had lowered the boom, the only thing Aurora had said before climbing the stairs to her room was that they'd be leaving in the morning.

Aurora sighed, the sound coming up from her toes. "I don't know why I thought this time would be different."

Mya had foolishly believed too, especially with Jonarel and Kire there to offer their input. But Libra hadn't even given them a chance to get a word in. "You're an optimist. And you've always hoped your mom would become one, too."

Aurora made a face. "Dumb move on my part."

Mya gripped Aurora's hand. "*Not* dumb. Courageous. You're trying to help the Suulh. Just like you helped Raaveen and Ren. And Paaw's family. And everyone else on Azaana. You're acting like the Sahzade. A leader."

Aurora's smile was weak, but at least it was there. "I don't feel much like a leader at the moment. I feel like a failure."

"You're not. You did your best. We couldn't control the outcome." She wrapped her arm around Aurora's waist and squeezed.

Aurora rested her head on Mya's shoulder like she used to when she was a child. "You tried talking your parents into telling you something, didn't you?"

Aurora knew her well. "Yes. They wouldn't say anything." She didn't comment on her mom's vague offer of help. No point in getting Aurora's hopes up if her parents couldn't come up with any solutions. "But I'm not giving up. We'll find another way. Together." She kissed the top of Aurora's head, the gesture another throwback to their childhood. Being home was pulling them both into old patterns. "But not tonight."

"No, not tonight." Aurora sat up, pushing a strand of loose hair out of her eyes. "Maybe things will look brighter in the morning."

Mya chuckled in spite of herself. "See what I mean? Born optimist."

Eight

She needed a plan B.

Aurora stuffed the remaining items into her pack with more force than was necessary to make everything fit. But she couldn't help it. The scene from the previous night had been playing in her head on a continuous loop since she'd woken up that morning, cranking up her frustration level each time she reached the inevitable conclusion.

Had she honestly believed her mom would see reason? That she'd get past her overwhelming fear and realize there was more at stake than their family?

Her comband pinged. She glanced at it and sighed. *Cade.* She'd sent him a short message the previous night, letting him know she'd be available to meet with him later today. She'd chosen her words carefully to avoid tipping her hand about the meltdown she'd had with her mom, but his reply had indicated he hadn't been fooled. He'd been equally brief, although she'd surmised that he'd struck out tracking leads on the Admiral at Council HQ.

Much as she longed to hear his voice, she just didn't have the energy to talk with anyone right now, even him.

I'll see you tonight. She sent the reply and then returned to her packing. After running into the same wall she'd been trying to scale since she was a child, she needed time to think.

"I'm sorry, Sahzade."

Aurora turned.

Gryphon stood in the doorway, a lidded container in his hands. He held it out. "I know it's a ridiculous way to apologize, but I brought you brownies. You didn't get a chance to eat any last night."

Aurora's heart melted a little bit. The gesture *was* ridiculous, trying to soothe her with chocolate like she was five. But it was also incredibly sweet.

She took the box and gave him a hug. "Thank you." It certainly wasn't his fault that he was caught in the middle of the civil war with her mom.

He hugged her back. "I added chocolate chunks in the batter and fudge ganache on top. Just the way you like it."

A hiccup of a laugh escaped her lips. Apparently, she *was* five, because his words brightened the dark clouds hanging over her.

He let go, his gaze intent. "You be careful out there."

She swallowed past the lump in her throat. Why couldn't her mom support her the way Gryphon and Marina did, with understanding and confidence in her ability to take care of herself? "I will."

"Good." He pointed at the container in her hand. "And eat those on the train. They're better when they're fresh."

She couldn't imagine eating anything right now, but she didn't have to tell him that. "Okay."

After he left, she finished packing, settling the box of brownies in last before sealing up her pack and heading out the door.

Mya met her at the top of the stairs and they walked down together. "You don't look like you got much sleep."

"Neither do you."

Mya grimaced. "Great trip home, huh?"

"Yeah. We'll have to do it again soon."

Jonarel and Kire were waiting by the archway with Marina, as was Aurora's mom, though she and Marina stood a good five meters apart. They weren't looking at each other, either.

Aurora's mom stepped forward to give her a hug. The embrace felt like two tin soldiers colliding. "I love you."

"I love you, too." What more could she say? Wishing things were different wouldn't make them so.

The drive to the station was uncomfortably silent. Even Kire, who could hold a stimulating conversation with a boulder, was mute.

When Marina dropped them off at the station, she pulled Aurora into a tight hug. "Be sure to eat the brownies on the trip down." She stepped back, her expression solemn. "They won't keep long."

A bubble of hysterical laughter tickled Aurora's throat. Those were Marina's parting words? With all the drama unfolding around them, she was worried about stale brownies?

Marina turned to Mya next, clutching her in what looked like a death grip. It was a far cry from the enthusiastic embrace they'd shared the day before. So much had changed since then. Because nothing had changed.

Marina's voice shook as she waved goodbye. "Safe journey."

Twenty minutes later Aurora was once again staring out the window at the passing scenery, this time heading south. And rather than battling anxiety, she was tamping down frustration.

She couldn't accept going back to her ship empty-handed. She'd played her hand and lost, but she still needed *something* to show for this trip. A plan or a starting point at the very least. Maybe it was time to—

Her comband buzzed, interrupting her thoughts. She checked the display. An incoming message from Celia.

Council HQ just sent a message for you. They want you to report to Admiral Payne ASAP for assignment.

For assignment? It took her a moment to make sense of the message. When she did, she wanted to bang her head on the tabletop.

The Suulh had dominated her thoughts for so long that she'd pushed all other considerations to the back of her mind. But the Council didn't know anything about that. They thought the *Starhawke* had been on Drakar for the past two months, being repaired after the confrontation with the Setarip ship on Gaia. That was the cover story the Admiral had circulated to give her crew time to find a homeworld for the Suulh.

Apparently returning to Earth had indicated to the Council that the ship was ready for a new mission. Which also reminded her that her crew hadn't been earning any money while they'd been on Azaana. No one had said a word. They might have been so focused on helping the Suulh that they'd forgotten. Or more likely, they had been unwilling to ask her when they knew she wasn't being paid, either.

"Sahzade?"

She glanced up. Mya, Jonarel and Kire were watching her with matching expressions of concern.

"Who's the message from?" Mya asked.

"Celia. Council HQ has an assignment for us."

Kire's thin brows lifted. "What type of assignment?"

"Don't know. But I'm supposed to report to Admiral Payne as soon as we arrive at the station." She made a face. "Which just reminded me that I haven't paid any of you since we left Gaia."

Mya exchanged a glance with Jonarel. "I can only speak for myself, but getting paid is the last thing on my mind at the moment."

Jonarel nodded. "You do not need to pay me. I only agreed to accept funds initially because you insisted."

"Of course I did!" A few of the other passengers glanced curiously in their direction. She took the volume down a notch. "You provided me with a *ship.* I couldn't let you work for free, too."

His gaze warmed. "Being on the ship provides everything I need."

She wasn't touching that comment. No way, no how.

"I'm with Jon and Mya," Kire said. "I didn't sign on because I thought it would be lucrative. I signed on for the adventure. And you've given me that in spades. Don't worry about the money, Roe. It's not important right now."

She had to swallow a couple times before she could speak. "Thank you." She gazed at her friends, their faces growing fuzzy as moisture gathered behind her eyes. "I couldn't do any of this without you."

Kire grinned. "Yeah, well, we'd be bored stiff if you weren't around. You keep life interesting." He sobered. "So, are we going to take the job?"

"I'll want to find out what it is, first. But since we're stalled on locating the Suulh, earning a little money might be a good idea while we formulate a new plan."

Her stomach picked that moment to growl, reminding her that she'd skipped breakfast. Reaching inside her pack, she pulled out the box of brownies. Might as well make good on her promise. "In the meantime, I say we take a chocolate break." She popped open the lid, plucked off the sheet of baking parchment covering the brownies and pushed the box to the center of the table. "Help yourselves."

They each selected one of the neatly cut squares as the rich scent of chocolate wafted across the table. Aurora placed hers on the parchment in front of her, but paused as she noticed marks showing through the semi-translucent paper. Something seemed to be written on the underside. Picking up the brownie, she flipped over the parchment. It was covered with writing in Gryphon's large, scrawling hand. Baking measurements, perhaps? Except the numbers and symbols looked like...

She sucked in a breath, unable to believe what she was seeing.

Jonarel's deep baritone rumbled near her ear. "What is it?"

She stared at the piece of paper, her breath hitching in and out as adrenaline pumped through her system.

"Sahzade?" Mya sounded worried. "What's wrong?"

"Nothing." Her voice came out like the croak of a bullfrog. She cleared her throat. "Nothing's wrong." In fact, things had just gotten a *whole* lot better.

The corners of her mouth lifted. Gryphon and Marina had found a loophole. Without saying a word.

"What are you smiling about?" Kire asked.

She lifted her gaze and slowly pivoted the paper so her friends could see it. "We have coordinates." Her smile widened as her gaze met Mya's. "For the original Suulh homeworld."

Nine

Cade was waiting for Aurora when she exited the monorail at the station. Her bright smile surprised him after the curt messages she'd sent while she was at her mom's house.

He fell into step beside her as they headed for the exit. "You look a lot happier than I'd expected."

"I got some good news."

"From your mom?"

"No. But the trip definitely ended well."

"Did it?" He glanced at Mya, who was walking with Clarek and Emoto a few steps behind Aurora. She had a Cheshire Cat smile, too. "How so?"

"Later. Right now I have a meeting with Admiral Payne."

"Admiral Payne? What does she want?"

"She has an assignment for us."

"An assignment?" They'd just gotten back and already the Council was sending her away? That didn't bode well. "What kind of assignment?"

"Her message didn't say. But she wanted to see me ASAP."

"I see."

Aurora frowned. "Is something wrong?"

Maybe he was overreacting, but given what he'd learned, he felt compelled to warn her. "It may be nothing, but do me a favor. Watch your back while you're there."

She stopped, allowing the flow of passengers to move around them like currents around an island. "Is there a threat?"

"Threat?" Clarek moved to Aurora's other side, much closer than Cade would have liked. "What threat?"

Cade folded his arms and lowered his voice, aware of the presence of Fleet and Council personnel passing them. "I don't want to go into it here. Just promise you'll stay alert."

Clarek's chest puffed up. "I will accompany—"

"No." Aurora cut Clarek off before he could finish. She speared him with a look. "I'll be fine." She turned back to Cade. "But thanks for the warning."

He nodded. "I've made a reservation at a tavern nearby where I know the owner. He's given us a private room so we can talk without being disturbed."

"Sounds good." She motioned to Emoto. "Why don't the rest of you head on over with Cade. I'll meet you there."

Emoto shot a glance at Clarek, who looked like he was sucking lemons. "Will do."

Cade gave Aurora the address for the tavern and took her bag so she wouldn't have to lug it with her.

She brushed her lips on his cheek. "See you soon."

Cade didn't bother looking at Clarek as Aurora walked toward the tram. The chill from the Kraed's icy stare registered just fine without that confirmation, thank you very much.

Ten

Buildings flashed past the tram window, interspersed with glimpses of the Pacific Ocean to the west. Aurora's mind kept pace with the rapidly moving scenery.

Despite Mya, Jonarel and Kire's assurances, she needed to seriously consider whatever Admiral Payne was offering. While the *Starhawke* provided for the crew's day-to-day needs, they'd have expenses now that they were back in Fleet space. She couldn't ignore an opportunity to bring in some money.

But the piece of parchment with the coordinates to the Suulh homeworld burned in her pocket like a red-hot coal. She didn't even need it anymore—she'd memorized the information—but having it close made the connection to the Suulh feel more real somehow. It was also pulling her in a completely different direction from the one the tram was headed.

How long could she keep things running without taking on another mission? Certainly long enough for them to visit the homeworld and find out what had really happened to the Suulh.

Celia would side with Mya, Jonarel and Kire. Money had never been a key concern for her. Kelly was another matter. She didn't have a long history with Aurora like the rest of the crew. If she knew she wasn't likely to get paid for the foreseeable future, she might decide to find a new post. And that would leave Aurora without a navigator.

Unless Cade took over the job. A tantalizing possibility. She wanted him on her ship. No doubt about that. But his first priority had to be finding Admiral Schreiber. She wanted that, too. Unfortunately, to do that, he'd need to leave the *Starhawke*. And her.

When the tram arrived at the Council station, she followed the flow of personnel into the HQ building, taking the lift to Fleet Command on the tenth floor. After checking in at the security station she proceeded down the hallway to Admiral Payne's suite.

The lieutenant behind the desk smiled in greeting as she entered. "May I help you?"

"Yes. I'm Captain Hawke. The Admiral is expecting me."

"Yes, of course, Captain. One moment, please." The PA touched his console. "Captain Hawke has arrived, Admiral." He listened to the reply, then gestured Aurora toward the door. "She'll see you now."

"Thank you."

It had been a while since she'd visited anyone at HQ besides Admiral Schreiber, and the sterility of Admiral Payne's office threw her off balance. Admiral Schreiber's suite was welcoming, his walls lined with pictures, many of them taken during the years he'd been a captain in the Fleet. The walls in Payne's office were conspicuously bare.

The Admiral stood as Aurora entered. "A pleasure to see you again, Captain." She extended her hand, the burgundy polish on her manicured nails flashing in the overhead lights. "Thank you for coming so quickly."

Aurora accepted the offered handshake, but her empathic senses snapped to attention. The Admiral's body language indicated friendliness and ease, but her underlying emotions were laced with apprehension and fear. And her palm felt clammy.

"It's nice to see you, as well."

"Please, sit." The Admiral gestured to the chairs in front of her desk. "I understand you recently returned from Drakar. Not many of us have had the opportunity to visit. How did you enjoy your time there?"

The question felt like a baited hook. Aurora's uneasiness grew, but she pasted on a smile as she settled into one of the chairs. "It was lovely."

"So the reports of dangerous predators are exaggerated?"

An image of an enormous greewtaith dragging down a relquir flashed in her mind's eye. "Not exactly. The Kraed have their share of...challenges."

"Sounds interesting." Payne paused, her expression expectant. But when Aurora didn't elaborate, she moved on. "And your ship? They were able to complete all the repairs?"

"Yes." The *Starhawke* had taken a lot of hits during the attack at Burrow, but Jonarel and Drew had worked with Star on repairs during the journey to Azaana and while en route to Earth. That was a distinct advantage to having a Nirunoc bonded with the ship. Star could access every millimeter of the ship and facilitate repairs that would ordinarily be impossible while traveling through space.

Payne smiled, her teeth white against her caramel skin. "That's wonderful news. I have an important research mission for your crew that's been on hold since you left Gaia."

Was it her imagination, or did Payne stutter a bit on that last word? "What's the mission?"

"A wonderful opportunity to study a binary system just beyond our borders. It's in Teeli territory, but they've given us special dispensation for a two-month research project."

It was a legitimate request given her crew's skill set, but Aurora didn't buy it for a moment. Not after Cade's warning. The Admiral's emotional grid had shifted, anxiety pushing to the forefront.

She needed to keep the Admiral talking. "What can you tell me about the system?"

The Admiral's unease ramped up by a factor of ten as she laid out the details of the mission parameters. Her outward behavior remained cool and professional—so at odds with what Aurora was sensing that only one conclusion made sense—Payne was setting her up.

Comments Admiral Schreiber had made the last time she'd talked to him filtered back. He'd been concerned that he couldn't trust anyone at the Council. Had the security breach infiltrated the Fleet, too? Was Payne compromised?

The idea took root and wouldn't go away.

"How soon can your crew leave?" Payne's enthusiasm came out a little forced, her emotions drawn tight as a bow.

Thank goodness she had no idea Aurora was an empath. Aurora kept her own smile in place. "I'll need to check with my crew before I can answer that question. We'll discuss it and I'll contact you to confirm our departure date."

The first cracks appeared in the Admiral's façade, her skin glistening with a faint sheen of perspiration. "The sooner the better. We're already behind on this project. We don't want to impose on the Teeli's generosity by pushing back the timetable more than we already have."

"I understand. I'll get back to you as soon as I can." Aurora stood to go, then paused as if something had just occurred to her. "I'm surprised Admiral Schreiber didn't contact me about this while I was on Drakar."

Bingo.

The cracks in the Admiral's composure turned into fissures as the comment pushed on a fault line. "He's...away...at the moment. Personal leave."

Aurora pretended surprise. "Oh, I hadn't heard. Do you know when he'll be back?"

"I couldn't say."

Uh-huh. But her emotions were saying plenty. Aurora shrugged as if Payne's reaction was perfectly normal. "It's not important. I was just hoping to see him." She headed for the door. "I'll be in touch."

On the way to the address Cade had given her, she analyzed the bizarre conversation. She'd been in too many mission briefings to accept the Admiral's behavior as normal. It had to be a setup. But for what?

The location for their proposed mission seemed odd, too. Studying a binary system in Teeli space? That was unprecedented. The Teeli had always been cordial in their dealings with the Fleet, but to her knowledge they'd never invited cooperation on matters of science.

The Council was deliberately maneuvering her crew out of Fleet space. She could think of several reasons why, none of them good.

The hum of conversation and background music drifted out of the tavern's worn wooden door as she entered. The manager directed her to a stairway near the back that took her to the upper level. The space was separated into a collection of cozy booths and several enclosed rooms. Following the directions she'd been given, she made her way to the last door on the right.

Justin Byrnes had joined the four others around the oblong table. He gave Aurora a wave of greeting as she claimed the vacant chair between Cade and Mya.

Cade set a glass of red wine in front of her. "Figured you might be in the mood for cabernet."

She smiled. "Good guess."

He held her gaze. "What did Admiral Payne have to say?"

"She has a mission for us." She took a sip of the ruby liquid, letting it glide down her throat. "Researching a binary system."

Kire perked up. "Sounds up our alley."

"Oh, it is. Unfortunately, I think it's a trap."

Cade set his beer down with a thump. "A trap?"

"The location is outside Fleet space, in Teeli territory." Which also put it as far from Kraed space as possible. Her gaze met Jonarel's briefly. The same realization showed in his eyes.

She returned her attention to Cade. "I sensed severe anxiety from Payne the entire time she was telling me about the mission. It bordered on panic, as though something terrible was going to happen if I turned her down. Considering Admiral Schreiber's recent vanishing act, I think we're being set up."

"But why would Payne do that?" Kire frowned. "I don't see the motivation."

"She's probably being coerced." Cade's lips thinned. "We found out Lieutenant Magee has been reassigned to the Teeli delegation, and Reanne resigned as Director of the RC."

Aurora blinked. Surely she'd heard wrong "Reanne resigned? When?"

"Not long after we left Gaia. Her assistant indicated the trauma of the shooting was too much for her to handle. But I'm not sure I believe that."

"No." Aurora couldn't picture Reanne overcome by trauma. "She's tough and ambitious. She wouldn't willingly resign, especially after reaching the Director's position."

"I doubt she was given a choice." Cade sighed. "Unfortunately, I don't have any way to confirm that. I never had her personal contact information. Everything went through the RC or the Admiral. Do you have any way to get in touch with her?"

"No. Before Gaia, we hadn't spoken in years." After graduation, she'd put her former friend out of her mind, partly because of Reanne's inappropriate behavior toward Cade. "What about the Admiral? Any promising leads?"

Cade exchanged a look with Justin. "According to the Council, he's on medical leave, but Williams couldn't find any records to corroborate that. We also searched his house. Nothing."

Aurora's brows lifted. "You have access to his house?"

"We bypassed the security." Cade shrugged. "Trust me, the Admiral wouldn't object."

Given the circumstances, he was probably right. She rested her forearms on the table. "What's your plan going forward?"

"That partly depends on you. Right now, without the Admiral or Reanne, my unit is grounded."

"Grounded?"

"They provided us with transportation. We don't have a ship."

"You have the *Starhawke*."

His expression softened. "*You* have the *Starhawke*. We've just been tagging along."

Aurora held his gaze. "And you can keep tagging along. We certainly won't leave you here." A thread of anger tickled her senses. She glanced at Jonarel, whose golden eyes had narrowed to slits. He clearly didn't want Cade back on the *Starhawke*. Well, he'd have to get used to the idea. If she had her way, Cade would become a permanent member of the crew.

She shifted her focus to Kire and Mya. "But first we have to decide if we're going to accept Payne's offer, knowing it might be a trap."

Kire shook his head. "We told you we don't care about being paid. And if we're being set up, the reception we'd get when we arrived at the system might make the attack at Burrow look like a cake walk."

Worry lines showed around Mya's dark eyes. "I agree. Besides, we need answers more than we need money."

Aurora turned to Jonarel.

"You know where you want to go." His voice rumbled with certainty.

"You do?" Cade glanced between Aurora and Jonarel. "Where?"

She met his gaze. "The original Suulh homeworld. Marina and Gryphon gave us the coordinates."

He stared at her. "I'll be damned. *That's* why you said the trip ended well."

"Uh-huh."

"Does your mom know?"

She grimaced. "No. Gryphon wrote the information on a piece of baking parchment he stuck in with the brownies he gave me."

The corner of Cade's mouth quirked up. "Smart man."

"Yes, he is." And she needed to be smart, too. They didn't want to draw attention from the Council that might undermine the secrecy of their plans. "Maybe I should tell

Payne we'll take her offer, even if we don't go to the system."

"Why?" Kire asked.

"If Payne believes we're going to the binary system, whoever's behind all this will be waiting for us there rather than hunting us. That buys us time."

"So we tell her we'll take it, but we go to the homeworld instead?" Kire frowned. "Won't that cause an issue when we return without any data?"

"Only if I'm wrong about it being a trap. Payne may not expect us to return at all." She glanced at Cade. "What's your next move to track down the Admiral?"

"We need to talk to Knox. Would you be able to set up a meeting without alerting anyone at Council HQ?"

A small smile tugged at her lips. Her former captain had established a system that would make granting that request a snap. "I'll contact him as soon as we're back on the *Starhawke*."

Eleven

The Firenze market on Osiris was alive with activity as Aurora and Cade made their way to a small café at the outskirts of town. The colony had started as a tiny hamlet, spearheaded by a group of like-minded citizens seeking free land and minimal Council oversight. But over the years the community had developed into a bustling trading hub on the edges of Fleet space.

For the most part the residents of Firenze maintained a harmonious balance, with those who wanted a sense of community living in town, and those who wanted more privacy settling in the countryside. The local law enforcement was tough but fair, keeping order with a firm hand and an impressive arsenal. Without the might of the Council and Fleet to back them up, they had to be prepared to handle any threat, including Setarip attacks.

Residents rarely left their homes without weapons strapped on their hips or slung over their shoulders. Visitors were strongly encouraged to do the same, which is why a stroll down the main concourse could serve as an object lesson on modern weaponry. The inhabitants accepted the risks of a frontier life as a fair trade for their personal freedoms.

Aurora had visited the colony a few times during her two years as the *Argo*'s first officer. Osiris was a supply stop for longer Fleet tours, a place for the crew to feel the sun on their skin and breathe fresh air. The vibrant colors and lively atmosphere of the streets of Firenze had called to Aurora, a welcome change to the utilitarian surroundings of the *Argo*. Like all Fleet ships, it had been designed for function rather than aesthetics.

Yet another reason Aurora loved the *Starhawke*. Her ship was a marvel of both.

The only downside to leaving the *Argo* had been resigning her post as Knox Schreiber's first officer. She'd respected him as her captain, but she'd loved him like the older brother she'd never had, one who looked out for her and encouraged her to reach her goals.

She'd sent her request to meet with him through Fleet channels, so she'd written it using the coding system he'd taught her while she was on the *Argo*. Anyone reading it would dismiss it as a note between friends sharing the latest news. Knox had responded in kind, but the decoded message had informed her the *Argo* would be spending a few days at Osiris, and Knox would meet her in Firenze. She couldn't ask for a better spot for a rendezvous.

She'd also informed Payne that her ship needed to proceed to the binary system at half its normal speed to break in the new engine parts they're received at Drakar. A total fabrication, of course, but it gave them more wiggle room for this side trip to Osiris.

"Think Clarek's still chewing nails on the bridge?" Cade asked as he strode beside her through the busy market.

Aurora bit back a smile. He sounded delighted. She didn't want to encourage him. "Probably."

Jonarel had wanted to accompany her on this trip, but he would have stuck out like a walking tree, destroying their plan to keep the meeting under the radar. Kraed never visited Osiris. They didn't have a reason to. Jonarel's presence would have been a flashing neon sign. He hadn't been able to argue the point, but he'd glared as she and Cade had headed for the *Starhawke's* shuttle.

They'd used the shuttle's camouflage to land covertly several kilometers from the town limits, hiking in and joining the bustle of activity in the busy market. Street vendors called out from their stalls as she and Cade passed by.

"Pretty necklace for a pretty lady." A middle-aged man stepped in front of Aurora and held up a flowing chain of gold embedded with sparkling cut stones. His booth was filled with similar treasures, although the materials were likely fabricated to look like gemstones.

"No, thank you." Aurora smiled at the man but kept moving down the aisle.

"He's pushing the wrong item." Cade commented. "If he'd enticed you with polished crystals instead, he might have made the sale. Especially if he had tiger's eye."

She glanced at Cade. "You remember my weakness for tiger's eye?"

"It's a stone of protection. How could I forget?" Cade flashed a devilish smile. "Besides, I remember all your weaknesses."

That smile made her hum like a live wire. She tingled...everywhere. "Is that so?"

Three women with baskets balanced on their heads came down the aisle toward them and Cade moved behind her to give them room. He slipped his arm around her waist as he bent his head, his lips brushing her ear. "Maybe later I'll prove it to you."

Sparks danced over her skin, but she shot him a mock glare. "Focus, Ellis. We have work to do."

He chuckled. "Oh, I know. But the captain needs to play, too."

And he was very good at bringing out her playful side. She hadn't realized how dormant it had been until he'd burst back into her life. Now her world felt as vibrant as the brightly colored cloths fluttering above their heads. "I'll keep that in mind."

The crowds thinned as they crossed a stone bridge overlooking the main river and moved into a more residential section on the far side. The café where they were meeting Knox had delightful food, but the atmosphere was even better. The unassuming stone façade opened onto a courtyard garden, with small café tables tucked among the greenery and fountains providing soothing background music to the visual beauty.

The café owners greeted them as they stepped inside and showed them to a table shaded by a flowering fruit tree. Knox was already waiting for them, his tall frame and broad shoulders making the petite café chair look like it was meant for a child.

"Aurora." He stood as she approached, leaning down to brush a kiss on her cheek. His perfectly trimmed beard tickled her skin.

"Hi, Knox."

He extended his hand to Cade. "Good to see you again, Cade."

"You, too."

After their server had taken their order and headed for the kitchen, Aurora turned to Knox, keeping her voice low to avoid drawing attention from the occupants of the two nearby tables. "Have you spoken with your father recently?"

"No, I haven't. I was hoping he might have contacted you." Knox rested his forearms on the tabletop. "The last communication I had with him was four weeks ago."

Four weeks? Her heart sank. So much for Knox being the bearer of good news. "We haven't heard from him since we left Gaia. We were under strict orders not to communicate with him until our mission was completed."

Knox's blue eyes clouded with worry. "I was afraid of that. I'd held out hope that he'd reconnected with you. I'm assuming your presence here means the refugees are safe?"

"Yes," Aurora said. "Siginal's the one who alerted us to your father's disappearance. He hasn't heard from him recently, either."

"Do you know anything about his movements prior to his disappearance?" Cade asked.

"He was investigating a lead regarding the Setarip connection to the attack on Gaia. He used the *Cassini*'s inspection tour as an excuse to reach the outer rim."

"What about the reports regarding his medical leave? Williams couldn't find any corroborating evidence."

Knox nodded. "That was his cover story so he could get off the Fleet radar for a while. He has an old friend who's head of medical at Hydra One. She filled out the paperwork and convinced Captain Montgomery that my father wouldn't be fit to travel. After the *Cassini* departed, my father booked passage on a supply freighter under an assumed identity. Last time he contacted me, he was heading for Gallows Edge, but I haven't heard from him since."

Aurora didn't like the direction this was going. "And because he's supposedly on medical leave and traveling under an assumed identity, you can't call for a Fleet investigation of his disappearance."

"That's right. Anything I do could put him in danger." Knox bent his head, staring at his hands. "Assuming the danger hasn't already caught up with him."

His soft words dropped like boulders in Aurora's stomach. "If he's using a false identity, he might be having trouble sending messages." She didn't want to contemplate the other possible reasons he wasn't in communication.

The lines of tension in Knox's face deepened. "I realize that. But my father was instrumental in creating the communication systems we take for granted. If anyone would know how to get a message out without being traced, he would."

"He's resourceful. And wily." Cade rested a hand on Knox's shoulder. "Wherever he is, I'm sure he's okay. We'll find him." He said it like it was a foregone conclusion.

Knox glanced between Aurora and Cade. "So, you're going after him?"

"That's right." Aurora laced her fingers together. "Sounds like we need to start at Gallows Edge. Was he meeting someone there?"

"Not that he mentioned."

"Was he tracking someone?"

"Not exactly." Knox shifted in his chair. "Did Signal share any information regarding his last communications with my father?"

Aurora shook her head. "Not with me."

"Me, either." Cade frowned. "And I didn't think to ask. I hadn't realized until recently that they were good friends. He calls your father by his first name. I've never heard anyone do that."

"They've been working together a long time."

Aurora hadn't been aware of the connection, either. The Admiral was even better at keeping secrets than she was. "Working together on what? I'm still not clear on how they met."

Knox's gaze flickered. He looked like he was weighing his options.

"Come on, Knox," Cade prodded. "You need to be straight with us if we're going to help your father."

"This isn't my story to tell. It's his."

"Unfortunately, he isn't here. You are."

Knox met Aurora's gaze. "You're not going to like it."

Her stomach tightened, but she managed to keep the agitation out of her voice. "Tell me."

He sighed. "My father was going to talk to you after you returned from your mission. After the Suulh were safe. It was...time."

She swallowed. "Time for what?"

"Time for you to know the history. To see all the connections. To understand where you fit in."

Where she fit in? Tension rippled out from her core. This couldn't be good.

He squared his shoulders, his chest expanding as he took a deep breath. "It started when the Teeli applied for membership to the Council. My father was concerned that they were sidestepping the procedures and protocols the Council had put in place to insure any potential new members would meet the standards set forth in the original charter."

"Wait a minute." Aurora held up a hand. "This is about the *Teeli?* They're what brought your father and Siginal together?"

"That's correct."

"But the Teeli have been respected members of the Council since I was a child."

"I'm aware of that."

"So your father's concerns must have been unfounded."

Knox's mouth flattened into a grim line. "Actually, they weren't."

Twelve

Cade planted his forearms on the tabletop as tendrils of unease snaked down his spine. "You're saying the Teeli manipulated the system? Fast-tracked their application and misrepresented themselves to the Council?"

"I'm saying there's a lot more to the Teeli than you realize. Unfortunately, it took my father six months to convince Signal to even start an investigation. They weren't friends yet, and my father's statements were at odds with the accepted facts. Signal finally agreed to look into it, but it was too late. The Teeli were approved for Council membership shortly thereafter."

"So why didn't your father lead his own investigation?" Aurora asked. "Why go through Signal?"

"You're forgetting this was more than twenty years ago. He was a newly appointed Admiral, and while he had friends and connections in the Council, anyone he spoke to dismissed his concerns. He even received a formal reprimand when the Teeli delegates objected to his attempts to gather more information. He needed a way to investigate without attracting attention. The Kraed provided that. Their ships are perfect for covert operations."

No kidding. Cade had witnessed the effectiveness of the *Starhawke's* hull camouflage during the battle at Burrow. "What did the Kraed learn during their investigation?"

"For starters, they discovered the Teeli homeworld is not in the system that's listed in the official record. It's an ice planet in an isolated star system fifteen light years from any other stars."

Aurora looked confused. "Why would the Teeli lie about that?"

Knox didn't answer her, his gaze shifting over her shoulder. Their server appeared with their drinks, setting down mugs of coffee in front of Knox and Cade and tea in front of Aurora.

"The food should be up shortly," the server said, smiling at Knox.

"Thank you."

Aurora repeated her question after the server headed back inside. "Why did the Teeli lie?"

"Because the real homeworld is guarded by orbiting space stations and a fleet of warships."

"Warships?" Aurora's eyes widened. "But aren't the Teeli pacifists?"

Knox's brows drew down. "Hardly. That's another lie they told the Council."

Cade couldn't believe what he was hearing. "If that's true, why isn't this common knowledge? Why are the Teeli still part of the Council?"

"Because the Council was never told. With the Teeli already accepted as official members, and my father's reputation tarnished by the objections he'd made previously, no one would have listened. Most of the Council members were firmly on the side of the Teeli. And sharing the information would have meant disclosing the extent of the Kraed involvement in the surveillance. My father and Signal realized such a revelation had the power to destroy the Council. Trust between humans and Kraed has always been essential."

"So they did nothing?" Cade couldn't imagine the Admiral or Siginal Clarek walking away.

Knox shook his head. "They focused on gathering information. During the original surveillance, the Kraed monitored the Teeli communications system. They worked to translate the fragments they uncovered, since most of the words in the communications weren't in the official dictionary, or had different meanings from what the Teeli delegates provided to the Council. Over time, they pieced together—"

"Hang on." Aurora sat forward. "Are you saying the Teeli language I studied at the Academy isn't accurate? Or complete?"

"That's correct. Compared to the language the Kraed uncovered, what you were taught is practically gibberish."

Aurora's mouth pinched at the corners. "Great."

"That's not all." He gripped his coffee mug in his hands, his gaze locked on Aurora. "Over the years, the Kraed uncovered a narrative woven through the messages. It detailed the ongoing search for two powerful females from another race who had evaded capture years earlier." He paused, his jaw working like he was struggling to get the words past his lips. He lowered his voice. "Females with the ability to shield others from harm and heal wounds."

Aurora went very still, her green eyes widening.

Cade's heart stopped in his chest.

Knox kept talking, the words coming faster and faster. "The Teeli believed the two females had fled to Fleet space. They followed them, which is how they ended up making first contact with humans. They'd been searching for the females. Encountering a Fleet ship was unexpected, as was learning that the humans onboard looked like they belonged to the same race as the females they were hunting."

Cade gripped the tabletop. All this time—

"Becoming part of the Council gave the Teeli access to resources and freedom of movement in Fleet space to continue their search. My father made it his mission to locate the two females before the Teeli did."

A blunt swear word slipped from Cade's lips.

Aurora looked like a carved statue. When she spoke, her voice was barely a whisper. "How long have you known?"

Knox hesitated, tapping his finger on the rim of his mug. "My father suspected who you were by your second year at the Academy."

Aurora's mouth hinged open.

"Siginal spearheaded the search for the original females, and found evidence they'd spent time on Gaia, and may have traveled to Earth. After that, the trail went cold. My father—" He halted as the server reappeared with their food.

She set the plates down with a smile, but it faded as she picked up on the tension swirling around the table. "Uh, enjoy." She backed away. "Let me know if you need anything else." She headed inside without waiting for a reply.

Knox picked up the thread without missing a beat. "My father theorized that the females might have produced children who would share their abilities. He asked the Academy professors to keep him informed of any students who excelled, especially in healing or self-defense. Mya drew his attention first."

"Mya?" Aurora's voice came out like a faint echo.

"Yes. But you were her roommate at the time, and from the same hometown, so he monitored your progress as well. You excelled at everything you tried, and showed natural leadership abilities, but it wasn't enough to prove his theory. That's why he arranged for Siginal to join the faculty—to make a personal connection with you and learn more about your family history."

Cade's fingers dug into his palms as he curled his hands into fists. "You're saying Siginal Clarek was *spying* on Aurora? At the Admiral's request?"

"Yes."

Heat climbed up the back of Cade's neck. "And you *knew* about it?"

Knox didn't flinch. "Yes."

The heat crested Cade's forehead and swept over his face. "And none of you thought to say anything to *Aurora* about this?"

"I wasn't at liberty to reveal what I knew."

The heat erupted into flames. "Like hell!"

Conversation at the nearby tables ceased. The other patrons glanced nervously in their direction.

He forced his voice down to a more socially acceptable level, although acid dripped from his lips. "Do you have any idea how hard she's worked to *hide* that ability? How much better her life would have been if she'd had your *support* rather than your *surveillance*?"

"She's *had* our support. Always."

Cade begged to differ. Right now, Aurora looked sick to her stomach. He placed his hand on her arm, but she pulled back, drawing into herself.

"Your *support?*" she snapped. "You and your father have known about Mya and me, our moms, our history, our abilities, *all* the things I've tried to hide, and you never thought you should say *anything* to me about it?" Her green eyes glowed with a feverish light as she stared at Knox.

His brow furrowed. "I'm sorry, Aurora. Truly, I am. We couldn't tell you what we knew. It was too risky.

Especially when we understood how powerful you could be. All we could do was protect you. That's why you were assigned to the *Excelsior* with Jonarel and Mya. And why you and Mya were transferred to the *Argo* when Jonarel came into his succession."

Two blooms of red appeared in Aurora's cheeks. "So I didn't earn that promotion? You were just protecting a potentially valuable resource?"

Knox held up his hands, palms out. "That's not true. You were the best in your class. You've always been a remarkable leader. It's in your blood. You deserved that promotion. We just made sure you were assigned to my ship when you received it."

The heat in Aurora's eyes rose several degrees. "How convenient. You just *happened* to have a command position open on your ship when Jonarel left the Fleet."

The pain behind Aurora's words fueled Cade's anger. Knox had played her for years, manipulating her rather than trusting her with information she'd yearned for since she was a child. He had the urge to plant his fist in the other man's face.

"I wanted you on the *Argo* from the beginning," Knox protested. "I would have moved you when the ship was first commissioned, but Siginal objected. He argued that you should remain with Jonarel. We couldn't move all three of you to the *Argo* at the same time. That would have been suspicious."

A possessive rage swept through Cade. Siginal had wanted to keep Aurora close to his son so he could manipulate her through Jonarel. Yet another reason to hate the Clareks.

Aurora folded her arms over her chest. "Right. You, your father and Siginal had to move the pieces strategically.

Didn't want to tip me off." Her fingers clenched her upper arms until the skin underneath showed white. "So what's your father's big plan for me, huh? You said he was going to tell me all this when he saw me. That it was time. Time for what? To put his valuable piece into play?"

Cade's heart ached for her. The people she trusted most had betrayed her. *Again.*

"I don't know. I'm not even sure he had a plan. He just wanted to protect you."

Aurora growled. "Protect me. Right. It was all about *me.*" Sarcasm punctuated every word. "I don't *need* his protection. Or yours."

"Maybe not. But there's a lot at stake here."

"And this is *my life* we're talking about!"

The diners at the nearby tables turned in their direction again, but Aurora didn't seem to notice.

"We're drawing attention," Cade murmured.

Her gaze snapped to his, fury burning in her eyes, but she glanced over her shoulder and lowered her voice. "You just admitted that you and your father have been lying to me the entire time I've known you. How can I possibly believe anything you've said to me? Ever?"

At least Knox looked chagrined. "This isn't how I wanted you to find out. Believe me. We never meant to hurt you."

Aurora deflated like a balloon. "No, you just meant to control me. Like everyone else." She looked at Cade, her expression bleak. "We're done here."

Thirteen

Was there anyone in her life who hadn't lied to her? Anyone she could trust?

Aurora's rage at Knox and the Admiral burned through her veins like lava, the scope of what she'd learned poisoning her mind. She stared at the emerging starfield as Cade guided the shuttle out of the planet's atmosphere. She hadn't spoken more than a dozen words to him since they'd left Knox. She wasn't upset with him. She just didn't know what to say. Or do.

But before they reached the *Starhawke*, she needed an answer to one important question. "Did you know?"

Cade glanced at her, his green eyes wary. "Did I know what?"

She shifted in her seat to face him. "Did you know that the Admiral and Knox were manipulating me?"

His jaw clenched, the cords of muscle in his neck standing out in sharp relief. He returned his attention to the navigation console. "What do you think?"

"I hope not, but..."

"But you don't know what to believe."

"Not anymore." She drew in a calming breath. "*Did* the Admiral tell you any of this when he sent you to spy on me at Gaia?"

His hands tightened on the controls. "Aurora, I swear I had no idea. I was supposed to keep my presence on Gaia a secret from you, but he didn't tell me why. And he certainly never told me he knew about your heritage and abilities. I would have warned you if he had."

"Are you sure?" She wanted to trust him. But after so many betrayals...

"I swear on my life." He met her gaze. "I didn't know."

The anger and frustration she sensed from him echoed her inner turmoil. The tension in her chest eased a bit. "If you weren't flying this shuttle, I'd kiss you right now."

The corner of his mouth lifted a fraction. "Can I have a rain check?"

"You bet." At least she had one ally in this. And her crew. Mya, Kire, Jonar—

She bolted upright, her hand going to her heart. "Do you think *Jonarel* knew? Before we met?"

The muscles in Cade's jaw twitched. "Probably. Siginal certainly did."

There wasn't enough oxygen in the cabin. She clamped a hand on the console to steady herself as the stars spun. *Please, no. Don't let it be true.*

But it made perfect sense. If Siginal had been at the Academy at the Admiral's request to observe her and Mya, what were the odds that Jonarel had been unaware? Slim to none. And yet, he'd never said a word.

It also explained Siginal's support for Jonarel's decision to build the *Starhawke* for her. She'd believed Siginal expected one day she and Jonarel would pair bond, which would bring the *Starhawke* back to the Clarek clan. It was a romantic notion, if unrealistic given the fact that she'd never viewed Jonarel that way.

But this put an entirely different spin on Siginal's motivation. If he wanted to keep a watchful eye on her, what better way than to have his son build a ship and gift it to her? With Jonarel and Star onboard, they'd be able to monitor her activities without arousing suspicion.

Heat flooded her face as she flashed back to Siginal's unexpected arrival on Azaana. He'd told her he was worried about Jonarel and the Suulh after the attack at Burrow. But that hadn't been his reason for being there. He'd been checking up on *her*!

She smacked the console with her palm hard enough to make Cade jerk in his chair.

He glanced at her with a frown. "What—"

She held up a finger to silence him and opened a comm channel to the *Starhawke*. She struggled to keep her voice even, but the words still came out clipped. "Hawke to Clarek."

"Clarek here."

"We're returning to the ship." But for the first time since she'd become the captain, she didn't want to be onboard. She just wanted answers. "Meet me in my office in fifteen minutes. And tell Mya to join us."

"What is—"

"I'll tell you when I see you. Hawke out." She smacked the console again, cutting off the channel.

She sensed Cade's curiosity, but he didn't question her. She told him anyway. "Mya needs to hear this. *All* of this. And Jonarel is going to tell me *everything* he knows about what his father and the Admiral have been up to. If he doesn't, he's going to become the newest resident of Osiris."

Fourteen

When Aurora stalked into the cozy office where Mya and Jonarel were waiting, her fierce expression reminded Mya of Hippolyta, the legendary queen of the Amazons, facing off against Hercules.

Aurora didn't bother with a greeting. "Jonarel's been spying on us."

The accusation struck Mya in the chest like an arrow. "*What?* That's not...that can't...spying?" She couldn't make the words come together. Jonarel spying? On them? He would never do such a thing. He just...wouldn't.

But he didn't roar with indignation. Instead, his gaze remained locked with Aurora's like a cobra sizing up a mongoose.

Mya pressed her hand against her chest to keep her heart from punching through. "Jonarel? It's not true. Is it?"

He didn't look at her. Didn't respond.

The steel in Aurora's gaze dared him to contradict her as her fists clenched at her sides. "He's known about us from the beginning. He knew about our moms. He knew about the Suulh. The only reason Signal came to the Academy in the first place was because of *us.*"

Mya's stomach rolled. It couldn't be true. She didn't want it to be true. "But how can that be? How could he know anything about us?" She directed the question at Jonarel, willing him to look at her.

When he finally met her gaze, his golden eyes revealed nothing. "It is a long story."

"Then I'll give her the short version." Aurora growled. "The Admiral and Signal were investigating the Teeli. They were the ones who invaded our homeworld. And they've been the ones hunting us ever since."

The room started to tilt. Mya sank into one of the plush chairs, needing the support. "The Teeli? That's impossible. They're not conquerors. They're pacifists."

"Wrong. It was a lie they told the Council. One of many."

Mya stared at Jonarel, but he didn't refute Aurora's words. And if that was true, he'd allowed them to flounder unnecessarily, to suffer through the recent confrontation with their moms, while withholding key pieces of information they needed. "You *knew*? You knew that the Teeli were responsible for attacking our homeworld? And you never said *anything*? *Why*?"

The first chinks showed in his stoic façade. "I was unable."

"*Unable*?" Sparks ignited. "What do you mean *unable*? Unable to be a loyal friend? Unable to provide the answers we needed to help the Suulh?"

"I had my reasons."

"I don't give a damn about your reasons!" She leapt to her feet and moved into his personal space. "Lies of omission are still lies!"

He stepped back.

She followed.

He held up his hands, palms out. "I know. I am sorry, Mya. I never meant to hurt you. Or Aurora."

Aurora snorted. "No. You just meant to manipulate us. You created this lovely gilded cage." She swept her arms wide. "And filled it with every enticement you could think of so that we'd never suspect it was a trap."

"That is not true!" Star's dark form shimmered into place beside Jonarel, her honey-colored eyes swirling as her voice filled the room. "Jonarel's only desire has been to help you."

Aurora swung to face the Nirunoc. "*Help* us? By *lying* to us? And what about you? You're the ultimate spy. You see and hear *everything* on this ship. How much of that are you reporting back to Siginal? How much did you tell him about what happened at Burrow?"

Star looked wounded. "I told him nothing."

"*Nothing?* You expect me to believe that? Your entire clan has been working to keep us complacent so we wouldn't resist your manipulations!"

"That is not—"

"We just—" Jonarel interrupted.

Aurora pointed a finger at him. "Don't even—"

Mya's stomach knotted as the rapid-fire argument intensified. Aurora was right. Everything about the *Starhawke* had been designed with their comfort in mind. The greenhouse. The med bay. The observation lounge. The ship provided her and Aurora with everything they'd ever wanted. It was a beautiful, elegantly concealed cage.

She backed away from Jonarel and Star, coming to stand beside Aurora. "Why?"

Her quiet question broke through the heated exchange. Aurora, Jonarel and Star all turned to her.

She kept her focus on Jonarel, fighting against the rising tide threatening to drown her. "Why did you do it?"

He and Star exchanged a glance. "To protect you," he said.

Aurora unleashed a particularly harsh string of swear words. "I am sick and tired of *hearing* that! Don't worry about us. You want to protect someone?" Her head lowered as she eyed him like a bull about to charge. "Protect yourself."

The threat wasn't implied. It was a promise.

He took a step forward. "Aurora, I—"

She held up a hand, halting him in his tracks. "I wouldn't do that if I were you." Her soft voice chilled the air. "Be grateful I'm not leaving you here to find your own way back to Drakar."

Star held out a hand in supplication. "Aurora, please, we—"

Aurora's lips pulled back in a snarl. "And *you*, I can't very well order you off the ship now can I? But nothing you say is going to fix this. Not now. Not ever. As far as I'm concerned, we're finished." She crossed her arms over her chest, her expression carved from stone. "Now both of you, get off my bridge."

Fifteen

Cade had never needed a drink so badly in his life.

He couldn't decide where to direct his anger—at the Schreibers, the Clareks, or himself. They'd all behaved like self-centered jackasses. And they'd steamrolled Aurora in the process.

He stared at his reflection in the oval mirror above the bathroom sink in Aurora's cabin while he scrubbed his hands, trying to wash away the stain of this awful day. How could he have been so blind? Why hadn't he figured out that the Admiral knew a lot more about Aurora than he let on? Or that the Clareks had been part of the equation from the beginning? It seemed so obvious now, but he'd never suspected the web of lies that surrounded Aurora. He'd let her down.

The man in the mirror didn't argue. He looked at Cade with well-deserved reproach.

He'd always prided himself on his observation skills. Yet when it really counted, when the deception had affected the woman he loved, he'd completely missed the boat.

Turning off the water, he shoved away from the counter with a growl. Aurora hadn't said much when they'd parted ways at the shuttle, just that she'd talk to him later. For now, all he could do was wait.

Being idle wasn't one of his strong suits. Especially when he was feeling like an idiot.

Maybe he'd go down to the training center. A workout might clear his head. He strode to the closet to pull out his exercise clothes, but a chime at the cabin door stopped him.

He padded over to open it.

Justin stood in the corridor. "You got a minute?"

"Yeah. Come on in."

Justin's gaze swept over him. "You sure? You look like you got drop kicked."

Cade grimaced. "I did. And so did Aurora."

"You want to talk about it?"

"Maybe later." He stepped back and gestured to the seating area by the viewport. "What's up?"

Justin sat on the couch while Cade sank into the nearest chair. "I was curious what you learned from Knox. But judging by your expression, it wasn't good news."

Cade sighed and rested his elbows on his knees. "Good and bad. We know where to start looking for the Admiral. But Knox dropped a bomb on Aurora." He gave Justin a brief summary of the conversation.

Justin whistled. "And Aurora's talking to Clarek right now?"

"That's right."

Justin glanced at the ceiling as if he could see through to the bridge. "I can't imagine that's going well."

"Neither can I." Cade objected to Aurora's friendship with Clarek as a general rule, especially when the Kraed acted possessive, but now he hated the bastard for lying to her.

"So where does this leave us?" Justin leaned back and crossed his ankle over his knee. "Do you think she'll take us to Gallows Edge?"

"Possibly."

Justin's eyes narrowed. "That sounded more like a no."

"Honestly, I can't say. Knox hit her hard. I can't predict how she'll react after she's had a chance to calm down."

"Any idea how long that might take?"

"Aurora has a long fuse, but when it blows..." Cade shrugged. "Could be a few hours. Or it could be a few days."

"In that case, you want to do some sparring in the training center while we wait?"

Cade got to his feet. "You read my mind."

He went into the bedroom to change. For Aurora's sake, he hoped she'd burn through her anger quickly and find some peace. She'd suffered enough already.

Either way, the *Starhawke* might end up minus an overgrown Kraed engineer. If that thought brought him a small measure of satisfaction...well, he was only human.

Sixteen

Aurora stared out the small viewport in her bedroom. The glitter of stars didn't soothe her the way it normally did. Not this time.

Cade hadn't been in the cabin when she'd returned, and she'd been too exhausted to wander the ship looking for him. She certainly wasn't going to ask Star to locate him. Not that she'd expected him to be waiting for her. She'd stayed in her office an hour after Mya had left, just sitting and...thinking. Or more to the point, *not* thinking.

The soft click of her cabin door opening made her turn. Her empathic senses alerted her to Cade's arrival before he appeared in the doorway.

He was dressed in workout clothes, a towel around his neck and his hair damp with sweat. "Hi."

"Hi."

His gaze swept over her. "Did I wake you?"

"No." She glanced down. Her tunic was crooked. She tugged it into place.

He joined her by the viewport. "Is there anything I can do to help?" He lifted a hand to touch her face, but hesitated, uncertainty in his green eyes.

Capturing his hand in hers, she drew him forward and twined her arms around his neck. She needed his touch, now more than ever. "Your presence is always a help."

"That's good to hear." He brushed a strand of hair out of her eyes. "Any problems with Clarek?"

"Not exactly."

"Is he staying on the ship?"

"For the moment."

"I'm not going to ask how you feel about that."

He knew her well. "Thank you." She stood on tiptoe and brushed her lips across his. Shivers of sensation spiraled outward from the point of contact. Maybe he *could* help her. More than anything, she wanted to blot out reality for a while. She licked her lips. "Wanna help me...let off steam?"

His arms tightened, but his gaze searched hers. "Is that what you need?"

She feathered another kiss over his lips. "Yeah. I really do."

He groaned. "Then lady, I'm all yours."

He pulled her flush against his muscled body, his mouth caressing hers, giving comfort and passion in equal measure. She tunneled her fingers into his hair, urging him closer. She needed this. And clearly, so did he.

She lost track of time after that, as well as the location of their clothes. When the delirium finally passed, she was on the bed, naked, and cradled against Cade's bare chest.

"That was unexpected," he murmured as he stroked her hair.

She placed a kiss on the warm skin of his neck. "I know. It just seemed like the right thing to do."

The corners of his mouth lifted. "So I gathered."

And it had worked. Her body no longer felt like it was wrapped in iron. "What were you expecting?"

"Actually, I wanted to find out if you're still going to the Suulh homeworld."

The homeworld. In all the emotional cacophony, she'd forgotten her original focus. And now it seemed coated in soot. She fisted her hands on his chest and rested her chin on top. "I suppose so."

He frowned. "You suppose so?"

"I'm just not sure that's the best move."

His fingertips trailed across her forehead, brushing strands of hair off her face. "Why not?"

She sighed. "Because my life has turned into a pack of lies."

His frown deepened. "That's not true."

"Oh, no?" She ticked the items off on her fingers. "My mom lied to me about the Suulh and is still stonewalling me about her past. Knox and the Admiral have lied to me about my career, turning it into a house of cards. And this ship—" She gestured around them. "Jonarel made me the captain so he could spy on me for Siginal. Think about it. I don't have anything left in my life that's real."

His body tensed beneath her. "You have me." He said it with a slight hitch, like he thought she might contradict him.

A flash of pain echoed in her empathic senses. She'd just given him a verbal backhand without even realizing it.

She cupped her palm against his cheek and brushed her lips over his. "I'm sorry." She followed the apology with tiny kisses at the corners of his mouth. "You're right. That was a terrible thing to say." She gave him a more lingering kiss before pulling back to look into his eyes. "Forgive me?"

His grip tightened as he pulled her close and kissed her with exquisite tenderness. "Always."

When he released her, she rested her cheek on his chest, drawing comfort from the steady thump of his heart.

He made small circles on her back with his palm, sending tingles of sensation dancing over her skin.

She turned her head to meet his gaze. "I just really hate knowing that ever since the Academy, I've been unwittingly following a path created by the Admiral and Siginal."

His brows drew down. "I don't believe that."

"Why not? You heard Knox. I've been watched and maneuvered every step of the way, like a pawn in a chess game. All the things I thought I'd worked for, all my supposed achievements and promotions, were designed to keep me on the track they wanted. I didn't earn them. They were given to me."

His hand stilled. "Whoa. Back up the train." He sat up, pulling her with him. "You can't be serious."

"I'm very serious."

"Then you're an idiot."

She jerked at the vehemence in his voice.

"You were *not* babied at the Academy. I was there, remember? You worked your butt off. And you sure as hell weren't given the command position on the *Argo* without earning it. That's not how the Fleet works and it's not how *you* work. I've read your service reports. You belonged on that ship, Aurora. Just as you're meant to be the captain of this one."

She swallowed as her throat closed.

But he wasn't finished. "You brought this crew together. You saved the Suulh on the Setarip ship. And again at Burrow. You're the most extraordinary leader I've ever known. You need to be that leader now." He pinned her with a pointed look. "Sahzade."

She stared at him, transfixed by the confidence shining in his eyes. He believed in her. One hundred percent.

There was only one thing she could say after a speech like that.

"Hawke to Emoto."

Kire's voice came over the cabin speakers. "Emoto here."

"Call a crew meeting for all personnel. Observation lounge. One hour."

Seventeen

"To accomplish our objectives—finding the Admiral and investigating the Suulh homeworld—we'll need to split up."

Murmurs of discontent followed Aurora's pronouncement. She avoided looking at Jonarel. She couldn't afford to let her anger break through. "But before we decide how to proceed, you need to know the information Knox shared with us." She gave a brief synopsis of the discussion, choosing to omit any mention of the Schreibers' manipulation or the Clareks' duplicity.

"The Teeli are the ones who attacked the Suulh?" Gonzo shook his head. "That's hard to believe. They're a peace-loving society."

"That's what they told the Council." Anger flowed through Cade's words. "It's the perfect smokescreen to keep the Fleet from asking questions about their true intentions."

"What *are* their intentions?" Reynolds asked.

"Enslavement of the Suulh, for starters," he said. "But that may be just the beginning. It's safe to assume the Teeli built the carrier and warships we ran into at Burrow. Those ships were designed for a very specific purpose."

"And that's why we'll need to use the *Starhawke*'s camouflage ability to reach the Suulh homeworld," Aurora said. "We'll be going deep into Teeli space. Now that we know they're the enemy, we'll have to be cautious."

Cade rested his forearms on the table. "If we're splitting up so my unit can track down the Admiral while you're investigating the homeworld, we'll need to acquire a second ship with interstellar capability. There's no guarantee we'll find the Admiral on Gallows Edge."

Aurora nodded. "I realize that. Any ideas on where to obtain one?"

"Maybe. But I doubt you'll want to be involved."

"Why not?"

Cade glanced at Drew. "I thought we'd pay a visit to Weezel."

Drew's nose scrunched up. "That reprobate? Have you forgotten that last time he propositioned me and put his hands where they didn't belong? Like I'm supposed to find his sweaty palms and enormous gut enticing." She shuddered.

"I'm with Bella," Justin said. "There has to be a better option than making a deal with Weezel. He's a public menace."

"A menace who owns the largest junkyard in Fleet space."

"That's because he's slimy," Drew said. "There's not a ship in that yard that wasn't obtained through some underhanded deal."

"Which is why you shouldn't object to removing one from under his nose."

Drew perked up. "You mean steal one of his ships?"

Cade shrugged. "It's not really stealing if he doesn't legally own it in the first place, is it?"

Justin gave a snort of laughter and Gonzo grinned.

Aurora covered her mouth with her hand to hide her smile. Her crew looked a little less amused by the conversation.

"Isn't there another way besides stealing?" Kire asked.

Cade met his gaze. "Not that I can see. You can't rent an interstellar ship unless you're willing to have a pilot and crew go along. That's not an option. And we can't afford to buy one."

Kire frowned, but didn't argue the point.

Cade turned to Aurora. "The real question is, would you be willing to drop my unit off at Weezel's shipyard before you head into Teeli space?"

She tapped a finger against her lips. "Of course. But I'm not sure your entire unit should go."

"Why not?"

"We need to be strategic with our resources. Infiltrating Teeli space and investigating the original Suulh homeworld won't be easy. If you're willing, I'd like to keep Reynolds and Gonzo onboard. We could use their talents."

They both looked surprised by her request. Intrigued, too. But they turned to Cade rather than responding.

He shifted in his chair. "That leaves my unit pretty shorthanded."

"Not necessarily. I'm going with you."

Cacophony erupted as her crew launched a flurry of objections. Even Star appeared beside her to join the debate.

"You must remain—"

"No way—"

"Sahzade, you can't—"

But Jonarel's roar drowned out the rest as he rose to his feet. "You cannot go!" His golden eyes blazed. "They are going to *steal* a ship."

She folded her hands, her gaze steady. "I heard."

"And you would help them?" He stabbed a finger in Cade's direction. "You would let *him* turn you into a criminal?"

Drew jumped into the fray before Aurora or Cade could respond.

"Hey!" She scowled at Clarek. "That's unfair. Weezel is the scum of the universe. He preys on the weak and ignorant. He deserves far worse than having one of his ships lifted."

Justin weighed in. "We might even be able to return whichever ship we take to its rightful owner."

Jonarel glared at them, his hands curling into fists.

"You see?" Aurora gestured to Justin and Drew. "I would be performing a public service."

He glowered, his dark hair creating a curtain around his face. "And what if you are caught?"

She stared him down. "I've faced far worse than a corrupt owner of a junkyard. I can handle it. And it's *my* decision." She packed a lot of meaning into those words.

Jonarel got the message loud and clear. His scowl deepened, but he sank into his seat.

Mya's plea was harder to ignore. "Sahzade, you can't leave the *Starhawke*." Worry shone in her dark eyes. "You're the captain."

"And Kire will be acting captain while I'm gone."

Kire stared at her. "I thought you wanted to see the homeworld."

She had. She did. But her priorities had shifted. Her instincts screamed at her to get away from Jonarel and Star's watchful gazes. And more important, she wanted to track down the man responsible for this mess. She had a few things to discuss with the Admiral after she found him. "Mya can lead the investigation. She knows more about our heritage than I do, anyway. I'll be more useful locating the Admiral."

Kire's neck looked stiff as he nodded. He clearly didn't like her plan one bit.

Mya's expression shifted from worried to bleak. "What exactly do you want me to do?"

"Find out if any Suulh are still living on the planet. If possible, make contact, and gather information about the current situation with the Teeli."

"What about you? If you leave the *Starhawke* we won't have any way to contact you while we're in Teeli space. What if you need us to come back to help you?"

Aurora gritted her teeth. Mya had just thrown down a gauntlet, implying *she'd* be the one who would need help. "I'll be fine."

Jonarel growled. "You are putting yourself at risk."

Cade backed her up, his face darkening like a thundercloud. "Cool it, Clarek. She said she'll be fine. Show a little faith."

She appreciated his support. "Besides, I'm not the one traveling into enemy space." She gave Jonarel and Mya a pointed look. "You're taking a much greater risk than I am. With any luck, we'll have the Admiral with us when you return."

Eighteen

How could Aurora do this?

Mya's thoughts kept time with her feet as she paced in her cabin. But it didn't help. Pivoting, she flopped onto her couch and stared at the ceiling. Like the answers she sought would be written there. Ridiculous.

The door chime startled her. She couldn't sense whoever was in the corridor, which meant it wasn't Aurora. She pushed to her feet. "Come in."

Jonarel's large silhouette filled the doorway.

Her heartbeat sped up. Not a good sign. Then again, her pulse rate tended to increase anytime he was around. It was an unfortunate reaction she'd developed not long after they'd become friends.

"May I speak with you?"

She crossed her arms. Part of her wanted to tell him to get lost. She was still smarting from the revelations in Aurora's office. But the look in his golden eyes called to her. She didn't have the strength to turn him away. "I suppose."

He stepped across the threshold. The spacious room immediately shrunk to the size of a closet, the air thickening, forcing her to focus on her breathing.

He stopped within touching distance. "I am concerned about Aurora."

She barely caught the sigh before it escaped her lips. Of course that's why he was here. He always sought her out when he wanted to talk about Aurora.

She motioned him to the couch and perched on the nearby chair. "So am I."

His muscular frame dwarfed her couch. He rested his forearms on his knees and stared at the floor while he ran his thumb along his fingers, pressing on the pads until a hint of his claws showed from the dark flesh. It was an unconscious gesture, something she'd watched him do dozens of times during their private discussions. It indicated he was gathering his thoughts.

He lifted his head and gazed into her eyes. "I am having trouble understanding her."

Such beautiful eyes. They were the color of spun gold, flecked with dark green that matched his skin tone. She could get lost in those eyes, which is why she never allowed herself to look at him for very long.

She forced herself to pay attention to his comment. "Things have been...challenging...recently." And she'd suffered collateral damage in the region of her heart. She didn't want to think about the lies he'd told her over the years. Or how foolish she and Aurora had looked, blindly trusting his good intentions. "Finding out about your...your..." She waved her hand in a vague gesture, unwilling to call him a liar.

"I never meant to hurt her." Pain etched his face. "Or you."

She swallowed. Talking to Jonarel when he was focused on Aurora was tough enough. When he looked at her with anything that resembled caring, her insides turned to jelly. "I believe you."

"Do you?" Doubt lurked in his eyes.

"Yes, I do." She could say it with conviction because her heart told her it was true. Whatever had motivated his actions, he never would have intentionally set out to hurt either of them.

"Thank you." He clasped her hand in his.

Red alert! His touch warmed her skin, making her think things she had no business thinking, especially now.

His thumb brushed the back of her hand as he gazed into her eyes.

He probably didn't realize that he was doing it, but it was seriously impacting her ability to draw in air. Or maybe that was her anxiety about what was coming next. He was clearly focused on one thing. *Aurora.*

His next words proved it. "We must change her mind."

She bit down on the inside of her cheek. It was either that or start screaming.

He was delusional if he thought he could change Aurora's mind considering how hostile she was toward him at the moment. Yet that didn't stop him from wanting Mya to jump into her usual role as mediator and work miracles. "What makes you think we can?"

His response was more snarl than speech. "We must. She is allowing Ellis to control her decisions."

Oh, boy. She was tiptoeing through a minefield. She didn't want to hurt him, but his objectivity was out the window when it came to Cade Ellis. And wasn't that the pot calling the kettle black?

But Cade wasn't the monster Jonarel wanted him to be. He'd hurt Aurora in the past, but his actions since Gaia had proven he'd learned from his mistakes. Everyone could see it, except Jonarel. Because he didn't want to.

She knew the feeling. "Her decisions as captain?" she asked gently. "Or her personal decisions?"

A menacing growl rumbled out of his chest. He released her hand as his claws protruded from their sheaths. "He will hurt her. One way or another."

Unfortunately, he could be right. There were no guarantees when it came to love.

She chose her words carefully. "Cade's a good leader. And his unit has been invaluable in helping with the Suulh. I don't believe he's a bad person. Do you?"

His lips pulled back from his teeth. "I do not trust him. And she should not, either."

Mya suppressed a sigh. Jonarel believed he knew what was best for Aurora, and that he was a better match for her than Cade. Mya didn't agree. Unfortunately, she couldn't trust her own judgment in that department.

"I know you love her. So do I. But she's a grown woman with the right to make her own choices."

His fingers curled as a shadow passed over his face. "It is not that simple. There are...consequences."

His tone made the hairs on the back of her neck stand up. "What do you mean, consequences?" When he didn't respond, she laid a hand on his forearm. "Jonarel, answer me. Is Aurora in danger?"

His expression hardened. "No. I will protect her."

Protect her? "From what?"

"From any threat she encounters. Her safety is all that matters."

Now *she* wanted to growl. "All that matters to you?" He was trying to tell her something important, but for whatever reason, he wouldn't say it directly. Because of his loyalty to his clan? To his father? To the Admiral?

"Not only me." His words came slowly. "I want Aurora with me. Even if she does not mate with me, I can keep her safe. But if she chooses Ellis, things will be...difficult."

Difficult? She fought the urge to grab the front of his tunic and shake him. He had a possessive streak longer than the Nile, but she didn't think that was prompting his little speech. His focus was on Aurora's wellbeing, not his own. Which meant there was an outside threat. That rang every alarm bell she had.

She gritted her teeth. "Care to be more specific?"

He gazed at her. "I cannot. But you must convince her to remain on the *Starhawke*. With us."

She pulled her hand back and folded her arms over her chest. "I can't. She won't listen to me. If I even broach the subject, I'll push her further down the path she's on." She held up a hand when he opened his mouth to object. "But I do have a suggestion." And he'd hate it. "The one person who might be able to talk her out of this is Cade."

Yep, his face resembled an ice sculpture. "He would not listen."

"Probably not. But if you want Aurora to stay, you'll have to convince him it's in her best interests. Get him to talk her out of going with his team." Even then, the odds were slim to none. When Aurora made up her mind, nothing short of a typhoon would move her.

Jonarel swallowed, the sound audible in the quiet room. "I will try."

Nineteen

Cade's fist connected, the punch jostling the heavy padded bag suspended from the ceiling. He followed with a flurry of blows, each one delivered with precision and focus. Shifting his stance, he struck with a kick that made the bag swing. He kept up the assault, the satisfying thump of each blow keeping time with his grunts of exertion.

But he still caught the sound of the door to the training room opening.

"Ellis."

He paused, balancing on the balls of his feet as he pivoted to face his new opponent. "Clarek." He'd expected to hear from his adversary sooner or later. No way would the Kraed let Aurora's declaration to leave the ship go unchallenged.

Clarek stood just inside the room, his large body positioned like he was bracing for a fight.

Cade would be happy to give him one. The Kraed had betrayed Aurora's trust, hurting her with his deception. That was unacceptable.

"We need to discuss Aurora."

Discuss? The Kraed was willing to talk first? That was a surprise. Cade grabbed the small towel hanging next to his jacket and mopped the sweat from his face. "Okay." He draped the towel around his neck and waited.

Clarek seemed uncharacteristically hesitant. "You must tell her to remain on the *Starhawke.*"

Cade barked out a laugh. "*Tell* her? Are you kidding? I can't *tell* her to do anything. This was her decision, not mine." And he'd applauded it. If he tried to change her mind, she'd tell him a thing or two. Like where he could shove his opinions.

Clarek bristled. "You can talk to her. She will listen to you. Convince her she is safer here."

Cade's eyes narrowed. "Safer because she's with you?"

Clarek didn't bat an eye. "Yes."

Arrogant jerk. "I'm not onboard with that idea. Your track record for protecting her isn't exactly stellar."

Clarek growled.

"And besides, she doesn't need your protection. She doesn't need *anyone's* protection. She can take care of herself."

"She does not *need* to take unnecessary chances. And she does not *need* to be involved in illegal activities."

Cade kept a firm grip on his temper. "I didn't hear you offering any brilliant ideas about how we could acquire a second ship. And we need one if we're going to track down the Admiral. You want to ask your father if he'll loan us one? After all, he wants us to find the Admiral, too."

That comment seemed to knock Clarek off balance. He shifted his weight as he considered Cade's suggestion. "He cannot provide you with a ship."

Cade shrugged. "Then taking one from Weezel is our best option. And Aurora wants to go with us. Finding the Admiral is more important to her right now than going to the homeworld."

"That does not make sense. She has been wanting to learn about her history all her life. Why would she choose to go with you instead?" Clarek looked genuinely perplexed.

Maybe the Kraed didn't know Aurora as well as he thought he did. "Because the Admiral's been *lying* to her all her life. Withholding information about her past. Manipulating her." *Like you,* he wanted to add, but didn't. He'd promised Aurora he wouldn't be the instigator of any fights with Clarek. Although that didn't mean he wouldn't engage if Clarek came after him.

"Then why would she seek him out? Why not go to the homeworld and send you to find him?"

Cade almost laughed. Clarek really *didn't* understand Aurora. "She wants to know what he knows. And once she's confirmed he's okay, she probably wants to yell at him for lying to her."

Clarek flinched. Judging by the Kraed's expression, he knew exactly how that felt. Aurora had probably hit him with both barrels when she'd returned from her meeting with Knox.

Cade had a question of his own. "Why did you do it?"

Clarek's brows lifted. "Do what?"

"Lie to her. Keep what you knew about her past a secret. You knew how desperately she wanted that information. How could you keep it from her?"

Clarek glared, but Cade got the distinct impression the anger was directed inward as much as it was at him. "I did not want to lie to her."

"But you did. Why?"

"I was protecting her."

Crazy as it sounded, Cade believed him. It fit with Clarek's attitude. "Protecting her from what?"

"From knowledge she was not ready to handle."

That got Cade's ruff up. "Who are you to decide what she can and can't handle? You keep talking about her like she's fragile. Weak. She's a lot stronger than you give her credit for. A lot stronger than *you.*"

Anger flashed in Clarek's yellow eyes, followed by something that looked like shame. He looked away. "Perhaps you are correct."

Cade's jaw hit the floor. Hell had frozen over. Clarek was agreeing with him? His odd capitulation prompted Cade's next question. "What exactly are you afraid of? If she comes with me, what do you think will happen to her?"

The glower was back. "You will hurt her."

Cade reined in his temper. "Not intentionally. I want her to be safe. I wouldn't—"

"You hurt her before. I will not allow you to hurt her again."

The commanding tone grated Cade's nerves, but for the first time, he understood the motivation behind it. Ten years ago, he'd left Aurora heartbroken. And Clarek had been justifiably furious with him. Now, the shoe was on the other foot.

Something passed between them, a flash of elemental understanding that hit Cade at his core. "We've *both* hurt her. We've *both* been idiots, making decisions without seeing things from her perspective. That has to stop. If you really care about her, you need to accept her choices." Was he actually giving Clarek advice? To improve his relationship with Aurora? Apparently it was snowing in Hell, too.

Clarek's lips lifted in a snarl. "I do not like you."

"That's okay." Cade's mirthless smile probably looked equally aggressive. "I don't like you, either. But we both love Aurora. And that's what matters. *Her* needs. *Her* happiness."

"You cannot make her happy. You will only bring her pain."

"And she'll be happy with you? I don't see that. You've tried controlling her, pushing her in the direction you want her to go, and look where it's gotten you. She doesn't even want to talk to you."

Direct hit. Clarek turned into a wall of fury as he stalked forward.

Cade shifted into a defensive crouch. Maybe this would end in bloodshed after all.

But Clarek halted before he was in striking distance, his gaze arctic. "Be careful, Ellis." He opened his palms. Wickedly sharp claws extended from the pads of his fingers. "I may accept Aurora's choice, but know this. If anything happens to her, I *will* kill you."

Cade had encountered those claws once before. He had a couple scars to prove it.

He met Clarek glare for glare. "You won't have to. If anything happens to her, I'll already be dead."

Twenty

Aurora was leaving her ship. Again. Only this time, she couldn't get away fast enough.

Reynolds and Gonzo had agreed to remain on the *Starhawke*, freeing her to join Cade in stealing—*obtaining*—a second ship. She didn't question her motivations. She was going on instinct, the one thing she could count on. And it was driving her to remain with Cade and locate the Admiral. What she'd do when they found him was still up for grabs.

One thing was certain. She wouldn't be worrying about keeping her abilities a secret anymore. Not from the Admiral, not from anyone. Knox's revelation had a lot to do with her change of heart, but the confrontation with her mom had been a factor, too.

The weight of the fears that defined her mom's life had burdened her for too long—she was sick of carrying those emotional chains. Leaving the ship was a step in the right direction. She needed to physically separate herself from Mya and Jonarel and their overprotective tendencies. Intentionally or not, they both fed that fear cycle.

She pulled another tunic from her closet and stuffed it in her pack. *Jonarel.* What was she going to do about him? The anger from his betrayal still burned, but she couldn't sustain that kind of animosity for long. And he'd looked so miserable the few times she'd seen him during the journey to Weezel's junkyard. He was punishing himself. She could feel it. Guilt and remorse covered him like a cloak.

She couldn't excuse what he'd done, but the words she'd spoken in anger haunted her. She'd annihilated him. And while his actions had caused her pain, she believed his intentions had been honorable. She just wasn't ready to talk to him about it.

Hefting her bag onto her back, she left her cabin and strode to the lift. As she descended, Star appeared beside her.

"Will you reconsider your decision?"

Aurora stared straight ahead. She didn't know how much of an accomplice Star had been in all of this, but she wasn't happy with the Nirunoc, either. "No."

"Jonarel fears for your safety."

Aurora clenched her jaw. "He should fear for his. I'm staying in Fleet space. He's the one heading into Teeli territory."

Star appeared in front of her, part of her image blending with the bulkhead since Aurora stood right in front of the lift doors. The lifted halted, but the doors didn't open.

"We want to help you, Aurora."

"Right. Help me. By lying to me about your real intentions. By concealing your knowledge about my heritage and your connection to the Admiral. I can see how that would help me. Thank you." Sarcasm wasn't her style, but the words tumbled out of their own accord.

"If Jonarel had told you what he knew, what would you have done?"

"I don't know. Maybe nothing. But at least I would have had a choice."

Star's eyes narrowed. "He is fighting very hard to give you the right to choose. And you do not even see it."

"See *what?*"

"He loves you, Aurora. Your happiness means everything to him. Even when it costs him what he wants most."

Aurora frowned. "He's not fighting *for* me. He *lied* to me."

"Because *he* does not have a choice."

That brought her up short. "What choice? I don't understand."

"If you do not understand, then you do not know the Kraed as well as you think you do." Star's image faded. "Be careful, Aurora. So much depends on you."

The doors opened onto the shuttle bay.

Jonarel was waiting on the other side. Without a word, he hauled her into a death grip.

And nearly collapsed her lungs. "Jonarel," she croaked. "I can't breathe."

He eased up a bit, but the sensation of being squeezed in a vise didn't go away.

He rested his cheek on top of her head. "Please, stay."

Fear washed over her, pouring off him in waves, drowning her. She needed space. Physically and emotionally. She pushed at his chest. "I can't."

He resisted for only a moment before dropping his arms to his sides. The look in his eyes matched the emotions breaking over her. "I never wanted to hurt you."

Her throat constricted. She was *not* going to get into this now. But she couldn't reject his overture entirely. "You had your reasons. And I have mine." She crossed her arms and drew in a calming breath. "I need you to do something for me."

His gaze burned like the sun. "Anything."

"Keep Mya safe. She won't see danger coming the way you will. Or be able to defend against it." *Like I can* she almost said, but didn't.

His spine straightened. "I will guard her with my life."

Of that, she had no doubt. She stood on tiptoe and brushed a feather kiss on his cheek. "Thank you." Ignoring the plea in his eyes as she pulled back took willpower, but she did it, turning away and walking to the shuttle.

Celia intercepted her halfway. "Take this." She held out a dark brown bundle.

Aurora accepted the cloth package. "What is it?"

"I figured you didn't have a good outfit for meeting with unsavory characters." Celia smiled, a knowing look in her brown eyes. "Now you do."

Aurora returned the smile. "You're right. I don't." And the gift said a lot about how Celia viewed her decision. Come to think of it, Celia hadn't voiced any objections during the meeting in the observation lounge, either.

She pulled her friend into a hug. "Thank you."

Celia hugged her back. "I'll watch out for Mya," she murmured. "Whatever she needs."

Tears pricked her eyes. From the day they'd met, she'd always been able to count on her friend.

As Celia stepped back, her gaze drifted to the shuttle where Cade waited. "He brings out the best in you."

Aurora blinked. She hadn't expected the comment. "I know."

Celia nodded in approval. "Good." She gave Aurora's shoulder a squeeze and made a shooing motion. "Now get out of here."

As Celia left the bay, Aurora slipped the compact bundle into her pack and joined Kire, Mya, Cade and Justin outside the doorway of the shuttle.

Mya stood with her arms crossed over her chest and her legs braced apart like she was facing a hurricane gale. The stance fit the sea of emotions Aurora picked up from her—frustration, worry, and fear chief among them.

Cade met her gaze over the top of Kire's head. "All set?"

"Ready when you are."

"I'll go warm up the engines." Cade inclined his head in a subtle nod as his gaze flicked to Kire and Mya. He and Justin stepped into the shuttle's interior, giving Aurora a moment alone with her friends.

Kire hugged her first. "Be safe out there."

He wasn't happy about her decision to decamp. She could feel it. "You, too."

"We could stay in orbit until you're ready to leave. In case there's trouble."

She shook her head. "Weezel may be a scumbag, but our plan still involves breaking Fleet law. You can't be a part of that."

If something happened that caused the *Starhawke* to be identified, and word got back to the Council, they could end up incarcerated. As it was, they were risking censure by ignoring the mission they'd contracted for with Admiral Payne. She wouldn't drag her crew down an even rockier road. "I'll send updates to the border buoy so you'll know where we are."

His hazel eyes were uncharacteristically somber. "We'll find you."

Mya looked like a deflated balloon. "Are you sure this is what you want to do?"

"Yes, I'm sure." She rested a hand on Mya's arm. "It'll be okay. Trust me."

"I *do* trust you." Mya sighed. "It's the rest of the galaxy that has me worried."

Aurora pulled her into a hug. "I'll be fine. I promise."
She stepped back. "And I'll want a full report on the
homeworld when I see you." She put emphasis on the
comment, hoping to lighten Mya's mood.

No such luck. "You could still see it in person."

She shook her head. "You know I can't. Not now."

Mya's fear struck her, as powerful and intense as
Jonarel's. "Be careful, Sahzade."

"You, too." She gave Mya an encouraging smile
before entering the darkened interior of the shuttle. Their
fears were acting like quicksand, sucking her down. She
needed to get out of here.

Justin, Drew, and Williams were already belted in.
Aurora stowed her pack and settled into the seat next to
Justin.

Cade sat with Kelly in the cockpit. He glanced back
at her. "Ready?"

She nodded. "Let's go."

They glided away from the *Starhawke*, the planet
below steadily filling the viewports. Aurora resisted the urge
to look back at her ship. She wouldn't be able to see it
anyway with the camouflage engaged. And it represented
the wrong path. At least for now. She'd made a choice she
believed in. She needed to keep moving forward.

The vista opened before them as they exited the
thin cloud layer. Desert stretched to the horizon, though not
nearly as stark as what she'd experienced on Burrow. A
mountain range rose in the distance, with a meandering
riverbed near the base. Small, scraggly trees and shrubs
dotted the landscape around the fenced enclosure that
housed the junkyard.

Cade made a high pass over the area, giving Aurora
a good look. Unlike a Fleet salvage yard, where ships were

lined up in orderly rows, the layout here looked more like a traffic jam.

Newer vessels with gleaming hulls sat side by side with stripped carcasses that would never fly again. A few open paths wound through the chaos, but how the owner ever found anything in the mess, or moved a ship in or out, was a mystery.

Justin must have noticed her puzzled expression, because he grinned. "Yeah, the yard resembles its owner. Weezel's not known for the cleanliness or maintenance of his domain. Or his body."

She made a face. "Charming."

"Yep."

Drew spoke up from the seat behind her. "And fair warning—Weezel's like an octopus, but nowhere near as smart. No woman is safe with him."

Aurora couldn't decide if she should be intrigued or horrified by their descriptions. But she didn't have long to contemplate it. Cade set the shuttle down behind a small hill a few kilometers from the yard's perimeter, making use of the hull camouflage to hide their approach.

Kelly opened the hatch and claimed the pilot's seat as Cade joined the rest of the team. Sunshine and a blast of heat radiated through the open doorway.

Aurora squinted against the glare. "Glad I brought sun gear." She pulled her shades from her pack.

Cade hefted his pack on his shoulder. "It'll get chilly tonight. If we don't locate a suitable ship to camp in, you'll be grateful for your jacket." The look in his eyes before he slipped his shades in place confirmed he'd be willing to help keep her warm, too.

She grabbed one of the supply bags and her pack before following him down the ramp. The sunshine pressed into her skin, intensifying the sensation of stepping into an oven. The dry heat might be good for preserving spacecraft, but her body objected to the assault. A memory of balmy tropical breezes blowing off the ocean on Azaana drifted through her mind like a siren song, reminding her of something she'd been meaning to ask Justin. "Have you talked to Raaveen lately?"

He nodded. "I got a message from her two days ago. The Suulh are doing great, and the settlement's coming along. Three more of the outbuildings are completed and they've finished furnishing the main house."

That was good news. "No problems to report?"

"Nope. I sent a message before we left the *Starhawke*, letting her know communication might be patchy for a while, and not to worry."

At least one part of her original plan was clicking along smoothly. "Thank you. She has plenty to focus on without worrying about us."

Kelly appeared at the shuttle hatch, her red hair turning into a crown of flame in the bright light. "Everything's unloaded, Captain. Any final instructions before I take off?"

Aurora shook her head. "Just make sure the *Starhawke* leaves for the homeworld as soon as you're back at the helm." She didn't expect Kire to disobey her order, but it didn't hurt to clarify the situation for Kelly, just in case. "And bring her back to me in one piece."

She'd meant the last comment as a joke, but the words didn't come out that way.

Kelly's pale eyes revealed an understanding way beyond her years. "I will."

Twenty-One

"What do you see?" Cade crouched beside Drew and peered over the top of the hill overlooking the junkyard. The crowded enclosure was shadowed, the weak glow from the scattered post lights barely visible through the hulking silhouettes of the ships.

She flipped up her night visor. "No surveillance of any kind."

"You're kidding. Nothing?"

"Nope. No cameras and no security personnel."

Justin snorted. "Typical Weezel. He's too cheap to pay someone to guard the place and he's too lazy to do it himself."

"What about the fence?" Aurora asked. "Is it as flimsy as it looks?"

"Uh-huh." Drew slipped her visor back into place. "It's basic wire mesh. A pair of bolt cutters will get us in. Getting out, however, will be the tricky part."

"What do you mean?" Cade glanced at the long stretch of metal fencing.

"Weezel's put all his efforts into keeping anything that's inside the yard from leaving. See the boxes along the top line?" She pointed to a series of square objects placed with military precision at intervals along the perimeter. "Those are EMP emitters. They're designed to send out a pulse whenever an object of sufficient mass breaks through the security grid. If we try to take off while that system is live, the ship will drop like a stone."

Cade frowned. Leave it to Weezel to figure out the one security measure he needed to keep his contraband safe. "Can you hack in and disable a few of the boxes? Create a window for us?"

Drew shook her head. "Not with this kind of setup. If one goes down, the others will trigger an alert. I'll need to shut down the entire system at the source."

"Which would be where?"

"Most likely the utility shed attached to Weezel's main building. Justin can verify that after we're inside the yard and have selected our ship."

"Do you have any prospects?" Cade asked.

Drew projected an image from her comband that she'd taken during the aerial pass over the junkyard. "I was thinking this one, since we're going for rugged but understated." She zoomed in on a smaller craft near the back of the yard. "It's seen some action, but the exterior looks well maintained despite the battle scars. And it's well-armed for a ship of its size. Might have been used for security detail in a previous life."

"That would be helpful." Cade glanced at Aurora.

Her gaze was locked on the image of the ship. "Can you tell if it's still spaceworthy?"

"Not until I'm inside."

Cade pushed to his feet. "Then let's get moving."

Getting past the fence was as easy as Drew had predicted. A few snips of the metal mesh and they were in. Finding the ship Drew had chosen took longer because they had to climb and crawl their way through the yard. When they reached it, the team formed a semi-circle around Drew while she worked her magic on the locking mechanism for the hatch.

"Come on, sweetie," she crooned, stroking a hand on the ship's hull. "I promise I'll take good care of you if you let us in."

Cade grunted. "Did Weezel spend money on an advanced lock for this ship?"

"No. I'm working with the ship's original security system. And it's a good one. I could break into it, but that might destroy it and some of the ship's related systems in the process. I'd rather convince the system I'm the registered owner."

As Drew continued wooing the security system, Cade's gaze drifted to the looming outlines of the nearby ships. The sharp edges and deep shadows cast by the smattering of yard lights and the pale moonlight gave the surroundings an eerie beauty.

A gentle whirring alerted him that Drew had achieved her goal.

She brushed her hands together and gestured to the opening as the gangway settled onto the ground with a thump. "Your turn."

Cade and Justin entered first, with Drew behind, while Aurora and Williams remained outside. Cade kept his pistol at the ready as he scanned the area with his night visor. Weezel wasn't the type to set booby traps, but that didn't mean the previous owners hadn't installed additional safeguards.

But a thorough sweep of the ship came up clean. Cade sent the all clear to Aurora and Williams to join them. By the time he returned to the central room, they were setting up camp, pulling food rations and water containers from their supply packs. The hatch had already been sealed, a red light on the control panel indicating the security system had been reactivated.

He glanced down the corridor. "Where's Drew?"

Aurora smiled. "Engine room. Getting to know her new friend."

"I doubt we'll see her again tonight."

"Probably not. What's our next step?"

"Let's check out the command center."

Cade led the way down the narrow corridor to the navigation pod at the front of the ship. He slid into the pilot's seat while Aurora claimed the co-pilot's chair. The layout for the controls reminded him of the training fighters he'd flown during his Academy days.

At one time, this ship had likely served as security for a luxury yacht or commercial passenger cruiser. Rather than sullying the pretty lines and precious interior space of their private vessels with armaments and ammunition, most ship owners preferred to hire security ships like this one to fly in tandem, acting as interstellar bodyguards.

Cade ran his fingers over the console, appreciating the more rudimentary layout that placed everything of value within easy reach without adding a bit of extraneous material. He pulled open one of the side panels and confirmed what he'd suspected—the ship was heavily customized. Drew was right. Whoever had owned this ship before Weezel acquired it had treated it with love and respect.

"I like this ship." Aurora peered over his shoulder. "It's nothing like the *Starhawke*, but there's a logic to its form and function that's appealing."

"I think the word you're looking for is *classic*."

Aurora nodded. "Yes, classic. That's perfect."

He reached out to capture her hand in his. "The ship's not the only one that fits that description."

The corners of her eyes crinkled as she fluttered her eyelashes at him. "Why Mr. Ellis, I do believe you're giving me a compliment."

He smiled as he urged her closer. "I'd like to give you a kiss, too."

Her eyelids slid to half-mast. "Be my guest."

The sound of footsteps interrupted them a millisecond before their lips made contact. They both turned as Justin appeared in the doorway.

"Drew says the engine is in decent shape. It needs a few minor repairs, and she still..." Justin trailed off as he glanced between them. "Never mind. It can wait."

Cade dropped Aurora's hand. "No, it's fine." He shot Aurora a look to let her know he'd be claiming his kiss later.

Her smile made him move that to priority number one.

Justin stayed in the doorway. "Drew's checking the ship's supplies to see if everything she needs is onboard. If not, we'll salvage items from the yard."

"Any estimate on how soon we'll be able to leave?"

"A couple days, assuming she doesn't run into any problems."

Good thing Weezel didn't believe in onsite security. "We'll check everything up here, make sure the command systems are operational. You and Williams get the tougher job—finding a solution to our EMP problem."

Twenty-Two

"We're passing the last Fleet comm station."

Mya glanced over her shoulder at Celia, who was seated at the communication console usually occupied by Kire. Now that he was acting captain, he had settled into Aurora's chair and Gonzalez had taken Celia's normal post at tactical. The musical chairs made Mya's head spin.

"Any messages from Roe?" Kire asked Celia.

"No."

Mya fought the knot of disappointment in her stomach. She hadn't expected a message from Aurora. Not really. But still...it would have been nice to hear from her before they headed into enemy territory.

She rested her chin in her palm and stared at the bridgescreen. She'd been having trouble focusing ever since Aurora had bolted off the *Starhawke* like the ship was on fire. Anxiety stalked her, and haunting images tumbled through her dreams, leaving her more exhausted when she woke up than when she'd crawled into bed. Ironically, when Celia had asked her how she was holding up, she'd responded with Aurora's favorite line. *I'm fine.*

She wasn't fine. She was coming unglued.

"How long until we reach the Teeli border?" Kire asked Kelly.

Kelly's fingers danced over the navigation console. "Fifteen minutes."

"Is the course laid in to the homeworld coordinates?"

"Aye."

The tension on the bridge clicked up a notch. There weren't any physical markers to designate the border, but there were definitely psychological ones. They were approaching the point of no return. After they left Fleet space, they'd be on their own.

Kire rested his elbows on the arms of the captain's chair and opened a ship-wide comm channel before addressing the crew. "We're about to cross into Teeli space." He glanced at Mya, his expression troubled but resolute. "Whatever we encounter at the homeworld or from the Teeli, it's imperative that we return to Fleet space safely. If you have to make a difficult choice, don't hesitate. Aurora believes in this crew. So do I. And Star?"

The Nirunoc appeared beside him. "Yes?"

"Our hull camouflage is critical. Monitor it continually. If we can't remain hidden, alert Kelly immediately. Kelly, if that occurs, you get us out of sight as quickly as possible. Understood?"

Star exchanged a look with Kelly. "Yes."

"Aye, Commander."

Commander, not Captain. Technically, Kire was the captain now, at least until Aurora returned. But no one had addressed him that way, and he hadn't encouraged it. They already had a captain. She just wasn't on the ship at the moment.

He gripped the arms of the chair and let out a slow breath. "Let's go see what the Teeli are hiding."

Twenty-Three

"I can't believe Cade talked you into doing this."

"He didn't." Aurora smiled at Drew as they walked along the junkyard's perimeter fence toward the main building. "It was Justin's idea. We had to convince Cade to go along with it." And it had been a hard-won battle. To say Cade hated this plan was a gross understatement.

Drew stopped in her tracks. "Justin's idea? Really?"

Aurora's smile widened. "Yep." She and Cade had been working side by side under the console in the navigation center, both sweaty and hot in the tight space. Her tunic had been plastered to her skin, outlining everything underneath. Cade had commented that the visual stimulation made it hard for him to concentrate. From the look in his eyes, he'd been extremely tempted to forget the repairs and focus on her, instead.

Justin had overheard Cade's comment. And hatched his plan. "Besides, Justin thought this would be good payback for all the inappropriate advances Weezel has made toward you in the past."

Drew grimaced. "But why would you volunteer to put yourself in Weezel's grubby paws?"

Aurora waved the question away. "I can handle Weezel. And I'm as eager as you are to slip *Gladiator* out from under his nose." Cade had suggested the name for the ship, which had been met with unanimous approval.

"Okay. But this." She gestured to Aurora's outfit. "It seems like overkill."

Aurora glanced down at the outfit Celia had loaned her. The low-cut tunic tied at her waist, exposing both her cleavage and her midriff, and the leggings fit like a second skin. She'd swept her hair up into an arrangement that bared her neck and shoulders. She'd end up with a sunburn if she stayed outside too long, but she was pleased with the effect she'd created. "You don't think Weezel will like it?"

"Oh, he'll like it all right." Drew rested her hands on her hips. "He'll like it even more if he can get it off you."

Aurora sobered. "I can assure you, that will *not* be happening." She had multiple ways to prevent it, with or without using her shielding ability.

"But the plan is for you to seduce him, isn't it?"

"Distract him. Keep his focus on me while you sneak into the control room and deactivate the EMP."

"Just remember Weezel doesn't have any reservations about groping a woman when she's unwilling. I can't imagine how he'll react if you pretend he has the green light."

"Actually, that might help. If he thinks he has a shot, he may not want to mess up a good thing by being pushy."

"I hope you're right."

So did she.

Maybe she should be nervous, but to be honest, ever since she'd left the *Starhawke*, she'd felt lighter and more playful. And this plan fit in perfectly with her current attitude. From what Cade's team had told her, Weezel could use a lesson in humility and self-control. She'd do her best to deliver it.

They rounded the corner of the mesh link fence and continued toward the main building. Not a single vehicle passed them on the barren road to their right.

"Will he think it's strange that we're arriving on foot?" Aurora asked Drew.

Drew snorted. "Not at all. Weezel's customers come here in all manner of ways. Our unit has made a habit of hiking in anytime we pay him a visit. As long as money changes hands, he doesn't ask questions."

So, it was discretion rather than business acumen that made him successful. And his willingness to take advantage of everyone he met.

They reached the main building and pulled open the scarred front door. The coolness of the small foyer felt heavenly after the unrelenting heat outside. Unfortunately, that was the only thing that could recommend the place. Two chairs with faded and torn upholstery sat underneath the window that faced the street. A large stain on the ceiling indicated a leak in the roof, and the rest of the small room was filled with an assortment of bins containing spare parts stacked haphazardly in vague rows.

"Cozy," she muttered under her breath.

"Just wait until you meet the owner." Drew raised her voice. "Weezel? You here?"

Aurora blinked. Drew had suddenly developed a twang to her speech and raised the pitch of her voice an octave. Her posture had changed, too. She slouched with her weight on one leg, the other canted out to the side and her hands on her hips. Apparently she had an alternate persona she used when dealing with Weezel.

A chair groaned in protest in the room off to the left, followed by heavy footfalls on the wooden floor.

Despite the warnings she'd received, Aurora wasn't entirely prepared for her first view of the man called Weezel. He was taller than she'd expected, almost the same height as Cade, but three times as wide. His girth barely fit through the narrow door to his office as he walked into the front room. The lower half of his flabby face lifted in a delighted smile that revealed crooked teeth.

"Why Suz, is that you? You're a drink of cool water on this hot day."

Suz was it? She'd remember that.

"How you doin', Weezel?" Drew's eyes sparkled like she was pleased to see the hulking man before her.

Aurora wanted to applaud. She hadn't realized Drew was such a talented actress.

"Oh, I'm doin' fine. Better now that you're here." He put his arms around Drew and pulled her against his chest. His hands somehow ended up on Drew's butt, which was a trick considering their height difference. He had to hunch to make it happen.

Drew turned her head sideways and made a face at Aurora before placing her hands on Weezel's chest and pushing. "Let me go, Weezel. I got someone I want you to meet."

Weezel's beady-eyed gaze shifted to Aurora, looking her up and down in a calculated motion that made her doubt the wisdom of her plan. But at least he released Drew.

"This here's my cousin, Sandy," Drew said. "She's lookin' to buy herself some transportation, and I told her you was the one to go see."

"Well, you got that right." Weezel puffed out his considerable chest. "No place better for a lady looking for a vessel to call her own."

Aurora did her best to imitate Drew's speech patterns. "That's what Suz told me. Had to come talk to Weezel, she said. Said you'd treat me right."

The hunger in his eyes made her skin crawl. "Oh, I assure you, I will." He grabbed her hand in both of his and raised it to his lips.

It was like being accosted by a Saint Bernard. His saliva dripped onto her skin. She almost jerked back, but that wasn't going to get her what she wanted. She forced herself to stay in character, but good grief, was that his *tongue* licking her?

Somehow, the back of his hand grazed her breast as he released her. She had seriously underestimated the slime factor of the man. But that only increased her determination to deprive him of *Gladiator.*

"Why don't you both step back into my office and we'll have ourselves a little chat?" he said, already moving in that direction.

Drew glanced at Aurora in alarm.

Aurora caught up with Weezel. "Hang on, sugar."

He turned, his gaze going to where her hand rested on his forearm. She sensed his emotional shift to surprise and confusion, confirming that if she initiated physical contact, he'd be more inclined to follow her lead.

She stepped closer. "You see, I got me some...*special* circumstances." She licked her lips in slow motion as she gazed into his eyes. His breathing changed. "I was hopin' you and me might be able to talk in private." She dropped her voice to a seductive purr. "Maybe help each other out?"

Weezel looked at a loss for words. Aurora would bet money he'd never had a woman proposition him before. And she couldn't have asked for a better reaction.

"Uh...yeah. *Yeah.* You come on back and we'll...talk." He glanced at Drew. "You don't mind waitin', do you, Suz?" The words came out as a plea.

"Sure don't. I'll just sit myself down here." Drew plunked onto one of the upholstered chairs. "You two go ahead." She waved them toward the office.

Now Weezel was *really* salivating. "Follow me."

Aurora flashed Drew a thumbs-up sign before stepping inside Weezel's office and closing the door behind her.

Twenty-Four

Cade gripped the navigation controls so hard they cut into his palms. Why had he allowed Aurora to talk him into this? Thanks to the concealed comm devices she and Drew wore, he'd heard every blessed word since they'd switched them on before entering the building. And right now he wanted to gut Weezel with his bare hands.

"Hey, buddy, you okay?" Justin glanced at Cade from the co-pilot's seat, where he was monitoring the communications.

"No," Cade ground out, his gaze locked on the speaker.

"Headed to the control room." Drew's voice was back to normal and all business.

"Roger that," Justin acknowledged.

The speaker fell silent. "Is Aurora's comm working?" Cade asked.

"Yes."

"Are you sending it to the speaker?"

"No."

Cade stared at his number one. "Why not?"

Justin shrugged. "No offense, but you can't listen to what she's doing and fly at the same time."

"Of course I can!"

Justin just gazed at him.

Cade grunted and turned back to the controls.

Drew's voice came over the speaker. "I'm through the security door. Having a bit of a challenge locating the EMP hardware. This place is worse than a packrat nest."

Cade focused on the startup sequence. He needed to be ready to lift off as soon as the EMP went down. "Systems online. Starting the engines."

The console vibrated slightly as a low hum drifted up through the deck. The sound shouldn't be loud enough to reach the main building, but he didn't want to count on it. He glanced at Justin. "Any reaction from Weezel?"

"He's a bit distracted at the moment."

Cade gritted his teeth. "Do I want to know by what?"

"Probably not."

Twenty-Five

Aurora perched on the edge of Weezel's desk, her legs crossed so that the tip of her toe brushed his thigh. He sat in his enormous padded chair, his gaze scrolling over her body like he was reading a book.

"You sure you wouldn't be more comfortable here?" He patted his lap with one beefy hand.

She fought to keep her smile in place. "Can't do that, sugar. Too distractin'. We need to talk business before movin' on to...other things." *Had she really just said that?* The bile rising in her throat assured her she had.

His leer indicated he'd bought the line. He folded his hands, seemingly content to view the whole scene as foreplay. It didn't hurt that she was leaning onto her palms, giving him an excellent view down the front of her tunic.

"This here's my problem, hon." She sighed dramatically.

His gaze followed the rise and fall of her breasts.

"I got sideways with a guy who treated me real bad. He promised we was gonna travel the galaxy together, and then he run off with the ship we'd bought. Left me stranded." She slid her tongue along her bottom lip and pouted.

Weezel tracked the movement like a dog eyeing his favorite treat.

"I need me a transport so I can get back to work."

"What kind of work would that be?" He didn't sound particularly interested in the answer, his attention alternating between her lips, her breasts, and her legs.

She slowly uncrossed her legs and looked at him through lowered lashes. "I provide fellas in need with...companionship." She trailed her fingers along the side of his face and brushing her thumb over his lips. It was like stroking a toad. "Think you can help me out?"

Weezel's eyes were as big as a toad's, too. But he wasn't looking at her face. His gaze was locked on the knot that was holding her shirt closed. "Maybe." He swallowed audibly. "What you got in mind?"

A faint vibration of the desktop alerted her that *Gladiator* had powered up.

Weezel must have felt it, too. His eyes shrank to the size of peas as he glanced out the window overlooking the junkyard.

She needed to redirect his attention. *Now.* She slipped off the desk, blocking his view of the window as she gripped his knees and swiveled his chair to face her. "I'd sure be grateful if you could help get me a ship, hon." She straddled his legs and reached for the knot at the front of her shirt to loosen it. "And I'm mighty generous when I'm grateful."

Weezel's hands gripped the arms of his chair. He'd apparently lost all interest in the vibration. He was staring at her breasts like a man who was enjoying an erotic dream and was afraid to move for fear he'd wake up. His gaze was so focused on the bare skin she was revealing that he didn't notice her palm the small syringe she'd tucked into the gathered folds of cloth.

Her shirt fell open as she wrapped her arms around his neck. "We got us a deal?" She glanced significantly at the front of his pants.

"*Oh, yeah.*" His voice was thick with lust as he reached for her.

"Good."

She struck, the needle sliding under his skin and delivering the drug before Weezel made contact. She used his shoulders and thighs as leverage to shove her body upright, sending the chair skidding in the opposite direction.

He slapped a hand against his neck like he was swatting a mosquito, but surprise quickly turned to anger as he glared at her. "What game you playin'?" He heaved his bulk out of the chair.

Aurora backed up, placing the desk between them. Williams had told her the drug would take effect immediately, but Weezel lumbered forward, seemingly unhindered. Maybe she hadn't injected the entire contents? The syringe was still in her hand, but she wasn't about to check it. She'd have to buy some time and hope for the best. "I didn't take you for a man who likes things nice and easy." She gave him a saucy smile.

His lip curled and the glitter of lust returned to his eyes. "You wanna make this rough? I can do that." He stumbled forward, but she couldn't tell if his lack of coordination was a result of the drug or the physical condition that was tenting the front of his pants.

"Ain't that more fun?" she taunted, circling the desk. She was close to the door, but she couldn't risk opening it. If the drug didn't work and he noticed Drew wasn't in the front room, things could turn ugly. Well, uglier.

He placed his hands on the desk. For support? "Fun furr me. But I'm gon make you pay furr thut pinch."

He was slurring his words. Definitely a good sign. She needed to keep him talking. "Oh, I want you to, sugar. I'm a bad, bad girl." She suddenly had a vision of Cade listening to this conversation and winced. Not the image she wanted planted in his mind.

"Vury baaad," Weezel agreed. But his eyes had lost focus. His upper body swayed while has hands remained stuck to the top of the desk like they'd been glued there. He took one step, and then toppled over like a felled tree, smacking the floor with a squishy thud.

She crept around the desk so she could see his face. His eyes were closed and his breath blew in and out in little snorts.

She pulled the ends of her shirt together and retied the knot with a decisive tug. "Actually, I'm very *good* Weezel. But I'm still taking one of your ships. After all, a deal's a deal."

Twenty-Six

"The EMP is down." Drew's voice carried over *Gladiator*'s comm system. "Go now."

Cade engaged the thrusters. The ship shimmied as it fought against the pull of gravity and climbed toward the top of the fence line.

"Here we go." Cade muttered as he eased the ship into the space formerly guarded by the EMP.

They didn't fall out of the sky. Instead, *Gladiator* rose like an eagle taking flight.

Justin shot Cade a grin. "Looking good."

"Yep. Tell Drew we're on our way. She can reactivate the EMP."

Justin relayed the message as Cade swept the ship in an arc that would bring them in front of the main building.

"How's Aurora?"

"Weezel's down. She's keeping an eye on him until Drew's out of the control room. They'll be waiting for us."

Cade's breath came a little easier. She was okay. The plan she'd cooked up with Williams and Justin had obviously worked. And now that he was moments from having her safely onboard, he could acknowledge the wisdom of Justin's decision to mute the speaker. Whatever Weezel might have said or done with Aurora would have driven Cade into a murdering rage. He certainly couldn't fly with that mindset. The mission would have ended before it began.

The buildings came into view, looking like tortoises camped out in the sun. He maneuvered the ship along the vast stretch of cleared dirt that passed for a road, checking first to make sure no vehicles were coming.

He spotted Aurora and Drew standing at the front entrance. Aurora had her back to the street, her posture indicating she was keeping watch on the front door.

Cade's heart thumped in anticipation as he brought the ship into a hover. "Tell Williams to lower the gangway."

Drew and Aurora disappeared from view, and a moment later Aurora's voice came over the comm system as the gangway lock light flashed green. "All set. Let's go."

He didn't need to be told twice. He punched the thrusters, guiding the ship past the mountain range and through the planet's atmosphere. When the glitter of stars opened before them, he keyed in the course that would take them to their jump window.

"Nicely done." Aurora said as she stepped into the command center and rested a hand on his shoulder.

"You, too." He glanced back. And did a double take. "*That's* what you were wearing?" His eyes almost popped out of his head. He'd never seen her wear anything so tight. Or revealing.

She glanced down, her expression nonchalant. "Sure. Celia loaned it to me. It was effective, too." She smiled at Justin, who grinned back at her. A flush crept into Aurora's cheeks as Justin waggled his eyebrows at her. She cleared her throat. "Weezel's sleeping like a baby, and with any luck, he'll think the whole incident was a weird dream. At least until he discovers *Gladiator* is missing. Which, going by the state of his yard, could take years."

"You knocked him out?" He hadn't realized that was part of the plan.

"Uh-huh. Injected him with a drug Williams gave me. Weezel thought I'd pinched him."

"Injected him?" She'd been close enough to inject him? "Did he lay his hands on you?" If so, he'd happily turn the ship around and hit Weezel with something harder.

Aurora looked bemused. "No. But he thought he was going to get lucky, so he let his guard down."

"Get lucky?" The words rumbled out in a growl. "What do you mean, get lucky?"

She shifted her gaze to Justin. "I'm gathering he didn't hear the conversation?"

Justin shook his head. "I turned off the speaker feed to your comm. Seemed like the smart move." He glanced at Cade. "And I was right." He stood and headed out the doorway. "Do yourself a favor, buddy. Don't be an ass about this."

He wasn't being an ass. He was being protective. Totally different.

But Aurora didn't take the seat Justin had vacated. Instead she remained standing, her arms crossed loosely over her chest. A chest that was quite prominent in the outfit she was wearing.

Cade swallowed. "I *am* being an ass, aren't I?"

"Little bit."

Which in Aurora-speak translated to *a lot.* She was just too kind to say so. He sighed. "I'm sorry. Apparently, I'm not very evolved."

She tilted her head, studying him. "Would you like to be?"

They were still a ways from their jump window, so he flipped on the autopilot. "If it means I get to be with you? Hell, yeah." When he held out a hand, she took it, allowing him to settle her crossways on his lap. He wrapped one arm around her waist and cupped her cheek with his other hand. "I'm sorry for going caveman on you."

The corner of her lip lifted. "Caveman? In a different context, that could be fun."

The flare of heat in her eyes raised his core temperature a few degrees. "Duly noted."

Her gaze grew serious. "But irrational jealousy indicates a lack of trust."

Whack! She'd pegged him like a stake through the heart. And he deserved it. "I trust you."

"Do you, really?"

He brushed his thumb over her cheek. "Yes. It's not you. It's me." He blew out a breath. "And I'll work on it." He drank in the beauty of her emerald green eyes. "I don't want to lose you."

"What makes you think you will?"

He sighed. "I did once before. Once an idiot, always an idiot." Even though he liked to think he'd matured in the past ten years.

"But you're not the same boy you were then. And I'm not the same girl I was, either." She stroked her fingers through his hair, sending tingles along his scalp. "We know ourselves now. And, we're a good team." She pinched him on the neck.

"Hey!" He caught her hand in his, laughing with her.

"I didn't want you to feel left out." Her green eyes sparkled with mischief, but her expression grew tender as she continued to gaze at him. "I believe in you, Cade. I always have."

He really didn't deserve her. But he'd thank the universe every day that he got to hold her.

He lifted her hand to his lips and pressed a kiss on her palm. "I love you, Rory."

Her smile was incredibly sweet. "I love you, too." She cupped his face in her hands and brushed his lips with a kiss he wanted to last for the rest of his life.

Twenty-Seven

Mya's nerves were at the breaking point.

Until a few days ago, she'd known her purpose. Ever since the moment Aurora had drawn her first breath, she'd stood beside her, watched over her. As a little girl, Aurora had held so much power and so little knowledge about who she was or what she could do. Mya had known all her secrets, including a few Aurora hadn't uncovered yet.

She'd accepted her role as Aurora's companion without question. It was the way of their race. Their connection defied any label she gave it.

But somewhere along the way, Aurora had stopped leaning on her for support. And Mya had failed to notice.

Aurora had departed the *Starhawke* with the confidence of a born leader, without hesitation or regret, leaving Mya to battle her growing anxiety alone. Only one other person on the ship could relate to what she was going through. Unfortunately, he wasn't talking to anyone right now.

Jonarel glowered like a bear with a thorn in his paw anytime he appeared among the crew. He'd spent most of the trip sequestered in engineering. She was pretty sure he was sleeping down there, too. He only came to the upper decks to gather food from the greenhouse.

She'd considered intercepting him during one of those visits, but what was the point? Aurora's absence was tearing him apart, too, but if they talked about it, that wouldn't help her. It would make her feel ten times worse.

"We'll be coming out of the jump in two minutes."

Kelly's announcement brought Mya's attention back to the bridge.

"As soon as we arrive in the system, I want you to calculate a return jump." Kire's normally smiling countenance was deadly serious. "Keep a course plotted to that window at all times."

"Aye." Kelly didn't bat an eye. She looked fully prepared to sleep at her post if necessary.

Kire left the captain's chair and crouched next to Mya, his hazel eyes clouded with concern. "How are you doing?"

She forced a smile. "Fine." Then she frowned. She was parroting Aurora's automatic response again, saying she was fine when she wasn't. Ironic, considering Aurora had been breaking that habit recently. In fact, she'd been breaking a lot of habits recently.

Kire clasped Mya's hand and squeezed. "I miss her, too."

Uh-oh. She must really be coming apart if Kire could see her pain. She'd been working hard to keep her bedside manner in place. Apparently she'd failed. "Is it that obvious?"

He shrugged. "We're all adjusting. Some more than others."

No need to ask who he was referring to. Jonarel was his best friend, but Kire had been shut out just like the rest of the crew.

Kelly glanced over her shoulder. "Entering the system."

The image on the bridgescreen changed, the starfield reappearing. Mya stood as her heart rate spiked. *They'd arrived.*

"Scanning for ships." Gonzo studied the readouts on the tactical console.

Kire moved behind Gonzo's chair. "Any readings?"

"I'm picking up strong energy signals from the second planet. Could be ships, or something larger."

"Star, how's our camouflage?" Kire asked.

"Fully functional."

"Make sure it stays that way." Kire nodded at Kelly. "Take us in. Your discretion."

The bright star in the distance guided their course as they approached the orbits of the inner planets.

"I've got a lock on those signals," Gonzo said. "It's definitely coming from a planet, not a ship. But it's unclear what's causing it."

"I'm picking up a lot of communication signals, too." Celia pivoted from the comm station. "Not sure what the language is, though."

Kire moved to the captain's chair. "Put it on speaker."

Snatches of conversation filled the bridge, most of it clipped and sporadic.

Kire cocked his head, his eyes narrowing. "That's Teelian. Start recording all communications. I'll analyze it later." He glanced at Gonzo. "Got a visual yet?"

"Coming up now."

Mya's gaze darted to the bridgescreen and her breath caught. She'd been terrified that she'd find a smoldering wreck of a world. The reality was entirely different.

The planet shone in the surrounding starscape like an exotic gem resting on black velvet. White swirls of clouds painted lazy patterns over a lush background of deep blue, with hints of green and brown dotting the surface. Definitely not dead.

"This is interesting." Gonzo stroked his goatee. "The signal's being produced by a geosynchronous satellite system surrounding the planet. The satellites are generating a static charge that's preventing sensors from penetrating."

"Is that even possible?" Kire asked.

Gonzo shrugged. "Looks like it."

Kire tapped the comm. "Jon, I need you on the bridge."

A slight hesitation preceded Jonarel's reply. "On my way." He didn't sound happy about it.

Kire frowned at the speakers, the first sign of irritation he'd shown at Jonarel's behavior. "Any ships?" he asked Gonzo.

"Hard to say this far out. That system's producing a lot of interference."

Mya watched over Gonzo's shoulder as he zoomed in on the visual.

"Think I've found one. Oh, ho!" His spine straightened. "I recognize you, my friend." He sent the magnified image to the bridgescreen. "Look familiar?"

Mya shuddered. *Too familiar.* She hadn't been on the bridge during the battle at Burrow, but she'd seen the images Star had recorded during the fight. Seeing one of the warships in real time was worse.

"So the ships that attacked us at Burrow were Teelian." Kire murmured.

"Looks like it. And they're a paranoid bunch," Gonzo added. "In addition to our friend there and the satellite screen, I'm picking up five additional warships and at least ten artillery satellites in a higher orbit. And that's only on the side of the planet we can see." He decreased the magnification, allowing the planet to take center stage again.

The lift doors parted and Jonarel stalked onto the bridge, his lips drawn down in a scowl.

Kire nodded toward the bridgescreen. "What do you make of that?"

Jonarel paused, his golden eyes narrowing as he focused on the image. The scowl disappeared. "A sensor web." He said it the way Mya might say *a unicorn.* He moved closer to the screen, his finger tracing a path in the air that followed the invisible lines between the satellites.

Kire joined him. "It's messing with our readings."

Jonarel glanced over his shoulder at Gonzo. "What are you seeing?"

Gonzo leaned back in his chair. "Nothing. Everything I send at it is being broken up like confetti."

Jonarel crossed his arms, the muscles in his back flexing. He looked like an oak tree planted on the bridge. A gorgeous, powerful oak.

Mya couldn't look away from the tantalizing image. "What's the web for?"

Jonarel's piercing gaze shifted to her. "It prevents anyone in orbit from scanning the planet's surface. And keeps ships from landing or leaving without authorization."

A chill chased across Mya's skin, raising goosebumps. Her parents had barely escaped from this planet with their lives. How many others had been trapped here ever since? "What would happen if we flew through it?"

"The system would send an alert and trigger the defenses."

She frowned. "But the hull camouflage would conceal us, wouldn't it?"

Jonarel shook his head, his thick hair brushing his shoulders. "Unlikely. We would be unable to keep the entire ship masked as it passed through the terminus line." His golden gaze held hers. "Your parents escaped through this?"

"I have no idea. It may not have existed when they were here. The only thing my mom said was that she and my dad stole a ship and made their escape with Libra."

"Alone?" Gonzo sounded incredulous.

Mya shrugged. "Must have."

"And one of your parents was able to pilot the ship through an interstellar jump?" Jonarel asked. "I was not aware the Suulh understood that technology."

He was looking at her with keen interest, which was doing funny things to her heartbeat. "My dad does. He's mentioned a few times that he misses flying."

"Did your people have their own ships?" Gonzo looked as fascinated as Jonarel.

"I don't think so, but honestly, I don't know." Mya blew out a breath. "That's part of the problem. There's so much that's blank. And this." She gestured at the web. "This was never part of the discussion." Her gaze met Jonarel's. "What do we do?"

Jonarel's eyes glowed with determination. "We find a way in."

Twenty-Eight

"For some reason, I didn't expect Gallows Edge to be so...*lively.*" Justin stumbled as he sidestepped to avoid being run over by a cargo vehicle that zipped past them.

Cade placed a hand on Justin's shoulder to steady him. "For the right clientele, it's a popular destination." Although Gallows Edge certainly wasn't *his* idea of Shangri-La.

Prior to its current incarnation, the moon outpost had been a mining operation. A tram still ran along a track in the center of the wide tunnel where he, Justin and Williams were walking, but instead of transporting mineral ore, it now carried visitors from the main shaft at the center of the facility to the ship docks at the outer reaches. Taking the tram would have been safer than dodging the cargo transports rumbling by on either side, but trams cost money and they were in resource conservation mode. They'd opted for walking instead. To the irritation of the cargo transport drivers.

"Be grateful the environmental controls are top-of-the-line," Williams said. "Otherwise mining dust would be coating your lungs."

The moon lacked an atmosphere, which was one reason the mining operation had been constructed almost entirely underground. Taking a walk outside wasn't an option if you wanted to keep breathing.

The airlock command personnel that controlled access to the outpost had been happy to allow them to land...for a price. They'd paid it with items Justin and Drew had scavenged from Weezel's yard.

Up ahead, the tunnel opened to a circular hub that connected with the main shaft. Lifts disgorged exiting passengers while new arrivals waited in a queue to pay and board.

Cade checked the map displayed on a large panel by the lift exit, then headed down the stairs, with Justin and Williams right behind. He paused when they reached the next landing, turning to Williams.

"Medical facility is that way." He gestured down the brightly lit tunnel lined with tiled mosaic floors. Williams planned to talk to the medical staff to see if they had a record of anyone checking in who matched the Admiral's description while Cade and Justin poked around the local watering hole in the lower tunnels. "We'll see you back at *Gladiator.*"

Williams set off along the path of colored tiles as Cade and Justin continued down the stairs. Drew had stayed behind to guard *Gladiator,* a necessary precaution on an outpost fueled by greed. Aurora was with her but would be joining them at the bar in a little while. She'd chosen to arrive separately to prevent their group from drawing unwanted attention.

The air grew thicker the deeper into the bedrock they went. The number of people hiking up and down the stairway increased as well, mostly ship personnel by the look of them, their clothing travel-worn and their expressions ranging from sullen resignation to manic excitement. The frequency of the passing lifts also changed, the hum becoming a subtle background whisper by the time Cade and Justin reached the tunnel that housed the bar.

"At least we'll have plenty of folks to talk to." Justin murmured as they followed the flow of humanity into the dim tunnel.

Very true, although Cade hoped they'd get a lead on the Admiral's whereabouts within a few hours. The sooner the better. How did miners tolerate these conditions, buried under meters of rock without the benefit of sunlight or fresh air? Of course, he didn't necessarily have that on a spaceship either, but he could always count on the vista of the stars. He'd only been on this moon thirty minutes and he was already feeling claustrophobic.

The strip of light that ran along the center of the half-moon shaped ceiling cast a yellowish glow that didn't do anything to improve the ambience of the tunnel or the appearance of the people walking along the cracked and stained concrete path.

A second tunnel on the left had been converted into storefronts, most of which advertised merchandise that would earn you a hefty fine or imprisonment in a Council court. But Gallows Edge was privately owned and operated, and located on the rim of Fleet space. Fleet patrols didn't pass this way unless they received a distress call, making the outpost an ideal spot for underhanded dealings.

A shaft of amber light cut through the gloom as a doorway opened to their left, the echo of noisy chatter and the clicks and thumps of gaming tables confirming they'd reached their destination.

Cade grasped the door handle before it could close. "Let's see what we can find out."

Twenty-Nine

"I'm looking for a man."

The bartender regarded Aurora with a frank stare. No doubt he'd heard that phrase thousands of times before, for a variety of reasons. He continued polishing the bar glass in his hand with a cloth that had seen better days. "And what type of man might ya' be looking for?" A Scottish burr tinged his words.

"Someone who might have been in here a few weeks ago. Older man, bald, average height, with a wiry build. Do you remember anyone like that?"

The bartender leaned against the counter. "Can't rightly say."

The emotions Aurora was picking up from him indicated otherwise. He *had* seen the Admiral. He just wasn't prepared to share that information. Yet.

"What was it this man did to ya'?"

Aurora folded her hands in front of her. "What makes you think he did something to me?"

The bartender gave her a knowing look. "Pretty woman like you comin' to a place like this." He indicated the crowded room behind her. "You'd need to have a mighty powerful reason. Figure he did you wrong, one way or another."

Might as well be honest. "He lied to me." She allowed some of her anger to come through. She had a score to settle with the Admiral. Her first priority was confirming he was all right. But after that, she intended to let him know exactly what she thought of his manipulative behavior. "And then he disappeared."

"That's a pity." The bartender shook his head. "Galaxy is filled with villains. Especially around these parts. Hate to see one preyin' on someone classy like you."

The compliment caught her off guard, especially since she'd dressed down for this assignment. Her hair was back in a braid, and her brown tunic and pants were intentionally non-descript. But compared to the tattered or revealing garments worn by most of the other customers, she supposed she stood out. "It's very important that I find him. Anything you remember would be helpful." She slid a credit square onto the counter.

The bartender pocketed the money before setting the glass on the rack behind him. He rested his forearms on the bar and lowered his voice. "Now that I think about it, I believe I did see this man you're seekin'. As I recall, he was askin' questions about the Setarips who frequent this area."

"*Setarips?*" She sucked in a breath. "There are Setarips in this system?"

"Oh, certainly."

She was surprised the outpost was still standing. But he acted like it was perfectly normal. "You don't seem particularly concerned by that fact. Aren't you worried that they'll attack the outpost?"

"Not especially. They don't bother us. We have an...arrangement."

Fascinating. "Do you know which faction?"

"Can't say. Never seem 'em myself. But sounded like your man was trying to make contact with 'em." The bartender left to attend to a group that had settled in a few seats down.

Aurora sipped the drink she'd ordered, which was supposed to be wine but didn't taste like it had even a passing acquaintance with a grape. *Setarips? Here?* What a revelation. How had the Admiral known?

She sensed Cade a moment before he slid onto the barstool beside her. He propped his back against the railing so he was facing her, a cocky grin on his handsome face.

He'd been playing pool with a couple of burly men in the gaming room when she'd arrived. She'd ignored him, keeping up the pretense that they were strangers, and he'd done the same.

His smile made her cheeks warm, even though she knew it was an act, intended to convince anyone watching them that he was a man bent on seduction. His murmured words dispelled that illusion. "Noticed you talking to the bartender. Did you learn anything?"

She gazed at him over the rim of her glass. "The Admiral was in here asking questions about Setarips."

"*Setarips?*" Cade leaned in closer. "What about Setarips?"

She filled him in on the information the bartender had provided.

"And they're somewhere in the system?"

"That's what he said. But I can't imagine why. They never stay in one area for long. They're like locusts, destroying everything in their path and moving on."

"The Setarips on Gaia were Etah." Cade pivoted on the stool so their knees were touching. "They weren't even supposed to exist anymore. What if they set up a home base here that they've used to rebuild th–" He broke off as a woman with flaming red hair sidled up next to him and placed a hand on his arm.

"Hey, handsome." The plunging neckline and tight fit of her outfit left very little to the imagination. And gave a clue to her profession. "Looking for company?"

Aurora stared at her. The woman had brass to approach Cade when he was clearly taking an interest in someone else. Business must be slow tonight.

Cade gave her his most charming smile, anyway. "Thanks, but I'm working on closing the deal with this young lady." He winked at Aurora. "Maybe another time."

The woman dismissed Aurora with a wave of her hand. Her fingernails were painted a bright red that matched her top and clashed with her hair. "You can bring her." She batted her lashes at Cade. "I'm not the possessive type. I can share."

The muscles around his mouth tightened. "Sorry. I *am* the possessive type. I *don't* share."

"You sure? I guarantee I'm more fun than she is."

Cade's eyes turned cold. "I doubt it."

The woman shot Aurora a look of annoyance. "Well, if you change your mind, I'll be here all night."

Aurora fought the urge to laugh at the look of discomfort on Cade's face as the woman trailed her fingers along his arm before walking away. "It's not her fault you're nice to look at."

He grimaced. "No, it's *your* fault for not giving off stronger signals that I'm taken."

Aurora's lips twitched. She fluttered her lashes in an imitation of the woman's gesture. "But we just met, handsome. What do you want me to do? Plaster a sign on your chest that says *MINE?*"

He snorted with laughter, his gaze warming considerably. "Fine with me." He glanced at the gaming room, where Justin was setting up the table for their next match. "I think the guys we've been playing saw the Admiral. Still trying to figure out if they're responsible for his disappearing act." He leaned closer, his breath on the sensitive shell of her ear. "I'll check back with you after the next game."

She tingled from head to toe as she watched him stride away. She really couldn't blame any woman for wanting to get Cade alone. She was counting the hours until she could do that herself.

She took another sip of her drink, forcing down the bitter liquid. If she didn't finish it, she wouldn't have an excuse to talk to the bartender again, and she was hoping she might be able to get a few more details from him.

As it turned out, she didn't have to empty her glass. A few minutes later he approached her, keeping his voice low. "There's someone you'll want to talk to."

"Oh?" She hadn't expected him to volunteer information.

"Those Setarips I mentioned? Well, their navigator just came in."

Aurora snapped her gaze to the front door. No sign of a Setarip. She glanced back at the bartender. "I thought you said you'd never seen the Setarips?"

He shook his head. "I haven't. Their navigator's human. She shuttles their supplies from the outpost to their ships."

Aurora's head spun. A *human* was working for Setarips as a navigator? What next? A white rabbit with a pocket watch? "Where is she?"

"Other end of the bar, sittin' alone. Dark hair. Petite."

She glanced down the bar. A young woman in a high-collared tunic and duster whose hair looked like it had been cut with pruning shears sat staring into a large mug of alcohol.

"The night that man you're lookin' for was in here? He talked to her before he left."

Aurora's pulse shot up. "Any idea what she told him?"

He gave her a warning look. "I'm not in the habit of listenin' in on my customers' private chats."

That probably wasn't true, but he'd already given her more information than she could have hoped for. "Of course not. Did you happen to notice if they left together?"

"Can't say. It was a busy night. But if you want to find your man, I'd start by talkin' to her."

Aurora placed another credit square on the counter. "Thank you."

This time he pushed it back. "Hope you can help each other out." He gave her a solemn look before heading off to take care of another customer.

An enigmatic comment. Aurora picked up her glass and made her way to the other end of the bar. The stools on either side of the woman were conveniently vacant. As she drew closer, she figured out why. A strong odor permeated the air. The scent was unfamiliar, but it had an earthy quality that reminded her of musk. Or rotting fruit.

She slid onto the stool to the woman's right but kept her gaze averted. The woman didn't make any move to acknowledge her, either, but Aurora sensed a flare of irritation. Too bad. She wasn't leaving until she'd found out what the Admiral had said to her. And where he'd gone afterward.

Judging by the level of alcohol in the woman's mug, it could be a long night.

Keeping her attention on the woman's emotions, Aurora sipped her own drink, barely aware of the taste now that it was overlaid with the noxious odor. She studied the woman out of the corner of her eye.

At first glance, she'd guessed her to be in her late twenties, but up close she looked younger, closer to Kelly's age. She had delicate features, although she appeared to be doing everything she could to downplay her natural beauty. The hack job on her hair and the pungent odor certainly helped achieve that goal.

The woman's irritation built, like a kettle on a stove. Aurora waited, nursing her drink.

The irritation shifted to anger a moment before the woman's words snapped out like pistol blasts. "You gonna ask me?"

Aurora turned her head slightly. "Ask you what?"

The woman continued to stare into her drink. "Whatever it is you came over to ask."

Aurora studied her. Everything about her screamed *go away!* And yet, her underlying emotional grid didn't support that. The anger had split, revealing an underlying melancholy. "What makes you think I came over here to talk to you?"

The woman finally lifted her gaze. "Because no one comes near me without a good reason."

The emptiness in her pale eyes made Aurora wince. "Is that so? Why not?"

She scowled. "Don't mock me."

"I'm not. I'm curious."

"Curiosity killed the cat," the woman muttered as she turned back to her drink. "What do you want?"

So much for small talk. "I'm looking for someone who was in here a few weeks ago. Older man, bald, average height. The bartender indicated you might have spoken with him. Do you remember him?"

The woman's emotions upshifted. Aurora had her full attention now. "Maybe." She kept staring at her glass. "Who's he to you?"

Aurora trusted her instincts to guide her, the lie tripping off her tongue effortlessly. "My father."

That got a reaction. The woman set down her drink and pivoted on the stool, her gaze analyzing Aurora like a scanner. "Is that so?"

"Yes. But he's disappeared. I need to find him." *And you know where he is*. That certainty flashed like a neon sign amid the jumble of emotions emanating from the young woman. Aurora waited, allowing the uncomfortable silence to chip away at her opponent's composure.

"You looking for Setarips, too?"

So the Admiral *had* talked to her about the Setarips. "No. I'm looking for *him*. Do you know where he is?"

The woman's gaze bored into her. "Yeah. I do."

Something was wrong. Chaos had exploded in the woman's emotional field, making her impossible to read.

"Can you take me to him?" Aurora prodded.

A glint appeared in the woman's eyes. "You're going to wish you hadn't asked me that." Her hand came out of the pocket of her duster, revealing a pistol aimed directly at Aurora's heart.

Thirty

Cade retrieved a cue from the rack on the wall as he rejoined Justin.

"You and I shoot for the break this time?" one of the men they'd been playing asked. He gestured to Justin, flashing a collection of metal rings across his fingers that looked more like brass knuckles than jewelry. A well-placed punch could break bone.

"Sure." Justin sounded like a happy-go-lucky kid eager to be included in the game. Not like the pool shark Cade knew him to be.

Justin had honed his communication skills in the gaming hall at the Academy, playing cadets and professors alike. Winning the game hadn't been the challenge for Justin. He'd routinely cleared the table. His goal had been to soundly defeat his opponents and still have them leave the table in a good mood. He'd usually succeeded.

"Same stakes?" Rings's companion asked, the expression on his hook-nosed face revealing his eagerness as he placed a couple credit squares on the table. The denomination of each flashed on the built-in screen.

"Guess so." Justin glanced at Cade. "Though we haven't had much success so far." They'd played four rounds, and lost all but one. Which made their opponents hungry to keep playing. And talking.

Clearly the two men saw Cade and Justin as easy marks. Looks could be deceiving.

"Okay with me." Cade set a couple of matching credit squares on the table.

While Rings lined up the cue ball to shoot for the break, Hook Nose moved closer to Cade. "That gal I saw you talkin' to at the bar. She with you?"

"You mean the one over there?" Cade indicated the redhead who'd propositioned him in front of Aurora. She was leaning against a pillar, talking to an older man whose gaze was fixed firmly on her cleavage.

Hook Nose scoffed. "Her? Uh-uh. I've sunk my anchor in that harbor. Most men here have. I'm talking 'bout the stacked blonde sitting at the bar."

Cade kept a tight rein on his temper as he glanced in Aurora's direction. She was sipping her drink, her gaze on the bartender. She looked like a faery trapped in a den of trolls.

Hook Nose definitely fit in the troll category. And Cade had a good idea where this discussion was going. To hell with acting like he and Aurora were strangers. He wasn't going to leave any doubt in this thug's mind. He injected a note of warning into his words. "Yeah. She's with me."

Hook Nose's eyes gleamed as he stared at Aurora. "Thought so. And that's good, 'cause I got a proposition for you." He wiped a hand across his lips, like he'd started to drool. "After this game, how 'bout you and I make a deal so I get a little time alone with your lady."

How about I break your neck? Fire poured into Cade's veins, but he clamped it down.

Justin stood from the crouch he'd assumed to shoot for the break. He held the pool cue loosely in his hand, but his gaze locked onto Cade, watching for a signal.

Cade forced a smile to his lips. This man was their best lead so far regarding the Admiral's whereabouts. Keeping the lines of communication open was a priority. At least, for now. And that meant resisting the urge to do bodily harm. "That would be up to her. But if you win this game, you can buy an introduction." He almost wanted the man to win so he could enjoy watching Aurora take out the jackass.

Hook Nose's lips lifted off his teeth in something that might have been a smile. "Deal."

Justin shared a look with Cade that confirmed their new game plan before settling back into his crouch. He sent the cue ball racing to the other end of the table, where it bounced and began the return journey. It stopped closer to the edge on the near side than Rings's ball had, giving Justin the break.

He took a moment to chalk up his cue before lining up his shot. "So, the man we're looking for." He sent the cue ball flying, sinking a ball on the break. "You said you saw him in here. Did you talk to him?"

"No," Rings replied. "He sat at the bar."

Justin sank another ball. "Think I'm getting the hang of this." He grinned at Cade.

"Did you notice if he talked to anyone else?" Cade asked as Justin's next shot fell with a soft thunk.

Rings scowled, ignoring Cade's question.

Justin had noticed, too, because his next ball bounced off the edge away from the pocket, ending his turn.

"Thought you was gonna run the table." Rings grumbled, glaring at Justin.

Justin's grin reappeared. "Nah. Just got lucky."

Rings took his time analyzing the table before lining up a shot. Justin had done a good job of positioning the cue ball, but Rings still managed to sink a ball on a ricochet and lined up another two shots that followed into the pocket afterward, bringing the count even.

The man's overconfidence cost him the next shot, which placed control of the table in Cade's hands. He wasn't as skilled a player as Justin, but he successfully dropped two balls into the pocket before missing a bank shot.

"Did you see the guy we're looking for talking to anyone at the bar?" Cade repeated as Hook Nose stepped to the table.

Hook Nose answered the question as he surveyed the layout, looking for a shot. "I did. Same woman who's talking to your gal."

Cade glanced at the bar. Aurora had moved to the far end of the room and was talking with a petite woman with short, dark hair. Aurora's back was to him, so he couldn't see her expression.

Hopefully she was getting the information they needed. Or confirming that Rings and Hook Nose had assisted in the Admiral's disappearance. "Who is she?"

Hook Nose sank a ball and lined up his next shot. "Don't know. And don't care. She stinks." He pocketed another ball.

"Stinks?" An odd comment when nearly everyone on Gallows Edge was a criminal of one sort or another.

Hook Nose stared at Cade like he was a simpleton. "She *smells*. Like a skunk." He returned his attention to the table, but his next ball rattled around the pocket and rolled away.

Justin glanced at Cade as he chalked up his cue, keeping his back to the two men. He could easily run the table at this point, but if he did that, there was a chance the men would walk away. And Cade had more questions he wanted answered.

On the other hand, if Justin let Rings shoot, they could end up on the losing side. And that would mean introducing Hook Nose to Aurora.

She could handle him. That wasn't the point. He just hated the idea of the troll getting within breathing distance of her. So much for becoming more evolved.

Shifting his gaze to the table, he folded his arms over his chest, tucking two fingers in the crook of his elbow and spreading two on his bicep.

Justin gave a hint of a smile before turning to the table.

"She come in here often?" Cade asked Hook Nose.

The other man shrugged. "Sometimes."

Justin pocketed the first ball.

"Did our friend leave with her?"

Hook Nose scowled. "Do I look like a tracking system to you?"

Probably not wise to answer that the way he wanted to. "Just thought you might have noticed."

Justin sank another ball while Rings and Hook Nose glowered. He missed the final shot, but left the cue ball without a direct line to any of the balls on the table.

Rings tried to do a ridiculous behind-the-back shot. He made contact, but the ball bounced harmlessly off the side of the table before rolling to the middle. The cue ball followed until they were nearly kissing each other. Spittle flew from the man's lips as he swore.

Cade slid a look at Justin before lining up his shot. Their opponents were getting hot. The game might turn physical.

But Justin was already watching for it. His grip on the cue indicated he could turn it into a weapon in a heartbeat.

Cade allowed his cue to glide through his fingers nice and easy, focusing on where he wanted the ball to go. With a smooth stroke he made contact, striking the remaining ball exactly where he needed to. The ball rolled in a straight line into the pocket, while the cue ball stopped dead center.

Hook Nose growled as Justin pocketed the credit squares.

"Good game." Justin's expression was pure innocence. "Want to go again?"

Hook Nose and Rings exchanged a glance. "You two—"

A female voice interrupted them. "Nice shooting, handsome."

The redhead was back. And she was invading Cade's personal space.

She licked her painted lips as she gazed at him through her lashes. "You deserve a reward, hon. How 'bout I give you one, on the house."

The woman was relentless. "I told you, I'm with the lady at the bar."

The redhead batted her eyelashes. Again. They were as fake as everything else about her. "I figured that deal had fallen through."

Cade held onto his temper with effort. "Why would you think that?"

She gestured behind her. "Because she left."

Cade's gaze snapped to the bar. Aurora was gone.

Thirty-One

Aurora had a split-second to decide what to do when the woman pressed the pistol against her ribs and ordered her to keep quiet.

She wasn't in any danger. Her shield would protect her. And she could disarm the woman with minimal effort. But that wouldn't bring her any closer to finding the Admiral.

The woman had said she knew where he was. Aurora believed her. But to reach him, she'd have to act like a captive.

The gaming room was behind her, so she couldn't see Cade. That was probably a good thing. He would disagree with her decision—strenuously—but she wasn't in a position to consult him.

"Hold your left arm toward me, palm up, and pull back your sleeve."

Aurora followed the instructions, revealing the comband on her forearm.

"Turn it off."

Aurora deactivated the device.

"Remove it and hold it out. Try anything, and I'll shoot."

"Wouldn't that draw attention?"

The woman's brow quirked up. "In this place? No one would even notice. And they wouldn't try to stop me if they did."

She was probably right. Aurora unfastened the comband.

The woman plucked it from her hand with the dexterity of a professional thief. It disappeared into the folds of her duster. "Now, get up slowly, and walk to the archway to the left of the bar."

Keeping her expression neutral, Aurora did as she was told, moving through the crowd while her would-be abductor shifted the pistol's business end from her ribs to her back.

"Through the archway, then halt."

Aurora entered a short hallway with several doors to the right and another at the end.

"Hands behind your back." The woman pressed the gun more firmly against Aurora's ribs in silent warning.

She complied. Cold metal bindings snapped around her wrists.

"Now move." The woman prodded Aurora toward the back door, her movements taking on a sense of urgency now that they were alone. She pushed open the door, revealing a corridor wide enough to accommodate cargo transports and refuse bins in between the curving wall of the tunnel and the back walls of the storefronts.

"This way." She grasped Aurora's arm and pulled her toward a small ground transport that had seen better days. She opened the passenger door. "Get in."

Levering herself into the tight space with her arms behind her back was a challenge, but Aurora managed to do it without stumbling.

The woman hurried around the vehicle and put it in motion toward the lifts before she was completely in the driver's seat, somehow managing to keep the pistol pointed at Aurora's torso.

Aurora shifted so she was facing her abductor, easing the pressure on her arms. "Who are you?"

The woman ignored her, focusing on the cargo lift up ahead. It stood open like it was waiting for her. Sure enough, as soon as she eased the vehicle inside, the doors closed and the lift rose.

"Where are you taking me?"

Still no response. However, the answer became self-evident as they exited on the docking level and raced past *Gladiator*, continuing down the row of ships.

Aurora's pulse spiked. The bartender had said this woman was a navigator for the Setarips. Was the Admiral onboard one of the Setarip ships?

Cade would pitch a fit if she allowed herself to be taken off Gallows Edge. Had he noticed she'd left the bar? Had he alerted Drew that she was headed this way? Did she want him to?

They halted next to a battered, late-model cargo shuttle. The woman turned to Aurora. "If you want to see your father, you'll go quietly."

Last chance to stop this insanity. But she didn't see any other way. Overpowering her abductor wouldn't get her what she wanted. The woman seemed to hold a privileged position on Gallows Edge. Aurora might find herself at the business end of a dozen weapons if she threatened the Setarip navigator.

No. If she wanted to find the Admiral, she had to strike a devil's bargain.

Which meant leaving Cade in the dark.

Thirty-Two

Cade grabbed Justin's arm. "Check the front. I'll check the back."

Don't panic. The words sounded hollow as he moved through the crowd to the spot where he'd last seen Aurora. He searched the nearby tables and booths on the off chance she'd simply moved to a new location. But he didn't see her.

A man had claimed the vacant stool where Aurora had sat.

"Did you see where the woman who was sitting here went?"

The man gave him a baleful stare, but he gestured to an archway at the back of the room.

Cade covered the distance in two seconds. The hallway was empty, but several doors opened off it. He hurried to the back door and threw it open, revealing the corridor that ran behind the storefronts. No sign of her. He tapped his comband. "Justin, she was seen leaving through the back. I'm heading down the corridor. Check the rooms along the hallway."

"On it."

Cade sent a ping to Aurora's comband. The automated reply indicated the device had been turned off. Anxiety crawled into his throat. Why would she turn off her comband?

He used the scanner on his comband to inspect the area, picking up faint residual heat signatures that indicated footprints. He fought to breathe normally as he tracked them. This was Aurora, after all. She could take care of herself. She was probably following a lead. But that thought did little to calm the primal urge that warned of impending danger.

Not far from the back door the footprints were replaced by vehicle tracks that ran down the corridor in the direction of the lifts.

He opened a channel to Drew. "Have you heard from Aurora?"

Drew sounded puzzled. "No. Why? I thought she was with you."

"We got separated. Is Williams back yet?"

Williams's voice replaced Drew's on the line. "I'm here."

"Aurora's missing. I think she took the lift, but I don't know where she got off. Looks like she's in a vehicle. Head for the cargo lifts and check vehicles exiting to the docks."

Williams was all business. "On my way."

Justin stood at the back door when Cade returned. "No sign of her."

Cade followed him inside. "There are vehicle tracks leading to the lifts." Exiting through the archway, he intercepted the bartender on his way to the kitchen and grabbed him by the front of his tunic, shoving him into the shadows. "Who was she talking to?"

The bartender's gaze darted in the direction of the archway, a definite tell. But he tried bluffing anyway. "Who?"

Cade's grip tightened. "Don't play dumb. Who's the dark-haired woman?"

The bartender's expression shuttered. "I donna know what you're speakin' of."

Cade growled, drawing the man so close their noses almost touched. "If anything happens to her, I'll—"

The bartender's face flushed. "She willna hurt your lady."

"*Who is she?*"

"She works for the Setarips. As their navigator."

Cade blinked. "Nobody works for Setarips."

"She does. And she knows the man your lady was askin' about."

"Knows him *how?*"

"He left with her."

The Admiral had left with her? Cade loosened his grip a fraction. If Aurora had learned the same thing, she might have seen an opportunity to locate the Admiral by going with the dark-haired woman. It didn't explain why she'd failed to alert him, or why she'd turned off her comband, but at least he understood what might have motivated her decision.

"Where would they go?"

The bartender swallowed. "She has a cargo shuttle at the docks."

Hope and worry battled for dominance in Cade's chest. "What's the shuttle's designation?"

"*Gypsy.*"

Thirty-Three

"*Gypsy*, you are cleared for departure."

Aurora's abductor gave her a sidelong glance before focusing on the shuttle's controls. "Heading for the airlock."

Aurora was strapped into the co-pilot's seat, her arms still pinned behind her back and her chest harness in place to keep her from moving. She stared out the viewport as the shuttle rose from its assigned slot.

As they gained altitude and pivoted toward the airlock chamber, she spotted a muscular man with a shaved head running down the tunnel in their direction, dodging oncoming traffic and waving his arms over his head. *Williams*.

The shuttle shot forward, leaving Williams far behind. But that one glimpse told her Cade had already figured out where she was. She didn't want to think about the anxiety she'd caused him. She'd owe him a big apology the next time they were together.

At least he'd be able to track her in *Gladiator*. The ship had a sensor array that rivaled most Fleet vessels, which would be a necessity if Setarips were part of her reunion with the Admiral. She'd also watch for an opportunity to get her hands on her comband again.

The shuttle hovered in the airlock chamber as the interior doors closed and the exterior doors opened. When the starfield appeared, the shuttle's thrusters fired, breaking them free of the moon's minimal gravity and putting them on a path toward the outer planets.

Her abductor let out a small sigh and leaned back in
her chair. The chaotic emotions that had dominated their
mad rush to the shuttle had been replaced by the
melancholy Aurora had sensed back in the bar. Maybe she'd
be in the mood to talk.

"You didn't tell me your name."

The woman glanced at Aurora in annoyance, but
didn't respond.

She tried again. "My name's Aurora."

More silence.

"What should I call you?"

The woman's lips pinched. "Call me whatever you
want."

"I'd rather call you by your name."

"Why?"

"Because *the woman who kidnapped me* is rather
wordy. And because names matter."

The muscles in the woman's jaw flexed, like she was
grinding her teeth. Her emotions shifted, too, a sense of pain
and loss twining through the melancholy. She gave an
irritated snort. "Nat."

"Nat?"

"That's my name. Nat."

And judging by her emotions, she was telling the
truth. It was a start. "Okay, Nat. Can you tell me where
you're taking me?"

Nat's gaze remained on the console. "You wanted to
see your father. You're about to."

But the flatness in her tone and the creeping
anxiety in her emotional field indicated that wasn't all Aurora
was about to see. "Are we going to the Setarip ship?"

Nat still didn't look at her. "Yes."

"And my father is there?"

"Yes."

"Is he okay?"

"He's...fine."

That wasn't encouraging. Aurora's heart stuttered as she flashed on an image of the cages she'd encountered on the Setarip ship at Gaia. Was that what Nat was referring to? "Is he a prisoner?"

Nat glanced at her. The empty look was back in her eyes. "We all are."

"What do you mean?"

Rather than answering, Nat snagged a finger under the collar of her tunic, pulling it down to her shoulder. A ring of metal encircled her neck.

"Take a good look." Nat's voice held the ghost of an apology. "You're about to get one, too."

Aurora stared at the metal ring. "What does it do?"

Nat's jaw tightened. "Keeps us in line."

"Us? Who's us? My father?"

"Him, and...others."

"What others?"

Nat shot her a look before returning her attention to the controls. "You ask a lot of questions."

"You've abducted me. Why wouldn't I want to know as much as possible about where we're going?"

Nat's breath slipped out on a weary sigh. "You'll see soon enough. We're almost there."

Within moments a shape appeared out of the blackness. The shuttle's lights flashed across the outline of a vessel that looked like three or four ships shoved together to form one solid mass. The entire thing was about half the size of the *Starhawke*, but still managed to look imposing, even with protruding parts that didn't seem to serve a logical function.

Then again, Setarips weren't known for their design skills.

"Home sweet home," Nat murmured, more to herself than Aurora.

The shuttle slowed as they approached the ship from underneath. Makeshift grappling arms extended to grab hold of the smaller craft. The shuttle trembled like it was caught in an earthquake when they made contact, throwing Aurora against her harness.

"Steady, *Gypsy.*" Nat patted the console.

The shuttle's hull protested as it was squeezed by the grappling arms, but eventually the shaking subsided.

Nat unsnapped Aurora's harness and helped her to her feet, then stepped behind her. "Hold still." She ran her hands over Aurora's back and legs, checking for weapons.

"I'm not armed."

Nat grunted and continued the pat down.

"Anything I should know before we go out there?" It might be foolish to expect compassion from Nat, but she didn't seem to be indifferent to the suffering her actions might cause.

Nat stood, her hands on her hips. "Keep your head down. Don't speak unless spoken to. Don't argue. Don't fight. And above all, be useful."

They exited through the back hatch and a makeshift airlock. The smell hit her first, triggering her gag reflex. She'd adjusted to the odors coming off of Nat, but here it was a hundred times worse.

Nat met her gaze, her pale eyes sympathetic. "You'll get used to it. They're a smelly species. It helps if you breathe through your mouth."

"Thanks for the tip."

As they exited into a cargo hold piled high with crates, two Setarips blocked their path, their weapons held loosely in their clawed hands.

The washed-out brown and grey patterns on the scales covering their faces reminded Aurora of a reptile, but their noses and mouths were shaped like a short-muzzled dog. Heavy protrusions of bone ran along their brow ridges and down their noses, framing eyes with vertical pupils like a cat's and heavy eyelids. It was a little hypnotic, gazing into those otherworldly eyes.

They both looked startled to see her with Nat. One of them spoke, the guttural quality of the sounds making them difficult to understand even if they'd been speaking Galactic English. But she got the gist of the question, anyway.

Nat's response confirmed it. "A gift for Tnaryt."

Tnaryt? Who was Tnaryt? Nat had neglected to mention anyone by that name.

Nat gave her a nudge, guiding her along the narrow path that wound through the stacks of crates. The Setarips followed close behind, bringing their pungent musk with them.

Nat stopped her at a metal ladder that led to the upper decks. "Turn around." She reached for the manacles around Aurora's wrists. "Don't do anything stupid," she warned in an undertone as she released the tension.

Aurora rolled her shoulders and flexed her fingers to restore circulation as Nat started up the ladder. The Setarips pointed their weapons at Aurora's back, motioning for her to follow. She began the climb, going slower than necessary while she analyzed her surroundings. Corridors branched off on each level they passed, but it was difficult to judge where they led.

Aurora reached the top deck and stepped off the ladder. The smell in this area was strong but different—musk with a sharper bite—with the nexus at a massive command console that sat like a throne in the center of the room.

Nat crossed to it and spoke in low tones to whoever claimed that place of honor.

When the figure rose, Aurora's breath caught. This had to be Tnaryt. Setarip males tended to be larger and more brightly colored than the females, but she'd never seen one like the male striding toward her. Even with the draping cloak that covered most of his torso and legs, he stood out like a hazard sign.

The scales around his eyes and cheeks were pumpkin orange, and a spiked crest of the same color ran along the top of his head and down his back. Large circular disks of black and grey lined the sides of his bulging neck, with more orange painting a stripe along his throat. His hands and feet were the same brilliant orange, with elongated fingers and sharp nails.

He stared at her, unblinking. His eyes were a paler orange-yellow. The vertical pupil made him look haughty and...dangerous.

Nat bowed her head. "This one should interest you, Tnaryt. She knows the engineer. And she's former Fleet, just like him. Useful."

Aurora's jaw dropped. How the hell did Nat know she and the Admiral were connected with the Fleet? Had the Admiral told her his history?

Tnaryt's lipless mouth opened and a slender tongue flicked out. "Yooou know Engineeeer?" His voice rolled over her like tumbling gravel, but his Galish was perfectly understandable.

She'd never heard of a Setarip who spoke Galish. And she had no idea how to answer his question. The Admiral must have shared some information with Nat, but how much did Tnaryt know? Had the Setarips pressed the Admiral into service as an engineer? And why hadn't Nat said Aurora was the Admiral's daughter? Was she intentionally keeping that to herself?

She glanced at Nat for clues, but her head was still bowed, her gaze on the floor.

Fine. She'd keep her answers vague and hope for the best. "I'm looking for him, yes."

"He issss friend? Or ennnnemy?"

That wasn't an easy question, either. She couldn't be certain whether Tnaryt would be more interested in bringing together two enemies or two friends. The general consensus held that conflict was a favorite form of Setarip entertainment, so he might be more inclined to produce the Admiral if he thought a fight was brewing.

She kept her tone frosty. "Neither."

"But yooou want to seeee him?" He seemed intrigued by her attitude, and the prospect of discord.

"Yes." She packed a lot of emotion into that one word, giving Tnaryt the opportunity to interpret it however he chose.

His tongue flicked out again. He motioned to one of the female guards and said something in his native language. The female headed for the ladder as Tnaryt's gaze returned to Aurora. He studied her for a long moment, like she was a piece of art he was trying to decide if he liked. "Yooou were Fleeeet?"

Was there any point in denying it? Probably not. "Yes."

"Not nowww?"

She could answer this one honestly. "No."

His pupils widened. A sign of eagerness? "Yoou have skillsss?"

She hesitated, sensing a flash of concern from Nat.

She'd lifted her head and was staring at Aurora with a plea in her pale eyes. *Be useful* she mouthed.

Useful. Right. Thanks to her Fleet training, her skill set was extensive. But what did Tnaryt need? She glanced around the bridge. No one sat at the consoles. Did he not have a command crew? Or were they somewhere else on the ship?

She'd play to her strengths. "I'm good with communications systems."

Two flicks from Tnaryt's tongue, and his pupils widened even more. "Yoou can fixxx?" His emotions had intensified, zeroing in on her like a laser.

Was his system damaged? It was easy to believe, judging by the state of the ship. "Yes. As long as I have the right parts and tools."

"You'll have whatever you need," a familiar voice said from behind her. "This ship is a treasure trove of spare bits and pieces."

The Admiral. Until that moment, Aurora hadn't been one hundred percent sure she'd find him. She turned slowly, her heart galloping in her chest.

He stood next to the Setarip female, looking thin and unkempt but otherwise unharmed.

Tension drained out of Aurora in a flood, the void filling with a flush of anger. She wasn't sensing any surprise from him, almost like he'd expected to see her here. How could that be? Was his presence on this ship just another step in his manipulative master plan?

Clearly she had a role to play, but she didn't know her lines. And she wasn't sure she'd say them even if she did. "We really should stop meeting like this."

The corners of his mouth lifted. "On the contrary. I'm delighted to see you."

That familiar smile and the warmth in his gaze pulled at her. She had the urge to hug him. And punch him. Her Setarip audience would definitely prefer the latter.

She allowed her anger to seep into her voice, the truth behind it giving it strength. "You disappear without a word and that's all you have to say to me?"

His brows lifted. "What would you like me to say?"

Her anger gained traction. "How about *I'm sorry*?" The words came out with a bite, the pain his deceit had caused rising to the surface.

His gaze slid to Tnaryt, who was watching the scene with rapt attention. "I *am* sorry. Upsetting you wasn't part of my plan."

Tnaryt was clearly enjoying the exchange. She could feel it. Good. Venting was easy. She'd built up a head of steam and she had a lot of things to square with the Admiral before this was over. She lobbed another question at him. "What *is* your plan?"

"Same as you. To find the Sovereign."

The Sovereign? That brought her up short. *Who the heck was the Sovereign?*

Tnaryt's mouth parted in a hiss, hatred coming off him like a firestorm. "*The beeetraaaayer.*"

Aurora almost laughed. The comment was absurd coming from a Setarip. Their race had destroyed their own planet in the process of fighting their civil war. They had written the book on betrayal.

However, if the Admiral was looking for the Sovereign, perhaps this was the mysterious person behind the attacks at Gaia and Burrow? The one who'd enslaved the Suulh?

She met the Admiral's gaze, tuning into his emotions. She sensed eagerness. He wanted her to continue her line of questioning. But she was walking on thin ice. She'd need to be careful. "Have you had any success locating the Sovereign?"

The Admiral's eyes sparkled. She'd asked the right question. "Not yet. I've been a little sidetracked. The engines on this ship aren't operational and the communication systems are down. Now that you're here, I could use your help with the repairs."

So the ship was dead in the water. That explained why he was stuck here, especially if he was a captive as Nat had indicated. A slight bulge underneath the neck of his tunic reminded her of the collar Nat wore. But how would restoring the ship's functions help them? Didn't he want to escape? Maybe if she asked the right question, he could give her the answer. "What's in it for me?"

The Admiral's gaze darted to Tnaryt. "Tnaryt wants to track down the Sovereign, too. But he needs the ship to be operational."

Oh, ho! The Admiral's plan was coming into focus. *The enemy of my enemy is my friend.*

Tnaryt's tongue flicked in and out like a whip. "Yooou want Sssovereign?" His pupils contracted to slits as he stared at Aurora.

She nodded. "Yes. I want to find the Sovereign."

His mouth parted in what could have been the Setarip version of a smile. Chilling. He glanced at Nat, who hadn't moved from his side. "Go. Unloooad shuuuttle."

"Yes, Tnaryt." She shot Aurora a warning glance before striding to the ladder and disappearing through the opening in the floor.

Tnaryt's attention returned to Aurora. "Uuuuuseful. Yessss." He walked to his chair and removed something from a compartment in the armrest. "Very uuuuseful." He held up a circular object.

It was a collar, exactly like the one Nat wore around her neck. But Aurora pretended ignorance. No point in tipping her hand. "What is it?"

Tnaryt made a gurgling noise. A Setarip chuckle? "I will shoooow you." Reaching over with one clawed finger, he touched a device on his arm.

The Admiral suddenly stiffened, his jaw clenching as his body went rigid.

Aurora could sense the electrical current the collar was sending through him, and the agony following in its wake. She stepped forward to channel the energy away, but halted before she reached him. She couldn't do it. Not unless she was prepared to fight her way off this ship. Once Tnaryt knew about her abilities, a battle line would be drawn. And the Admiral seemed to think Tnaryt had information they needed to locate the Sovereign.

But she couldn't stand by and do nothing. She turned on Tnaryt. "Stop it!"

Tnaryt touched the device. The electrical intensity went up, not down. The Admiral's eyes rolled back in his head as his body jerked in response.

Don't argue, don't fight Nat had said. Fine. She'd beg. "Please." She bowed her head like Nat had, watching the Admiral out of the corner of her eye. "Please, stop. I'll do anything. Just stop hurting him."

A few seconds passed before Tnaryt tapped the controls, ending the pulse.

The Admiral dropped to all fours, his head bent, his body shaking in the aftermath.

She sank down beside him, resting her hands on his shoulders to steady him. "Are you okay?"

He lifted his gaze. His smile was strained, his voice weak. "I will be. Now that you're here."

The confidence in those words punched her in the gut. He trusted her to get them safely through this. That didn't wipe away the pain of his manipulations or her anger at his deceit, but witnessing his suffering had successfully redirected her ire to the Setarip bully standing over them. A bully who was watching them with obvious glee.

His pleasure in the Admiral's pain infuriated her. She resisted the impulse to give him a charge he'd never forget. "That wasn't necessary."

"Necccessssary?" Tnaryt's tongue flicked out. "Yeeesss, necessary. Cooome." He motioned for her to stand.

She obeyed, even though every instinct she possessed rebelled.

"Goood."

She bit back a growl as Tnaryt stroked a finger down her cheek to her neck.

"Yeesss. Goood." His unblinking gaze bored into her as he held up the collar. With a deft movement he slipped it around her neck and snapped it into place. He stroked the collar lovingly, his claws scratching her skin. Then he tightened his grip around her throat and pulled her forward so their faces were millimeters apart.

"Noooow miiiine."

Thirty-Four

"The energy trail is getting stronger," Drew said from the co-pilot's seat. "Evidence of braking thrusters ahead."

Cade stared at the starfield through the viewport. Aurora was out there somewhere. And he would find her.

He darted a glance at the sensor images Drew was studying. They were following the trail left behind by the cargo shuttle as it had circled a moon orbiting the fifth planet in the system.

Drew had already pulled the dock tower's flight plan for *Gypsy* by the time he and Justin had returned to *Gladiator*. They'd obtained clearance to depart along a similar trajectory. The energy trail had deviated from the plotted path not long after leaving Gallows Edge, and they'd altered their course to follow it.

Williams had confirmed the shuttle Aurora was on was a short-range vessel. It couldn't get out of the system without help. Somewhere in the blackness, a larger ship waited. Hopefully they'd spot it before it spotted them.

Aurora's comband was still non-responsive. Justin was transmitting every fifteen minutes, but nothing had gotten through. It wasn't like her. If she'd left of her free will, she should have sent him a message by now. And if she hadn't....

"New readings." Drew peered out the viewport. "Ship ahead. At present speed, visual range in three minutes."

If they'd be able to see the ship, it would be able to see them, too. The moon's electromagnetic field might mask their energy readings if he took them close to the surface, but it wouldn't hide their movements. And *Gladiator* couldn't camouflage like the *Starhawke*.

Cade scanned the moon's surface, which was softly lit by the distant sun. An impact crater with sheer walls sixty meters high looked like his best bet for cover. He fired the braking thrusters and took them down, gliding over the rim of the crater and maneuvering into the shadows cast by the far wall. The ship settled onto the moon's rocky surface with a thump.

"Take us to low power mode," he told Drew.

She tapped the console. "Low power mode initiated."

"Running lights off."

"Lights off," Drew confirmed.

"Time to visual?"

"Thirty seconds."

He rested his forearms on the console and searched the blanket of stars for any sign of a ship.

"I have visual," Drew said. "And it's...interesting."

Cade switched his attention to the image she'd pulled up on the screen. He tilted his head to the side, but it didn't improve the view. The ship looked like the collected remains from a trash compactor. "Is that the front of a Fleet medical freighter?" He pointed to the ship's nose, which looked a little like the *Nightingale*.

"Uh-huh. And here," she indicated the ship's blocky T-wings, "are sections from a personnel transport and part of an old frigate, too." She shook her head. "This thing seems to have been assembled from parts of other ships they added to their original frame."

"It's a wonder it flies at all."

"Probably doesn't if you get it in atmo." Drew pointed to a lump on the ship's belly. "That's the cargo shuttle." Her lips pinched. "The contraption holding it in place isn't designed for this model, either. I'm surprised it hasn't punched a hole through the shuttle's hull."

Cade glanced over his shoulder to the auxiliary station behind the co-pilot's seat. "You getting anything?"

Justin pressed a hand to his ear as he listened to whatever was coming through the earpiece. "They're not transmitting. At least, not anything we can register. Either they know we're here and they're on radio silence, or their comm system isn't operational."

Cade returned his attention to the ship in the distance.

"There's no energy trail other than the shuttle's, so I think the ship's been here a while," Drew said. "Their main engines are cool. I doubt they're planning to leave any time soon."

Cade folded his arms over his chest and leaned back in his chair. "Which begs the question of *why* they're here." He'd been afraid they'd encounter another slave ship like the one on Gaia, but this vessel was too small to house a large group of Necri. The environmental systems were probably incapable of supporting more than fifty individuals, including crew. It didn't look like it would be effective for anything except interstellar transport. "What's the armament on that ship?"

Drew flipped through the scanner information. "Multiple torpedo bays and artillery but no cohesive layout. The weapons appear to have been added as haphazardly as the rest of the exterior. And they don't look like they're any better maintained than the rest of the ship."

"And the hull?"

"Layers of plating from the various components. Each chunk from the other ships has thickened the outer skin and provided mounting stations for the weapons. The ship can probably take quite a bit of fire without losing hull integrity."

The cobbled together design fit in with what he'd see on the Setarip ship at Gaia. Maybe they *were* dealing with the remnants of the Etah Setarip faction. The question was, did they have Aurora and the Admiral onboard?

"Do you think the Admiral's onboard?" Drew asked, echoing his thoughts.

"Possibly. I think Aurora believed that. It's the only reason I can imagine for taking off without alerting us." Her abandonment still stung, no matter how much he tried to rationalize it. He'd believed they were a team, but when push had come to shove, she'd pushed him aside. That hurt.

"She must have a plan."

Was Drew trying to convince him, or herself? "I hope so." But staring at the ship wasn't helping his attitude. To have Aurora so close and yet unreachable gnawed at his self-control. He massaged the back of his neck, where thick cords had taken up permanent residence. "For now, we'll wait and see if she contacts us."

"And if she doesn't?"

He gazed at the hunk of metal orbiting overhead. "We'll blow up that bridge when we come to it."

Thirty-Five

The collar around Aurora's neck pressed against her skin, a cool reminder that Tnaryt believed she was his captive. It was a misconception she'd encourage until she figured out her next move.

What she needed was time alone with the Admiral. He was still kneeling beside her, his hands braced on his thighs as he sucked in shuddering breaths. Rotating her wrist, she brought her hand in contact with his shoulder and sent a flow of soothing energy. His audible sigh told her it was helping.

Tnaryt's nails pricked her skin as he stroked her neck. "Youuu did not reesissst." His tone indicated he'd hoped she would.

She held his gaze. "What would be the point? There's nowhere to go."

He made that unpleasant gurgling noise again. "Truuuue." He waved his free hand at the Admiral. "Leave ussss."

It took the Admiral a few tries, but he managed to stagger to his feet. He swayed for a moment, resting a hand on Aurora's shoulder. At first she thought it was to keep his balance, but the reassuring squeeze he gave her told her something else. Dropping his hand, he shuffled to the ladder and started down.

Aurora kept her gaze on Tnaryt. His touch made her flesh crawl, which she suspected was the point. He wanted to dominate her.

He changed the angle of his hand, bringing the side of it in contact with her skin and hair, the musky odor growing stronger.

Was he *marking* her? That was the only logical explanation for the intense smell that surrounded her like a gas cloud. She focused on breathing through her mouth so she wouldn't gag.

He stepped back, giving her a sliver of personal space. "Tellll me about Fleeeet."

He wanted intel about the Fleet? Fat chance. She kept her tone cool. "Not much to tell. I was only with them for a short time. It didn't work out."

"Whyyyy not?"

She shrugged. "I'm very...independent. When an opportunity came up to get out on my own, I took it." Which was true.

He studied her. "Yesss."

She couldn't tell if he thought her attitude was a good thing or not. "You speak Galish well."

The grey and black patches on his neck puffed out at the compliment. "It isss...neccccessary."

Necessary? Why would a Setarip believe learning Galish was necessary? It's not like they ever talked to humans.

Except *he* did, didn't he? He kept human captives. Maybe he didn't want them saying things he didn't understand. "I suppose it's useful for communicating with the...crew." She didn't think it was wise to call them prisoners.

"Yeeess. And otheeersss."

Others. Meaning at some point he'd talked with humans who were not his captives. The leaders on Gallows Edge? The bartender had indicated the Setarips had an arrangement with them. Or perhaps he worked with slave traders? The Fleet worked hard to stamp out the practice, but it persisted in the outer rim. Was that how Nat had come under his control?

Turning, he pointed to one of the consoles at the front of the bridge. "Yoouu fix cooommm."

Right. She'd told him she was good with communications. His system definitely looked in need of repair. The display was completely dark.

Stepping past him, she settled onto the seat and studied the panel. The design of the markings was vaguely familiar, calling to mind what she'd been taught in her Academy classes, although not much was known about the Setarip written language. Even the spoken language was tough for the translators, since the Fleet's experiences with the Setarips rarely involved conversation. She'd have to let her intuition guide her.

She flipped a prominent switch in the upper left and waited to see if any of the connections responded. A few lights glowed across the panel, but not enough to give her much hope.

She looked around for a headset, and spotted a curved band of metal tucked into a slot in the wall. She pulled it out and examined it. Definitely a headset, with a small disc on one side and a long metal spoke on the other. But it was designed for the long, narrow skull of a Setarip, whose ears sat close to the top of their heads. She couldn't use it. She'd have to adapt it or see if she could borrow a headset from Nat's shuttle that she could rig to interface with the panel.

"Iisss working?"

Tnaryt's hiss so close to her ear made her jump. She'd temporarily forgotten he was there. "Not exactly." She slid off the seat and crouched on the floor, running her hands under the console to locate the access panels. There. The fastenings were unfamiliar, though. She looked around for a tool that could open them, but the bridge was bare of any extraneous parts. "I need to get this panel open. Where would I find tools?"

"Toools?" Tnaryt sounded annoyed, like a request for tools was unreasonable.

"Yes. Is there a utility compartment where they're stored?"

Flick-flick, flick-flick from Tnaryt's tongue. "liinn engiiiine room."

Aurora's pulse picked up. This was exactly the opportunity she'd been hoping for. If the Admiral was working in the engine room, she might be able to talk to him alone. "May I go look for what I need?"

Tnaryt's unblinking gaze pinned her. He wasn't an idiot. He knew she wanted to see the Admiral. "Theee engiineeer. Whooo iisss heee to yoouu?"

The lie she'd told Nat had worked to get her here. Hopefully it would work on Tnaryt, too. "He's my father."

"liiis he?" Tnaryt's pupils widened.

"Yes." She didn't elaborate. Less was more when it came to concealing the truth.

He stared at her for a long moment before gesturing to the stairwell. "Enngiiine room. Ooonnneee doooown. Gooo."

She didn't wait for him to change his mind.

"Do nooot waaanderrr," he called to her as she reached the ladder.

She paused, meeting his gaze.

His hand brushed over his control device in a silent threat. "I will knoooow."

Thirty-Six

Aurora descended the rungs quickly, stepping off one level down and halting when she encountered one of the armed female guards.

"Engine room?" Aurora asked, keeping her hands where the female could see them.

The female's slit-pupils narrowed, her tongue flicking like Tnaryt's, but she motioned Aurora down one of the corridors. Apparently Tnaryt wasn't the only Setarip who had learned some Galish.

Aurora hurried along a narrow, twisting corridor to the back of the ship, following the subtle echo of clanging metal until she located the engine room. Stepping through the hatchway, she spotted the Admiral's legs sticking out from underneath one of the massive cylinders at the center of the compact space. "Fixing or sabotaging?"

His body jerked. In seconds he'd worked himself out of the tight compartment. Grease smeared his cheek. "Fixing. Otherwise we'll blow up or run out of air. This ship is a disaster waiting to happen."

"So I gathered."

The exchange could have been friendly banter, except neither of them smiled. The warmth she'd seen earlier in his gaze had been replaced with wariness. Without Tnaryt's threatening presence to contend with, they were both acting like mannequins captured in an awkward tableau. Too many unanswered questions filled the room with their bulk.

She glanced around. "Are we alone?"

He nodded. "If you stand near the hatch, you'll hear anyone coming down the corridor. And the comm system hasn't worked since I arrived." He wiped his hands on a dirty piece of cloth and stood. "I'm surprised Tnaryt let you out of his sight."

"He wants me to fix the comm console. I need tools."

"I can help with that." But he didn't make any move to fetch them. Instead, he studied her. "How did you find me?"

"Knox."

"Ah." His brows drew down. "Judging by the way you're looking at me, I assume he shared certain...information...with you?"

"Yes." The betrayal cut anew, though the intensity had dimmed. "Information I should have had a long time ago."

He ran a hand over the smooth skin of his head in a gesture that was achingly familiar. "I made a choice, Aurora. A difficult choice." His mouth set in a line. "It may have been the wrong one, but it was made with the best of intentions."

She folded her arms over her chest. "You know what they say about good intentions."

He nodded. "I know. And I'm sorry."

The apology helped, but the wounds still ached. "Why did you do it? Why lie to me all these years and withhold knowledge of my past? Of my family?"

He looked like the weight of the universe rested on his narrow shoulders. "It was the only way to protect you."

She blew out an exasperated breath. "Why is everyone so damn fixated on protecting me? I can take care of myself."

"I know that. Now. I didn't back then."

"You could have said something."

"I didn't want to hurt you."

She leveled her gaze at him. "You *did* hurt me."

Regret flashed in his eyes. "I'm sorry. Truly, I am."

She could feel the truth of his words. But in some ways, that made the situation even harder. He'd meant so much to her for so long. She'd feared that the trail she'd been following would end with a memorial service.

Now that she knew he was alive, she'd run out of steam. Where did that leave her? Her gaze fell on the bulge around his neck. "How many times has he shocked you?"

His hand drifted to the collar, halting before making contact. "A few."

But he didn't look at her when he said it. Odds were good he was underestimating.

"I stay out of his way as much as possible. Not that he needs a reason. Has he used it on you yet?"

"No. But I'm sure it's just a matter of time."

His gaze grew thoughtful. "Will you be able to do anything to stop it?"

She blinked. He didn't know the answer? That surprised her, given how much he'd researched her past. Then again, he'd never had an opportunity to talk to her about her abilities. He might not know the particulars. "He can't hurt me."

"Really?" He looked intrigued. "How exactly does your energy field work?"

"That's a discussion for another time." She wasn't prepared for a lengthy explanation. Her emotions were too raw. "Right now I want to know what led you here. And who this Sovereign person is we're supposedly looking for."

"Ah, yes. The Sovereign. That's the name Tnaryt used to describe whoever is behind the attack on Gaia. The Setarips who died there were all from his clutch."

"Clutch?"

"That's the closest Galish term for a Setarip societal group. It's a complex concept."

"And Tnaryt is in charge of this particular clutch?"

"Yes. This ship is all he has left. The Sovereign commandeered his other one for the attack on Gaia."

"Commandeered it? How?"

"I'm not sure." The Admiral rested his hip against the engine housing. "But from what Tnaryt's navigator told me, he gave it over willingly."

"Why would he do that?"

"No idea. Maybe the Sovereign offered him something valuable in exchange."

"If so, he doesn't seem to have received what he was promised."

"No. His hatred of the Sovereign is very real."

"Do you know the identity of the Sovereign?"

"Not yet. Tracking down the Setarips who were involved in the attack on Gaia seemed like a good way to get some answers."

"But you ended up a prisoner. Was that part of the plan?"

He grimaced. "Definitely not. Although it may still work to our advantage. Tnaryt had personal contact with the Sovereign. If we fix his ship, we may be able to convince him to go after the Sovereign. Revenge is a powerful motivator."

"So he knows who the Sovereign is?"

"He should. But he doesn't encourage questions, and his navigator doesn't volunteer information. I haven't made much progress. I suspect it's one of the Teeli Council delegates."

"That would fit with what we've learned. Lieutenant Magee was reassigned to them."

The Admiral took a step back. "*What?* When?"

"After you disappeared."

His eyes darkened. "That can't be a coincidence." He rubbed a hand along his jaw. "This just keeps getting better and better."

"That's not all. Someone strong-armed Reanne into resigning as RC Director."

His eyes widened. "She quit? But she coveted that job. I can't imagine her resigning."

"Neither can I. Not unless her life was on the line. I don't think they gave her a choice. I was afraid you'd gone on medical leave for similar reasons."

"No. My disappearance was voluntary." His gaze sharpened. "Has anyone threatened you?"

"No. But I think Admiral Payne's compromised. She offered my crew a mission that had *trap* written all over it."

"You turned her down?"

"No, we accepted it to avert suspicion. And then came looking for you instead."

The corners of his mouth lifted a fraction. "Thank you."

"Don't thank me yet. We're still prisoners here."

His smile grew. "A temporary situation." He folded his hands. "What about the Suulh? Can I assume your presence here means the refugees are safe?"

An image of Azaana flashed through her mind, the scent of salt air tickling her nose. She smiled for the first time since she'd arrived on the ship. "Yes. They have a new homeworld. The Clarek clan is still finishing up the settlement, but I left Raaveen in charge. Justin's keeping in contact with her and reporting to me."

"You're still in communication with Cade's unit?"

"You could say that. Reynolds and Gonzo are on the *Starhawke* with my crew, following up on a lead. But Cade, Justin, Drew and Williams are somewhere nearby, probably formulating a plan to rescue us."

The Admiral's eyes widened. "Cade's with you?"

She nodded.

His cheeks creased in delight. "Well, I'll be damned. Good for him." But his smile quickly turned into a frown. "If that's true, how did you end up here alone?"

She waved the question away. "Long story. Suffice to say I ran into Nat and figured out she knew where you were. I tagged along."

"Nat?"

"Tnaryt's navigator."

"Ah. So that's her name." His hand drifted to his collar. "And you came here voluntarily?"

Aurora shrugged. "She pulled a gun on me, but I could have stopped her. I didn't want to. Finding you was my priority."

His gaze softened. "I'm honored."

"Yeah...well." She cleared her throat. "How did you end up here?"

"I met Nat in a bar on Gallows Edge. She was looking for someone to fix the engines on this bucket before the ship died. She'd been maintaining them as best she could, but her knowledge was limited. From the questions I asked her about the Setarips, she pegged me for a former Fleet officer with engineering experience."

"She figured out I was Fleet, too."

He nodded. "I'm not surprised. She's sharp." He folded his arms. "Unfortunately, I didn't pick up on that at the time. She doesn't miss a trick. One minute we were talking, the next she had her pistol jammed in my ribs. She made it clear she'd shoot me without a second thought if I didn't come with her. I believed her."

Interesting. Aurora had never truly believed Nat would shoot her. But she had the advantage of sensing Nat's emotions. "How did Tnaryt get his claws into her in the first place?"

"I've only gathered bits and pieces. She's very close-lipped, even when we're alone. I think she's been a captive for a while, before the Sovereign relieved Tnaryt of his ship and the rest of his crew. She has skills in a lot of areas, although she uses some unconventional methods."

"Is she loyal to Tnaryt?"

"She's loyal to herself."

Which made her untrustworthy, but predictable. "Are there other human captives onboard? One of Nat's comments indicated there might be."

"Yes. A cook, who's also responsible for cleaning duties. The Etah are lazy, especially Tnaryt. They use captives to do the work they can't or won't do."

That fit with Tnaryt's attitude. "I'm surprised there aren't more captives."

"I think there were others brought onboard after the Sovereign took Tnaryt's main ship, but...they didn't..." He seemed unwilling to finish the sentence.

Aurora could easily fill in the blanks. Tnaryt wasn't a tolerant master. "What about the Setarips? I've only seen two females and Tnaryt. Are there more?"

"Five females total. Tnaryt enjoys his little harem." He eyed the collar around her neck. "And speaking of Tnaryt, his patience is probably gone. I'll get those tools you need."

He moved to a compartment built into the bulkhead and hauled out a battered carrying case. Metal clanked within. "This is a hodgepodge of stuff they've stolen, some from Fleet, some I don't recognize. You should be able to get started on the repairs." He pointed to four additional compartments. "I also have all manner of spare parts, cables, and connectors available when you—"

A slight tingling around Aurora's neck warned her a millisecond before the collar sent out a charge. The Admiral was right. Tnaryt was tired of waiting for her.

She engaged her shield, capturing the energy and circulated it through the field, testing just how much power the collar gave her. Quite a bit. If she channeled it, she could fry a few consoles. Or take down one oversized Setarip bully. She tucked that information away for future consideration.

"You're doing it right now, aren't you?"

She jumped, like a kid caught with her hand in the cookie jar. The Admiral was staring at her. "Yes." She'd reacted on instinct, forgetting he was there. "You can't see it, can you?" Most humans couldn't, but there were exceptions. Cade being one.

"No. I just saw you go still and get a focused look on your face."

The collar shut off, and she dissipated the energy before releasing the shield.

He gazed at her. "That's amazing."

She'd never heard the Admiral speak in that tone before. Her cheeks grew warm. "That's nothing. You should see me deflect boulders." She'd meant to be flippant, but the words came out sounding strained. She hadn't expected to demonstrate her abilities in front of him. "I'd better get going."

She took the case from him and headed for the door, but paused at the opening. "By the way, I told Tnaryt that you're my father."

She enjoyed the stunned look on his face as she left the room.

Thirty-Seven

Because names matter.

Natasha Orlov couldn't escape the echo of those words as she shifted crates in the cargo hold, making room for the latest shipment.

She didn't want to hear those words. Didn't want to think about Aurora on the bridge, facing Tnaryt. Didn't want to think about Aurora at all. But she couldn't help it.

Aurora had claimed she wanted to see her father. Nat didn't believe that for a moment. A professional liar could spot the tells of an amateur, and Aurora was definitely an amateur. Whoever the engineer was, he wasn't her father. But she hadn't been faking her concern for his welfare. He meant a great deal to her. Why?

She grabbed another crate from the stack by her feet and shifted it into place closer to the back wall. It was a never-ending battle, making room for the incoming supplies. Tnaryt had been using Gallows Edge as his home base for years. He'd been a legitimate threat to the outpost back then, and the leaders had worked out an arrangement with him where they provided regular pickups of fresh food and supplies to maintain the peace.

Problem was, the supplies were designed to support the original crew compliment of the large cruiser the Sovereign had taken. Nat couldn't tell the suppliers to decrease the amount without tipping her hand. Instead, she had to get creative with storing it. If the residents caught onto the fact that Tnaryt's cruiser hadn't put in an appearance in a while, the flow of food might get cut off.

With no habitable planets in the system, and no working engines to get them out of the system, they'd be stranded.

She kept as much of what they gave her on hand as possible, rearranging the cargo bay to put any perishables that were no longer viable into the airlock and jettisoning them into space. The waste gnawed at her, but she didn't see an alternative.

With a section cleared for the new arrivals, she returned to *Gypsy* and patted the shuttle's frame. "How you doing, girl?" Entering *Gypsy*'s cargo area always felt like coming home. She snagged the first crate by the hatch and carried it to the clearing she'd created.

Because names matter.

The problem was, she believed that, too. She'd named *Gypsy*, hadn't she? But why had she told Aurora *her* name? She could've made something up. Or given Aurora her last name, Orlov. That's what everyone had called her on the *Sphinx.*

The last person who'd called her by her first name was—

No. Not going there.

She went back for another crate.

She hadn't wanted to know Aurora's name. Hadn't wanted to know the names of any of the women and men she'd brought up here since the day the Sovereign took away Tnaryt's ship. It was easier that way.

Easier for you.

She flinched. The voice in her head had changed, becoming deep and masculine. She knew it well. She'd heard it often enough in her daydreams, and sometimes, calling out for help in her nightmares.

She shoved it aside. Thinking about the pain Tnaryt had doled out to the humans onboard this ship wasn't a productive use of her energy.

And what about Aurora? Is he hurting her right now?

Shut up.

She'd had far too many conversations with this voice. It kept her sane, and drove her mad. She talked to *Gypsy*, too, but those were one-sided conversations. *Gypsy* never talked back or pushed her to see things she didn't want to see. This voice delighted in keeping up his side of the conversation, always happy to pose questions. Especially the difficult ones. Happy to say things she didn't want to hear.

A face appeared in her mind's eye, the dark eyes haunting her—

Stop it!

She pushed the crate onto the stack with too much force. It slid over the side, smashing to the floor and popping the fasteners. Red and yellow tomatoes tumbled out, oozing their innards onto the deck.

She swore, pounding her fist against the top of the stack. Pain radiated up her arm. She welcomed it. Pain was the only thing that felt real anymore. As long as she could feel pain, she was still alive.

Because names matter.

Please, stop. Clapping her hands over her ears, she sank to the floor, drawing her legs up to her chest and burying her head against her knees.

How much longer could she keep this up? Hour by hour, day by day, her soul was slipping away. It was only a matter of time before she became a human shell. Empty. Lost.

Tears leaked from the corners of her eyes, soaking the fabric of her leggings. She didn't try to stop them. What was the point? Nobody cared if she cried. Including her.

Aurora had gotten to her. With those simple words, she'd reminded Nat what it felt like to be *seen*. And what had Nat done in return? Turned her over to Tnaryt to be tortured and abused until she too, became an empty shell. Or died. Just like all the others.

Was that all the future held for her? An endless stream of deception and torment? How many more lives was she willing to sacrifice just so she could continue in this sham of a life, this existence without meaning or hope?

Self-loathing and bitterness clogged her throat, choking her. No more. It had to end.

Natasha—

She silenced the voice. Whatever it had to say, she didn't want to hear it. She knew what she had to do.

Rising to her feet, she walked to the shuttle. She hesitated at the hatch, placing both palms flat against the hull. Her chest felt like it had been scooped out and filled with ash. Resting her forehead against the cool metal and squeezing her eyes shut, she blocked out everything but the connection with the only friend she had left.

"I remember what I told you, *Gypsy.*" She pressed closer, allowing the solid feel of the shuttle to calm her racing heart. "When we were captured, I promised you that we'd get out of here. That one day we'd fly free again. I meant it then. But there's only one way to keep that promise now." She pushed back, her fingers trailing over the smooth surface. "I'm sorry."

A chill spread through her limbs as she reached the cockpit.

The shuttle's weapons systems had never been restored following the abrupt crash-landing on Troi, but she didn't need weapons to achieve her goal. An overload of the engines would create an impressive explosion, tearing a gaping hole in Tnaryt's ship, opening the interior to the vacuum of space. Tnaryt would meet the end he deserved. And she and the other captives she'd condemned to a living death would finally be free.

Forgive me, Aurora.

"Piiiilot!"

Nat spun around, startled by the hiss of the female Setarip who stood directly behind her. She hadn't heard her enter the shuttle.

"Y...yes?" Her teeth chattered as adrenaline poured through her veins.

"Caarrry beeed briiiidge."

She was so focused on her course of action that it took a moment to make sense of what the Setarip had said. "Bed?"

"Beeed tooo Comm."

Bed? Comm? The Setarip had to be talking about Aurora. Tnaryt referred to the captives only by function. Pilot. Engineer. Cook. And Aurora had told Tnaryt she was good with communications. Hence, Comm.

That still didn't explain why Tnaryt wanted a bed brought up to the bridge. But the female was waiting for her, weapon aimed at her torso, so she'd have to go and find out.

Following the Setarip to the ladder, she climbed to the deck that housed an assortment of small compartments where the females slept. Snagging one of the thin pallets from an empty compartment, she carried it down the corridor and wrestled it up the ladder to the bridge.

The sight that greeted her stopped her in her tracks. Aurora knelt by the communication console, with one wrist encircled by a manacle and the other end attached to the frame of the console, tethering her. Her head was bowed as Tnaryt stood over her.

Nat's throat constricted. She'd done this. It was all her fault. Aurora didn't deserve this. No one did. And it was only the beginning of the torment Tnaryt would inflict. But not for long.

I'm sorry, Aurora.

Nat avoided Tnaryt's gaze as she approached with the pallet, afraid he'd read her intentions on her face. She focused on Aurora, instead.

"Gooood," Tnaryt crooned as she set the pallet down.

Aurora lifted her head, and Nat braced for the hatred she'd see in her eyes. It was always the same.

Except...

Aurora's expression was calm as a forest glade.

No hatred.

No pain.

No reproach.

Only empathy. And a determination that melted Nat's despair like ice in a bonfire.

The corner of Aurora's mouth tilted up in a smile so subtle Nat might have imagined it. But she hadn't. And that smile sparked an emotion she hadn't felt in a very long time.

Hope.

Thirty-Eight

Mya worked her trowel along the edge of the clay pot, loosening the soil that clung to the surface. Engaging her energy field, she surrounded the root system of the rosemary shrub, keeping the cellular structure protected as she transferred the plant to the larger container that sat on the potting bench.

Over the past two days she'd spent most of her time in the greenhouse, interacting with the plants. She needed the solace they provided. As a result, the plants were outgrowing their containers at breakneck speed.

The rest of the crew was working on the problem of gaining access through the sensor web, but her knowledge was of no value in those discussions. And with Aurora gone, she was at loose ends. Hence, the greenhouse's rapid transformation into a jungle.

"Can I help?"

She glanced up. Celia stood just inside the entrance from the med bay. "Sure." She handed Celia a pair of pruning shears and pointed at an overgrown vine.

Celia took the shears, her gaze sweeping the room. Evaluating. Analyzing.

Mya picked up her trowel. "Is there a problem?"

Celia turned toward the trellis, her face in profile. "We still haven't found a way through the sensor web." She plucked a trailing vine off the ground and clipped it.

Mya studied her friend. She didn't believe Celia had come down here to discuss the sensor web. She was on a personal mission. "That's not why you're here. What's up?"

Celia kept her gaze on the vine tendrils as she snipped. "You're very good at helping things grow."

That was an odd comment. "I know."

"You've helped Aurora grow, too. To a point."

Mya set down her trowel. "What do you mean, to a point?"

Celia continued clipping. "She's strong-willed. Determined. When she was younger, she probably needed guidance to keep her from barreling down the wrong track. But she's not a kid anymore. And neither are you."

What the hell was that supposed to mean? She rested her hip against the potting bench and folded her arms. "And you're telling me this because?"

"Because Aurora knows what she wants. What she's striving for." Celia glanced over her shoulder. "Do you?"

Mya opened her mouth, but nothing came out. Her brain had stalled.

"That's what I thought." Celia stood, motioning to the wooden bench beside the trellis.

Mya joined her as she sat down, but only because she didn't know what else to do.

Celia folded her hands in her lap, looking more like a counselor than a security officer. "You haven't been yourself lately."

"I—" She couldn't even summon a decent protest. "No, I haven't."

"And you've been unhappy because Aurora's gone."

"I miss her." Although the emotional spiral pulling her down was a lot more complicated.

"Of course you do. We all do. She's an important part of our lives. But you've made her the *focus* of your life, probably since she was born. She's growing. Changing. You need to grow, too."

Mya straightened. "I'm growing."

The look in Celia's eyes told her what she thought of that statement.

"I *am*. Really."

"Then what is it you want from your life? What are you growing toward?"

"Working with Aurora. Keeping her safe."

Celia snorted. "That's not your job. It never was. And you're not answering the question. What do *you* want. Independent from Aurora."

"I want..." Images, feelings, memories tumbled through her mind. She tried to hold onto them, but they slipped through her fingers like grains of sand. "I want..." But no matter how hard she tried, she couldn't finish the sentence. She had no idea.

Celia's sympathetic gaze said it all. "Exactly. You don't *know* the answer. And that's why you've been at sixes and sevens ever since Aurora announced she was leaving."

Mya stared at Celia as the words sunk in.

"You've spent so much time pushing your own needs and wants aside, accommodating Aurora, that you've lost track of what's best for you. It weakened you. And her. She finally realized that, which is why she left. Now it's your turn to find your focus."

Mya wanted to protest, to tell Celia she was wrong, but she couldn't. Everything she'd said was true.

When was the last time she'd considered what *she* wanted? Had she ever done that? An image of Jonarel flashed through her mind, and she flinched. Well, yeah. She knew exactly what she wanted when it came to him. But it would never happen.

Celia cleared her throat. "He's never going to figure it out."

"*Who's* never going to figure out *what?*"

"Clarek. He's never going to figure out how you feel about him."

Mya's stomach contracted like she'd been punched. Celia *knew*? How was that possible? She'd been so careful. Panic seized her in an iron grip. If Celia knew, then maybe—

Celia rested a hand on her arm. "Don't worry. No one else has figured it out. Including Aurora."

Mya's heart continued to pound. "But Jonarel—"

"Is as clueless as everyone else. You've covered your reaction well. But I know you. And I'm trained to notice details."

Mya swallowed. She'd never expected to have this discussion with anyone. But better Celia than Aurora. Or Jonarel. "You won't say anything, will you?" She'd planned to take the secret to her grave.

Celia looked offended. "Of course not. I wouldn't sabotage your chance at happiness." Her lips pursed. "However, you might want to consider doing something about it."

"About what?"

"About Clarek. Tell him how you feel."

The pounding turned into a full drumline. "But he's in love with Aurora." Something he'd made abundantly clear on Drakar. And every day since. She couldn't bear the thought of seeing pity in his eyes if he learned her secret.

"Perhaps."

Perhaps?

"But Aurora's in love with Ellis. Even if she wasn't, she's not interested in a romantic relationship with our strapping engineer. Which means they're never going to end up together."

Never?

The drumline picked up the tempo. Could Celia be right? Was it conceivable that Jonarel and Aurora wouldn't end up together?

The possibility lifted Mya's spirits…for a fraction of a second. Then she plummeted. How selfish could she be? She wanted Jonarel to be happy. And being with Aurora made him happy. She should wish for Aurora to fall in love with him, not take pleasure in the idea it would never happen.

"Hey." Celia squeezed her arm. "It's okay to want something for yourself. You deserve to be loved, too."

"But I'm not the one he wants."

The corners of Celia's mouth turned up. "Clarek doesn't know what he wants. All he knows is what he's been told. I talked to Siginal while we were on Drakar. As far as he's concerned those two are already mated. That's the message Clarek's been getting ever since he and Aurora met. He's never considered a different path because he's only been given that one option. You could give him an alternative."

Celia's words tantalized her with images she'd only imagined in her wildest dreams. Dreams she kept safely locked away where no one would ever find them.

"It may seem like a radical idea now, but it's something to consider. Unless, of course, you *want* him to spend the rest of his life alone." Celia lifted her brows in a subtle challenge.

"Of course not." She wanted him to have everything life could offer. She'd always assumed that would mean mating with Aurora. But if what Celia said was true, and Aurora wasn't going to be the one, then maybe…

Celia squeezed her hand. "See? You *do* know what you want. You just have to give yourself permission to go after it. Think about it." With a parting smile, she rose with the grace of a cat and left the room.

Mya stared at the closed door long after she'd gone.

Maybe.

Thirty-Nine

They finally had a plan.

Mya leaned against the bulkhead behind the science station on the bridge, watching Jonarel as he analyzed the data from their most recent test. His mood had improved considerably over the past few days. Having a problem to focus on seemed to be working as a distraction. He and Kire had been coordinating with Star, formulating a way to trick the sensors.

The *Starhawke's* hull could keep them hidden before they reached the web, and should theoretically keep them hidden after they entered the planet's atmosphere. It was crossing the sensor line that was the sticking point.

The hull's camouflage worked by mimicking the surroundings. However, in the case of the sensor web, the line would bisect the ship as it passed through. When that occurred, the hull would have to mimic the surroundings at every point except where the line touched. There, it would have to mimic the sensor itself.

Achieving that would require perfect precision. They'd only get one shot at this. It had to be right the first time, or they'd alert the Teeli to their presence.

Mya slipped her hand into her pocket, resting her palm against the piece of parchment Aurora had given her that contained the galactic and planetary coordinates. She didn't need the paper—the coordinates were burned into her memory—but she liked the tactile connection to her parents. Especially now.

What would they find on the other side of the web? The site of the original attack? The village, town or city where her parents had grown up? A Teeli base? She had so many questions, and the answers dangled just out of reach. All she could do was wait.

Jonarel turned to Kire, who sat in the captain's chair. "Run the—"

"Commander," Gonzo broke in. "We've got incoming ships."

Mya's attention snapped to the bridgescreen as Gonzo switched the image to a point in the starfield.

"How many?" Kire asked.

"Seven. A cargo freighter and six warships."

Celia pivoted from the communication console, where she and Reynolds were keeping an eye on the planetary defenses. "The orbiting warships are moving to intercept."

"Attacking?"

"No. Weapons systems are not engaged."

The six arriving warships split off from the incoming freighter as the six planetary warships took up positions parallel to the freighter's path.

"Changing of the guard." Kire murmured as the newly arrived warships headed for high orbits around the planet.

Jonarel glanced up from the science station. "A section of the web has deactivated."

"So the freighter can pass through?" Kire asked.

"Most likely."

"Can we follow it in?"

"As long as we remain on its flank."

Kire turned to Kelly at navigation. "Get us alongside that freighter."

"Aye."

The image of the freighter filled the bridgescreen as they drew closer, its design looking more like a marine vessel than something meant for space.

"There's another freighter exiting through the web from the planet's surface." Celia shifted the image on the bridgescreen.

This one looked identical to the freighter that was approaching the planet.

Kelly guided the *Starhawke* to flank the first freighter as it slowed its approach, giving the exiting freighter time to clear the web. The six warships moved into formation around the departing freighter, leading it out of the system.

"Kelly, do you have a course plotted to the jump window if this doesn't work?" Kire asked.

"Aye."

"Gonzo, weapons on standby."

"Roger that."

The *Starhawke* sidled up next to the freighter as it made its approach to the web.

Mya moved directly behind Jonarel's chair, her hands gripping the back as she stared at the screen. She wasn't accustomed to being on the bridge during moments like this. She was usually in the med bay, keeping her mind and body occupied preparing to receive any wounded personnel. Now she remembered why she'd never wanted to be an officer. How did Aurora stay calm while tiptoeing through a potential minefield?

"Fifteen seconds to the web." Jonarel's deep baritone acted as a balm on her frayed nerves, as did his solid presence. He shifted in his chair, bringing his shoulder blades in contact with her fingers. Was that intentional? Had he realized she was on edge?

Kelly had positioned the *Starhawke* close enough that Mya could see the markings on the freighter's hull. An image popped into her mind of a baby dolphin swimming alongside its mother, triggering a nervous laugh that bubbled up at the absurdity of the comparison.

Kire glanced at her with a quizzical look. "Stay with them," he told Kelly, returning his attention to the screen.

"Five seconds to the web." Jonarel leaned back, his torso trapping her hands, his thick hair caressing her forearms. Definitely intentional. He'd picked up on her anxiety.

And no wonder. Despite her death grip, her arms were still trembling. Aurora actually enjoyed this? She was nuts.

"Passing through the web."

Mya held her breath. So did everyone else, judging by the hushed silence that fell on the bridge.

But no alarms sounded. No dire warnings flashed on the consoles. No jolts rocked the ship.

"We have cleared the web."

Mya exhaled on a gusty sigh, her chin dropping to her chest. They'd leapt the first hurdle.

"Follow the freighter down," Kire said. When Mya glanced at him, he lifted a brow. "Unless you have another destination in mind?"

Another destination? Oh, right. She was in charge of the mission now that they were through the web. The weight of responsibility landed on her shoulders with a thump.

The coordinates her parents had provided called to her, but the freighter stood out like a huge exclamation mark, demanding her attention. "Let's see what we can learn about this freighter. And what it's carrying."

Kire's cheeks creased in a reassuring smile. "You've got it. Gonzo, check for ground artillery or patrol ships. Cardiff, scan for cities and technology. We need to know what we'll encounter before we get there."

Mya returned her attention to the image on the bridgescreen as they followed the freighter's descent. They'd come through the web on the night side of the planet, so there wasn't much to see on the surface. If there were cities down there, they weren't illuminated.

Celia turned to Kire. "I'm picking up communications between the freighter and someone on the ground."

"On speaker."

Voices filled the bridge, the clipped words hitting like artillery fire.

Kire frowned.

"Can you understand it?" Mya asked.

Star had provided Kire with the Kraed's revised Teeli language logs, formulated from Siginal's original investigations of the Teeli. The data wasn't sufficient for a full translation, so Kire had been studying the logs, working to correlate what he'd learned at the Academy with the authentic Teeli language. If he couldn't translate what they were hearing, they were out of luck.

"Some. They're talking a lot faster than what I'm used to. But it sounds like landing instructions. We should see a dock soon."

A faint glow appeared on the horizon, growing brighter and more distinct as they continued to track the freighter. They were over water, but a landmass had appeared on the port side.

"Looks like they'll be docking there." Kire murmured. "Gonzo, anything we need to be aware of?"

"Not that I can see. No weapons systems visible to sensors. Just lots of cargo containers stacked along the dock."

Kire turned to Mya. "We won't be able to land the Starhawke within visual range without risking detection. Too much water displacement. Do you want to assemble a shuttle team while we set down further out to sea?"

Finally a task she could get excited about. Putting together a team was what she did best. "Absolutely. Jonarel, Celia and Reynolds, you're with me."

Forty

The cargo dock hadn't provided many insights, except to confirm the workers were Teeli. Their white hair and pale skin was easy to spot, even in the dim lighting.

A steady flow of cargo transports had arrived and departed while the freighter was being unloaded. Her team had followed one of the vessels as it left the dock. Thanks to the *Starhawke* shuttle's camouflage, the other ship had no idea they were there.

Mya had sent a short communication to Kire before they departed to let him know their plan and to alert him to their general direction.

They'd been traveling inland, heading toward the rising sun, which had revealed a marshy terrain thick with jungle growth. The cargo transport descended as a clearing appeared at the top of a terraced hill, surrounded by large swathes of crop vegetation.

Figures moved in the lush landscape. Mya's heart stuttered. Their bodies were enveloped by a pastel rainbow of energy fields. *Suulh!*

She sucked in air, the sharp rasp audible in the small cockpit.

Jonarel glanced at her. "They are Suulh?"

Mya nodded, unable to push words through the constriction in her throat. *They were here. She'd found them.*

"Would you like to land?"

She forced air out of her lungs as pressure built in her chest. She needed to focus, not come unglued. Jonarel was waiting for an answer. But a quick scan of the area didn't reveal any other clearings. "Can we?"

His golden eyes held a hint of amusement. "Of course."

A river flowed past the base of the terraced clearing, playing peek-a-boo in the heavy foliage that encircled the area. Jonarel followed its course for about half a kilometer before touching down. The transition was seamless, the shuttle going from airborne to gliding through the current in an instant, their motion carrying them to the bank on the starboard side.

Before she'd unhooked her harness, Jonarel had the craft anchored in the tumbling water, as if the shuttle were a boat, not a space vessel.

He reached over and clasped her hand in his, sending squiggles of sensation dancing over her skin. "Come with me."

He took the lead position as their team left the shuttle and made their way through the trees. Mya followed Jonarel, with Celia and Reynolds guarding the rear. Jonarel seemed to know exactly where he was going. The terrain wasn't as extreme as what Mya had experienced on Drakar, the Kraed homeworld, but the lush growth and tall trees had a certain similarity. He probably felt right at home.

The hoots and calls of small creatures in the trees and undergrowth provided accompaniment to their footsteps as they climbed along the hillside, moving around fallen branches and avoiding muddy quagmires. When they reached the crest of the hill, Jonarel held up a hand. Guiding Mya forward, he motioned for her to crouch next to him.

The terraced clearing opened up directly in front of them, a cluster of rough-hewn huts winding down the center of the crop clusters. The small village followed the terrain from midway up the hill down to the river's edge, where a dock moored several canoe-like boats.

The cargo transport sat like a giant toad above the village, its hatch a gaping maw that revealed stacks of crates inside. A handful of Teeli directed the Suulh, who were unloading the crates and carrying them to a large building at the heart of the village.

"That looks suspiciously benevolent," Celia said.

Mya agreed. *Suspicious* being the opportune word. It was impossible to know what, if anything, was in the crates, but they weren't heavy. Some of the Suulh were carrying two or three with minimal effort.

As the shuttle emptied out, the flow changed direction, with Suulh exiting the building carrying crates toward the shuttle. This time, the crates were obviously full. No one carried more than one, and some of the crates required two people to haul.

Reynolds scowled. "They're arriving with empty crates and leaving with full ones?"

"Looks that way," Celia said. "Any chance the Teeli paid for what they're taking?"

"The Suulh don't seem to be offering any objections." If only Aurora were here. She would be able to get a sense of how the Suulh felt about the exchange. Mya didn't have that advantage.

"The Teeli are not assisting with the loading. They are in the position of power." Jonarel didn't sound happy about that.

Mya wasn't, either. She didn't see any exchange of money or other sign of barter between the Teeli and Suulh, but as soon as the last crate was loaded, the Teeli left and the Suulh returned to the fields.

As the cargo ship disappeared into the distance, Mya faced her team. "Recommendations?"

"Do you want to make contact?" Celia asked. "We have Justin's translation for the Suulh language coded into the combands."

"I'd like to try talking to them." However, she probably wouldn't need the translation. She'd learned enough of her native language as a child that spending time with the Suulh on Gaia and Azaana had given her a solid foundation for speaking it. She glanced at Jonarel. "But I don't want to scare them, either." As beautiful and striking as he was, he was also intimidating at first glance. If he stepped out of the trees, the Suulh might panic.

He lifted one brow, understanding in his eyes. "I will remain out of sight."

"Thank you. I'll keep a channel open on my comband so you can listen in." Mya turned to Reynolds and Celia. No problem there. They could pass for Suulh just as easily as Mya passed for human. "Ready?"

They both nodded. "We'll follow your lead." Reynolds said.

Mya made her way along the tree line above the village, with Celia and Reynolds at her side. Shouts rose from the fields as the Suulh spotted her small group leaving the cover of the trees. She slowed her steps, gauging their reaction.

Adults and children streamed out of the fields and the huts, forming a crowd that flowed up the hill toward them.

Mya halted, waiting patiently, her hands at her sides.

All the Suulh were barefoot, their feet coated with a thin layer of mud up to the ankle. They were dressed in lightweight clothes, tunics and knee-length pants predominantly, the cloth looking homespun. The expressions on their faces ranged from curiosity to excitement, but no fear. Interesting. Whatever their situation was with the Teeli, they hadn't been taught to beware of strangers. At least, not those who looked like them.

A young woman at the head of the group stepped forward, a tall male remaining just behind her.

Mya made a gesture of greeting and said the Suulh word for hello.

A small frown creased the woman's face as she returned Mya's greeting.

"We are visitors," Mya said, grateful she didn't have to rely on her translator.

The woman replied, but her words were heavily accented, the dialect subtly different from the way the Suulh on Azaana spoke. Mya couldn't quite follow it. "Forgive me. I did not understand. Can you please repeat?" she prompted in the Suulh language.

The woman spoke slowly, enunciating her words. "Who are you?"

"My name is Mya. This is Celia, and Reynolds."

The woman's frown smoothed out a bit. Her eyes were an unusual color that resembled amber tinged with green. "I am Faahn, leader of our village. This is Buk, my mate." She gestured to the male behind her. "We have heard of Suulh who live in villages far from here, but we have never seen them. You must have traveled a great distance."

"Yes, we did." Farther than Faahn could possibly imagine.

Faahn glanced at Mya's feet, her raised brows indicating she'd taken note of the boots Mya, Celia and Reynolds wore. "Did you travel by foot?"

"No. We came in a ship."

"A ship?" Faahn glanced at the river. "You sailed along the river?"

Mya shook her head. She'd used the wrong word for ship. Unlike Galish, the Suulh didn't have a word to denote space vessels. At least, not one she knew. "A transport. Like the one that was just here." She gestured to the clearing where the cargo transport had sat.

Faahn's expression changed to excitement. "Then the White Hairs brought you to us?"

Now it was Mya's turn to frown. "No. We have our own transport."

"But only White Hairs have transports."

Mya gritted her teeth. She had no trouble believing the Teeli kept the Suulh far away from any means of transport. "That is untrue. The one we came in is ours." Technically it was Aurora's, but she wouldn't mind the slight liberty.

"Yours?" Faahn's eyes widened. She pressed her palms together and bowed low. "*You are Gifted.*"

"*Gifted?*" Mya had never heard that term used by the Suulh. "I don't understand."

Faahn lifted her gaze. "Gifted. The strong who work with the White Hairs to protect us." She bowed again. "You honor us with your presence."

A whispered murmur rose from the Suulh like the chatter of excited children, although it was the adults who looked awestruck.

Faahn gazed at Mya expectantly.

She'd been in enough diplomatic situations to figure out the proper response. She returned the bow. "We are honored to be here."

Faahn beamed at her, then pointed to one of the larger huts. "Please, will you join us? We can offer you nourishment after your long journey."

She wasn't about to pass up the opportunity. Her questions were mounting, and Faahn might be able to provide answers. She motioned to Celia and Reynolds to follow her. "Thank you, Faahn. We would be grateful."

The crowd parted to allow them through, Faahn and Buk leading the way. But as they walked to the hut, Mya noted something odd about the Suulh they passed. Every single one looked younger than thirty. Children, teenagers and young adults abounded, but the older generations were conspicuously absent. Where were the parents and grandparents? Yet another question to add to her list.

Faahn's hut was built on stilts, which kept the foundation above the damp ground. They entered through a door woven from narrow branches tied with vines. A sturdy broom propped near the door and pencil-thin streaks on the floorboards indicated the area was swept regularly. The furnishings inside the single-room structure were sparse, with sleeping pallets on the floor in one corner. A doll crafted of a straw-like material lay on one of the smaller pallets. Villagers, including a few small children, crept into the room and settled themselves on the floor along the walls.

"Please, sit." Faahn gestured to a collection of worn crates gathered around a low table. Buk set carved wooden mugs in front of each of them while Faahn fetched a pitcher. As she poured a pale brown liquid into Mya's mug, her gaze settled on Celia. "You are also Gifted?"

Celia gave Mya a questioning look. "Should I turn on my translator?"

Mya paused with her mug halfway to her lips. She'd forgotten that neither Celia nor Reynolds had understood a single word she and Faahn had said, although Celia had probably followed the conversation through the non-verbal cues. "Go ahead."

Celia tapped her comband. "Can you please repeat the question?" she asked Faahn.

Faahn stared at Celia's arm, where the Galish words had been reproduced by the translation program in the Suulh language. "What is that?" She peered closer when the comband repeated her words in Galish.

Celia held her arm out for Faahn's inspection. "It's called a translator. It allows us to understand each other even though we don't speak the same language."

Faahn's brows drew down. "Do all the Gifted speak a different language?"

Celia glanced at Mya for help in fielding that question.

"She speaks a different language because she's from somewhere far away." Mya hoped Faahn would accept the vague answer.

Faahn turned to Mya. "But *you* speak our language."

"I was taught both languages as a child."

Faahn nodded in understanding. "By the White Hairs."

Mya grimaced. "No. By my parents."

Faahn backed up a step at the bite in her words. "Did I say something wrong?"

Mya lifted a hand, palm out. "No. It's not you. But the White Hairs have hurt a lot of people I care about."

Faahn's lips parted in surprise. "No. That cannot be true. The White Hairs take care of us. They guard us from the Pebble Skins."

"Pebble Skins?"

"Yes. The violent monsters that would destroy us without the protection of the White Hairs."

It clicked. *Setarips.*

Now they were getting somewhere. "How do the White Hairs protect you from the Pebble Skins?" Setarips would never attack a planet as heavily guarded as this one. They were opportunists. They went for easy prey.

Faahn looked completely perplexed. "You do not know?"

Mya shook her head.

"But you are Gifted. Do you not work with the White Hairs to guard the borderlands?"

"No, we don't."

Faahn frowned, exchanging a glance with Buk before continuing. "The White Hairs have told us many stories of the battles they have fought to keep the Pebble Skins out. They take great risks to protect us."

Reynolds snorted.

Faahn's frown deepened.

"And what price do you pay for this protection?" Celia asked. A hard glint had appeared in her brown eyes.

"We share the bounty of our lands. We are happy to give to our protectors."

"Is that what we witnessed earlier?" Mya asked. "The White Hairs coming to collect their payment?"

Faahn nodded.

"And how often do they come?"

"Every seventh sunrise."

Judging from the number of crates the Suulh had loaded, growing that much food each week would be a full-time occupation.

"Has your village ever been attacked by the Pebble Skins?" Celia asked. Her expression indicated she already knew the answer.

Faahn shook her head. "No. But we have heard the tales of the monsters with flattened heads and scaly skin that terrorized our world."

Mya hesitated to ask her next question, but she needed to know. "Is that what happened to your parents and grandparents? Were they killed fighting the Pebble Skins?"

Faahn looked puzzled again. "Our parents and elders are not dead."

But the village didn't have any older generations. "Where are they?"

"They are with you. At Citadel."

Citadel? Mya didn't recognize the Suulh word Celia's comband had translated as *citadel.* "What is Citadel?"

Tension lines formed around Faahn's eyes. "That is not where you are from?"

"No."

"But all the Gifted live there." Faahn said it like a child insisting dragons lived in the forest.

Mya chose her words carefully. "We have lived apart from the others for some time. What can you tell me about Citadel?"

Faahn's gaze darted to her mate. He looked as concerned as she did.

"Citadel is where all Suulh go after their children come of age."

That explained the missing elders. "How do they get there?"

"The White Hairs take them."

Mya worked to keep her voice steady. If the Teeli had gathered all the older and more powerful Suulh in one place, she needed to know as much about it as possible. "Why would your people want to go to Citadel rather than remaining here, with their families?"

Faahn looked at her like she'd sprouted another head. "Because living at Citadel is a great honor."

"An honor? Why?"

"At Citadel, they work with the White Hairs and Gifted to protect us." Faahn raised her chin a notch. "They keep our children and our homes safe."

Clever. The Teeli had convinced the Suulh that being separated was a noble and selfless choice. "Has anyone ever returned from Citadel? Do they visit you here?" Mya could predict the answer.

"No. But when my children are of age, I will join my parents there."

Mya's heart sank at the unshakable certainty in Faahn's voice.

"Do you know where Citadel is located?"

"No. But it is far from here, close to the borderlands, where the White Hairs keep watch for the Pebble Skins."

Faahn's description made it clear she didn't even realize the Setarips and Teeli weren't indigenous to the planet. Which meant Citadel, if it existed, might not be on the planet, either. "What—"

A crack and thud followed by a child's sharp cry shattered the morning air.

Mya was on her feet and out the door between one breath and the next, clearing a path through the Suulh gathered on the stairs.

A boy of about nine lay on the ground, his arm at an unnatural angle between the shoulder and elbow. A large branch lay beside him. A quick glance at the hut revealed a gap in the railing for the stairway. It must have given way.

Mya dropped to her knees beside him and placed her hands on his arm.

His light brown eyes were etched with pain and fear.

"It's going to be okay," she murmured, engaging her energy field and numbing the pain.

The tension in his body eased, but his eyes widened as he stared at his arm. Under her guidance, the bone realigned almost as quickly as it had broken, the cells shifting into their proper state and reuniting, reversing the damage.

A harsh whisper broke Mya's concentration. "*Nedale.*"

Mya glanced up.

Faahn stood beside her, her face a mask of shock as she stared at Mya and the boy.

Mya bit back a groan. Healing the boy's injury had been instinctive. She hadn't considered that the Suulh might recognize the distinctive dark green of her energy field that marked her as Nedale, the Healer of the race.

Faahn's mouth hung open as a murmur swept through the gathering crowd.

Now what? If the Suulh told the Teeli that their Nedale had visited the village, Mya's mission would end. And the hunt would begin.

Faahn dropped to her knees beside Mya and bent her head. "Forgive me, Nedale. I did not know." When she lifted her gaze, tears shimmered in her eyes. "*You are legend.*"

Mya didn't know whether to laugh or cry. If this was how Faahn reacted to her presence, she could only imagine the uproar Aurora would cause.

The young boy was staring at her with a similar look.

Mya gave him a soft smile. "Why don't you join your mother?" she suggested, gesturing to a dark-haired woman standing behind Faahn, her gaze locked on the child like a tractor beam.

The boy scrambled to his feet, touching his arm in wonder as he hurried to his mother's side.

Mya returned her attention to Faahn. "I'm a Suulh, Faahn. Like you. There's nothing legendary about me."

"But, you are *Nedale*," Faahn protested.

Mya sighed. Maybe fighting this was the wrong approach. After all, the Suulh on Gaia had reacted in much the same way. "Yes, I am. And that's why I need you to listen to me very carefully." She clasped Faahn's hands in hers and pulled her to her feet.

"I need you all to listen to what I have to say." Mya addressed the crowd, including Celia and Reynolds, who stood at the bottom of the stairway watching her. "The White Hairs have convinced you *they* are your guardians. But they are not. I am Nedale, consort of Sahzade, the true guardian of our race. She and I have witnessed atrocities committed by the White Hairs against the Suulh. They have imprisoned our people, and are using them as weapons of destruction."

Faahn's gasp was the loudest amid the multitude that greeted that statement. The Suulh looked shell-shocked.

"We want to free our people from a life of torture and pain, but the White Hairs will do everything they can to stop us. They must *not* know I was here."

Mya was asking them to make a leap of faith. The Suulh had spent their entire lives believing the Teeli were their friends. The specter of betrayal was not something they would face willingly.

But they also would not want to go against the wishes of someone who, as Faahn had made clear, was considered a living legend. Whatever the Teeli had told them, it had not overridden their inborn connection to their heritage and beliefs. Their reaction to her presence told her that. She prayed their faith in her was stronger than their loyalty to the Teeli.

"I know this is difficult. But I can assure you that the Setarips—Pebble Skins as you call them—are not waiting on your borders. And the White Hairs are not your protectors. They're manipulating you, taking advantage of your abilities for their own benefit."

Faahn swayed, her legs no longer supporting her.

Mya wrapped an arm around her shoulders and surrounded her with soothing energy.

Faahn's breath stopped coming in hitching gasps, but she still looked like she was on information overload.

"Use your energy," Mya prompted.

Lines appeared around Faahn's eyes, but she complied. A subtle red joined Mya's green, the color nearly transparent compared to the deep richness of Mya's field.

Her mate stepped beside her and added his energy, an anemic yellow that Mya could barely see.

The rest of the villagers crept forward, one by one adding their energy to the mix. Even combined, it was a drop in the ocean compared to what she'd experienced with the Suulh on Azaana.

The energy field of the boy she'd healed was as pale as the rest. Now that she thought about it, he hadn't engaged his energy field to assist with his healing, either.

Is that why these Suulh lived in the village and produced food? They would be useful to the Teeli in that capacity, but their minimal energy abilities would make them terrible Necri soldiers.

Silent tears streamed down Faahn's cheeks as she met Mya's gaze. "Citadel?" she whispered. "My...parents?"

Mya's heart ached for her. For all of them. They were facing a new reality, one that came with painful revelations. And she didn't have any answers to give.

"I don't know."

Faahn trembled, the tears coming faster. "Will you...find them?"

This was her fault. Until today, the villagers had lived in blissful ignorance. Now they were suffering, because of her.

Aurora, I wish you were here. Mya could heal physical wounds with ease, but healing emotional wounds was Aurora's specialty. Without Aurora's empathic abilities to guide her, she did the only thing she could do. She spoke from her heart.

"I will not abandon you. I promise."

Forty-One

The shuttle trip to the *Starhawke* passed in silence. Jonarel had been waiting for them in the trees after they'd said their goodbyes to Faahn and the other Suulh.

He hadn't asked any questions. He seemed to understand that Mya needed time to process. But he'd rested a comforting hand on her shoulder before settling into the pilot's seat.

Kire met them in the shuttle bay. "What did you find?"

"A village of Suulh. And a pack of lies the Teeli have told them to keep them under control."

Kire's thin brows lifted. "You were able to talk to them?"

She nodded, filling him in on the details as the team made their way to the bridge.

"So, what's our next move?"

Mya pulled the slip of paper with the planetary coordinates out of her pocket. "Finding out if the Citadel Faahn talked about is located at the coordinates my parents wanted us to investigate."

A quick meal and thirty degrees of longitude later, Mya was back in the co-pilot's seat of the shuttle. Celia and Reynolds were in the main cabin, directing the shuttle's fore and aft cameras as Jonarel made an aerial pass over the coastline.

Mya had envisioned a plethora of scenarios for what she'd find. The reality cut deeper than she'd expected.

The city below them had been her ancestral home. The massive structure at its heart told her that. It was an enormous version of Stoneycroft, with the two half-moons on either side of the central dome.

A shiver danced over her skin. Forty years ago, her mom would have called that building home.

It was one of the few recognizable structures left. Remnants of the buildings that had been part of the original Suulh settlement were scattered here and there, but they'd been repurposed by the Teeli. The simple, graceful lines that had once opened their arms to the elements were now enclosed in walls of glass, cutting them off from what they'd been designed to embrace. Additional buildings had supplanted what would have been gardens and greenspaces, the angular metal and glass structures standing out like boils on the landscape's skin. They dominated their surroundings, demanding obedience rather than nurturing harmony.

On the outskirts of the city, the greenery reappeared, but in carefully controlled agricultural centers. Natural, free-flowing elements didn't exist. Instead, regimented rows of plants and trees stretched out to the base of the mountains to the east. The overall effect was one of lifelessness, despite the bustle of activity in the city streets and the fields. Such a harsh contrast to the vibrancy of the Suulh settlement on Azaana. And to what this city must have been like before the Teeli changed the course of the Suulh's lives forever.

Mya swallowed around the tightness in her throat. The tragedy of what had been lost sank into her soul, weighing her down. And she was only seeing the end result. She still didn't know what had happened here forty years ago that had convinced her parents to abandon this world to its fate.

The repercussions of that decision rocked her. If the Teeli hadn't come to this planet, this city would be her home.

Her parents would be living in the cultural center with her, and she would be the Nedale of this entire world, a leader of tens or hundreds of thousands, caring for and nurturing her people alongside Sahzade.

Except Sahzade...Aurora...would never have been born.

That brought her train of thought to a screeching halt. Yes, Libra would have mated and had a daughter, but that child wouldn't have been Aurora. She would have been a child of two Suulh, not a Suulh-human pair. And she would have been steeped in the Suulh culture from the day she was born.

That child would have been so different from the precocious girl Aurora had been, and the independent woman she'd become. The gifts that made her so unique among the Suulh were special precisely because her father was human. She'd inherited so much from him, including his indomitable spirit, even though she didn't realize it.

A gentle touch on her shoulder startled her.

"Are you all right?" Jonarel murmured, compassion shining in his golden eyes.

"No." Her voice sounded hollow. Well, that fit. Her insides felt hollow, too. She'd been prepared for the crumbled ruins of a battle zone. Or even a barren wasteland. But not this. It was like watching a murderer dancing on her parents' graves.

"I am sorry." Deep lines etched Jonarel's face as he returned his attention to their flight path.

Heat sparked in Mya's belly, and her hands clenched. The Teeli had stolen this world from her family. And now they were using it as their personal playground, uncaring of the scars they were leaving on the land and the people they'd conquered.

"I think we've found the older Suulh." Celia called from the main cabin.

Mya glanced over her shoulder.

Celia was staring at the camera monitor, her lips curled in distaste. Anger flashed in her eyes as she met Mya's gaze. "Take a look."

An image appeared on Mya's console, a magnification of one of the sectors they were passing. Figures moved along the main promenade, most of them Teeli, their white hair prominent in the aerial view. However, other figures scuttled along the edges, their darker hair and drab rags a sharp contrast to the flamboyant clothing worn by the Teeli.

Mya stared at the images. "What are they doing?"

"Garbage patrol." Celia zoomed in, focusing on two of the Suulh, a middle-aged man and an older woman, who looked like they hadn't eaten a decent meal in weeks. They were using long-handled brooms to gather the trash that littered the ground of the walkway.

The woman stumbled when one of the Teeli knocked into her. She fell on her knees in front of another of the passing Teeli and was rewarded with a smack across the face that sent her sprawling. She received a kick from another Teeli before her middle-aged companion reached her and helped her retreat to the relative safety of the outer edge of the walkway.

Mya's breath came out on a hiss.

"Charming race." Reynolds's voice dripped with sarcasm.

"So they use the younger Suulh to provide their food, and the older ones to do their dirty work." Celia's disgust was written all over her face.

Mya's belly churned. "Apparently." And there was nothing she could do to help them. At least, not right now.

Jonarel banked the shuttle to the right, taking them closer to the agricultural fields. Celia and Reynolds adjusted the cameras, pulling up images of Suulh moving among the plants.

The video images didn't show Mya what she needed to see, so she peered out the shuttle's viewport. Sure enough, she could make out subtle color variations as the Suulh generated energy fields around the plants. However, the colors were almost as pale as the fields produced by the Suulh in Faahn's village. Mya could barely sense the resonance of their energy at all. If the Teeli were keeping powerful Suulh on this planet, they weren't here.

She chewed on her lower lip. She'd hoped they'd find the Citadel Faahn had spoken of at these coordinates, or at least something to point them in the right direction. No such luck. "Where are you keeping them?" she murmured. Had all the powerful Suulh been moved off planet? Were those with weak skills who could be easily manipulated by the Teeli the only ones who remained?

She didn't want to believe it. Tracking down the Suulh on the planet would be hard enough. Tracking them through Teeli space would take a lifetime. "Let's head back to the ship."

After they arrived, she gathered the crew on the bridge. "We still need to find the powerful Suulh." She focused on Kire in the captain's chair. "What have you learned from the Teeli comm channels?"

He laced his fingers together on his stomach. "Not much. From what I can make out, it's all personal chatter. Like listening to an extended cocktail party. The Teeli living here don't seem to be interacting with anyone except other residents."

Reynolds nodded. "That fits with what we saw. The city looks like a pleasure palace, not a government or military hub."

"No ships arriving or departing, either," Gonzo said. "Pretty self-contained."

"Which doesn't give us anything to go on." She turned to the bridgescreen, staring at the waves of the ocean stretching to the horizon. If only she could get close to the powerful Suulh, she'd sense them. Especially if they were engaging their energy fields. But searching the entire planet could take—

An idea popped into her head and she spun around. "Star?"

The Nirunoc appeared in front of her. "Yes?"

"If you analyze my energy field and use it as a template, can you attune the ship's sensors to identify similar energetic patterns produced by other Suulh?"

Star exchanged a look with Jonarel, who stood to Mya's right, his arms folded over his broad chest.

He gave an almost imperceptible nod.

"Yes, I can."

Mya's eyes narrowed. Something had passed between those two in that moment. Unfortunately, she didn't have the time or energy to find out what. "Then we'll start there. Kelly?" Mya turned to the navigator. "Plot a search pattern, starting with a heading to the west. Pay particular attention to any isolated areas, like high altitude mountain ranges or large islands." Based on the Teeli's desire to control the powerful Suulh, she was willing to bet that if Citadel existed, it would be in a remote location. And her instincts told her to head west.

Kelly nodded.

Mya headed to the lift. "Star, I'll meet you in the med bay."

Forty-Two

Tnaryt was driving Aurora crazy.

Not only had he chained her to the comm console
before he'd retired to his quarters for his sleep cycle each
night, but during his waking hours, he was planted on his
throne, watching her every move.

She'd spent most of her first full day accessing and
evaluating the communication system, the hours of sweaty
work broken only by the appearance of an older man with
greying curly hair who brought her a nasty-tasting mash. He'd
scuttled down the ladder as soon as he'd delivered the meal,
refusing to meet Aurora's gaze. After he'd gone, she'd
choked down every bite even though her stomach had
rebelled. She needed to maintain her strength.

Tnaryt had been served several meals throughout
the day, always by the same older man. The food on his
plate had looked and smelled far more appetizing than what
Aurora had consumed. Tnaryt had clearly enjoyed taunting
her with what she couldn't have.

He'd returned to the bridge after his second sleep
cycle, shocking her with the dramatic change in his
appearance. His coloring had been the same, but what she'd
taken for a permanent row of spikes running along his head
and back had collapsed into a thin strip of darker orange.
His neck had also deflated, giving him the appearance of
heavy jowls and flabby skin. Not a flattering look. She wisely
did not point it out.

As he had the previous morning, he'd removed the
manacle and given her permission to use the sanitation
facilities in his cabin. She'd climbed through the hatch on the

bridge that led directly into the compact space. The facilities had allowed her to relieve one point of discomfort, but the tradeoff had been surrounding herself with his overpowering musk. When she'd returned to the bridge, the pungent odors from another bowl of mash had greeted her, making her stomach churn. But she'd eaten it anyway.

The sleeping pallet Nat had brought was only moderately cleaner than the floor, but at least it had provided a slight buffer from the cold metal of the deck. Finding a comfortable sleeping position with one hand tethered had been a challenge, though. Both nights she'd woken a dozen times with her arm asleep and her shoulder aching.

This morning, Nat had been pressed into service as her assistant while she sorted out the inner workings of the communication system. From the comments Tnaryt had made when Nat arrived on the bridge, Aurora had gathered she'd spent the previous day down in engineering with the Admiral, helping with the main engines.

Nat had indicated they'd be operational in a few days, which lit a fire under Aurora to get the comm system functioning. She'd need the comm to contact Cade and alert him that she'd found the Admiral. Ironically, if Tnaryt continued to shackle her to the console, it would make that task easier.

She was also hoping to gain access to the ship's communication logs, which might shed light on the Sovereign's identity. Or at least give her a path to follow. She could ask Nat about the Sovereign, but only if Tnaryt left them alone. She wasn't very optimistic about that possibility. He seemed to enjoy watching them work.

Nat was a different person today. When she'd delivered the pallet that first night, her emotions had been a whirlpool of darkness, dominated by pain and despair. *Tortured.* That's how she'd looked. Like someone had been flaying her with a whip only she could see.

Aurora had wanted to reach out to her, to comfort her, but Tnaryt's looming presence had made that difficult. She'd managed to send a subtle flow of energy to Nat through the pallet, coaxing her back into the light while she'd knelt in front of her, though the effect had been muted without a direct physical connection. However, Nat had responded, her emotions shifting dramatically when she'd seen Aurora's small smile. At the time it had been enough. Whether the change would hold was still up in the air.

"Hand me that thing that looks like a socket wrench." Aurora waved a hand at the array of tools she'd spread on the deck before she'd ducked into the crawlspace beneath the communications console.

Nat held up a bulky contraption for Aurora's inspection. "This one?"

"Yep." Aurora took the tool and returned her attention to the panel above her. "It's a wonder this species ever made it into space," she muttered, keeping her voice low so Tnaryt wouldn't hear her.

He was sitting on his throne, as usual. So far he was allowing them to work in peace, without making use of their collars. It probably helped that they were focused on the job he wanted them to do. Shocking them would only slow them down.

The interface for the communications system wasn't nearly as cooperative. Despite her best efforts, the console remained dark, which necessitated her presence in the tiny crawlspace, attempting to rewire the connections.

Her task was hampered by the unfamiliar tech and the Setarips' appalling lack of structural design. They'd placed key components in areas that were virtually impossible to reach. The damage she was seeing to the system also didn't look like normal wear and tear or faulty wiring. It looked like carefully executed sabotage. Someone had wanted Tnaryt's ship out of commission.

Her money was on the Sovereign.

She stretched her hand toward Nat. "I need the thick grey cable and those small pliers with the wire cutter."

Nat handed them down, her voice as quiet as Aurora's. "Any success?"

"Not yet. It's a mess." And this was only the first step. The internal comm stations weren't functional, either. Repairing those would give her a way to talk to the Admiral without leaving the bridge. She'd need that ability if they were going to coordinate a plan to outmaneuver Tnaryt.

A scraping sound followed by two thumps came from the direction of Tnaryt's chair.

Aurora paused, her hand in mid-air. What now?

The color washed out of Nat's cheeks as she tensed, but she kept her gaze on Aurora.

Aurora waited, expecting Tnaryt to approach them, but instead his cloak swirled past them as he moved to the stairwell. His gravelly voice drifted back to them. "Keeep at wooork."

Her eyes widened. He was leaving them alone on the bridge? That was a first. And he hadn't chained them up or posted a guard. She glanced at Nat as the echo of his footsteps faded. "Any idea where he's going?"

"Pleasure tour." Nat's voice didn't give a hint of inflection. It was like talking to an automaton.

"Meaning what?"

Nat's gaze skittered away. "Mating with the female Setarips. Intimidating the prisoners." She swallowed. "Shocking whoever he feels like tormenting."

Aurora's grip tightened on the tool in her hand. "Does he do this often?"

"Every few days." She shrugged, the gesture stiff and unnatural. "More often if he's in a bad mood."

"Lovely." Aurora prayed Tnaryt wouldn't pay the Admiral a visit. Or the older man who brought her food. The thought galvanized her back to work. They needed this comm system up and running ASAP.

Nat surprised her by asking a question. "How long have you been a Fleet officer?"

Aurora's hand stilled. "What makes you think I was an officer?"

"Come on, Aurora. Don't play games. You and the engineer were both officers. Might still be, in fact. Is that why you're here? Because of the Fleet?"

Nat wasn't wrong, except for the part about the Fleet being involved. "No. My reasons for being here are...personal." She kept her tone conversational as she asked the question that had been burning in her brain since she'd arrived. "What can you tell me about the Sovereign?"

Nat didn't answer for so long Aurora poked her head out of the crawlspace to check on her.

She looked like she'd seen a ghost. "You don't want to have anything to do with the Sovereign."

"Why not?"

"Because bad things happen."

Aurora studied her. "Is that how you ended up here? Because of the Sovereign?"

Nat's lips pulled down. "No. I have Tnaryt to thank for that."

"What happened?"

Nat shook her head. "Doesn't matter. At least, not while we're stuck here." She rested her elbows on her knees and leaned closer. "So, what's your plan for getting us away from Tnaryt?"

Aurora's mouth dropped open. She closed it when she realized Nat was waiting for an answer. "I don't have a plan." Not much of one, anyway. And she wouldn't trust Nat with it if she did.

Nat's scrutiny intensified. "Of course you do. You're not reacting like any of the other people I've brought up. You're not afraid of Tnaryt, even with that collar around your neck. Why not?"

Aurora scrambled for a reasonable reply. "I don't give up easily. Especially when dealing with bullies."

Nat snorted. "It's more than that. I felt that way at first, too. But with you, there's something different. You have an out. What is it?"

Aurora had seriously underestimated the young woman. "I don't have a plan. My plan was to find my father."

"He's not your father."

"W-What?" Aurora stammered.

"He's *not* your father. He means something to you, but it's not because he's family. You're not as good a liar as you think."

And how good a liar are you? Was she a mole for Tnaryt? Nat's emotions didn't indicate duplicity, but a really good liar might be able to fool her. "What exactly do you expect me to do?"

"Get us safely away from the ship."

Which brought to mind another question she'd pondered during her restless hours chained to the comm console. "Why haven't you escaped already? You have the shuttle, and the range of the collars must be limited. Tnaryt couldn't activate it when you're on Gallows Edge. Why do you keep coming back?"

"Because if I don't, I'll die. The collars have an autodestruct tied to a remote signal generated by the ship."

An autodestruct? Great. As if she needed another challenge to work around.

"If a collar travels out of signal range, an internal countdown triggers. When it reaches zero, the collar self-destructs, killing whoever it's attached to."

Aurora's breath caught. The collar around the Admiral's neck had just turned into a viper. "What's the signal range?"

"Not far. Mine triggers less than halfway to Gallows Edge. But Tnaryt can change the lag time for the autodestruct of each collar. He's been extending mine to allow me time to make the run and acquire new ca—" She cut off and looked away.

"New captives?"

Nat's jaw tightened as she nodded.

Either Nat was the best liar Aurora had ever met, or she hated the role Tnaryt had given her.

"What about removing the collars? There must be a way."

"Not that I've seen. A few of the early captives tried." Nat's voice dropped to a murmur. "It...didn't end well."

"Meaning what?"

The haunted look was back in Nat's eyes. "There's more than one way to trigger the autodestruct. Tnaryt made me clean up the remains of the last captive who tried."

Aurora shivered. She *really* wanted to get that collar off the Admiral's neck. "You said the signal is tied to a system on the ship. Do you know where it's located?"

Nat shook her head. "I've been all over engineering, and it's not there. I used *Gypsy's* sensors, too, but no luck. I think the system's generating an interference pattern. The sensors couldn't lock onto anything." She grimaced. "It could be tucked in a million odd corners of this ship."

And the hits kept coming. Deactivating all the collars at the source would have freed her to deal with Tnaryt. His control over the other captives was the one thing keeping her from acting against him.

But Nat's knowledge might be valuable in other ways. "If I help you escape, will you help me track down the Sovereign?"

Nat's fear struck Aurora like a sledgehammer. "*No.* You don't want *anything* to do with the Sovereign."

"Yes, I do."

"Are you insane? Suicidal?"

"Neither. The Sovereign has hurt a lot of people I care about."

"So you want revenge?"

"Justice. I want the suffering to end. And I want—I *need*—to free my people from the Sovereign's grip."

Nat stared at her. "Who *are* you?"

Aurora stared right back. "Your best hope to get off this ship."

Forty-Three

Cade was going out of his mind.

Four days without any contact from Aurora or the Admiral. The Setarip ship hadn't moved, which was the only item in the positive column. But that begged the question of why he hadn't heard from Aurora.

Her comband was still turned off. He'd tried contacting her. Repeatedly.

"It's awfully quiet up there." Justin turned in the co-pilot's seat to face Cade. "Maybe you should take a break."

Cade grunted in response. Williams had tried to convince him to get some rest in one of *Gladiator*'s bunks, but he couldn't force himself to leave the controls until he knew Aurora was safe. He'd dozed fitfully in the chair, but his body felt like he'd been sleeping in a rock tumbler. His conversation skills were deteriorating along with his mood.

What are you doing up there, Rory? She had to be okay. Anything else was unacceptable. But what was her game plan? Did she know he was here, waiting for her?

"Something's coming through." Justin shifted, his attention returning to the comm. He pressed a hand to his ear, then switched on the speakers. "Aurora? Is that you?"

Static filled the cockpit, followed by the sound of Aurora's sweet voice flowing from the speakers. "Hi, Justin. Figured you'd be listening. Is Cade with you?"

Cade sat up so quickly his spine cracked. "I'm here." He flattened his hands on the console as though he could reach her through the speaker. "Are you on the Setarip ship?" Amazing that his voice sounded calm and reasonable when his internal organs were whacking each other with croquet mallets.

"Yes. I'm on the bridge." Her voice was faint, like she was whispering.

"Did you find the Admiral? Is he with you?"

"Yes, he's on the ship, but I'm alone on the bridge. At least, right now."

A monolith tumbled off Cade's shoulders. She'd found the Admiral. And they were both okay. "What's going on? Why did you take off?" Lack of sleep wasn't helping his diplomatic skills, either.

Aurora sighed. "Sorry about that."

"Sorry? You scared me to death. I didn't know—"

"Cade, please. I had to make a choice. I didn't have time to alert you."

"Then why didn't you contact me later? Why did you switch off your comband?"

"Nat took it."

"Nat?" He exchanged a puzzled glance with Justin. "Who's Nat?"

"Another captive on this ship."

Another... Cade's heart began to pound. "Are you saying you're a *prisoner?*"

"Sort of. At least, Tnaryt thinks I am."

The pounding moved to Cade's head. "Who's Tnaryt?"

"The Setarip leader. A real prince." Her words had teeth. She really didn't like this Tnaryt.

Two sets of footsteps echoed down *Gladiator*'s corridor. "Is that Aurora?" Drew asked as she and Williams appeared at the hatch.

"Hi, Drew," Aurora replied.

"Hi, yourself. You okay?"

Cade was glad she'd asked. He hadn't gotten to that question yet.

Aurora sighed. "I'm smelly, dirty and tired, but otherwise I'm good."

Her words went a long way to calming his fears. If she was admitting to hardships, then she really was okay. She hadn't defaulted to *I'm fine.*

"Do you want us to come get you?" He didn't have a plan, but if she said yes, he'd fire up the engines. Assuming she needed rescuing. With Aurora, he could never be sure.

"Not yet. We have a few...complications to work out first."

Her vague comments buzzed in his head like wasps. "What do you mean?"

"Tnaryt met with the person responsible for the attack on Gaia—someone he calls the Sovereign."

That was big news. "Do you know who this Sovereign is?"

"No. But the Admiral's hoping to convince Tnaryt to track down the Sovereign after we complete the ship repairs. The cruiser we encountered on Gaia belonged to Tnaryt. The Sovereign took it."

"Took it? They're not working together?"

"They might have been originally, but Tnaryt seems to have been cheated out of whatever he was promised."

"Then maybe we could help you. I could make contact with him—"

"Not a good idea. Tnaryt's easily provoked. He'd see you as a threat, especially if he figured out you knew me and the Admiral. He'd end up getting control of you, too."

Cade stared at the speaker. Surely he'd misheard. "How?"

"He has all the captives wearing shock collars to keep us in line."

"You're wearing *what?*"

"Shock collars. And they'll self-destruct if any of us leave the ship."

Her words didn't make any sense. "Why would you—"

"Because I didn't want Tnaryt to know about my abilities. And the collar can't hurt me."

"What about the Admiral?"

"That's a different story. The collars generate an electric pulse, a potentially lethal one. Nat and the cook are wearing them, too. I have to disable the collars before I can move against Tnaryt."

Cade shared a glance with Justin. A million questions raced through his mind, but only one mattered. "What can we do to help?"

"Stay close. Most of the systems on this ship are inoperable, so you won't be picked up on sensors. The Admiral's working on repairing the engines. When he's finished, if all goes well, Tnaryt will be moving the ship. You'll need to be ready when that happens."

His hands closed into fists. He wanted to see her, to hold her in his arms and assure himself she was in one piece. He also wanted to wrap his hands around the neck of the Setarip who'd dared to take her captive.

"Is there any way we can contact you?" Justin asked.

"Not yet. I don't want Tnaryt to know the comm is working. But I'll be in touch as soon as the Admiral and I have a plan."

More waiting. Not that he had a choice. "Be careful."

"I will. And Cade?"

"Yeah?"

"I miss you."

He swallowed. She'd said *miss*, but that's not the word he heard. "I miss you, too."

The static cut out, shrouding the small space in silence again.

He drew in a long breath, slowly unclenching his hands.

Justin clapped him on the back. "She's okay, buddy."

"That's good news," Williams said as he rested his hand on Cade's shoulder, his grip firm. "It also means I finally get to order you out of here." He pointed down the corridor. "Don't show your face for at least six hours."

Cade glared at Williams, still reluctant to leave his post.

Williams's eyes narrowed, making him look less like a kindly doctor and more like a professional wrestler. "I mean it. You'll need to be sharp and rested when Aurora makes a move. Right now you're a lead balloon."

Much as he hated to admit it, Williams was right. Exhaustion would slow his reaction time, and might cost Aurora when she needed him. But still.... He glanced at Justin. "You'll alert me if she contacts you again?"

"Immediately. I promise." Justin made a shooing motion. "Now go."

Cade stood, which took a lot more effort than he'd expected. His legs were none too steady, either, even with Williams's support. He'd been running on pure adrenaline, and his body was letting him know it.

With a nod of thanks at Justin and a quick glance at Drew and Williams, he walked down the corridor, through the small common area, and collapsed onto a bunk with a sigh.

Forty-Four

Hearing Cade's voice had gone a long way to improving Aurora's mental and emotional state. He was nearby, waiting to back her up. That gave her a much-needed boost.

She'd nixed the idea of asking Nat to smuggle her comband to her so she wouldn't have to rely on the ship's comm. Beside the risk of Tnaryt seeing the exchange, she didn't want to confirm Nat's suspicions that she was working on a plan to escape. At least, not yet. Nat's name was still penciled in on the untrustworthy list.

She'd deactivated the short-range comm as soon as she'd closed the channel. She didn't want to tip off Tnaryt that the system was operational. It had taken two days of solid work to get the comm running, but she'd finally sorted it out. Now she was focusing on the long-range communications, which were proving to be a tricky nut to crack. Whoever had sabotaged the system had focused most of the damage there. But she needed to fix it soon. She wasn't sure how long Tnaryt's patience would last.

He reclined in his throne, his gaze locked on her.

Nat was working as her assistant again today, after spending the previous day helping the Admiral complete the physical modifications to the interstellar engines. The occasional rumble from below indicated he was performing preliminary diagnostic testing to confirm the system was functional.

Aurora poked her head around the lip of the console. "Any change?"

Nat sat in the chair, monitoring the panel while Aurora made adjustments to the inner workings underneath. "No."

"Damn." Dealing with the unfamiliar tech was like working with one hand tied behind her back.

She wiped her palms on her pants as she stood, leaving streaks on the dark brown material that blended with the stains already covering her clothes. She glanced at her hands and sighed. She'd never craved a shower and clean clothes so much in her life.

Nat vacated the chair so Aurora could slide in front of the console. Using her sleeve, she wiped some of the grime off the panel, giving her a clear view of the Setarip symbols. A few lights flickered, but none of the commands responded to her touch.

The system was as stubborn as the Setarips.

She turned to Tnaryt. "The comm still won't respond. I need a few more parts. I could also use some input from my father. May I go down to engineering?"

His unblinking gaze pierced her, his tongue flicking in and out.

She waited while he weighed the pleasure of refusing her request with his desire to have the system running.

He rose from the throne and stalked closer, the spikes along his head and back lifting and his neck puffing out. He pointed a long finger at Nat. "Yooou staaay." He motioned to Aurora. "Yooou go."

Nat's face paled as she changed places with Aurora. Being the focus of Tnaryt's attention wasn't a position either of them wanted, and Nat had just lost the coin toss.

Aurora made it down to engineering in record time. She didn't feel good about leaving Nat alone with Tnaryt, but she needed parts. She also wanted to alert the Admiral to her successful communication with Cade.

He was studying diagnostic readings on the main control panel when she entered the room. He looked up. "Here for parts?"

"Among other things." She quickly filled him in on the situation with Cade and her conversation with Nat as she gathered what she needed. "If you're not able to convince Tnaryt to take us to the Sovereign after we finish the repairs, then I'll have to find a way to quickly immobilize him. If he was out of the way, I could disable each collar individually."

His brows lifted. "Nat seemed to think that was unwise."

"Nat doesn't know what I can do. The real problem is the female Setarips. They're armed, and I can't protect everyone unless we're in the same room. Do you know where the cook and Nat sleep?"

He shook his head. "My movements have been as restricted as yours. Tnaryt's made it clear I'm not to leave the engine room without permission. The only parts of the ship I've seen are on the path from here to the bridge. The limited interactions I've had with the cook have occurred when he brought me food. I've spent the most time with Nat because she was able to help with the repairs."

"Same here."

"In any event, we're outnumbered. And it's unlikely the cook would help us, regardless."

Aurora paused with her hand halfway in one of the storage bins. "Why not?"

"Fear. From what I've seen, he's given up on living. He's just existing."

Aurora pressed her lips together. "Maybe we can change that. What about the Setarip females? Have you noticed any pattern to their movements?" She hadn't seen any of them on the bridge in a couple days, but she'd passed the one guarding the stairwell on her way to engineering.

"They only come to engineering when they lock me in during their sleep cycle. I don't know where they spend the rest of their time. I gather they're not on the bridge?"

"No."

"Then they may be supervising the cook. Or they may be lying around waiting for Tnaryt. Nat says he...visits them...regularly."

Aurora grimaced. "So I heard." But that gave her an idea. "How much freedom does Nat have to move around the ship?"

"Quite a bit. She's responsible for hauling and delivering all the supplies from the cargo hold. Unfortunately, Tnaryt can track the position of all the collars. He'd know if she went somewhere he hadn't told her to. And he'd deliver a harsh correction."

So they were back to the damn collars. "Then if we have to make a move, it would need to be during his sleep cycle. You said the females lock you in here. I'm assuming they lock up the cook, too. What about Nat?"

"I have no idea."

"We need to find out. She strikes me as...resourceful. Do you think she could find a way to bypass the locks?"

"Possibly. She's—" The control panel chimed, interrupting him. He studied the readings. "Better," he murmured, more to himself than to her. "This bucket's only good for short hops, but it shouldn't blow up when it makes an interstellar jump." He glanced up. "Assuming we'll be here when it does."

"I guess that depends on whether Tnaryt will take us to the Sovereign."

"Indeed. The next time he sends Nat down here, I'll talk to her about the females and the locks. Just in case."

She nodded and picked up the crate of parts. "Should we ask her about our combands, too? I've been reluctant because it means trusting her to smuggle them to us and to keep that information to herself."

"Do you think she'd tell Tnaryt?"

"If it meant avoiding punishment? She might."

"I see your point. But if we could get those back, it would help with communication. Would you be able to hide yours from Tnaryt?"

"I could stuff it in the crawlspace."

"Then let's consider it. I'll see how she responds to my other questions first."

"Good. Speaking of Nat, I need to get back to the bridge. She's up there alone with Tnaryt."

When she returned, Nat was slumped over the comm station, gripping the edge of the console like she needed it for support. She didn't even lift her head as Aurora stopped beside her. Pain radiated from her like flames.

Tnaryt lounged in his chair, a glint in his eyes and waves of euphoria rolling through his emotional field.

The bastard had been having fun tormenting Nat while she was gone.

Anger poured through her. If Tnaryt wanted to shock someone, it needed to be her. She could handle it. Ironically, except for her first trip to engineering, he'd never activated her collar.

She set the parts she'd gathered next to the console and stood between Nat and Tnaryt. "My father could use help running the engine diagnostics." She gestured to Nat. "I won't have anything for her to do for at least a few hours."

She held his gaze as she waited. That was the easy part. Keeping the loathing out of her expression took more effort.

His pupils contracted as his excitement ebbed. He rose from his chair, looming over her.

She had to tilt her head back to hold his gaze.

His tongue flicked out, centimeters from her face.

She didn't budge.

His gaze slid in Nat's direction. "Gooo to engiiineeer."

Nat stumbled getting up, her breathing labored as she struggled to follow his command. He'd really worked her over.

Aurora's anger kicked up another notch.

Tnaryt must have caught the change, because his lips parted in the hideous expression she'd come to recognize as his smile. "Coooome." He stroked his palm over her hair. "Siiiit."

His hand landed on her shoulder and he shoved, throwing her off balance. Her knees caught the edge of the chair and she sat down hard, grabbing onto the console to steady herself.

The soft clang of the ladder rungs indicated Nat had made it off the bridge.

"Weee taaalk." He remained uncomfortably close, crowding her. He clasped his long hands behind his back and stared down, like an owl watching a mouse.

He wanted to talk? That was new. "What about?"

"Whyyy seeeek Soveeereign?"

She'd been expecting him to ask about the repairs. Or maybe the Admiral. She made a rapid mental shift, sorting through possible responses that wouldn't trip her up. She came up with one he'd relate to. "The Sovereign hurt me. I want revenge."

"Reeevenge?" His awful smile reappeared. "Yeeess. Gooood." He rested one of his scale-covered hands on the console and leaned closer. "How huuurt?"

The hiss of his voice right next to her ear made her shudder. He was seriously invading her personal space. She swallowed down bile as his noxious scent filled her nostrils. "The Sovereign attacked my ship." True, assuming the Sovereign was behind the ambush at Burrow. "And took me prisoner for a while." Technically the Setarips had done that, and only for a very short while, but she wasn't about to explain that to him. Especially since those Setarips had been part of his clutch and were now deceased. Because of her.

"Yoou esssscaaape?"

"Yes."

"Hooow?"

Uh-oh. She'd backed herself into a corner. She didn't want to put the idea in his head that she'd freed herself, or that she'd had help from the other prisoners. She needed him to underestimate her. But it might not hurt for him to believe she wasn't without resources. "My friends rescued me."

"Friieeends?" His pupils contracted. "Where arrre friieeends nooow?"

"I don't know." She was able to say it with absolute sincerity. Other than the Admiral, she didn't know the exact whereabouts of *any* of her friends. Although Cade wasn't far. And he'd throw a fit if he could see her right now.

Tnaryt brought his face closer to hers, his unblinking eyes filling her vision. "Goooood."

She jerked as he rested his hand on top of her head and began stroking her hair again.

"Yeeesss. Gooood."

Her stomach pitched. He'd never been this close before, and her body was rebelling. She needed to distract him before she tossed up the remnants of the mash. It tasted vile going down. She didn't want to experience it in reverse. She pulled back slightly and gestured at the console. "Would you like me to get back to work?" *Please, please, please say yes.*

But instead of looking at the console, his grip on her hair tightened, holding her in place. "Not yeeet." He lifted his other hand off the console, brushing it along her cheek and down her neck.

Aurora forced air in and out of her lungs. If Tnaryt had been human, his behavior would have indicated a sexual advance. But that wasn't what she was getting from him. He'd never shown that inclination with her, thank goodness. What she was sensing was a desire to dominate.

He fondled the collar around her neck as his gaze bored into her. His tongue flicked. In. Out. In. Out. Abruptly he released her, his hand moving to the control band on his arm.

She'd had a feeling this was coming. Activating her shield, she clenched her jaw and closed her eyes as the energy leapt out of the device.

At least it gave her an excuse to jerk away from him. She tensed her muscles and twisted her face into an expression of intense pain. But her focus remained on the powerful emotions flowing off Tnaryt. The bastard was in ecstasy. The longer the torture continued, the more gleeful and excited he became.

Her stomach began to churn for an entirely different reason. This is what he'd been doing to Nat. Possibly for most of the time she'd been in engineering. She kept her gaze averted. It was the only thing that prevented her from slamming the full brunt of her shield into his skull.

The pulse continued, steadily building in her field. She was going to have to find an outlet soon if he didn't stop. And pretend the shock had rendered her unconscious. She was about to simulate that reaction when the charge ceased. She slumped across the console, drawing air in and out of her lungs in a pretend pant as she slowly dissipated the energy into the air. She waited another minute before she turned her head and glared over her shoulder. "That...wasn't...necessary."

That hideous smile taunted her. "It waaas gooood. Yeeess. Gooood."

He was a sadist. Pure and simple.

And she was done. No more negotiating. As soon as she could coordinate with the Admiral and Nat, Tnaryt was going down.

Forty-Five

After four days of searching. Mya's determination to locate Citadel had shifted to apprehension. She'd had plenty of time to process what had become of her ancestral home, and she wasn't entirely certain she was prepared for what they might find at Citadel. Would it be a Teeli prison colony, with the Suulh turned into Necri and trapped in tiny cages?

The image raised goosebumps on her skin. She didn't want to face that again. But it didn't matter what she wanted. The Suulh were out there. She could feel them. And the ship was getting closer.

"I'm picking up something on the sensors." Gonzo glanced over his shoulder. "An island to the southwest." He sent the sensor image to the bridgescreen.

One section of the large landmass showed a scattered pattern of red dots, each point indicating an activated energy field similar to Mya's.

Her pulse sped up. *They'd found them.*

"Adjusting course." Kelly said.

As the ship glided closer to the ocean's surface, the fading light of the setting sun cast shadows over the verdant green of the island's peaks, making it difficult to identify specific features.

Mya didn't need the visuals. Or the sensor readings. The energetic vibration of the Suulh wrapped around her like a loving caress, so unlike what she'd experienced from the Necri at Gaia.

She exhaled, releasing the breath she'd been holding. She glanced at Kire. "They're here."

He nodded, understanding in his hazel eyes. "Kelly, land out of visual range, then take us in nice and slow."

"Aye."

Despite the choppy waves, the ship settled into the water with the grace of a swan, continuing in a wide arc that brought them back in line with the island. As they drew closer, the shadows lengthened, the island's silhouette growing fuzzy as darkness crept in. The glow of warm lights appeared like fireflies in the foliage near a small beach visible at the water's edge.

Kelly guided the ship along the coastline. The foliage parted to reveal a brightly lit, multi-level structure sitting on a promontory near the center of the island. The building was constructed of mostly glass with metal supports, the intensity of the light pouring out of the structure illuminating the surrounding terrain and foliage for a hundred meters in all directions.

It reminded Mya of the buildings constructed over her ancestral home. The Teeli seemed inordinately fond of glass and metal, which fit the personality profile she'd developed for their race. Cold and hard.

"I'm picking up all kinds of tech readings," Gonzo said from the tactical station. "Underwater, underground, and aerial. Security and artillery. All hidden, and designed to destroy any vessel that approaches the island."

"A carefully concealed citadel." Celia gazed at the bridgescreen from her post at the comm station. "Or a prison."

Mya's money was on the prison, whether the inmates realized they were captives or not.

"Do you want to drop anchor?" Kelly asked Kire.

Kire glanced at Mya, giving her the choice.

"Let's circle the island first. Get more readings on the terrain and defenses." If they were going to make it onto the island, which she fully intended to do, they'd need as much information as they could gather.

Kelly continued the ship's circular path, the island off to starboard. The glass building slipped out of sight, replaced by thick foliage and low mountain ridges.

"Switching to night vision." Gonzo tapped a command into his console.

The trees and shrubs popped into green-tinged relief. A winding road appeared through the gaps in the foliage, weaving through the thick trees as it followed the coastline around the island. A peninsula appeared in the distance, jutting into the water to form a natural dock.

"There's a landing pad." Gonzo indicated a cleared space on the edge of the peninsula. It was spacious enough to accommodate a large Fleet personnel transport or cargo freighter. He let out a low whistle. "And a whole lot of extra hardware to protect it. The weapons array they have concealed underwater and beneath the landing pad could take out a ship the size of the *Starhawke*."

Kire rested his elbows on his knees. "The Teeli's most valuable resource is on this island. They wouldn't want anyone landing without permission."

"Which begs the question of how *we'll* make it onto the island." Gonzo met Mya's gaze. "I assume that's the goal?"

She nodded. "It is." But planning an infiltration into a heavily guarded compound wasn't something she'd studied at the Academy. For the hundredth time, she wished Aurora was standing beside her. "I'll need some guidance on how to accomplish that."

Gonzo grinned. "No problem. We'll get you there."

Forty-Six

To Mya's great surprise, she slept like a baby during her off hours. The energy vibrations from the Suulh had mellowed to the low-grade hum she associated with being around Aurora or her parents. It reached her on a subconscious level, making her feel connected in a way she hadn't since Aurora had left the ship.

By the time she returned to the bridge, Gonzo and Kire were off rotation and Jonarel had taken their place.

He glanced over as she stepped onto the bridge. "Good afternoon."

"Afternoon."

He looked tantalizing as he reclined in the captain's chair, with his long legs stretched out and his chin resting on his closed fist. His hair was slightly damp, like he'd showered recently, and the dark green tunic that matched his skin tone stretched over his broad chest, emphasizing every ripple of muscle as he shifted to face her.

He looked completely at home in the captain's chair. And it wasn't difficult to picture him in that role. Which begged the question—did he ever regret his decision to give the ship to Aurora, rather than keeping the *Starhawke* for himself? Would he have asked her and Aurora to be part of his crew? Would Aurora have accepted a position, knowing she wasn't the captain, and never would be?

Mya had trouble picturing Aurora taking orders from Jonarel. Kind of ironic, considering he didn't seem to have any issue taking orders from her. Even the complication of Cade Ellis joining the crew hadn't altered his unswerving devotion.

But Mya doubted Aurora could have been happy in the reverse situation. She would have chaffed at being under someone else's command without the possibility of advancement. One quality that had always defined Aurora— she liked being in charge.

But her empathy made her a very different leader than the others Mya had met during her years in the Fleet. Aurora wanted control for all the right reasons. Her need to protect was so strong that she had an overdeveloped sense of responsibility. If someone had a problem, she wanted to fix it. And that got her into trouble, especially when she ended up needing help herself.

Cade Ellis was the only person who seemed to consistently break that pattern, to pull Aurora back and help her gain perspective. Mya failed to rein her in more often than she succeeded. And Jonarel seemed to feed Aurora's obsessive behavior, not lessen it.

He fed Mya's private obsession, too. His current pose was having a very predictable effect on her. Celia's comments whispered in the back of her mind, taunting her. Was she being noble to squash those feelings? Or cowardly?

"Mya?"

She snapped out of her reverie. "What?"

The pad of his thumb grazed his jaw as he studied her, his golden eyes thoughtful. "When you are introspective, I cannot tell what you are thinking. It puzzles me."

"You can always ask." She slammed her mouth shut as soon as the words tumbled out. She didn't want him asking about her most recent thoughts. That path led to a galaxy of black holes.

His gaze held hers. "I might."

Her heart rate kicked up a notch and she looked away. It was either that or risk spontaneous combustion. She moved out of the danger zone and sat at the science console, pulling up the sensor readings for the island. "Have we made any progress on a plan?"

He brought temptation with him as he followed her, leaning over the back of her chair with one hand braced on the console. "Yes. We have analyzed the fortifications."

"And?" She didn't dare turn her head to look at him. They were way too close and she needed to focus on what he was saying.

"It is a complex system. The Teeli have created an effective deterrent for unexpected visitors."

"So we're locked out?" Mya dared a quick glance at his face.

His eyes gleamed. "No. We will just have to be...creative." The corner of his lips lifted a fraction. "I am good with creative."

This was why she rarely allowed herself to be alone with him. She didn't need to hear something like that out of his mouth. It sent her mind in very unprofessional directions. She reminded herself to breathe. In. Out. Focus.

Thankfully, Jonarel didn't have any clue about the effect he was generating. He tapped a command on the console that produced a 3D composite of the island in the space in front of the bridgescreen. He moved to stand beside it, giving her a reprieve.

"An approach from the water would trigger submerged barriers that circle the island at the half-kilometer mark." He indicated a blue line that surrounded the island. "That is the first defense. The sensors have a range of ten meters above the water, so skimming the surface is not an option."

She stood to get a better look, but kept her distance from him.

"A tower on the main peak provides aerial defense. It is tied into ground artillery. If the sensors are triggered, the ground systems will activate."

"What about the shuttle's hull camouflage? Won't that confuse the sensors and allow us to slip through?"

"You are correct." He enlarged a section of the image. "We can land the shuttle offshore within the underwater perimeter, but not on the beaches or the landing pad. Plates underground are calibrated to measure mass and pressure and will detonate an explosive charge on contact with any vessel large enough to trigger them."

Mya frowned. "So we land in the water? Then what?"

"We swim."

"And no one will notice us emerging from the water like nymphs?" That seemed unlikely, given the robust defenses.

"Their systems are focused on ships, not individuals. There is no indication of visual surveillance on the island itself. The side of the island opposite the glass building is mostly sheer rock, making it a natural barrier. However, several locations have trees with branches that drape close to the waterline. I will get you on the island from there."

He said it like it was a done deal. His confidence gave her hope.

He leaned against the nav console and crossed his arms, making his biceps bulge. "What do you hope to learn while you are on the island?"

She mirrored his pose, leaning against the tactical console. "How the Teeli are treating the Suulh, for one. And whether anyone has been taken from here recently. I want to find out if any of the Suulh we rescued grew up here."

"Did you ever talk to the Suulh on Azaana about their history?"

Mya shook her head. "They're still recovering from the trauma of their Necri existence. I didn't want to open wounds I wouldn't be around to heal. But it's possible some of their relatives are on this island."

Which brought up another important point. If she learned the Suulh on this island were related to the Suulh on Azaana, what then? Would she tell them the truth about what the Teeli were doing, like she had in Faahn's village? Would she tell them about Azaana? About Aurora? It seemed irresponsible, since she wasn't in a position to rescue anyone. But she shuddered at the idea of leaving them behind, knowing the Necri existence that awaited them.

"You are introspective again."

She jumped. Jonarel had moved next to her while she was lost in thought.

"Will you tell me what you are thinking?"

She forced herself to meet his gaze while her stomach did cartwheels. "I hate that we can't help the Suulh. The thought of leaving any of them here, at the mercy of the Teeli..." She gestured at the image of the island.

He rested a hand on her shoulder, his warmth seeping into her skin through the material of her tunic.

"We *will* help them. The more we learn, the better prepared we will be when we return."

She swallowed around the lump in her throat. "You sound so certain."

"These are your people. Aurora's people. Your ancestral home." His eyes darkened and the muscles around his mouth tightened. "We will end the Teeli's persecution of the Suulh. You and Aurora will free them."

"With one ship?" As amazing as the *Starhawke* was, she couldn't take on the entire Teeli fleet. They'd barely made it out alive during their last encounter.

Jonarel's grip tightened. "You and Aurora will not fight alone. You have allies who will stand by your side. Always."

The intensity of his gaze made her tremble. Sometimes she forgot that at his heart, Jonarel was a warrior, one with a protective streak that ran to the bone. Thank goodness he was on their side.

She placed her hand over his. "Thank you."

"You two plotting something?"

Mya turned as Celia stepped off the lift. She dropped her hand and moved away from Jonarel. "Jonarel was explaining the infiltration plan."

"I see." Celia's eyes narrowed as she gazed between the two of them. With her ability to read body language the way most people read books, she was probably getting a whole library from the scene she'd just walked in on. "Did he tell you Reynolds and I will be joining you? Gonzo's going to stay with the shuttle, just in case."

"Can he fly the shuttle?"

"It might be a little bumpy, but he said he can bring one home in a pinch. He spent a lot of time in the simulator at the Academy."

Mya glanced at Jonarel. "But it's a Kraed shuttle."

"This morning I gave him an overview," Jonarel said. "It should be sufficient for him to power up and reach our location if we run into trouble. I can take over from there."

Mya sincerely hoped that wouldn't be necessary. But they were short on navigators now that Cade and Drew had left with Aurora. And Jonarel's plan required his presence on the island.

Not that he'd allow her to set foot on the island without him, anyway. His behavior since they'd arrived at the planet indicated he'd appointed himself as her protector during Aurora's absence. It was sweet, but she wasn't used to having him watching her every move. It made hiding her normal reactions that much harder. "When do we leave?"

Jonarel's golden eyes gleamed. "Before dawn."

Forty-Seven

The sensor panel in *Gladiator*'s cockpit lit up. Cade tapped the comm. "Drew, get up here."

He scanned the incoming data while keeping the magnified view of the enemy ship in his peripheral vision. Sure enough, the running lights for the shuttle clamped to the ship's underbelly were shining, the engines beginning to glow.

"What's happening?" Drew slid into the co-pilot's seat and tucked her dark hair behind her ears.

"Movement from the shuttle."

"Got it."

Drew focused on the sensor readings while Cade maneuvered *Gladiator* toward the moon's surface. After Aurora had confirmed the Setarip ship's sensors weren't operational, he'd positioned *Gladiator* in a synchronous orbit behind the other ship, far enough away that they wouldn't be visible if someone looked out a viewport, but close enough that their cameras and sensors could detect any movement from the other ship.

He settled *Gladiator* into a hover in the shadows of the moon's surface before returning his attention to the image on the display.

The shuttle had dropped below the belly of the Setarip ship, making a lazy arc that took it away from the moon and in the direction of Gallows Edge.

"Do we follow?" Drew asked.

"No. Aurora would have alerted us if she or the Admiral were onboard." Unless she'd been unable to contact him. But he couldn't start second guessing himself now.

He searched the nearby terrain for a good landing spot. "But I'm going to keep us out of sight until the shuttle returns."

Followed by more waiting. He was getting a master class on patience.

When are you going to make your move, Aurora?

Forty-Eight

Aurora had kept a rein on her temper through sheer force of will.

Tnaryt's malevolent tendencies had continued the rest of the day and into the next. He'd followed up the abuse he'd directed at her and Nat by making another of his pleasure tours. He'd manacled her to the console, using a longer, thicker chain so she could continue working while he was gone.

When he'd rejoined her, he'd stayed on the bridge well past his normal sleep cycle, keeping her hard at work on the comm system. She'd managed a few hours of sleep after he'd retired to his cabin, but she'd woken to the stroke of his hand on her hair and the stench of his musk. She'd jerked away, which had only encouraged him. The sight of his grotesque smile made her stomach roll.

The minimal sleep had left her dragging. Keeping her eyes open had become a continual struggle. She'd dozed off once already while patching a connection, and had woken with a jolt when Tnaryt had triggered her collar. Her energy shield had snapped into place, protecting her, and thankfully she'd had the presence of mind to react as though she was being shocked.

Tnaryt had eventually tired of watching her twitch and moan, but not before she'd turned into a furnace about to blow. She could deal with the torment he was directing at her. But knowing he was doing the same things to the Admiral, Nat, and the cook was pushing her over the edge. She had to free them. Soon.

Tnaryt had sent Nat on a shuttle run to Gallows Edge, which at least put her temporarily out of his reach. Picturing her sitting at the bar with a drink in her hand lightened Aurora's heart a little.

She'd spoken to Cade briefly last night, filling him in on the changes in their status. She'd left out the details of Tnaryt's behavior, but Cade was a smart man. He'd sounded like he wanted to storm the ship and take care of Tnaryt personally. In other circumstances, she might have agreed. But not when everyone onboard was in danger from the collars.

With a sigh, she returned her attention to the system assembly. It still wasn't functional even though everything seemed to be in place. She had to be missing something. Her vision blurred as she stared at the circuits and wires. Something had to be—

She jerked her head up and blinked rapidly. Dammit! She'd dozed off again. She'd probably only been out for a few seconds, but she was fighting a losing battle with her body. The mash Tnaryt was giving her wasn't providing nearly enough nutrition for the amount of physical labor she was doing. And now she was running dangerously low on sleep.

She could sense the pleasure he was deriving from watching her struggle. It bit into her like millions of tiny teeth.

Clenching her jaw, she shone the light into the dark recesses of the panel. And spotted something. She peered closer. There. In the shadows. A loose connection. She worked her hand into the narrow space and carefully attached the wire firmly to the panel.

A tone sounded from above. She scrambled to her feet and checked the display. Sure enough, the dark section of the console now glowed with a new array of Setarip symbols. *Yes!*

She studied the panel, parsing how to send and receive messages through the system. Maybe she could call up a log of past communications that would—

"liiss wooorking?"

She jumped at the sound of Tnaryt's hiss. She'd been so focused on the panel she hadn't noticed he'd moved behind her.

He placed his hands on either side of the console, caging her in.

She kept her gaze forward and drew air in through her mouth. "Seems to be."

"Gooood. Yeesss." He used one hand to navigate the console while he stroked her hair with the other.

She suppressed a shudder as his nails scraped her scalp. But she also watched every move he made. He was obviously comfortable working the controls. Information flashed by quicker than she could identify it.

He paused on one particular set of data, and the gurgling noise she'd identified as a chuckle rasped out of his throat. "Yeesss. Veeerrry gooood." He stroked his hand down her back and along her arm, then wrapped it around her wrist. "Cooome."

She resisted as he tried to pull her out of the chair. "Come where?"

"Cooome," he hissed, yanking her to her feet.

Unease curled in her belly. This was different. And different with Tnaryt was always bad.

"Where are we going?"

He didn't reply, but in a few short steps she had her answer. He unlocked the hatch to his cabin and shoved her toward the opening.

She dropped to her knees and grabbed onto the ladder rungs to keep from tumbling over the edge. Her pulse beat furiously but she focused on calming her breathing. Nothing had changed. The collars were still active. Whatever Tnaryt had planned, she'd have to deal with it. He couldn't hurt her unless she let him, and she didn't plan to let him.

He sealed the hatch after following her down, shutting them in together. She'd been in the room many times, since it was the only area on the bridge with sanitation facilities. But he'd always waited for her at the top of the ladder. She'd never been in here when he was with her. It was a totally different experience.

The room was tiny by Fleet standards. Only a few meters separated the sleeping platform from the sanitation station in one corner and the shelving unit in the opposite corner. Tnaryt's noxious odor surrounded her, his crest rising and his neck puffing out as he watched her. She returned his stare, waiting. The first move in this new game would be his.

"Gooood. Yeeesss. Gooood." He reached into a cubby in the wall and pulled out a pair of bindings identical to the ones he'd used to chain her to the comm console. Grabbing her arm, he snapped one end of the manacle around her wrist, then yanked her forward and attached the other end to the main pipe for the sanitation station. The chain that tethered her gave her about a meter of play, enough so she could touch the edge of the bed with her fingertips if she stretched, but not enough to reach the ladder.

Tnaryt checked the bindings to make sure they were secure, then trailed one clawed finger along the side of her face. His eyes glowed with excitement as he moved his finger to the control band on his arm.

Aurora's pride screeched in protest, but her hands were tied. In more ways than one.

When the collar activated, she crumpled to a heap on the ground and went through the same acting routine she'd done previously when Tnaryt had tried to shock her. But since he was looming over her, she couldn't resist the opportunity to give him a taste of his own medicine. Keeping her eyes closed to slits, she jerked her leg forward in a pretend spasm, bringing it in contact with his ankle and channeling the energy to that point.

He leapt back, stumbling against the wall.

She rolled sideways to hide her grin. It might be petty, but she felt a little better. She kept her back to him as the pulse continued. When it finally stopped, she let her body melt to the floor, her head lolling.

"Gooood. Yeeesss." The glee in his voice was unmistakable, as was the thump of his feet on the ladder as he climbed up, sealing the hatch behind him.

She didn't move for a few minutes, just in case he returned. When the room remained quiet, she rolled onto her back and stared at the hatch.

Why had he left her chained in his room? His actions didn't make any sense. Clearly he could run the comm console now that it was operational, but why chain her up? Why not give her a different task to complete? The other bridge systems were in bad shape. What about the sensors and weapons? Didn't he want those operational?

She groaned as a new realization hit her. If she wasn't on the bridge, she wouldn't be able to communicate with Cade, or anyone else for that matter. With this one move, Tnaryt had effectively isolated her.

She slammed her palm on the floor. Why now? One more day and Nat might have been able to smuggle a comband to her. Then they could have coordinated an escape plan. "Tnaryt, you creepy, scaly bastard." She said the words in an undertone even though he wouldn't be able to hear her.

She wouldn't be able to hear him, either, unless he opened the hatch. That was one of the things that had made it easy to communicate with Cade during Tnaryt's sleep cycle. The thick decking and heavy hatch made the room soundproof.

She'd appreciated that fact when she'd been on the other side, talking with Cade. Now, she resented that particular feature.

Pivoting, she took an inventory of the room. The chain allowed her to take two steps in each direction, enough to make use of the sanitation facilities or lie down on the floor, but nothing else.

And the only way out was through the hatch.

At least she'd see him coming. Stretching out on the floor facing the door with her back against the wall, she pillowed her head against her arms and closed her eyes. Whatever Tnaryt had planned, she wanted to be well rested when he made his next move.

Forty-Nine

"I'm picking up a pulse from the Setarip ship." Justin frowned as he stared at the comm panel.

Cade leaned over for a better look. "What kind of pulse?"

"It looks like a homing signal."

Cade's brows lifted. "Are they signaling other Etah?"

Justin's gaze met his. "I certainly hope not."

Cade seconded that. The last thing they needed was a fleet of Setarip ships descending. "Maybe they—"

"Wait. I'm getting something on the comm channel. It may be Aurora." Justin tapped the console.

"Commander Ellis?"

Cade lurched to his feet. "*Admiral.* It's good to hear your voice, sir."

The Admiral's reply sounded strained. "I wish it were under better circumstances."

Cade flattened his palms on the console, bringing his face closer to the speaker. "What's wrong? Is Aurora with you?"

"No, I'm in engineering, using my comband. Nat returned it to me so I could contact you. Aurora's not on the bridge."

Cade's pulse hammered. "Where is she?"

"We don't know, although Nat suspects she's in Tnaryt's cabin."

The hammering doubled. "Why would she be there?"

"I have a theory. But we may need your help."

"Anything."

"Tnaryt may move the ship soon. If he does, we need you to follow us. Nat's turned on the homing signal for the shuttle so you can track us."

Cade shared a glance with Justin. They'd been right about the signal. He resumed his seat, switching into problem-solving mode. "Any idea where he's headed?"

"It can't be far. I've patched the engines as best I can, but we can't travel for more than a day without stopping to cool and recharge. And the ship's slow."

Cade pulled up the navigational charts for the area. "How slow?"

"Just getting the ship up to speed could take an hour. At top speed, we'd still be at half of Fleet standard. And that's if we push the upper limits, which I hope Tnaryt won't do."

Cade checked the nearby star systems. They were in luck. It was a short list. "At that speed, there are only six systems within a few days journey."

"Any inhabited?"

"Not according to the Fleet. The farthest of the six has a planet that's listed as habitable, but no one has tried to colonize it. At least, that we know of."

"And no stations or outposts?"

"Other than Gallows Edge? No, sir."

"Then we'll have to wait and see what he does. He's relied on Gallows Edge for his survival up to now, but he has a powerful reason to leave. I think he's making contact with the Sovereign."

The Sovereign. He'd like to get his hands on their mysterious adversary himself.

"Why would Tnaryt reach out to the Sovereign? As I understand it, the Sovereign took his cruiser and left him stranded on that rattletrap you're on."

"He may be brokering a deal. He grilled Nat
yesterday about Aurora and her connection to the Sovereign.
Nat didn't tell him what little she knows, but from the
direction of his questions, I think he's figured out Aurora's
identity. And what she can do."

Cade sucked in a breath. "How is that possible?"

"According to Nat, he talked to the Sovereign
extensively during their initial meeting. The Sovereign may
have shared details about the Suulh's abilities to gain his
trust, and to prepare his crew to take charge of the Suulh
during the attack on Gaia. They would have needed to know
what to expect. If he's figured out Aurora has the same
ability, he would rightly believe she's valuable to the
Sovereign. He's egotistical, not stupid. He might be planning
to strike a bargain to get his ship and crew back."

"But they're dead. And the ship's at the bottom of
Gaia's ocean."

"Tnaryt doesn't know that. He hasn't been able to
communicate with anyone since the Sovereign sabotaged his
systems."

A chill crept down Cade's spine. "We need to get
you both off that ship. Now." He'd rather deal with Tnaryt
than face the Sovereign's warships. His team wouldn't have
the *Starhawke* to back them up this time.

"And how do you propose we accomplish that, Mr.
Ellis?" The Admiral sounded strangely calm. "Tnaryt still has
control of our collars. He's a bully. He will not hesitate to use
them if he feels threatened."

Cade stared at the speaker. "We can't allow him to
turn Aurora over to the Sovereign."

"Perhaps we should."

His jaw dropped. "You can't be serious."

"Quite serious. We need to find out the Sovereign's identity. It's why we're here. I cannot think of anyone better equipped to handle that task than Aurora."

Cade bit down on his tongue to keep from voicing his response to that one. He'd watched Aurora face off against the Sovereign's minions twice now, and both times he'd been terrified she wouldn't survive the experience. He didn't want to see round three.

Unfortunately, he didn't have an alternative. They'd never be able to board Tnaryt's ship covertly, and an assault would spell disaster for the Admiral and anyone else wearing one of Tnaryt's collars. Like it or not, he'd have to let the drama play out.

But that didn't mean he'd be a bystander.

"What do you want us to do?"

Fifty

Tnaryt returned to the room late, barely giving Aurora a glance before toppling onto the bed with a thump. His slight stagger indicated he was inebriated or exhausted. Maybe a little of both. His musky odor was stronger than ever and heavily blended with the scent she associated with the Setarip females. He'd obviously been busy below decks.

Aurora buried her nose against her sleeve to block the smell as much as possible, although her clothing was saturated with the odor, too.

The pale glow from the control panel by the hatch gave her just enough light to see his outline on the bed. She stretched her hand as far as she could, but wasn't able to make contact with any part of his body.

A blast like a train whistle made her jump, but Tnaryt didn't react. A few seconds later, the blast repeated. She peered at him as the sound came again, in perfect sync with his breathing.

She let out a gusty sigh. Perfect. Tnaryt snored.

The shrill whine grated across her eardrums. Wrapping her arms over her head, she curled into a tight ball. Maybe she could convince herself she was lying on a stone outcropping on Azaana, rather than the cold metal floor of Tnaryt's cabin. Sure. And maybe she'd add in a few faeries and rainbows while she was at it.

Still, the fanciful daydream must have taken hold at some point, because she awoke with a start when Tnaryt lumbered out of bed. The lights for the day cycle had already come on. She kept her eyelids lowered to slits so she could watch him covertly.

His crest was down, his heavy jowls flapping as he stepped past her to reach the sanitation facilities. She averted her gaze as he made use of them. That wasn't an image she wanted seared into her brain.

Fabric rustled as he changed clothes, discarding the soiled garments he'd slept in and replacing them with clean ones pulled from a storage bin under the bed. The hem of his cloak brushed over her as he strode to the ladder and climbed to the bridge. The hatch closed with a thud.

At least he was gone. But she was still shackled to the wall. Might as well make use of the sanitation facilities. She scrubbed the accumulated grime off her skin as best she could, considering Tnaryt didn't believe in soap. Or towels.

Her stomach rumbled, reminding her she hadn't eaten since the previous morning. Was Tnaryt planning to feed her? The sanitation facilities would allow her to stay hydrated, but she'd need something to eat if she wanted to keep her strength up.

On the plus side, thanks to Tnaryt's late night revels, she was well-rested for the first time since she'd arrived on the ship. But now she was left cooling her heels.

She stared around the small space. Might as well do something useful.

Settling on the floor, she started the sequence of yoga postures she'd made part of her daily routine since the Academy. She had to modify them to accommodate the manacle around her wrist, but the familiar motions and focused breathing helped her muscles relax.

She had both palms flat on the floor, her torso aligned in a push-up position, when a heavy vibration in the cold metal made the pads of her fingers tingle. *The ship's engines were running!*

She scrambled to her feet. Judging by the force of the tremors, this wasn't a diagnostic test. The ship was leaving orbit.

Fifty-One

"Locked onto the homing signal."

Cade gave Justin a short nod of acknowledgement but kept his focus on Tnaryt's ship. The engines glowed in the surrounding darkness, providing a clear target. He matched *Gladiator* to the larger vessel's course and velocity.

He was gripping the controls too tightly, but he couldn't help it. He hadn't talked to Aurora in two days, and despite the Admiral's assurances, he was worried. Only one thing kept him from doing something stupid. His ship was fast, and Tnaryt's was not. Wherever they were headed, he wouldn't lose them.

He glanced at the readout on the display as the other ship straightened its flight path and accelerated. "Have you sent a message to the border beacon alerting the *Starhawke* to our situation?"

"Just did." Justin's voice was tight. "No response to my previous messages, so they must still be in Teeli space."

"Hopefully they'll pick up the trail soon. We could sure use their help."

The Setarip ship's slow pace would buy them some time. Cade had already plotted out the most likely heading based on their current trajectory. Sure enough, the ship appeared to be lining up for a jump that would take them to the star system with the habitable planet.

Justin leaned over to peer at the display. "Think the Sovereign's on that planet?"

"If so, Tnaryt's not very bright. His ship would be easy to pick off while it crawled through the system."

"Then what's his plan? Land on the planet and use it as his stronghold? Make the Sovereign come to him?"

"Possibly. While he's on his ship, he's vulnerable. On the ground, the odds would even out. Especially with Aurora as a bargaining chip." His jaw clenched. He didn't want her in that role.

"If she and the Admiral were on the ground, it would be a lot easier for us to pull them out."

Williams's footfalls came down the corridor. He stopped behind Cade's chair. "I thought we were leaving the system."

Cade glanced at him. "We are. Just really slowly."

"Really, *really*, slowly," Justin said.

"So I see." Williams peered through the viewport. "At least they'll be easy to follow."

Tnaryt's ship continued to accelerate as they approached the jump window, the engines giving a telltale flare indicating the interstellar systems were warming up.

Cade checked the headings. Yep. Still on target. Power thrummed under his fingers. Unlike Tnaryt's ship, *Gladiator* seemed eager to make the leap.

"I think they're about to—"

Williams's words cut off as the engines on Tnaryt's ship pulsed and the ship disappeared.

Cade took a deep breath before engaging *Gladiator*'s interstellar engines. "Let's go see what's out there."

Fifty-Two

Aurora stared at the hatch in the ceiling, willing it to open.

But it remained stubbornly closed.

The ship had been in motion for at least thirty minutes. Where was Tnaryt taking them?

She paced, two steps forward, two steps back, the only outlet for the nervous energy percolating in her system. The vibration through the deck increased. Gearing up for an interstellar jump?

The lack of control of her situation was driving her insane. Her gaze drifted to the shackle around her wrist. She might be able to use her shield to break through it. But then what?

She gave up on pacing and settled into a seated position. Closing her eyes, she tuned into the emotional fields emanating from the bridge.

Tnaryt's was easy to pick out. Hatred flowed like venom, a toxic stream poisoning everything it touched.

She recognized Nat's emotional grid, too. Fear and anxiety predominated, but a mess of other emotions sloshed together in the swirling soup.

The hum of the engines changed, moving to a high-pitched whine. She engaged her shield and grabbed hold of the supports for the sanitation station before the interstellar drive kicked in.

The transition was surprisingly smooth. The ship's inertial stabilizers adjusted to compensate and the interstellar engines took over. The noise radiating through the hull wasn't pretty, but at least they hadn't blown up. Too bad she didn't know where they were going.

She continued to track Tnaryt's emotional field, noting a shift a few moments before the hatch opened and he made his way down.

She didn't like the look in his eyes when he faced her. Or the sight of the two heavily armed female Setarips who followed him down.

"Yooou. Cooome."

The females kept their weapons aimed at her head as Tnaryt knelt beside her.

He unlocked the manacle from the wall and pulled her to her feet, pointing to the ladder. "Cliiimb."

He didn't have to tell her twice. Getting out of his personal lair seemed like a great idea. He followed right behind her. When she reached the top, she found two more of the Setarips waiting for her, weapons drawn.

Stepping onto the deck, she moved away from the hatch as Tnaryt rose beside her. A quick glance toward the bridgescreen confirmed they were in an interstellar jump, and that Nat was seated at the navigation console.

Nat turned her head a fraction, just enough that Aurora could see the corner of her eye. And be seen in return.

Tnaryt grabbed the chain attached to Aurora's wrist and yanked her past his throne to the opposite side of the bridge. He opened a seal that looked identical to the one for his room and swung it open. He pointed to the ladder. "Doooown."

The bridge lights barely touched the darkness inside the cavern. It didn't smell like Tnaryt's room, but she didn't favor trading one prison for another.

She grabbed onto Nat's original recommendation. *Be useful.* "Wouldn't you rather have me on the bridge? I could repair one of the other stations. The sensors? Or the weapons?"

Tnaryt loomed over her, his pupils closing to slits as the guards got serious about aiming their weapons at every vital part of her body. "Gooooo!" He shoved her to her knees beside the hole.

Her gaze darted to Nat, who was watching her closely. Now wasn't the time to take a stand. Tnaryt or one of the females could kill Nat before Aurora brought the rest down. She wasn't willing to take that chance.

Giving Nat what she hoped was a reassuring look, she grasped the top rung of the ladder and descended into the pit. When she reached the bottom, she glanced around. This room was a mirror of Tnaryt's, with two exceptions. It was completely empty except for the sanitation station in the corner. And it was cold enough that she could see her breath.

The light from the bridge dimmed as two of the guards descended, followed by Tnaryt, who brought his musky odor with him.

Now what?

He grabbed the chain for her manacles and dragged her over to the far wall, securing the loose end to the sanitation station just as he had in his room. He seemed reluctant to touch her, which was a change. After he finished, he stood and stared down at her.

She stared back. When he didn't say anything, she prompted him with a question. "Where are we going?"

"To seeee Sooovereeeign."

Her heart thumped. He'd made contact with the Sovereign? "Why?"

Flick, flick went his tongue. "Traaade."

Trade? Trade what?

The air rushed out of her lungs as the answer sucker-punched her. Her. He was trading *her*. "You're selling me to the Sovereign, aren't you?"

Tnaryt's lips shifted into his sickening smile. His pupils widened like a cat's before it was about to pounce, eclipsing the iris so that his eyes turned black. "*Yesss.*"

Fifty-Three

The cool water lapped at Mya's neck as she used a breaststroke to glide toward the rocky outcropping in front of her.

Despite the chill, keeping warm wasn't a problem. Not with Jonarel swimming beside her. His coloring provided him with natural camouflage in the pre-dawn shadows, so she couldn't see him very well. However, she didn't need the visual. The image he'd created before they'd entered the water was already burned into her retinas.

He'd slipped off his tunic and leggings to reveal the Kraed version of swimming trunks, which molded to his body like a second skin and emphasized a part of his anatomy she wasn't supposed to notice.

She'd noticed.

She'd studiously avoided looking at him as they'd gathered to enter the water, but swimming beside him, so close they almost touched, was pure torture.

Jonarel reached the rocks and pulled himself out of the water. The pale light of the approaching dawn caught the movement of droplets as they cascaded down his sculpted torso and thighs.

Mya dunked her head under the water in an attempt to banish her inappropriate thoughts. When she surfaced, he'd turned toward her, his arm outstretched. She stifled a groan. She didn't want to make contact when he looked like Poseidon risen from the deep, but she didn't have a choice.

Sure enough, as soon as his grip closed on her hand he plucked her out of the water like she weighed no more

than a feather, settling her at his feet so that their bodies
brushed against each other.

Breathing became a real chore, but she couldn't put
any space between them without risking a nasty fall on the
slippery rocks.

He didn't have that problem. The claws in his feet
had anchored him like an oak. He brought his lips
centimeters from her ear. "Are you okay?"

"Sure," she mumbled, staring with exaggerated
interest at the branches of the trees that draped over the
water's edge.

Celia and Reynolds joined them a moment later.
Reynolds rose to her feet, an Amazon warrior ready for
battle, while Celia looked like a swimwear model, even with
the knapsack on her back that matched the one Jonarel
carried. Their dark tank-style suits were exactly the same as
the one Mya wore, but she felt like a wet cat by
comparison.

Jonarel released his grip on Mya and shifted to face
Celia, cupping his hands together to provide a foothold for
boosting her up. She snagged one of the low-hanging
branches above them and began climbing hand over hand
toward the cliff edge. He repeated the process with
Reynolds, who followed Celia steadily up to the base of the
tree ten meters above the waterline.

Mya stared at them in dismay. When Jonarel turned
to her, she shook her head. "I can't do that." She was
reasonably fit, but the thought of supporting her weight
while swinging over jagged rocks made her stomach flip. A
fall wasn't likely to kill her as long as she remained
conscious, but it would certainly hurt like hell when she
landed. She didn't have Aurora's ability to shield her body
from the impact. And even after she'd healed any damage,

she'd have to figure out a way to get herself *off* the rocks and back into the water without reinjuring herself. Not something she wanted to experience.

Jonarel's golden eyes glowed in the semi-darkness. "There is no need." Taking hold of her arms, he guided her around behind him as he crouched. "Place your arms around my neck."

Oh, no. She saw where this was going, and her body shook in reaction. Maybe risking the rocks wasn't such a bad idea.

"Mya?" Jonarel glanced over his shoulder. "You will not fall. I promise."

She swallowed. Her safety didn't concern her anymore. Her sanity did.

Slipping her arms over his broad shoulders, she clasped her hands together in front of his collarbone.

"Good." He rose. "Wrap your legs around my waist."

No. No. No. No. No. Her mind rebelled, but her body didn't have any problem obeying Jonarel's command. His warmth flowed into her like honey as bare skin met bare skin in all kinds of interesting places, only slightly mitigated by the press of the knapsack against her chest. She rested her cheek on his shoulder and closed her eyes, trying to block out the maelstrom of sensations bombarding her. *Hell, party of one.*

"Hold on."

Like she needed the reminder. She tightened her grip as his muscles coiled.

He sprang with the grace of a panther, catching the branch with ease, supporting their combined weight without so much as a grunt. His back and shoulders flexed as he made the journey up to the base of the tree, reaching the ledge in half the time that Celia and Reynolds had taken.

The claws embedded beneath his fingertips certainly gave him an advantage.

He dropped down next to Celia without making a sound.

Mya released her hold immediately, regaining her feet and putting some distance between them. "Thank you."

He nodded, but he was giving her that same puzzled look he'd had on the bridge. Not a good sign.

She turned to Celia as Jonarel pulled their sensor suits out of his knapsack. "Where do we go from here?"

Celia pointed to the left. "The energy signals all came from that direction." She tugged the top of her sensor suit on and fastened it, the dark material blending with their surroundings.

Mya worked her way into her own suit. "And the glass building is over that ridge?" She indicated the rocky promontory to the right. The outline of the aerial defense tower at the peak was visible in the grey dawn.

Celia nodded. "We'll need to stay out of sight of the tower as we cross the ridge, but that shouldn't be hard with all the foliage."

They started the uphill trek, reaching the summit as the sun peeked over the horizon, painting the ocean in strokes of azure and the foliage in verdant green. It was a tropical paradise. Unfortunately, Mya didn't believe for a second that the Suulh who lived here were free to come and go as they pleased.

Jonarel led the way down the far side of the ridge, followed by Mya, Celia and Reynolds. Mya focused on where she put her feet, since hiking wasn't one of her fortes. But walking behind Jonarel when he was wearing a form-fitting sensor suit was distracting, especially since he kept glancing over his shoulder to check on her. She stumbled several times, causing him to slow the pace of their descent and prolong the torture.

Celia caught Mya by the arm after she tripped over a tree root that almost put her face down on the ground.

"You okay?" she murmured.

"Fine." Mya averted her gaze. "Just a little clumsy."

"Uh-huh." Celia's next question indicated she knew exactly why Mya was tripping up. "You want to walk behind me?"

"No, I'm fine." Which proved she was an idiot. Or a masochist.

The woven circular roofs of huts appeared through breaks in the tree canopy and Jonarel changed course, leading the group in a curved path away from the huts. The density of the trees increased and the chatter of voices reached them as they arrived at the cove harboring the beach they'd seen from the *Starhawke*.

They halted in a thicket of trees overlooking the beach. Mya, Celia and Reynolds crouched behind the greenery. Without a word, Jonarel grasped the trunk of one of the trees and disappeared into the upper branches in a virile display of flexing muscles.

Mya stared after him.

"Your mouth is open." Celia whispered.

Mya snapped it shut, turning her attention to the figures gathered on the beach.

At least a hundred Suulh moved over the packed sand at the water's edge, forming pairs as they engaged in some type of physical exercise.

Celia slid her surveillance visor into place. "Looks like training. Defensive combat."

Mya blinked. "The Teeli are training them to fight?" She hadn't expected that part of Faahn's description of

Citadel to be true. The Suulh on Gaia had been treated like mindless Necri drones, not trained soldiers.

"Or they're training themselves. I don't see any Teeli down there." Celia pulled another visor from her pack and handed it to Mya. "Take a look."

Sure enough, the groups of teens and younger adults were engaged in sparring matches, some with carved practice weapons, but most unarmed.

Why would the Teeli allow the Suulh to develop fighting skills? Wouldn't that make them harder to control?

"They're pretty good," Reynolds said, watching them through her visor. "Although I'm not familiar with the methods they're using."

Neither was Mya, but that didn't mean much. Aurora and Celia had both tried to convince her to train with them, but she couldn't imagine striking another person, even in self-defense. She was a healer, not a warrior. Why train if she never planned to use her skills?

The sparring session shifted, the Suulh forming groups of four or five. Half the groups lined up along the beach with their backs to the water's edge while the other groups faced them.

Mya's breath caught as one by one, the groups by the water activated their energy fields, the bands of vibrant color weaving together to form a stunning tapestry. The energy pulsed, calling to her, beckoning her to join in.

She'd never encountered such intensity except from Aurora, Libra, and her parents. Even the Suulh on Azaana hadn't been capable of this strength. Whoever these Suulh were, they were powerful.

The energy fields continued to flow, weaving tighter and tighter, the colors blending to white in some places.

The opposing groups lifted their weapons and charged. They slashed and tore at the energy field tapestry, halting only when they reached the Suulh inside the web.

"What are they doing?" Reynolds sounded mystified.

As the groups separated and reformed, activating their energy fields once more, the answer struck Mya like a thunderbolt. "They're trying to create a shield."

"A shield?" Celia echoed.

Mya nodded, her head swimming from the ramifications. "Like what Aurora can do. But Aurora's family line is the only one that has that ability. These Suulh are trying to recreate it by blending their energy together."

"Is it working?" Reynolds asked as the groups attacked and defended a second time.

"Not very effectively." In most cases, the attackers were able to reach their opponents fairly quickly. But a few groups succeeded in holding them off, even if for just a few seconds.

Was it possible this was a natural response to the loss of their Sahzade? While other family lines might develop the same abilities as Aurora's over time, it could take centuries for the biological adaptations to occur. What these Suulh were attempting to create was a shortcut.

Was it their idea? Or something the Teeli had convinced them they needed to perfect to defend themselves from the Setarips? The Teeli would be interested in protecting their investment. And if the most powerful Suulh could be trained to shield, that would be another weapon in the Teeli arsenal.

Mya shivered. They had to figure out a way to free the Suulh from the Teeli. If they didn't, she could end up facing off against her own people. She'd already had that experience with the four Necri on Gaia, and it had almost killed her. She never wanted to go through anything like that again.

Jonarel dropped out of the tree beside her, startling her out of her dark thoughts. "We are within three kilometers of the glass building to the northeast. Do you want to investigate it?"

Her gaze drifted back to the Suulh. Shouted taunts and laughter filled the air as they continued to practice. They were so happy, so full of life. So different from what she'd expected to find. And so unaware they were living in a bubble that could burst at any moment, drowning them in despair and torment.

Aurora, I wish you were here.

Turning away, she met Jonarel's gaze. "Let's find out what the Teeli are up to."

Fifty-Four

Celia Cardiff kept a close eye on Mya as they followed Clarek through the dense foliage. Mya stumbled a couple times, but the cause seemed to be her preoccupation with the Suulh, rather than the large Kraed leading the way toward the glass structure on the promontory.

Celia ducked under an overhanging frond of a palm-like tree and sidestepped a thick fern. The plant life on this island grew with wild abandon, most likely with the help of the Suulh. She'd seen what Mya's presence did to the plants in the greenhouse on the *Starhawke*. This island took that lushness to an extreme.

As they continued uphill, the foliage gave way to rock protrusions, forcing them to zigzag to remain hidden beneath the overhanging branches of the trees. The sun had crept a quarter of the way across the sky, shortening the shadows as it pushed closer to its zenith.

Clarek raised a hand to call a halt as the foliage opened to their left.

The glass building sat on a natural plateau halfway to the peak at the center of the island. The area around the building had been cleared of foliage, making the interior easy to see. It housed what looked like administrative offices stacked on top of each other. The floors were semi-opaque, but the walls were clear, allowing visibility from one side of the building to the other.

To the northwest, a smaller ridge blocked the view of the peninsula that housed the landing pad. Celia had been itching to set up surveillance on that pad ever since they'd arrived. When a ship landed there, it would be important. And she wanted to be prepared when it did.

Clarek slipped off his knapsack and removed a scanner from the interior pocket. He panned the device across the plateau. "The foundation for the building is uneven. Readings indicate an opening that leads underground." He turned to Mya. "They may have converted existing caves."

"Any idea what's down there?"

Clarek shook his head. "The mineral content of the surrounding rock is blocking sensors. But the formation of the rock on this island is consistent with the existence of natural caverns and tunnels."

"So this building may be the tip of the iceberg?" Mya didn't sound happy about that idea. She stared at the structure, the strangest look appearing on her face, like she was listening to music only she could hear.

Clarek tilted his head, his brow furrowing as he noticed the change, too. "Perhaps."

"Hmm." Mya's gaze became unfocused, her breathing slowing. She was concentrating on *something*.

When she remained silent for a full minute, Celia gave her a nudge. "Do you want us to investigate?"

Mya jumped, as though she'd forgotten they were there. "Investigate?" She frowned as she stared at the ground like she was trying to see through it. "I don't know," she murmured, more to herself than to them.

Celia exchanged a look with Clarek. He seemed as puzzled by Mya's behavior as she was.

If Mya wanted to remain here to check out the building, then they needed to split up. It would take at least as long to hike to the landing pad and set up the surveillance as it had to reach this point, and they'd still have to make the return trip to the shuttle. They could accomplish it before nightfall if they didn't dawdle. Right now, they were dawdling. "With your permission, I'd like to take Reynolds and scope out the landing pad."

Mya blinked like an owl. She didn't seem to understand the words.

What was going on with her? Celia rested a hand on her shoulder. "Mya? What's wrong?"

"Nothing." Mya said it with conviction, but she looked distracted. "You and Reynolds go ahead. We'll stay here."

Celia glanced at Clarek. "Are you good with that?"

He nodded. "Alert us if you encounter any problems."

Celia pulled two short-range comm devices out of her pack, handing one to Reynolds and attaching the other to her ear. Emoto had set the signal to a frequency that should look like background noise, just in case the Teeli were paying attention. "Keep us posted if you learn anything interesting."

At least she didn't have to worry that Mya's distracted behavior would get her in any trouble. Clarek would die before he'd allow any harm to come to her.

The sun was past the midpoint before she and Reynolds crossed the peak. They halted briefly for a water break and a quick snack of dehydrated fruit before descending toward the peninsula that housed the landing pad.

The trees thinned out, giving a clearer view but less cover. Celia crouched behind one of the tree trunks and pulled out her visor. "No sign of personnel." She panned along the length of the landing pad, noting the seams for the anti-aircraft weapons buried beneath the surface.

The pad itself could support a ship about half the size of the *Starhawke*. Much larger than most terrestrial transports. Had it been designed for interstellar ships? If so, who was permitted to land here?

She turned to Reynolds. "Let's check ou—"

Static crackled over her earpiece. A moment later Gonzo's voice came over the line. "We have an interstellar vessel coming in from the southeast."

Her question was about to be answered.

Fifty-Five

A Suulh was down there. Someone strong. Powerful.

Mya couldn't say how she knew that, or what exactly she was sensing, but every instinct held her captive, focused on the building. She wasn't sure she could leave if she tried.

Jonarel's voice rumbled near her ear. "What is it?"

She turned. His puzzled expression indicated he couldn't figure out what she was thinking. Well, right now, neither could she. "I'm sensing someone. A Suulh. Or several Suulh. I'm not sure. But the pull is strong. And it's coming from below that building."

Jonarel's gaze swept the open plateau. "Which is inaccessible from here." He studied his scanner, then motioned to her. "Come with me."

"Where are we going?"

"The cavern beneath us is likely a lava tube. It should have a natural entrance. If we locate it, we may find a way in."

That was good enough for her. Turning away from the building, she followed him through the thick foliage as he cleared a path that took them below the plateau. The sensation of...*someone*...stayed with her, nagging her footsteps. She kept glancing around, expecting to see a face appear through the greenery. But all she saw was sunlight and shadow dancing over the ground.

They walked in silence as the sun shifted so that the plateau's shadow fell across their path. Jonarel seemed to know exactly where he was going, moving purposefully in front of her. But this time she didn't stumble. Even his

presence wasn't a strong enough lure to draw her attention
away from the sensations pulling at her.

When his steps finally slowed she moved beside him,
peering through the trees in the direction he was gazing.

A jagged oval in the rock face showed through the
foliage, roughly the width of the *Starhawke*'s shuttle and
covered by a solid metal door that matched the coloring of
the surrounding stone. A dirt road led from a break in the
trees to the entrance.

Mya looked from the plateau above them to the
road, trying to get her bearings. "Does that road lead in the
direction of the landing pad?"

Jonarel's gaze remained locked on the entrance.
"Yes."

Must be nice to have an innate sense of direction.
Then again, on Drakar, it was probably a survival skill. "Do
you see a way in?"

The corners of his mouth turned down. "Not yet."
Lifting his scanner, he studied the readings. His frown
deepened. "We will not be able to access if the door
remains closed."

"Why not?"

"Scanners do not show any controls for the door on
this side. I cannot override the system. And there are no
other entrances in the area."

Disappointment pricked her. "So what do we do?"

"For now, we wait." He gestured to a boulder a few
meters behind them. "And eat." When she didn't move, he
cupped her elbow in his hand, guiding her to the boulder.

She let him, although she had the childish urge to
go bang on the massive door and demand to be let in. The
idea was ludicrous, but that didn't keep her from considering

it. This island was having a decidedly strange effect on her. She needed to be careful.

Jonarel pulled two pouches from the knapsack and handed one to her. She opened it and began nibbling on the dried fruit, even though she wasn't the least bit hungry. She just knew he'd object if she didn't.

The breeze ruffled her hair, blowing it across her eyes and mouth. She shoved it aside. She usually kept it short enough that it wasn't a problem, but she hadn't found an opportunity to get it cut since the day she'd set foot on the *Starhawke*. Her ocean swim hadn't helped matters.

She stared in the direction of the metal door as she ate. How long could they afford to wait? The sun had already passed midday. Should they consider—

The rattle of grinding metal launched her to her feet. Jonarel was beside her in a heartbeat, a hand on her arm as he guided her into the shadows by the roadway.

The gaping maw had peeled open, metal teeth now poised to snap shut on the unwary. The dirt road disappeared into the semi-darkness beyond. But any view of the interior was eclipsed as a series of transports rumbled out of the opening. Mya counted five total as they sped down the winding road and were swallowed by the trees.

Voices drifted out of the entrance, the words in the clipped language of the Teeli. Jonarel glanced at her. "Do you want to get inside?"

Yes, she did. But she hesitated. He could probably sneak in unnoticed, but stealth wasn't a skill she possessed. Doctors didn't generally need to sneak up on their patients.

"I don't think—" She paused as the sensation of a Suulh presence shifted, like they were moving away. Her gaze drifted in the direction of the glass building.

"What is it?" Jonarel asked.

She shook her head, unable to put it into words. "We need to go back." She didn't question her certainty. Time was of the essence. But she had to alert Celia about the transports, first.

She didn't get the chance.

Her comm crackled to life, Gonzo's voice coming over the line. "We have an interstellar vessel coming in from the southeast."

Fifty-Six

Celia glanced at the sky, but the trees blocked her view. "Warship?" she asked Gonzo.

"No, personal transport. Although it looks armed."

"What about the island's aerial defenses?"

"They just shut down."

So this visitor was expected. The rumble of distant engines reverberated through the air, but the sound was coming from the island, not the sky. She focused on the road, spotting movement through the trees. "The welcome wagon is on its way. Five transports."

Mya's voice came over the line, her words coming out in short bursts, like she was winded. "We located a cavern...under the plateau. The transports came...from there."

"Are you monitoring the cavern?"

"No." Mya's breath puffed over the connection. "We're heading...back to the...glass building."

That explained why she was out of breath, but not why they were returning to their starting point. However, when it came to the Suulh, she trusted Mya's instincts. "Okay. We'll monitor the landing pad."

"Be careful."

"Always." Closing the connection, she turned to Reynolds. "Let's see who's coming to call."

They set off through the trees, staying low as they made their way to the edge of the landing pad. Celia glanced toward the sky, expecting to hear the roar of the approaching ship soon, but the only mechanical sound was the rumble of the transports as the last two joined the three already parked near the treeline. Maybe the ship was farther out than Gonzo had thought.

Taking advantage of the delay, she slipped a miniature surveillance camera out of her pack and attached it to the trunk of one of the trees, pointing it at the landing pad. She checked her comband, confirming the image was clear, and began recording the feed. More information was better than less.

A dark shadow passed overhead, blotting out the sun. Celia snapped her gaze up as a transport ship swooped down like an owl snatching prey, the whoosh of displaced air the only indication of its passing. Apparently the Kraed weren't the only ones who had figured out stealth for their ships.

Reynolds crouched beside her. "That's unsettling."

"Uh-huh." She'd be sharing that information with Clarek and Star when they got back to the *Starhawke*.

As the ship settled onto the landing platform, two lines of Teeli formed to either side of the ship's nose, standing at attention as the ship's gangway lowered.

The expanse of open space between Celia's position and the hulking vessel made any thoughts of getting onboard impossible. But there were other ways to learn more about the ship.

The four figures who emerged looked exactly like the Setarip guards they'd encountered on Gaia. Their bodies were covered head to toe in mesh fabric, which likely concealed their Setarip features and the body armor they wore underneath. They carried impressive weapons, the stocks as thick as her calf and probably twice as heavy.

The Setarips were followed by a hooded figure wrapped in a dark cloak that draped to the ground, effectively hiding any indications of age, race or sex. The figure strode between the columns of Teeli without giving any acknowledgment of their presence, proceeding to the transports with four additional Setarips close behind. Two more took up positions in front of the gangway.

The Setarips were acting like bodyguards, which left the question of the cloaked figure's identity. It had to be a Teeli of great importance. Was this the person responsible for the attacks at Gaia and Burrow?

She opened a channel to Mya. "A cloaked figure and eight Setarip guards headed your way."

"Setarips? How can...there be...Setarips here? The Suulh...think they—"

"*Concealed* Setarips. Like the ones we saw on Gaia."

"Oh."

And the cloaked figure was the one to watch. She and Reynolds needed to join the convoy. "We're going to catch a ride back to your location."

"How?"

"Leave that to us. See you soon."

She closed the channel and turned to Reynolds. "Get on one of those transports. I'll join you in a moment."

Reynolds gave a curt nod and disappeared into the trees.

Pulling a tracking device and airdart from her pack, Celia took aim at the ship. The Teeli had closed ranks behind the visitors, clearing a path to the gangway. She fired. A moment later, a flash on the display indicated the device had successfully attached to the sidewall of the door.

The robed figure climbed into one of the transports, followed by four of the Setarips. The remaining four split up between the transports in front and behind.

The Teeli, meanwhile, were watching the Setarips with thinly disguised fear and contempt. Taking advantage of their distraction, she slipped through the late afternoon shadows to the line of vehicles.

The first three, including the one with the cloaked figure, pulled out and headed along the road. She couldn't see Reynolds anywhere, but she trusted her companion had found a way onto one of the transports. Dropping to all fours, she rolled underneath the last vehicle in the line, grateful that the uneven dirt road forced the Teeli to use high-profile transports. Locating handholds and lifting herself off the ground took only a couple seconds.

The doors opened and the vehicle rocked slightly as the Teeli climbed in. The engine came to life as the transport rolled off the landing pad onto the road.

The vehicle bounced over a rut and she tightened her grip. She didn't have much of a view, but they were climbing, shadows now covering the road as they drove through the trees. She'd need to make her exit before the vehicles reached either the glass building or the cavern Mya had mentioned. She couldn't risk getting caught in the open or trapped underground.

The vehicle slowed. A quick glance to the side showed the first three transports turning left at a fork in the road. But her transport and the one in front continued straight ahead.

Great. She'd just lost visual on the cloaked figure.

Her vehicle took a curve, skirting a dropoff to the right and giving her a good look at the ocean. Judging by the distance, they were getting close to parallel with the promontory for the glass building, but at least a kilometer below. The next curve ended in a steady rise, and the vehicle lugged down as it made the climb.

This was it. Shifting her grip, she lowered her body close to the ground but didn't make contact. Turning her head, she used her peripheral vision to watch the road. *There.* A deep rut, followed by a level patch. She touched down, the sensor suit protecting her skin as she allowed the transport to drag her a couple meters. She let go when they reached the rut, dropping into the indentation as the vehicle continued on and disappeared around a curve.

As soon as it was out of sight she was on her feet, racing into the trees and making her way uphill. She tapped her comm device. Time to find out where her companion had ended up. "Cardiff to Reynolds."

No response, at least from Reynolds, but Clarek's voice boomed over the line. "Problem?"

"Not yet, but we got separated. I'm coming from the trees below. ETA in ten minutes."

"Understood."

Nothing more she could do for Reynolds until she made contact. Leaving the channel open, she focused on setting a new cross-country sprint record.

Fifty-Seven

The glass building dominated Mya's field of vision as she crouched beside Jonarel in a grove of trees overlooking the promontory. A seventy-meter stretch of dirt and gravel separated them from the front entrance.

The Teeli working inside had abandoned their tasks a few minutes earlier, gathering on the lower level. As they filed outside, they formed lines on either side of the main doorway, facing away from the building.

"Do they look nervous to you?" she murmured to Jonarel.

"Indeed."

The rumble of the transports reached them before the first one appeared out of the late-afternoon shadows. It continued past the building and made a one hundred eighty degree turn so that it was facing the road. A second and third vehicle followed close behind, halting after making the turn, with the middle transport directly in front of the main entrance.

Four figures appeared from the front and rear vehicles, taking up positions by the central vehicle, their bodies covered head to toe in a mesh fabric that concealed their features. *Setarips.*

Two more figures stepped out of the middle vehicle. They flashed their weapons at the waiting Teeli as a robed figure emerged behind them, followed by two more Setarips. They flanked the robed figure, effectively blocking Mya's view.

However, she really didn't need to see to understand what was happening. The reactions of the Teeli said it all. Most were so rigid their bones were in danger of snapping. The robed figure clearly inspired fear.

The cadre of four Setarips and the robed figure walked to the front entrance. Two Teeli hurried to open the doors, their gazes averted as the group passed. The Setarips led the way to a staircase in the center of the main room, disappearing from view as they descended into the subterranean depths.

So much for spying on the robed figure.

The Teeli filed back into the building slowly, returning to their tasks with obvious reluctance. The aura of tension followed them.

Jonarel opened a comm channel. "Cardiff? Reynolds? Report."

Celia's voice came over the line first. "Just reached the spot where I left you."

Reynolds replied a moment later. "Took a tumble getting off the transport, but I'll be there shortly."

Mya breathed a sigh of relief. They'd made it back safely. "Three of the transports are parked in front of the building. The cloaked figure and four of the Setarips went inside. Jonarel and I are keeping an eye on the other four." Not that they were doing anything, other than imitating stone statues of Titans.

"Good," Celia said. "I'll monitor from here."

"And I'm coming along the road," Reynolds said. "I'll keep an eye on this side."

Mya returned her attention to the glass structure, willing the robed figure to reappear. It would give her something to focus on. Right now it was taking a concerted effort to remain in her hiding place. Every instinct she possessed told her to walk through those doors and find the Suulh she sensed inside.

The breeze picked up as the sun dropped closer to the horizon, rustling the leaves of the trees. Strands of hair danced in front of her eyes. She shoved them behind her ears, but her hand stilled as a tingling spread along her skin, giving her goosebumps. *They were getting closer.*

An iron grip locked around her wrist. "*Mya!*"

The harsh whisper barely registered. But the firm tug that followed did.

She cranked her head around. Jonarel had his hand wrapped around her wrist, pulling her back. No, that wasn't right. She was pulling against him, leaning forward. And she was on her feet. *When had she stood up?*

"Mya, what is it?" Concern showed in his golden eyes and the tight lines on his face. "What are you sensing?"

Focusing on Jonarel helped cut through the mental haze. The warmth from his fingers spread along her arm. She dropped back into a crouch. "I think it's the Suulh. They're...affecting me."

She'd witnessed this reaction once before. Aurora had done the exact same thing in the orchard on Gaia when they'd first encountered the Necri. Mya had been the one to hold her back. Were there Necri down in the caverns? Was that what she'd been sensing? But that didn't fit. Their presence on Gaia had weakened her, not drawn her.

Jonarel studied her. "Affecting you how?"

"Drawing me to them." She glanced at the building as the sensation intensified.

"I see." His hold on her wrist tightened.

Probably a good idea. It would prevent her from doing something stupid. It also worked as a distraction, helping her stay present in her body. She couldn't tune him out when he was touching her, no matter how strong the pull was from the Suulh.

Movement at the stairwell preceded the return of two of the Setarips and the robed figure, followed by...*two more robed figures?* It was impossible to tell which of the three figures was the one who had first entered the building. They were all the same height, all dressed identically.

Jonarel's arm locked around Mya's waist from behind. He pulled her flush against his chest, his voice rumbling in her ear. "You cannot go."

She wanted to answer him. To explain that she had to reach the robed figures. But the words wouldn't come together.

The Setarips escorted the robed figures through the entrance, blocking her view. She heard a low whine, like a whimper. *Had that come from her?*

Apparently so, judging by Jonarel's reaction. One minute she was in front of him, the next he'd spun her around behind him, wrapping her arms around his shoulders. He held her wrists in his strong grip with one hand while he used the other to haul them both up the trunk of the nearest tree.

Instinct took over. She locked her legs around his torso without shifting her focus from the figures.

"You will have a better view," he murmured as he took them silently to the upper branches.

Sure enough, the extra height allowed her to see past the Setarips. The three figures had stopped outside the middle transport, the two behind now facing each other. Their movements indicated an intense discussion, but she couldn't hear a word.

Jonarel's superior hearing solved that problem. "They are speaking the Suulh language." He sounded surprised.

So they *were* Suulh, not Teeli. Her heartbeat pounded in her ears. "Can you translate it?"

"No. They are talking quickly. I—" He broke off and his body tensed.

"What?"

"One of them said Nedale."

Tiny shards of ice struck Mya's skin. Had the Suulh in Faahn's village said something to the Teeli? Had they tracked her to this island? "We have to go."

"Agreed." But Jonarel didn't move.

The cloaked figures split up, two climbing into the center transport, leaving the third standing alone by the entrance. The Setarips returned to their transports and all three vehicles moved off, leaving the lone figure facing in the direction of the departing vehicles.

Mya's grip on Jonarel's shoulders tightened. The sensation of...*connection*...didn't fade as the vehicles disappeared from view. The intensity remained constant, focusing on the figure standing in front of her.

"Mya?" Jonarel's tone indicated he'd noted her reaction.

"That one. That's the Suulh I've been sensing."

She'd whispered the words, but the figure turned in her direction.

Mya's heart stopped. The hood concealed the figure's face, but she had no doubt that the Suulh was staring right at them.

Fifty-Eight

Mya held her breath. *Don't panic. Don't panic. Don't panic.* She remained motionless for what felt like years, but may have only been a few seconds.

With slow deliberation, the cloaked figure pivoted to the right and walked past the building into the trees.

The air left Mya's lungs in a rush. She took a step to follow and found herself dangling in thin air. She'd forgotten she and Jonarel were up a tree.

Thankfully, he'd kept one hand wrapped around her arm, anchoring her. He shifted her back into place with little more than a shrug of his shoulders.

Heat flooded her face. "Sorry. Forgot where I was."

"So I surmised." He descended rapidly, dropping lightly to the ground. He turned her in his arms. "What is our next step?"

The pose was as close to an embrace as she'd ever experienced with him, and it short-circuited her brain. She had to look away before she could focus on his question. "I need to know who that Suulh is."

He released his hold on her shoulders but captured her hand, as if he didn't trust her to stay beside him. "Follow me." He tapped his comm device as he set off through the trees in the direction the cloaked figure had disappeared. "Cardiff, a robed figure entered the trees near you. We are moving to intercept."

"Already tracking. Reynolds?"

"I'll be there shortly."

As they wound through the trees, an unwelcome idea pushed into Mya's mind like a weed. "Do you think this is a trap? To capture me?"

Jonarel halted long enough to meet her gaze. A flash of hurt showed in his eyes. "I would not lead you into a trap."

"Oh." The caring in his words made her feel all warm and fuzzy inside. Not a good thing.

He squeezed her hand and urged her forward.

But she didn't need his help tracking the figure. Her sense of the Suulh grew stronger with every step, drawing her like they were connected on a line. She spotted the figure through the trees, standing in a small clearing overlooking the ocean, the setting sun painting the clouds in shades of pink, fuchsia and gold.

Jonarel released her hand, nonverbally returning control of the situation back to her as he slipped into the shadows.

She spotted Celia, who gave her a short wave as she took up a defensive position to guard their backs.

The cloaked figure didn't move as Mya crept forward. The sensations washing over her were nearly overwhelming, saturating the air and making every cell in her body pulse. She'd never felt more vibrantly *alive*. And she wanted...no *needed*...to know why.

She stopped a few meters away and waited.

The figure slowly turned to face her. An inarticulate sound, part-gasp part-sob, drifted out from beneath the cloak.

Tension coiled in Mya's belly like a snake, but she forced herself to take a step forward. "Who are you?"

Instead of responding, the figure reached up and folded back the hood, revealing an older woman with dark hair and brown eyes. And a face that, in fifty years, could be Mya's own.

The woman sank to the ground, tears spilling over her cheeks as she stared at Mya with wide eyes.

Mya took a step and stumbled, dropping in front of the woman. Her entire body shook as she extended a hand, not even sure why.

The older woman caught it in hers, a brilliant emerald green glow surrounding them both.

Blood roared in Mya's ears, deafening her. *It can't be*. And yet, what other explanation was there? Only one possibility fit the facts.

Her mind rebelled, threatening to check out at any moment. But the hauntingly familiar pulse of the energy that surrounded her kept her grounded. She drew in a shuddering breath. "What is your name?"

The woman's grip tightened. "I am Breaa. The Nedale."

Mya's head dropped to her chest as tears filled her eyes. *Nedale.*

Breaa squeezed Mya's fingers until she lifted her head. "What is your name?" Hope and fear warred for dominance in her eyes.

"I am My—" She caught herself. That wasn't the name her parents had given her. "Lelindia."

"Mylelindia?"

Mya shook her head. "Just Lelindia. I am Marina's daughter."

Breaa pulled back slightly, a frown creasing her forehead. "Marina?"

Mya's heart skipped a beat. Had she jumped to the wrong conclusion? "You are not Marina's mother?" If not, then who the hell was she?

Breaa shook her head, a shadow crossing her face. "No. My daughter was Maaree."

Was. Past tense. But the names were close. Maybe—

An image popped into Mya's head of a young woman of sixteen or seventeen, with long dark hair and a vivacious smile. The face was more rounded, without the lines of experience. But she'd know that smile anywhere.

"My daughter." Breaa's voice cracked, distorted by the pain of loss only a parent could understand.

Mya gripped Breaa's hands. Calling to mind an image of her mom as she'd looked at the train station, she projected it to Breaa.

Breaa tensed, her eyes wide.

Mya followed it with an image of her mom and dad laughing together.

Breaa's body shook. She held Mya's hands in a death grip. "They live?" she whispered.

"Yes. They do." Tears tumbled over her cheeks as she smiled. "They are my parents."

Breaa cried out a word Mya didn't recognize and yanked her into a bone-crushing hug, burying her face against Mya's shoulder and rocking her like a baby. She started crooning, too, the words muffled against the fabric of Mya's sensor suit.

They remained like that for a long time. Breaa released her with reluctance, swiping her damp cheeks as she gazed at Mya. "Maaree. She is with you?"

Mya shook her head. "No. She is on a planet far from here."

Breaa released her breath on a sigh. "She is safe?"

"Yes."

"And Sahzade?"

"She's on a m—" Mya paused as she realized Breaa was referring to Libra, not Aurora. "She is with them. Also safe."

Breaa's shoulders slumped in relief. But then her head snapped up. "Why are you here?"

Where to begin? "We came to learn what had become of the Suulh homeworld. We rescued three hundred enslaved Suulh who were being used as weapons of destruction."

Breaa's hand went to her throat. "Which Suulh?"

Would Breaa know them? "The two oldest are Ren and Zelle. They have children—"

"You *found* them?" Breaa gasped. "*Rescued* them?"

"Yes. They are safe, too."

Tears poured down Breaa's face as she embraced Mya again, murmuring words of gratitude.

Images flashed through Mya's mind in a jumble. She recognized younger versions of many of the Suulh on Azaana, including Ren and Zelle, as well as Raaveen, Sparw and Paaw as small children, playing on the beach of this island.

Mya's heart constricted. They *had* come from here!

But the images turned dark, revealing scenes of screaming and crying and pain, which abruptly ceased as Breaa pulled back.

The look in her eyes had shifted to match the fear and anxiety in the images. She released her grip on Mya and stood. "You should not have come here, dear one. You are in great danger."

Mya rose beside her. "But that's *why* I'm here. We want to help you. To help *all* of you." She swept her arm to encompass the entire island.

Breaa shook her head. "No. You cannot. It is too dangerous. You must go. Remain safe."

She'd just found her grandmother. She wasn't about to walk away. "I can't lea—"

"They will *capture* you! You must go. *Now!*" Breaa punctuated her words with a blast of energy that shoved Mya backward.

She stumbled, losing her balance, but strong arms came around her from behind, steadying her. *Jonarel.*

"Are you all right?"

His low growl made her glance up. He was glaring at Breaa with his lips pulled back from his teeth.

"I'm okay."

Breaa stared at Jonarel with eyes the size of saucers. Her grandmother would not have seen a Kraed before. His imposing physique, dark green skin and blazing golden eyes were a powerful visual.

Celia's voice came over the comm. "I hate to interrupt, but the surveillance feed from the landing pad shows they're finishing up loading supplies on the ship. If we have any plans to use the tracking device I planted, we need to get back to the shuttle."

Mya stared at Breaa. How could she possibly leave? She'd just learned her grandmother was alive.

But they also needed to know who the figures were who were on that ship. And where they were going. Her eyes narrowed. Maybe her grandmother already knew the answer.

Mya squared her shoulders. "The two hooded figures who left the building with you. Who are they?"

Breaa's expression closed down like a portcullis, shutting Mya out. "I cannot say."

Can't? Or won't? She tried a different question. "Are they White Hairs? Teeli?"

Breaa's lips pressed together. "They are our end."

Well that was cryptic. She'd known her grandmother less than an hour and she already had the urge to throttle her. "Do they control the Setarips?"

"They control everything."

Mya wanted to screech in frustration. But it wouldn't do any good. And she was out of time. "They don't control me." She pointed a finger at Breaa. "And neither do you. This isn't over. Not by a long shot." She faced Jonarel. "Let's go."

Tears stung her eyes, blurring her vision, as she turned and ran through the trees, with Jonarel by her side. Each step took her closer to the shuttle and farther from her grandmother. The grandmother she hadn't even known was alive.

For now, that would have to be enough.

Fifty-Nine

Celia ran just behind Mya, watching her back, with Reynolds right beside her.

Mya had to be reeling. Meeting a grandparent you'd assumed was long dead tended to do that to a person. And there was no doubt that's who she'd found. She looked like an older version of Mya.

But Mya was pushing hard to keep up with the rest of the team. They were racing against time to reach the water's edge before the Teeli ship took off. Clarek had sent word to Gonzo to get the shuttle prepped and to lock onto the tracking device Celia had planted.

Mya's breath was coming out in hitching gasps. How much longer could she keep up this pace?

Clarek must have had the same thought, because he glanced at Mya, concern in his eyes. Without breaking stride, he opened a channel to Gonzo. "Lock onto my signal and bring the shuttle into a hover over the next rise."

"Roger that."

Mya stumbled going up the incline and Celia clasped her elbow, steadying her. Her face was flushed and her chest was heaving, but she kept moving. Clarek moved closer, supporting her on the other side, and together they helped her reach the top of the rise.

Below, the tops of the trees were blowing in a strong wind that only touched a small area, announcing the shuttle's presence, even though it was completely invisible against the darkening sky.

"How are we getting up there?" Celia asked Clarek. They hadn't brought any grappling equipment with them, and

Gonzo was busy piloting the shuttle, so he couldn't leave the controls to assist them.

"We climb." He said it like the answer was obvious.

Climb? Celia glanced at Mya. She was having trouble walking. Climbing trees was out of the question. Hopefully Clarek had a plan for helping her.

He led the way until they were directly under the rustling leaves. He turned to Reynolds. "Hold onto me."

Ah. *He* would be doing the climbing.

Reynolds complied without a word, wrapping her arms and legs around his shoulders and torso. In seconds they'd disappeared up the tree.

Celia glanced at Mya. Her breath was coming in ragged gasps, but her gaze was steady as she watched Clarek descend, alone. He reached for her, and she hesitated for a split second before taking her turn as his passenger. She had to be suffering in a special hell, being that close to him physically, especially after the emotional turmoil of meeting her grandmother.

Celia didn't hesitate when Clarek returned. She couldn't see the claws in his hands or feet, but she could feel the force of the grip they gave him as he propelled them up the tree with impressive speed.

The wind whipped against her face when they broke through the canopy. A pale arc of light shone in the sky, outlining Reynolds standing at the top of a retractable ladder.

Clarek vaulted up the ladder and into the shuttle's interior, his claws clacking against the metal floor when he landed. He paused a moment for her to disengage before striding to the cockpit.

"We're locked onto the tracking device," Gonzo said as he shifted to the co-pilot's seat so Clarek could take the controls.

"Good. Strap in," Clarek called over his shoulder as he guided the shuttle away from the island.

Celia dropped into the seat beside Mya and locked her harness into place.

Mya stared straight ahead, her knuckles white where she gripped the armrests. "I can't believe she's alive."

Celia placed her hand over Mya's. "I can." With the incredible healing gift Mya's family line possessed, Celia had often wondered just how long her friend might live. A hundred and fifty years didn't seem outside the realm of possibility. "And now she knows you are, too."

Mya nodded, but her brown eyes remained focused on the patch of sky visible through the cockpit. "And she's not a Necri."

They should all be grateful for that. Celia didn't want to contemplate the apocalyptic nightmare Mya or her grandmother could unleash if their power to heal was twisted into a destructive force by the Teeli.

Sixty

Mya stared over Jonarel's shoulder, searching the sky for the Teeli ship. It was easier than thinking about the island. About who she had left behind.

Jonarel opened a comm channel. "Kire, we need the *Starhawke* in the air. Now."

"Already there." Kire replied. "Had a feeling you'd want to follow that ship."

"Indeed. Setting an intercept course."

A melodic chime sounded from the console.

"What's that?" Mya asked.

Jonarel glanced back at her. "Tehar's homing signal."

"Homing signal?"

"To guide us in. Both vessels are still camouflaged."

Mya swallowed. "You're going to dock in the air? While camouflaged?"

"Yes." Jonarel didn't show a hint of hesitation as he returned his attention to the controls.

Docking the shuttle while both ships were in atmosphere would be challenging enough. Now he was doing it without a visual? She had to see that.

Releasing her harness, she moved to stand behind Gonzo's chair. "Gonzo, do you mind if I—"

He glanced up. "Not at all." He relinquished the chair, stepping out of her way and taking a seat in the main cabin beside Reynolds.

Mya claimed the vacant seat and strapped in.

Jonarel glanced at her, the hint of a smile on his lips.

Mya peered into the growing darkness. "Is the *Starhawke* behind us or ahead of us?"

"She is to port." He motioned to his left. "But not for long."

The running lights of the Teeli ship shone in the distance, a pattern of pinpoints in the inky sky. But no sign of the *Starhawke*.

Jonarel adjusted their course as the frequency of the musical chime increased.

She kept her gaze out the viewport. Jonarel brought the shuttle's nose up and increased their speed. The lights from the Teeli ship winked out as the homing signal became a sustained note, like the call of a pan flute.

The transition was seamless. One moment she was staring at the sky, the next the interior of the *Starhawke* snapped into focus like someone had dropped a matte painting over the viewport. The docking clamps drew the shuttle up into the ship's belly without any jostling or jolting, bringing them to rest in the main shuttle bay.

She turned to Jonarel. "That was amazing!"

He met her gaze. "Thank you."

The friendly warmth in his eyes sent a jolt through her body. Her tongue stuck to the roof of her mouth, rendering her mute, so she shifted her focus to unfastening her harness.

While Jonarel powered down the shuttle, she joined the rest of the team as they hustled to the bridge where Kire and Kelly waited. Gonzo slid behind the tactical console, Celia and Reynolds moved to communications, and Mya sat at the science station.

Kire pivoted the captain's chair to face her. "The ship is accelerating toward an opening in the sensor web. Do you want to catch up to them?"

Did she? If they were going to make it through the sensor web, she didn't have long to decide. But that meant leaving the planet. And giving up any hope of helping her grandmother. At least, for now.

They are our end her grandmother had said.

She wanted to know why. "Stay with the ship."

Kire turned to Kelly. "Get us as close to that ship as you can. We need to make it through without triggering the web defenses."

"Aye."

The view on the bridgescreen shifted as they accelerated, drawing closer to the other ship as they followed it through the upper atmosphere. The image of the ship grew, filling the bridgescreen and blotting out the glitter of the starfield.

"Five seconds to sensor web." Gonzo sounded as tense as Mya felt. "Four, three, two, one."

Silence reigned for a beat.

"We're through."

Mya exhaled, her shoulders dropping away from her ears.

"Cruiser, straight ahead."

And went right back up. A ship at least ten times larger than the one they were following waited on the other side of the web.

"Have they spotted us?" Kire asked.

"I don't think so. Their weapons aren't armed. They may be the transport's escort."

"Warships closing in." Reynolds called from the comm station.

The tactical image appeared on the bridgescreen, showing six warships marked in red and the transport and cruiser in yellow.

"Back us away," Kire said to Kelly. "Give them room to maneuver."

The warships moved into formation around the cruiser, four in a diamond pattern and two more above and below. The transport glided over the cruiser's back, settling down like a bird on a tree branch, before disappearing into the interior.

Gonzo glanced over his shoulder at Kire. "Their trajectory will take them out of the system."

"They're going to make a jump, aren't they?" Mya's question wasn't directed at anyone in particular, but Gonzo nodded.

Kire rested his elbows on his knees. "Kelly, can you plot their projected course so we have some idea where they might be going?"

"Aye." Her fingers danced over the console, working on the trajectory. "If they maintain this heading, they'll enter Fleet space."

A chill crept across Mya's skin. Nothing good could come of the robed figures entering Fleet space. She glanced at Celia. "Is the tracking signal working?"

"Yes. But we can't trace it during a jump. And we have to be in range when they drop out of their jump to pick it up again."

Mya tapped her fingers against the arms of her chair. She didn't like any of her options.

"Do we follow them?" Kelly asked, turning to face her.

What would Aurora do? She wouldn't give up, that's for sure. "Yes. Plot a course to their most likely destination."

"Aye."

The cruiser's engines flared before it made the jump, vanishing from sight. The warships followed a moment later.

Mya settled in her chair, her jaw set. "Let's go find them."

Sixty-One

Aurora stood at the top of the stairs, looking down at her parents and My-a.

She'd been here before. She knew how this turned out.

She wouldn't let it happen again.

She scrambled down the stairs, but with each step, her feet grew heavier, her movements slower. Her legs froze, locking her in place.

She reached out a hand toward My-a, but something tugged on her arm, pulling her in the opposite direction.

Daddy picked up My-a and turned away.

"My-a!" Aurora screamed.

But Daddy didn't turn. Didn't stop. He kept walking, taking My-a away from her.

The stairs crumbled beneath her feet, pitching her into the yawning blackness. She pin-wheeled her arms, searching for something to grab onto. Out of the darkness, strong hands reached for her, gripping her shoulders. She looked up into Mya's familiar face.

"Sahzade. I'm here."

Mya's hold on her shoulders tightened, her fingers pressing into Aurora's skin. She grabbed Mya's hand to pry it away, but jerked back when she came in contact with rough scales.

Aurora woke as the clawed hands hauled her to her feet. She pried her eyes open, getting a close-up view of the pale orange scales on the underside of Tnaryt's forearm, millimeters from her nose.

She hadn't heard him climb down the ladder or unhook the manacle from the wall. The lack of sustenance was catching up with her.

Four days. Four days in this icebox and only two bowls of mash to sustain her.

At least he'd blown the tendrils of the dream away. She'd hated it the first time she'd had it. A repeat performance while Tnaryt yanked her around didn't improve the experience.

He jerked the chain attached to her wrist. "Yooou coooome."

The command raised Aurora's hackles, but she wasn't about to argue, especially with two guards pointing their weapons at her. "I'm going," she muttered, her boots striking the floor with a dull thud as she stumbled after him to the ladder.

She scrubbed her eyes to clear the grit. What she wouldn't give for a glass of water. Her mouth felt like the Sahara. Tnaryt hadn't bothered to switch on the water for the sanitation station she'd been tethered to. The mash had provided her only hydration.

Her stomach grumbled, reminding her she hadn't eaten at all the previous day. The only reason she knew how many days she'd been down here was by tuning into Tnaryt's emotions, which ebbed to low tide when he slept.

He pointed up the ladder. "Cliiimb."

Biting the inside of her cheek to keep from snapping at him, she gripped the first rung and pulled herself up, wincing as the bright lights of the bridge blinded her. It took a moment to adjust after the days of unceasing twilight.

Two of the females waited at the top, weapons at the ready, just as they had when she'd gone down. But they weren't alone. The Admiral knelt beside them, his breathing labored. Exactly the way he'd looked after Tnaryt had shocked him the first day she'd arrived.

She glanced at the bridgescreen. The curved surface of a small planet or large moon filled the space. The vibrations from the engines had stopped. They'd arrived at their destination. But where were they?

Tnaryt stepped off the ladder and grabbed the dangling end of the chain attached to her wrist, pulling her off balance. She stumbled, her head swimming at the abrupt movement. Not a good sign. She focused on her breathing as she worked to clear the cobwebs from her mind. Dehydration and stomach cramps weren't helping matters.

"Yooou miissss faaaatheeer?" Tnaryt placed his hand on top of the Admiral's head and stroked his skin the same way he'd often stroked her hair.

She was tired of his mindgames. "What do you want?"

"Waaant?" His lips parted in his sickening smile. "Yooouu. Obeeeey."

Heat burned the back of her neck. "I *have!* But you still shocked me with the collar and tossed me in solitary."

"Collaaar. Yeeesss." Tnaryt pulled something out of an inside pocket of his cloak, then wrapped his long fingers around her neck. When he stepped back, the collar was in his hands. "Collaaar nooot wooork on yooooou."

Her jaw dropped before she could hide her reaction. *He knew!*

The gleam in his eyes grew brighter. "Yeesss. Nooot on yooou. But hiiim." He gestured at the Admiral. "Yeess."

Her gaze met the Admiral's. They were so screwed.

Sixty-Two

Aurora couldn't offer any resistance as Tnaryt forced the Admiral down into the room she'd just vacated. She had no doubt that if she lifted a finger, Tnaryt would electrocute the Admiral until his heart gave out. And if Aurora intervened, the guards would open fire on them both. Considering how much effort it took for her to stand, she wasn't convinced she could sustain her shield under the onslaught. They could both end up dead.

Tnaryt didn't follow the Admiral into the hole. As soon as he disappeared into the darkness, Tnaryt swung the hatch into place and locked it. Turning to Aurora, he pulled a curved blade out of a sheath strapped to his thigh. He placed the tip under Aurora's chin. "Yooou fiiiight. Heee diiiees."

Aurora swallowed, but didn't respond.

Tnaryt made the gurgling noise she'd grown to hate. He was enjoying this *way* too much. Placing the knife back in its holder, he grabbed onto the chain attached to her manacle. "Coooome." He hauled her toward the stairwell where two of the females had already started down.

Aurora grabbed onto the ladder and descended, the other two female guards following her, with Tnaryt coming down last. When they arrived in the cargo bay, he took the lead, with Aurora sandwiched in between the four female Setarips.

Light poured out of the open hatch of Nat's shuttle, illuminating her petite form as she hauled crates from the cargo hold into the shuttle. The fifth Setarip female kept watch from just inside the hatch.

Nat paused as Tnaryt approached. "I still have six crates to load. Then we'll be ready to leave." Her gaze flicked to Aurora, zeroing in on her neck. Her eyes widened.

Tnaryt had returned the key for the collars to the pocket in his cloak. If Aurora told Nat where it was, she might be able to get her hands on it and free herself.

Tnaryt brushed past Nat and continued into the shuttle. "Goood."

For that brief moment, he was out of sight. Aurora did the only thing she could think of. She tripped, stumbling to the ground as she walked by Nat.

Nat immediately dropped to her knees beside her.

"*Key. Cloak. Inside right pocket,*" Aurora whispered as Nat placed a hand under her elbow to help her up.

The female Setarips shoved Nat aside, grabbing hold of Aurora with rough hands and propelling her forward. But the message had been successfully delivered. Hopefully Nat would have a chance to make use of it.

Sixty-Three

Tnaryt had the key to her collar.

Nat's heart pounded as she settled the next crate beside the growing pile filling *Gypsy's* storage compartments. Tnaryt hadn't told her what was in the crates she'd been ordered to drag down here, but most of them were heavy.

A few minutes ago, figuring out what she was hauling had seemed important. Not anymore. Tnaryt had a key. That's all that mattered. She could finally get the blasted collar off and take a shot at freeing herself. Or die in the attempt. At this point, she was fine with either option.

But first she had to relieve him of that valuable trinket. Easy enough. The challenge would be waiting until their next sleep cycle to use it. But she'd learned a lot about patience during the past year.

What she couldn't figure out was why Tnaryt had removed Aurora's collar. Was he using the engineer as a bargaining chip instead? He must have locked the engineer up somewhere on the ship. The cook, too. Possibly in the hole where he'd kept Aurora for the past four days.

She'd figured out where Aurora had disappeared to the first time the cook had arrived on the bridge with mash. He'd brought her one bowl and left a spare with Tnaryt. She'd pretended indifference, but she'd been acutely aware of Tnaryt's movements when he'd unlocked the hatch and descended the ladder. He'd kept the hatch open, but she hadn't heard anything from below. If he'd been torturing Aurora, the sounds hadn't carried. But she'd looked pretty ragged when she'd passed by a few moments ago.

Nat hadn't seen the engineer since the ship had left Gallows Edge, but he'd kept in contact with her during the sleep cycles through Aurora's comband. He'd alerted her that Aurora's friend Cade was tracking them, ready to launch a rescue operation when an opportunity presented itself. Now that she had a chance to get rid of her collar, she'd do everything in her power to create one.

With the last crate stowed, Nat sealed the outside hatch, pressurizing the interior. The presence of the Setarips turned the compact space from cozy to noxious, but she'd become an expert at ignoring her olfactory senses. She needed to focus on Tnaryt.

He'd strapped Aurora into one of the cargo seats and was smiling at her with obvious glee. Aurora looked like she wanted to spit in his face.

Slipping past Tnaryt on the way to the cockpit, she dipped her hand into the folds of his cloak. Years of practice had brought mastery. He never suspected a thing. In a heartbeat, the small metal disc went from his pocket to hers.

Her nerve endings thrummed as she settled into the pilot's seat and powered up *Gypsy*'s engines. One step closer to freedom.

Tnaryt's odor preceded him. His cloak smacked her leg as he wedged himself into the co-pilot's seat, leaving the five female Setarips to guard Aurora.

"Engines online. Disengaging docking clamps." *Gypsy* groaned until the clunky mechanism finally released its grip.

Tnaryt remained blissfully silent as Nat guided the shuttle into the planet's atmosphere. When they dropped below the cloud layer, she adjusted their course, bringing the shuttle into a glide, heading for the coordinates Tnaryt had given her. As they descended, the topography came into focus, showing a thicket of trees, towering rock formations, and cascading waterfalls.

No sign of technology, though. The sensors remained mute. And no sign of a landing platform, either. She glanced at Tnaryt.

He pointed with one scaly finger. "Theeeere."

She followed the line of his gaze and spotted a protrusion amid the trees. Rock peeked through the thick greenery that covered most of the surface. *He expected her to land on that?*

The cold look he shot her confirmed it. She made another pass of the area, calculating the best trajectory. She'd have to avoid the surrounding vegetation and land on the outcropping without tumbling off the edge of the precipice. Much as she wanted to get away from Tnaryt, dying in a shuttle accident wasn't what she had in mind.

"Landing gear down." She decreased their speed and fired the reverse thrusters to bring them into a hover. Even so, metal scraped and the shuttle lurched sideways as they made contact with the uneven surface and came to an abrupt halt.

Nat rubbed her left elbow where she'd banged it against the bulkhead.

Tnaryt stood, placing a heavy hand on Nat's shoulder when she moved to follow. "Yooooou staaaay."

She blinked. Was Tnaryt really leaving her alone on the shuttle? Could she be that lucky?

"Waatch for shiiips. Reepooort." He indicated the comm device attached to his forearm.

She bowed her head in complete obedience. "Yes, Tnaryt."

He motioned to one of the females and ordered her to remain behind, too.

Damn. So much for being alone. But it was far better than going anywhere with Tnaryt.

She entered the command to open the back hatch. A soft whirring was followed by a clang as it connected with the ground—unevenly. Poor *Gypsy* had to be at least five degrees off level. But the Setarips didn't seem to notice.

The four remaining females grabbed packs out of an open crate near the cockpit and exited the shuttle while Tnaryt knelt in front of Aurora to remove her harness.

Aurora's gaze flicked to Nat, awareness in her eyes and a tiny smile on her lips, just like the one she'd given her that first day. The one filled with hope.

Nat's heart rat-a-tat-tatted as Tnaryt hauled Aurora to her feet and shoved her ahead of him out the hatch.

She watched them disappear into the foliage.

Aurora knew she had the key. And expected her to make use of it. But that still left one burning question.

What happened after she was free?

Sixty-Four

Aurora dug her fingers into the congealed mash Tnaryt handed her and popped it in her mouth, swallowing as quickly as she could to keep from gagging. It tasted even worse when it was cold, but her body craved what little nourishment it provided.

Tnaryt's features were cast in bands of light and shadow from the small lantern hanging above his head. He watched her, a gleam in his eyes as he took a bite out of a plum-like fruit. Juice dribbled over his chin and down his flaccid neck.

They'd hiked through the jungle for hours. Well, not literally. But it had felt like hours. Her perception was based on the effort it had taken for her to keep up, not the actual distance covered. Her body was crying out for sustenance, water, and rest, which were all in short supply. Every minute with Tnaryt was an eternity.

They'd finally arrived at their destination, a ramshackle conglomeration of platforms and ladders built into the trees. It looked like something schoolchildren would construct, with no rhyme or reason to the design, and structural instabilities that made it a hazard in most places.

But Tnaryt was right at home. He'd climbed into the trees with surprising agility, making use of the steps only when absolutely necessary. The shifting light would have made him difficult to spot if he hadn't been wearing his dark cloak. The brown and grey scales of the females had blended even better.

From their behavior, it was clear they'd spent quite a bit of time here at some point. When and why were still questions without answers.

The females had pushed and prodded her up the steps to the platforms. Her hands had still been bound, making every movement a challenge. But Tnaryt had enjoyed watching her struggle.

They'd set up a rudimentary camp and then settled in for an evening meal. She, of course, had been given cold mash.

Tnaryt grabbed a piece of fruit off the vine dangling near the platform and held it poised centimeters from her mouth. "Yoooou waaant?"

Rich aromas that spoke of sunshine, warm breezes and damp earth wafted off the fruit, enticing her. Did she want it? Oh, yeah. With the force of a typhoon. Saliva pooled in her mouth.

But she wouldn't fall for the oldest bully trick in the universe. She turned her head away and forced down another handful of the mash.

His guttural chuckle told her she wasn't fooling anyone.

It didn't help that an entire row of the fruits dangled just out of her reach. The vine that produced them was wrapped around the thick branch of the tree that Tnaryt had tethered her to.

Night had descended an hour ago, turning up the volume on the chirps, squawks and buzzing from the surrounding trees. Occasionally a larger animal plodding through the undergrowth, but nothing she could see.

Tnaryt didn't seem the least bit concerned with any of it. His focus was on the sky above, and his comm device. He'd checked in with Nat twice since they'd left the shuttle, but from what she'd overheard, Nat didn't have any news to report.

Which brought Aurora back to the question that weighed heaviest on her mind. What exactly did Tnaryt have planned for the Admiral? He hadn't given him any food or water rations when he'd forced him into the prison where she'd been kept. She had to assume the cook was similarly locked away.

It could be a golden opportunity for Cade's team to free them, assuming they could figure out a way to link *Gladiator* to Tnaryt's ship. There was nothing standard about the Setarip design, and no one onboard to assist.

Except the Admiral and the cook couldn't leave the ship. They were still wearing their collars. She'd been relieved of hers, and hopefully Nat's would be gone soon, too, but the Admiral and the cook were still in danger. Maybe Drew could locate the central control for the collars and deactivate it.

If Cade wasn't in the system already, he would be here soon. She didn't doubt that for a second. And if he figured out she was on the planet, he'd come looking for her. On the ground, his team could outmaneuver Tnaryt blindfolded.

Nat might be able to help, too. She'd felt Nat's emotional shift when she'd successfully snagged the key from Tnaryt's cloak. Nat was resourceful. She would find a way to use the key without tipping off the guard who was watching her.

Aurora swallowed the last scoop of mash and set the container aside. Shifting so her back was to Tnaryt, she lay on her side, gazing into the darkness. Warm, moist air caressed her cheek, soothing and comforting.

She must have dozed off, because a soft patter in the distance roused her, the tap-tap growing steadily louder as it came nearer.

A drop of moisture landed on her cheek. *Rain!*

She opened her mouth and turned her face to the sky. The drops that fell onto her tongue tasted sweeter than the finest wine. The sprinkle turned into a steady cascade, the water bathing her face and hair. She sat up and scrubbed her hands over her eyes and cheeks, washing away the accumulated grit and grime. The rain soaked her clothes, sticking them to her body, but she didn't care. For the first time in weeks, she felt alive.

Closing her eyes, she engaged her energy field and placed her hands on the trunk of the tree. Its energetic vibration responded to her nurturing touch, its lifeforce sharpening her senses.

Which is why she anticipated Tnaryt's next move long before the blow fell.

She didn't summon her shield, but as the scales of his hand connected with the side of her face, she followed the motion as Celia had taught her. She landed on her back as he towered over her. Her cheek stung, but he hadn't inflicted any damage.

He glowered at her. "Nooo."

She almost laughed. *No?* That's the best he could come up with? He didn't even understand what he was forbidding her to do. He'd just wanted her to stop being happy.

But she wouldn't stop. Not anymore. On his ship, she'd been isolated from other living beings, drained of vitality. Here, she was surrounded by vibrant, nurturing life.

He'd seriously miscalculated by bringing her to this planet. In an attempt to use her as his pawn, he'd given her exactly what she needed.

Sixty-Five

"Do you trust Nat?"

Cade ducked under an overhanging frond before glancing at Justin. "Do I have a choice?"

Nat's homing beacon had allowed them to follow Tnaryt's ship at a discreet distance and track the shuttle to the planet's surface. When they'd arrived, Cade had contacted the Admiral via comband. When he hadn't received a reply, he'd tried sending a message to Aurora's comband instead, and had been rewarded with a typed message from Nat.

That's how he knew Tnaryt had taken Aurora away from the shuttle and left Nat alone with one guard. And that the Admiral was still on Tnaryt's ship. Assuming Nat was telling the truth.

The Admiral had vouched for her, which went a long way to building trust. But he couldn't forget that Nat was the reason the Admiral and Aurora were in Tnaryt's clutches in the first place.

A gentle rain kicked up, pattering on the leaves. A drop fell on Cade's neck and traced a path down his back. "How far to the shuttle?"

Justin checked the tracking device in his hand. "Three point four kilometers."

Since *Gladiator* didn't have the *Starhawke*'s stealth capabilities, they'd been forced to land a safe distance from the shuttle to prevent the roar of the engines from tipping off the Setarips to their presence. He'd left Drew in charge of the ship while he, Justin and Williams headed for the shuttle.

Cade glanced over his shoulder at Williams. "Any sign of critters we need to worry about?" Since both Reynolds and Gonzo were on the *Starhawke*, he'd placed Williams in charge of security. Trekking through a jungle on an unknown planet could pose unanticipated challenges. He wanted to be prepared.

"Nothing larger than a cat. And most of those are scurrying away from us."

Good news. His team had dealt with their share of predators during their time in the Elite Unit, but he preferred avoiding a confrontation whenever possible. Especially since sounds from an altercation might carry.

They were half a kilometer from their destination when the rain ceased. The clouds cleared, allowing pale moonlight to shine through.

"What's the plan when we reach the shuttle?" Justin asked.

"First we contact Nat. That shuttle is Tnaryt's only way off planet. If we gain control of it without alerting him, we gain control over him."

Justin frowned. "What about the collars? Won't those be an issue?"

"Yes. But we could—" He paused as his comband pinged with an incoming message. A quick glance indicated Nat had beaten him to the punch.

Where are you?

He halted so he could type his reply. *Half a kilometer northwest.*

Hurry. Chained in cockpit. Guard asleep.

He glanced at Justin and Williams. "We need to move. The guard's asleep."

They picked up the pace until they reached a rocky promontory pushing out of the trees with the shuttle at its center.

Cade and Justin darted across the open space and pressed against the shuttle's hull on opposite sides of the sealed hatch.

He texted Nat. *Outside. Hatch closed.*
Not for long.

The hiss of air servos followed. Cade and Justin crouched while Williams covered them from the trees. Shouts from the Setarip guard indicated she'd woken up and was standing close to the hatch. But her voice was directed at Nat in the cockpit, which would put her back to them. Perfect.

As soon as her outline was visible through the opening, Cade fired. Justin's blast followed, both finding their mark. The Setarip crumpled to the deck as the hatch thumped onto the ground. The smell that wafted out of the opening was musky and unpleasant, reminding him of a trash compactor.

Justin kept his weapon trained on the Setarip while Cade made his way to the cockpit.

He recognized the petite woman with unruly dark hair he'd seen in the bar. She knelt on the floor, a chain threaded through the supports for the console and attached to manacles around her wrists.

Cade approached cautiously. "Nat?"

Her pale-eyed gaze was equally wary. "Cade?"

"Yep." He pulled off his visor since the running lights in the shuttle provided enough illumination to see. He studied the cuffs around her wrists. "Is there a key for these?"

"The guard has it."

"Be right back." He found Justin and Williams securing the guard with a length of freight rope. "We need the key to the cuffs."

Justin made a quick search of the Setarip's pockets and produced a key.

Cade returned to the cockpit and crouched beside Nat. Inserting the key, he sprang the lock.

She slipped her wrists out and rubbed the red marks on her skin. "Thanks."

Cade spotted a circle of metal sitting on the console beside her. He glanced at her neck and back at the metal band. "Is that your collar?"

Her gaze followed his and her expression darkened. "Uh-huh."

"How did you get it off?"

She pulled a small object out of the interior folds of her duster. "Pinched the key from Tnaryt's pocket."

So she was a skilled thief, too. Fascinating.

"What about Aurora? Is she still wearing hers?"

Nat shook her head. "Tnaryt removed it. I don't know why. She's the one who told me where to find the key."

Cade's heart squeezed. Sounded like Aurora. "And the Admiral?"

"*Admiral?*" Nat's eyes widened. "What Admiral?"

Ah. So she didn't know Admiral Schreiber's identity. No reason to hold back now. "The man who's been working as your engineer is Admiral Schreiber, head of the Galactic Fleet."

Nat's eyes looked like small moons. "But...he's..." She swallowed. "What the hell is the head of the Fleet doing out here? *Alone?*"

"It's a story for another time. Right now we need to help Aurora. Come on." But when he started to stand, Nat grabbed his arm.

"I can't. I have to get back to the ship and pilot it out of the system."

"Why?"

"The Sovereign is coming."

"I know. That's why we need to backup Aurora."

"If you want the Admiral to live, you have to let me move Tnaryt's ship."

Alarm bells rang in his head. Her motives weren't as altruistic as she was making them sound. What was she hiding? "But Tnaryt and Aurora are down here. That's where the Sovereign will go. And where we need to be."

Nat looked at him like he wasn't playing with a full deck. "Wrong. At best, the Sovereign's minions will board the ship and take the Admiral and the cook prisoner. More likely, they'll use the ship for target practice."

Justin appeared in the cockpit doorway. "Problem?"

"Nat thinks the Admiral's in danger from the Sovereign." Cade waved a hand between Justin and Nat. "Nat, Justin. Justin, Nat."

They nodded at each other. "So what do we do?" Justin asked.

Nat blew out an exasperated breath. "You leave. Go help Aurora. I'll take *Gypsy* back to the ship. Now that Aurora's not wearing a collar, I can take the ship out of the system without triggering the autodestruct. You do your thing to rescue Aurora, then come find us."

Cade didn't correct Nat's assumption that Aurora had been at risk while wearing the collar. If she hadn't confided in Nat, he wasn't about to, either. He also didn't point out that her plan kept her neatly out of the line of fire. With freedom in her grasp, she didn't seem likely to put herself in jeopardy.

"Okay. Send me a message as soon as you're on the ship."

The lines of tension eased from Nat's face. "One more thing."

"Yeah?"

She snagged the collar off the console and moved past him into the main cabin. "Grab her and follow me," she told Williams, pointing at the Setarip female. She strode out the back hatch, stopping in front of one of the trees and snapping the collar around a low-hanging branch. She motioned for Williams and Justin to place the Setarip a few meters away. "Tnaryt tracks the collars. This way he'll assume I'm still here."

That brought up another important point. "Won't he hear the shuttle leave?"

She looked insulted. "*Gypsy* was designed for smuggling. I can sneak her out without alerting him."

He'd have to take her word for it.

Sixty-Six

He'd gone for it.

Nat hadn't been convinced he would. The look in Cade's eyes as he'd agreed to her proposal had indicated he saw a lot more than she wanted him to.

But he couldn't argue with her logic. The engineer—*Admiral—was* in danger from the Sovereign as long as the ship remained in orbit. If helping him allowed her to remain out of the Sovereign's reach...well, that was a bonus.

Tnaryt's ship came into view, hanging above the planet like a discarded toy. She shuddered. The idea of setting foot on it again made her skin crawl, but it was her only option. *Gypsy* couldn't get out of the system on her own. They needed the interstellar engines.

As soon as the grappling arm secured *Gypsy* in place Nat headed for the back hatch. The silence that greeted her when she exited into the cargo bay wasn't unusual. The ship had always resembled a tomb. Fitting, since the Sovereign had stuck them in the worthless hunk of metal and left them to die. It would have been kinder to blow them into space. But kindness wasn't a quality the Sovereign possessed.

Living under Tnaryt's control had been hell, but at least she'd known what she was dealing with. His abuse was physical. The Sovereign abused people's minds, warping their reality.

When Nat had flown the six Setarips over to this ship in *Gypsy*, leaving Tnaryt's battle cruiser and the rest of the captives and crew in the Sovereign's control, it had seemed like the most logical thing in the world. It had taken several days before she'd started to question the self-destructive stupidity of her actions. The Sovereign's power over her had been absolute. She hadn't even known how helpless she'd been.

She never wanted to be in that position again.

She climbed the ladder and exited on the engineering deck. Her footsteps echoed as she hurried down the corridor, but when she reached the engine room, it was empty. A quick check indicated the engines were on standby and life support was still on. Tnaryt hadn't abandoned the ship completely.

But the Admiral wasn't there. And she didn't trust the engines to run smoothly without someone to watch them. She couldn't afford to have them conk out while she was at navigation.

Racing back down the corridor to the ladder, she made the ascent to the bridge in record time. Scrambling onto the deck, she hurried to the hatch for the room that had served as Aurora's cell. "Admiral! Are you in there?" She smacked the hatch with her hand a few times.

Moments later, a muffled sound that might have been an answering bang from the other side reached her. But when she keyed the hatch to open, it refused to obey her command. She hit the pad again. Nothing. Tnaryt must have locked it. Good thing she knew a few things about hotwiring.

The stash of tools Aurora had been using to repair the comm console sat in a collection of crates against the wall. Nat snagged what she needed and crouched on the floor beside the panel. Getting to the wiring was easy. Figuring out the right combination to override the lock wasn't. Logic didn't seem to factor into how the Setarips designed their systems.

Sweat trickled down her cheek by the time the seal cracked open with a little pop.

The Admiral's bald head appeared above the lip. "Nat?" He looked startled to see her. He glanced around the bridge. "Where's Aurora?"

She backed up to give him room to climb out. "On the planet with Tnaryt and the females."

He frowned. "I didn't think Tnaryt could fly your shuttle."

"He can't. I did."

His look of bewilderment increased. "And he sent you back here?"

She snorted. "Hardly. Cade's team helped me escape."

His brows rose. "Cade's with you?"

"No. He stayed to help Aurora."

"You're alone?"

She nodded.

His eyes narrowed. "What's your plan?"

"We need to move the ship before the Sovereign arrives."

His gaze shifted over her shoulder to the bridgescreen. "I don't think that's going to happen."

"Why not?"

"Because the Sovereign's already here."

Sixty-Seven

Aurora kept a close eye on Tnaryt as he prowled the platform. He was dangerous when he was relaxed. Now he looked like a walking landmine.

The rising sun highlighted the orange in his crest, which stood at attention along his neck and back. His heavy cloak swirled around his legs with each pivot. It also snagged on the nearby branches, but he seemed determined to keep it on, his vanity overriding his common sense. The cloak didn't serve a practical purpose down here. In fact, there was a good chance it would make him overheat.

He'd had a terse conversation with the females a while ago, and had sent two of them off in the direction of the shuttle. Something wasn't going to plan. Aurora hoped that meant Nat had successfully removed her collar and incapacitated the guard.

Tnaryt halted his pacing and glanced at his comm device. His breath hissed through his teeth and anger flared in his emotional field. He tapped on the device, then his gaze shifted to Aurora. His tongue flicked. "Sooovereiiign iiisss heeere."

Aurora looked up at the sky, where the grey of dawn had given way to blue. No sign of any ships, but they wouldn't be visible in orbit.

Tnaryt grabbed the chain that tethered her to the tree and unhooked it, adjusting the fit on her manacles before hauling her to her feet. He yanked her braid back with one hand and pressed the point of his knife against her neck with the other. "Yooou fiiight. Yooou diiie."

Subtlety was not his strong suit.

He marched her down the rickety walkway to the ground. The knife pressed between her shoulder blades, a continual reminder that he believed he controlled her. His misconception gave her the advantage.

The two females followed behind. The path through the trees looked like something that had been cleared at one time, but the jungle had reclaimed most of it. That didn't prevent Tnaryt from shoving her through the greenery like she was his personal battering ram.

She lifted her hands in front of her abdomen and created an energy shield a few centimeters in front of her body to knock the plants out of the way.

A shadow swooped over them, blocking out the sun. She glanced up. The dark shape of a ship glided by as silent as an owl, with wings that cut through the air like scythes.

A shiver raised goosebumps on her forearms. Very soon she'd find out whether the Sovereign wanted her dead or alive. She wasn't sure which possibility concerned her more.

Tnaryt gave her a shove, propelling her forward. She pushed through the foliage, continuing along the overgrown path until it terminated at a rocky overlook. A shallow river cut through the clearing eight meters below, with mini waterfalls creating small pools in a wide stair-step.

Tnaryt motioned to the two females. They spread out on either side, disappearing into the trees. He moved so his back was against a tree trunk, pulling Aurora flush to his body so they both faced the water, his knife at her throat.

His proximity overloaded her senses, as did the churning hostility and fear seeping out of him. "Now what?"

His voice hissed in her ear, making her flinch. "Waaaaiiit."

Wonderful.

The temperature had climbed with the sun. A slight breeze blew across the river, keeping the post-rain humidity from becoming oppressive. Her skin had soaked up the moisture like a sponge, as had her clothes. She smelled almost as offensive as Tnaryt.

Breathing through her mouth, she tuned into her surroundings. Life energy vibrated all around her from the plants and small creatures who called this planet home. It fed her yearning for connection and calmed the butterflies playing tag in her stomach. She expanded the scope of her senses, seeking and finding amidst the foreign sensations the caress of a familiar emotional field from the direction she'd arrived with Tnaryt.

Cade. He'd found her.

But he wasn't the only one. From the other side of the river, she sensed a group approaching, more than a dozen spears of hostility piercing the foliage. And within that group, another energy field that felt strangely familiar, though she couldn't place it. It tugged at her, like snatches of a long-forgotten melody. She leaned forward, stopping only when Tnaryt's grip tightened and the tip of his knife bit into her skin.

"Waaaiiit."

The sensation of familiarity grew stronger, taunting her. What was—

The branches of the trees across the river rustled and several figures emerged into the clearing at the edge of the water. Every single one was covered from head to toe, most in mesh outfits that matched what the Setarips had worn on Gaia. However, two figures wore hooded cloaks that draped their bodies, making it impossible to identify any physical characteristics.

The familiar energy field was emanating from them.

One of the hooded figures spoke. "Greetings, Tnaryt." The voice had an artificial quality to it, the tones modulated by a vocal manipulation device.

"Soovereeign." He made the name sound like a curse.

The figure's head tilted to the side. "I see you were truthful in your claims regarding my prize. Are you prepared to trade?"

"Traaaade. Yeesss." Tnaryt wrapped his arm tighter around Aurora's ribcage, positioning her so she acted as a human shield. No way was that an accident.

She didn't fight him, though. Now that the Sovereign was standing thirty meters away, nothing would convince her to run. She had unfinished business with the hooded figure.

"Wheeere iiis my shiiip?"

"In orbit. Just as we agreed."

So Tnaryt was trading her for a ship? Maybe she should be flattered. At least he wasn't giving her up on the cheap.

He made a guttural barking noise that might have been a growl, followed by a word she didn't recognize.

"Really, Tnaryt. Such language. There's no call for incivility."

"Wheeere iiis my shiiip?" he repeated, hostility in every syllable.

"I told you. In orbit."

"Yoooou liiiiie!" His grip tightened involuntarily, putting pressure on the knife.

Aurora engaged her shield to keep the blade from cutting into her skin.

"Careful, Tnaryt. If you harm my prize, our negotiations will end."

Aurora didn't believe a word. Tnaryt couldn't hurt her, and the Sovereign should know that. Why was the Sovereign toying with him? To buy time?

"My shiiip iiis nooot heeere."

"Of course it is. Right where you left it. At least, for now."

His body jerked. He wasn't paying any attention to the knife. If she'd been anyone else, he would have slit her throat without even realizing it.

"Myyyy shiiip! Theee ooonnneee yooou tooook!"

"Ah, yes. That one. It was useful to me. Sadly, thanks to the woman you're squeezing like a grape, that ship was destroyed. And all your crew with it."

Aurora's jaw dropped. The Sovereign was blaming the destruction of the ship and Tnaryt's crew on *her*?

Tnaryt's rage washed over her. He grabbed her chin from underneath and forced her head up so he could see her face, shifting the knife like he was preparing to plunge it into her heart. "Yooou kiiilll theeem?"

"No! I didn't!" Well, she had killed one. But only in self-defense.

"Yoooou liiiie!" He lifted the knife.

"Stop!" She barked the command like he was an insubordinate crewmember.

He froze.

She lowered her voice so it wouldn't carry across the river. "The Sovereign is manipulating you."

His pupils closed to slits and his tongue flicked out. He didn't lower his hand, but she could feel a slight shift in his emotions. He was listening.

"I'm not the one who took your ship and crew. And I didn't destroy the ship. I tried to save it. But it was sabotaged."

Flick, flick. "Whaaat iiiis...saaabootaage?"

"The Sovereign planted explosives on the ship and set auto-destructs on the shuttles. They blew without warning."

His rage ramped up again, but his gaze shifted to the Sovereign. Pulling Aurora tight against him, he took a step around the tree. "Nooo traaade."

The Sovereign sighed dramatically. "That's unfortunate."

"Yooou liiiie to meee."

"Actually, I've been distracting you."

The attack came without warning. One moment Aurora was in Tnaryt's grip, the next his body crumpled to the ground in a lifeless heap. Two Setarips stood over him with their weapons trained on her, their vivid green scales and sloping foreheads marking them as members of the Ecilam faction.

"Ah, that's better."

Aurora slowly turned her head, her neck creaking in protest.

The Sovereign had taken a few steps closer to the river's edge. "Now, if you'll be kind enough to join me, we can get down to business."

Sixty-Eight

Aurora ignored the two Setarips. They were no threat to her. The figure across the river was another story.

Having her hands manacled didn't help, especially now that the Sovereign's full attention was on her. Freeing herself would take time she didn't have. "And what business is that?"

The Sovereign's artificial laugh poured ice through Aurora's veins. "Business involving an old friend."

Old friend? What the hell did that mean? "What old friend?"

The Sovereign made a tsking noise. "How quickly you forget those you claim to care about. What would the Admiral think?"

Oh. That old friend. Aurora's heart thumped. Did the Sovereign know the Admiral was on Tnaryt's ship?

The Sovereign gestured to Aurora's rumpled and stained clothing. "Although I must admit I'm reluctant to be near you in your current state. You really should take better care of yourself. You look like you crawled out from under a rock. Rather appropriate, don't you think?"

Aurora bit back a retort. The Sovereign was trying to rile her.

"But where are my manners? I haven't introduced you to my companion yet." Even with the vocal manipulation, the Sovereign's patronizing tone came through with perfect clarity. "I'm eager for you to come down and meet her." The Sovereign motioned to the second hooded figure. "Step forward, my dear. Show our guest your face."

The figure moved onto the sand, pausing at the water's edge before throwing back the hood with a dramatic flourish.

Aurora's breath caught. Not a Teeli.

The statuesque woman who stood before her didn't have the white hair and pale skin of the Teeli. She looked human—beautiful—with artfully arranged blond hair and tanned skin.

But that wasn't what had stolen the air from Aurora's lungs. As she held the woman's gaze, she knew why she'd sensed a familiar energy, a connection.

This woman was a Suulh.

The haughtiness in the woman's voice matched the pinched expression on her face. "Surprised?"

"A little." *Floored, actually.* She hadn't expected the Sovereign to bring a Suulh to this meeting. And they were both speaking Galish, not Teelian. "Who are you?"

Even though Aurora was standing eight meters above her, somehow the woman managed to look down at her. "I am Kreestol." She said the name like it should mean something to Aurora.

It didn't.

Kreestol's chin rose a notch. "The Sahzade."

Aurora blinked. "What?"

Kreestol's lips curled in a mockery of a smile. "The Guardian of the Suulh."

Aurora blinked again. Whoever this woman was, she was off her rocker. "You're not the Sahzade."

"Yes, I *am*, you insignificant *glussepac*." Kreestol's anger slamming into Aurora like a blow. "I shall enjoy watching you suffer."

Suffer? Forget delusional. The woman was psychotic. "That may be harder to achieve than you think."

"Maybe not," the Sovereign said, sounding positively giddy. "Kreestol, a little demonstration."

Kreestol shot a look at the Sovereign before returning her attention to Aurora. She raised her arms, palms out. An energy field bloomed to life around her.

A *pearlescent* energy field.

The ground tilted under Aurora's feet. She stumbled back a step. *No. It can't be.*

The Sovereign laughed, an ugly, harsh sound. "Oh, this is better than I had anticipated. You should see the look on your face, Aurora."

The sound of her name triggered a sense of déjà vu. She'd heard a comment like that before, said exactly that way. But when?

"Kreestol *is* the Sahzade. She's your mother's sister."

"Sister?" *Air. She needed air.*

"Yes. The one your mother abandoned when she ran away like a coward."

No. The Sovereign was lying. Manipulating her. Had to be.

But the glow of Kreestol's energy field wasn't a lie. She'd never even known her mom *had* a sister.

"Kreestol is the rightful leader of the Suulh. You, Aurora, are a worthless mongrel." The Sovereign stepped next to Kreestol. "One I will take great pleasure in bringing to heel."

Sixty-Nine

Cade couldn't believe what he was seeing. And hearing. *Aurora had an aunt?*

The pearlescent energy that surrounded Kreestol left no doubt that the Sovereign's words were true. And the revelation had stunned Aurora into immobility. She looked like a statue placed on the rocks above the river, her attention focused completely on the pair of figures on the opposite side.

If Kreestol had been brought along as a distraction, it had worked perfectly. Aurora's body language indicated she wasn't aware that the two Setarips behind her had become a pack of ten, all with their weapons pointed at her. They'd formed an arc along the path to cut off her escape route.

"What now?" Justin murmured from where he crouched next to Cade.

Cade answered without taking his gaze off Aurora. "We wait for Aurora to make a move. The Setarips can't hurt her." But he wasn't nearly as certain whether Kreestol could.

Aurora's stance shifted to a subtle defensive posture. Maybe she'd sensed the Setarips after all. "What makes you think I'll go along with your plan?" she called out to the Sovereign.

The Sovereign swept one mesh-covered arm toward the sky. "My cruiser's weapons are locked onto Tnaryt's ship. With a single word, I can turn it into a fireball."

Cade swore. Nat had been right. He'd already sent Williams back to *Gladiator* and told Drew to follow Tnaryt's ship as soon as Williams arrived. Now they'd end up defending it, instead.

But it wouldn't make much difference if the Sovereign had brought an entourage like the one they'd seen at Burrow.

Even at this distance, Cade could see the look of alarm that passed over Aurora's face as she glanced skyward.

The Sovereign's chuckle made Cade's skin crawl.

"You wouldn't like that, would you? Perhaps because your precious Admiral is up there? He's almost as much of a thorn in my side as you."

Aurora stepped closer to the ledge. "If you planned to blow up Tnaryt's ship, why didn't you do it when you arrived?"

"To insure your cooperation. If you don't come quietly, Tnaryt's ship will fall from the sky."

"How do I know you won't blow it up anyway?"

"You don't."

And based on their previous experience with the Sovereign's tactics, that's exactly what would happen.

Aurora glanced at the sky, then back at the Sovereign. "So you want me to come with you?"

"Oh, yes. Much as I would enjoy stranding you on this planet, I can't take the chance your crew of overachievers will find you. Besides, I have plans for you."

"Plans that involve a tiny cage?"

The Sovereign waved the question away. "We'll get to the details later. For now, there's only one question that matters. How badly do you want your Admiral to live?"

Seventy

"Any power to the console?" the Admiral asked from his prone position on the floor.

"No." Nat glared at the tactical console, which remained stubbornly dark. She'd had it on her list of items to fix during the months when the ship had been stranded in orbit, but something else had always taken precedence. The engines and life support, mostly, or maintenance on *Gypsy* so she'd be able to make the supply runs. The weapons and shields hadn't seemed important.

Well, they seemed pretty damned important now. Her gaze shifted to the sleek cruiser and six warships sitting off their starboard side. Not much she could do about them at the moment. Moving the ship would be suicide. It was slower than a turtle, and fleeing would only encourage the Sovereign to fire on them.

So, she and the Admiral had focused their attention on getting the defenses online instead.

The Admiral's collar sat on the floor beside him. She'd removed it as soon as they'd confirmed the other ships weren't about to blow them into space dust.

She sat up as a light flashed on the console. "I've got something." A few more lights appeared, and the console's main panel began scrolling through what looked like a diagnostic cycle.

The Admiral got to his feet with surprising agility for a man his age. "Any of it make sense to you?"

The layout was as illogical as all the other Setarip designs she'd encountered, but a few of the commands matched the icons on the navigation console. "A little." She pointed to a green bar. "I think that's the shield strength indicator. And this row of orange dots should be the torpedoes and cannons."

"Are they functional?"

"Your guess is as good as mine." She met his gaze over her shoulder. "But if they start firing at us, we'll find out."

He nodded, his lean face somber.

The comband on Nat's arm pinged, startling her. She opened the channel.

"Nat, it's Cade. Did you reach the ship?" His voice was barely above a whisper.

"Yes. But not before the Sovere—"

"We know. Is the Admiral with you?"

"I'm here, Mr. Ellis."

"What's your status?"

"Facing off against the Sovereign's cruiser and six warships. We restored power to the defensive systems, but there's no guarantee they'll work."

"Understood. Williams and Drew are headed your way. *Gladiator* is well armed and shielded. They'll do everything they can to protect you."

"Thank you, Mr. Ellis, but Aurora is the primary concern. Keep her safe."

"I will." The connection closed.

Nat grimaced. "One ship won't make much difference."

The Admiral's sparse brows lifted. "It might."

Nat's gaze swung to the Sovereign's ships. A few weeks ago, she hadn't thought her life was worth much. How ironic. Now that she wanted to live, she was one well-aimed torpedo away from oblivion. "Can you boost the energy to our shields?"

The Admiral grunted. "Perhaps. I'll head down to engineering and see what I can do."

Seventy-One

Aurora focused on her footing as she made her way down to the water. Having her hands bound didn't make the task any easier. But it gave her time to think.

Cade was nearby. She'd sensed his emotional shifts as she'd talked with the Sovereign. In fact, at one point she could have sworn he'd whispered a warning, alerting her to the Setarips at her back. She'd been so startled by Kreestol's appearance she hadn't realized they were there. She did now. They were following her down the decline, blocking her retreat.

It was wasted effort on their part. Even without the threat to the Admiral, Kreestol's energy would have pulled her like a magnet. That's why she'd sensed a familiar presence earlier. Kreestol's energy was a lot like her mom's— except for the vibrant hostility. That was completely different. The depth of Kreestol's rage was impressive. Her gaze was focused on Aurora like a laser that was burning a hole in her chest.

But Kreestol's behavior was a paradox. She claimed the role of Sahzade, guardian of their people, yet she'd sided with the Sovereign, who was capturing and torturing the Suulh. How did she justify the Sovereign's actions?

Aurora reached the water's edge and stepped into the slow-moving current, her shield preventing the moisture from reaching her skin. She kept her attention on the Sovereign as she waded across, which cost her when an underwater plant drifted under her foot. She slipped and went to one knee, the water swirling past her hip.

"Careful, Aurora," the Sovereign chided. "Wouldn't want you washing away."

Aurora rose to her feet, her gaze on her adversary. Who was underneath that cloak? She could sense everyone gathered around the river—Cade and Justin, the Setarips, the guards behind the Sovereign, and Kreestol most of all—but not the Sovereign. Not a flicker of emotion came through, as though Aurora was approaching a machine, not a person.

That bothered her more than anything else. If she couldn't read the Sovereign's emotions, she lost the ability to anticipate. And she needed that advantage. There was only so much help Cade could provide in this situation.

He knew it, too. She could sense his unease. She wanted to assure him that everything would be okay, but the truth was, she didn't have a plan. Except buying time. Hopefully Cade or Nat would devise a way to help the Admiral. Aurora couldn't, other than keeping the Sovereign's attention on her rather than Tnaryt's ship.

The Sovereign and Kreestol stood like twin sentinels as she reached the opposite bank, preventing her from stepping out of the water.

The Sovereign's mechanical laugh scraped up Aurora's spine. "My, my, my. You *are* a sight. What would Cade think if he could see you now?"

Cade? Aurora's heart thumped like a bass drum. How could the Sovereign know about her connection to Cade? Unlike her ties to the Admiral, her history with Cade wasn't in any Fleet or Council records. And yet, the Sovereign knew. How far did the Sovereign's tendrils reach? How much of Aurora's past had been laid bare?

Her fingers itched to snatch off the Sovereign's cloak, to reveal whoever—*whatever*—lay beneath.

The Sovereign didn't seem to notice her scrutiny. "The manacles are a nice touch. We may need to make those permanent."

Aurora matched the Sovereign's conversational tone. "And stuff me in a cage? Just like the rest of the Suulh you've imprisoned?"

That comment got a reaction from Kreestol. Her eyes narrowed. "Imprisoned?"

Was Kresstol unaware of the Sovereign's actions? That would explain a lot. "The Sovereign is turning the Suulh into weapons of destruction."

Uncertainty flickered in Kreestol's emotional field before anger swept it away. "You lie."

Aurora held her gaze. "It's the truth. Their own children were used as blackmail to keep them in line. I rescued hundreds—"

"That's impossible."

"No, it's not. They were forced to use their energy abilities to kill—"

"Enough!" The Sovereign's sharp command made them both turn. The Sovereign rested a gloved hand on Kreestol's arm. "Remember who you're talking to. She's a deceiver. Her mother betrayed you. And all the Suulh. You cannot trust her."

And wasn't that the pot calling the kettle black. Unfortunately, Kreestol had no reason to believe her, either.

Kreestol's face turned into a thundercloud as she pointed a finger at Aurora's chest. "You will pay for your lies."

"Later." The Sovereign waved a hand at Kreestol as if she were an annoying fly. "Right now, Aurora has a choice to make. Surrender to me willingly to save the Admiral, or watch him get blown to bits and be taken by force?"

The Sovereign sounded confident of the outcome in both cases. Kreestol's presence probably had a lot to do with that.

Only one option would buy Aurora more time. Much as she hated the idea, she'd have to—

Cade's abrupt emotional shift caught her off guard. His anxiety had been a solid presence at the edge of her senses since he'd arrived on the scene. But it had vanished in an instant, replaced with a surge of relief that washed over her, blocking out Kreestol and the Sovereign like a curtain. The vivid mental image that followed made her heart skip a beat.

She dropped her chin to her chest to conceal her reaction. *The rules of the game just changed.*

Taking a deep breath, she sank to her knees in front of the Sovereign.

The Sovereign managed to sound smug even through the vocal manipulation device. "I always knew one day you'd bow before me."

Aurora lifted her head, revealing the smile she'd hidden. "Don't count on it."

Seventy-Two

"Fifty thousand kilometers and closing."

Mya barely registered Kelly's words. She was still reeling from the mental image Aurora had just sent of a woman wearing a familiar cloak, her body surrounded by a pearlescent energy field.

It was one of the figures they'd followed from Citadel. Had to be. But how could she be generating a field that matched Aurora's? The woman bore a slight resemblance to Aurora—same blonde hair, same strong cheekbones—but she wasn't old enough to be Aurora's grandmother. Who was she?

The image vanished abruptly. Mya blinked, her gaze focusing on the cluster of ships visible on the bridgescreen.

The cruiser and warships they'd followed from the Suulh homeworld faced a battered transport that looked like something a child had assembled, all mismatched pieces and odd angles. A smaller but heavily armored vessel sat off the transport's starboard side. That would be *Gladiator*, the ship Cade's team had stolen from the junkyard. Justin had responded to their hail when they'd entered the system, and had given them a brief rundown of the current situation.

Even without that, Mya would have known Aurora was down on the planet with the cloaked figures. And that's all she needed to know. She left her chair without conscious thought, moving to stand next to Kire. "I want to take a shuttle down to help Aurora."

He frowned. "You can't fly a shuttle."

"No, but Jonarel can." And she needed his particular skill set to reach Aurora.

Kire studied her. "You're communicating with her, aren't you?"

She nodded.

Kire's gaze shifted to the ships on the screen. So far, no one had moved. But it wasn't likely to stay that way. "Do you have a plan?"

No. "Yes." But the shuttle's camouflage would allow them to sneak past the ships, just as the *Starhawke's* hull defenses kept the Teeli from knowing they were here now. That was step one. Step two? She'd figure it out when they got there.

Kire's mouth thinned, but he tapped the comm. "Emoto to Clarek."

"Clarek here."

"Jon, Mya wants to take a shuttle to the surface to help Roe. She needs you to pilot it."

Jonarel didn't hesitate for a moment. "I'll meet her in the shuttle bay."

Mya rested her hand on Kire's arm. "Thank you."

He placed his hand over hers. "Be safe."

"You, too." Mya hurried to the lift, but Reynolds intercepted her before she reached it.

"Permission to join you. Ellis and Byrnes are down there. And I'm not needed here." She gestured to Gonzo at the tactical station and Celia at communications.

Mya wasn't about to turn down the addition of another skilled fighter. "Glad to have you."

Jonarel was already in the bay when they arrived, prepping the shuttle. Mya paused before settling into the co-pilot's chair. "What about the *Starhawke*? Will she be okay if you're not in engineering?" A battle seemed inevitable, and Jonarel had always been at his post during their previous altercations.

Jonarel's gaze met hers. "I turned the critical systems over to Tehar. Aurora is our priority."

She didn't see a hint of doubt in his eyes. Good. They were on the same page. "Then let's get her back."

Seventy-Three

Dropping her palms to the sand, Aurora shifted her weight to one side and kicked out with her opposite leg, connecting solidly with the Sovereign's knee.

The mechanical shriek of pain that followed lifted the tiny hairs on her arms as the Sovereign collapsed.

Kreestol's roar drowned out the Sovereign's cry as she slammed her shield into Aurora's, generating a flare of light and a crackle of energy.

The pressure pinned Aurora on her hands and knees, immobilizing her. It was bizarre, like fighting her own shadow.

Kreestol's eyes burned as she pounded against Aurora's shield, but her movements were jerky and ineffective. She clearly wasn't trained in hand-to-hand combat.

Unfortunately, with her hands bound, Aurora didn't have the freedom of movement she needed to maximize her own power.

Weapons blasts streaked past her, slamming into the guards surrounding the Sovereign. They staggered and fell, drawing Kreestol's attention. She shrieked like a banshee, abandoning her attack on Aurora and flinging herself in front of the Sovereign, deflecting the next few shots.

Aurora took advantage of the distraction to roll away and leap to her feet. But she needed to get the manacles off her wrists. And she knew just the man to help her. "Cade! The cuffs!" She lifted her hands into the air, hoping he would understand her request.

Two blasts followed, scorching the metal and knocking it away from her wrists while her shield protected her skin. Perfect shot. Stellar light she loved that man.

She flexed her shoulders and lowered her arms, pivoting as she caught sight of the group of Setarips who'd followed her across the river moving into attack formation.

These Setarips didn't look like Tnaryt and his females. They all had the green scales and smoother features of the Ecilam faction. She'd engaged in a face-to-face confrontation with that faction once before, years ago. She'd lost that battle because she'd been unable to use her shield. This time, the outcome would be different.

Four of the Setarips attacked with weapons that resembled bayonets, stabbing at her from all sides. She struck with her shield, the weapons shattering and the Setarips staggering as they made contact with the impenetrable wall.

A few blasts from Cade and Justin hit the Setarips, and they immediately changed their stances, going on the defensive and taking cover. They disappeared into the trees and opened fire, but not at her. The weapons blasts struck the trees across the river.

Cade and Justin could handle the Setarips. With the cuffs gone, she needed to focus on her main problem.

Kreestol stood like a sentinel in front of the Sovereign, her shield creating a protective barrier. But her attention was on Aurora, her lips pulled back in a snarl.

She was standing between Aurora and her goal. Time to find out what her aunt could do.

Seventy-Four

When the full force of Aurora and Kreestol's energy shields met, the flash lit the trees like lightning, temporarily blinding Cade. The afterimage bounced in front of his eyes, making it impossible to see the Setarips or the Sovereign. He blinked rapidly to clear his vision.

By the time he could make sense of what he was seeing, Aurora had taken several steps toward the waterline while Kreestol pushed forward. Their shields sparked at every point of contact, the pearlescent glows saturated with the flow of energy.

Aurora's next step brought her in contact with the water, her boot sinking below the surface.

Cade ducked as blasts from the Setarips burned holes in the foliage above his head. He returned fire, but the green of the Setarips' scales blended perfectly with the trees, making it impossible to pinpoint their locations.

Another flash came from the water as Kreestol struck again, the brute force of her attack driving Aurora deeper into the river.

Justin fired off a couple shots at the Setarips. "She's in trouble."

"I know." But what could they do to help her? Their weapons were useless against Kreestol's energy shield.

However, as Kreestol followed Aurora into the water, her shield moved with her—and left the Sovereign exposed.

He snapped his pistol up to take a shot, but the Sovereign's guards had noticed the weakness, too. They shifted positions, clustering in front of the Sovereign, forming a physical barrier to replace Kreestol's shield.

He fired at the guards, striking one in the neck. The guard tumbled forward but another moved to fill the space. The remaining guards stood en masse and opened fire, the cloaked figure of the Sovereign a dark shadow in their midst.

Cade and Justin kept up a constant barrage as the guards pushed into the shelter of the trees. But the Sovereign's shrill command cut through the roar of weapons fire.

"Annihilate that ship!"

Seventy-Five

The *Starhawke*'s shuttle had just cleared the bay when flashes lit up the cockpit.

Mya's gaze snapped to the Teeli warships as they opened fire on the Setarip ship and *Gladiator*, the blasts slamming into their shields like cannonballs. *Gladiator* returned fire and moved to engage, but the Setarip ship sat like a rock, firing erratic shots that mostly missed the intended targets.

The *Starhawke* made her presence known, sending a powerful barrage that struck the aft shields of the warships and the Teeli cruiser.

Jonarel banked as one of the warships changed course, turning to engage the *Starhawke* and cutting across the shuttle's path.

Mya flinched. She hadn't anticipated the danger of an accidental collision because the warships couldn't see them.

Jonarel seemed unconcerned with the chaos erupting around them, his focus on the planet as he brought the shuttle back in line with their original trajectory.

Mya followed the movements of the *Starhawke* on the aft camera monitor, her heartbeat thundering in her ears. The ship had dropped the hull camouflage when it opened fire. Two of the warships and the cruiser had now moved into attack position. Seeing the battle from this vantage point was much worse than being on the ship. She glanced at Jonarel. "What should we do?"

"Help Aurora."

"But—"

"They will handle it." His tone brooked no argument, determination etched in the firm set of his jaw.

Mya's fingers dug into her thighs as she watched the battle unfold. He was right. Aurora needed backup. But that didn't make abandoning her friends any easier.

Seventy-Six

"Shields at forty-eight percent!" Nat shouted into the comband as another burst of firepower pummeled the shields. The ship groaned in protest.

She returned fire, doing her best to avoid striking the two ships that were blasting the Sovereign's cruiser and warships. She had no idea where the second one had come from. It had appeared out of nowhere, looking like a flying work of art, but it had an impressive arsenal. It had already destroyed one of the warships.

"Almost ready for burn!" The Admiral's voice boomed out of the comband, the background noise from the engine room rivaling the cacophony on the bridge.

His plan was suicide. She'd told him that when he'd laid it out for her, but she'd agreed to it anyway. If she were going to die, she'd rather take her fate into her own hands.

She flinched as one of the warships made a pass so close the shields kissed. A klaxon blared as the warship's weapons hit their mark. "Shields at thirty-four percent."

"Engines primed. Go, Nat!"

She darted from the weapons console to the nav station. The course was already laid in. Bracing a hand on the panel, she threw everything they had into the engines. The back of the chair shoved against her shoulder blades as the ship lurched forward, the engines whining at the rough treatment.

The ship lumbered past the cruiser and warships along a low orbit trajectory, charging ahead like a three-legged rhinoceros. The battering on the shields shifted to the aft then abruptly ceased. A quick glance at the aft cameras showed the two ally ships laying down a line of cover fire and forming a blockade in front of the Sovereign's ships.

A warning flashed as the ship's wobbling trajectory carried them closer to the atmosphere. She nudged the ship's nose out a bit to compensate for the pull of the planet's gravity. No way was she taking them down to the surface. She didn't trust the ship to survive reentry. If they were very lucky, they'd reach the opposite side of the planet without getting caught by the warships, enabling them to use the planet as a buffer. Another five seconds and the engine burst would—

The ship bucked, an ominous boom echoing up from the lower levels. Klaxons blared and a flashing light on the console indicated a hull breach...*near the engine room.*

She sent the command to seal off the compartment. "*Admiral!* Admiral, can you hear me?"

No response.

She shoved away from the console, but paused in mid-step. The vibrations from the engines had ceased. Spiders crawled up her spine as she turned to the bridgescreen.

Sure enough, the view of the planet had shifted, now filling half the image as the ship listed sideways, falling toward the planet's atmosphere.

And without power to the engines, there wasn't a damn thing she could do about it.

Abandoning the bridge, she raced to the stairway, reaching the deck for the engine room in record time. She covered her nose and mouth as she plowed through the acrid smoke that filled the corridor. The section outside the engine room was a mess of twisted metal and dangling

wires, the dim light from the emergency reserves creating
shadows that moved like ghosts at the edge of her vision.

She peered through the gloom, the smoke making
her eyes water and blurring her vision, each inhale burning
her lungs. "Admiral? Can you hear—" She broke off as a
coughing fit doubled her over.

The engine room hadn't been the nexus of the
explosion, but the damage had carried through the system,
creating the chaos blocking her path. And the Admiral had
been inside.

She shoved a broken panel out of her way and
stepped over a downed support beam, gaining a meter on
the engine room entrance. She searched for a safe path
over or through the debris, lifting another panel and setting
it aside.

A low sound reached her, making her pause. Was
that a moan? Or just the debris settling? Crouching down,
she shifted a hunk of warped metal and uncovered a pale
hand sticking out from underneath another beam.

"Admiral!" She clasped his hand, his skin warm
beneath her fingers. She checked his pulse. Weak, but his
heart was still beating. "Admiral?" No response. He was either
unconscious, or too injured to talk.

Working her fingers under the metal piece closest
to her, she lifted and pushed until she was able to see the
rest of his arm and part of his back through the haze of
smoke. The collapsed beam rested across his hip, pinning him
to the deck.

An erratic banging started up from the deck below,
reverberating through bulkhead. *The cook.* He must be trying
to get out of whatever space Tnaryt had chosen as his cell.
She needed to help him, too, but she didn't want to leave the

Admiral's side. Crazy as it sounded, she believed her
presence would keep him alive.

But she couldn't get him off this ship without help.
Tapping the comband on her forearm, she opened a channel.

Seventy-Seven

"—falling out of orbit. Do you copy?"

Kire's words came over the comm as Jonarel brought the *Starhawke*'s shuttle into the lower atmosphere.

Mya's breath caught. *Not the Starhawke*. "Kire, it's Mya. Please repeat."

"The Setarip ship's engines blew during a hard burn. The ship's falling out of orbit."

The news did nothing to ease the tension in her chest. "What about the Admiral? Is he okay?"

"Caught in the explosion. He's trapped under a downed beam. The navigator contacted Cade for help."

Mya squeezed her eyes shut. She'd been in the Fleet long enough to know the damage a downed beam could inflict. And the Admiral wasn't a young man.

She glanced at Jonarel. His large hands gripped the controls, his gaze fixed on the lush greenery of the jungle gliding below them.

She swallowed. "What do you want to do?"

He met her gaze for a fraction of a second. But it was long enough to see the turmoil in his golden eyes. "It is your choice."

She looked over her shoulder at Reynolds.

The same conflict shone in her eyes. Her friends were on the planet, too. "Your call."

Her call. She didn't want it to be her decision. Not like this. She could sense Aurora's energy, drawing her like a magnet.

Aurora was battling a Suulh with abilities that might surpass her own. She needed Mya by her side.

But without Mya's help. the Admiral would die.

Her heart told her where she needed to be. It was the most difficult choice she'd ever made.

"We're on our way."

Seventy-Eight

Kreestol was tiring.

Aurora lifted her arm to block her aunt's attack. The impact jarred her, but not enough to move her. She stepped back anyway.

Kreestol followed, her breath blowing in and out like a bellows. She swung from the shoulder, like she was wielding a club, wasting precious energy with each blow.

"I'm not your enemy." Aurora held her ground as Kreestol wound up again, retreating only when Kreestol made contact.

Kreestol's arms pinwheeled as she lost her balance on the rocks. "Yes...you...are."

"No." Aurora took another step backward, drawing Kreestol into the middle of the river. "I don't want to hurt you."

"You want...what's...*mine!*"

"I want to help the Suulh." Aurora deflected the next blow. "*All* the Suulh. Including you."

Kreestol sneered. "I...don't need...help."

"You do if you're trusting the Sovereign."

"You know...nothing!" Kreestol changed her approach, lunging in a flying tackle.

Aurora sidestepped, but not fast enough. Kreestol plowed into her, knocking her off balance and tumbling them both into a deep pool in a flail of arms and legs.

Kreestol struck first, pinning Aurora to the rocks at the bottom. She was taller, with a longer reach, which gave her leverage as she held Aurora down. Underwater, she looked like an avenging nymph, strangely untouched by the water thanks to her shield.

Aurora kicked her in the shins, but the water stole the force from her movements. Kreestol's shield pressed down from above while the rocks to either side blocked her in, making it impossible to slide out of Kreestol's grip.

Her aunt's lips contorted in a malicious grin that matched the emotions pouring out of her. Whatever her weaknesses as a fighter, she'd taken full advantage of the situation. Her shield was open to the air, allowing her to breathe while Aurora was trapped underwater.

Aurora's mind rebelled at the idea that her mom's sister was prepared to kill her. But her burning lungs made the truth undeniable.

She could see only one way out. And it would hurt her almost as much as Kreestol.

Drawing on the core of her power, she channeled energy into a blast that struck like a tsunami.

Kreestol's weakened shield deflected some of the energy, but she was no match for the assault Aurora had unleashed. Her arms flew out like wings as she fell backward, her body rigid with shock.

The agony racing through Kreestol's body echoed in Aurora's, locking her muscles and obliterating her shield. Water rushed into the void, soaking her skin. Her lungs screamed for air, but her limbs resisted her commands to move.

Fighting against the tension and pain, she forced her feet under her hips. Controlling her breathing reflex took every ounce of willpower. If she lost the battle, water would fill her lungs.

Her vision greyed at the edges as she pushed off. She broke the surface of the river with a gasp. Air and cool water flowed into her mouth, choking her and setting off a series of hacking coughs that burned her windpipe. She placed a hand on the rocks to steady herself until the coughing subsided.

Droplets of water clung to her eyelashes. She brushed a hand over her face and blinked to clear her vision, searching for Kreestol. *There.* Clinging to a rock beside the pool. Five Setarips and two guards lay in the water nearby, unmoving. What had—

"Aurora!"

The familiar voice brought her head around. Justin knelt at the edge of the opposite bank next to another prone figure.

Cade!

A strangled cry ripped through her throat. She clawed her way onto the rocks, slipping and sliding on the slick surface as she stumbled to Cade's side.

She sank to her knees and placed a hand on his chest. *No heartbeat.* Her gaze snapped to Justin's. "What—"

"He stepped into the water to help you. And collapsed."

"Did he get hit by—"

"No. It was like touching the water did something to him."

She stared at Cade, uncomprehending. Why would he collapse?

The answer came to her as she registered the aftertaste in her mouth from the water she'd ingested. *Salt.* Her breath caught, and her gaze shifted to the river. *Salt water doesn't flow in rivers.* But maybe—

She plunged her hand into the water and brought her cupped palm to her lips. More salt.

She closed her eyes as her throat tightened. By sending a massive energy charge through a saltwater river, she'd electrocuted every living being in contact with that water. Including Cade.

Her fingers clenched on the front of his tunic. He wasn't going to die. She'd stopped his heart. She would start it again.

"Stand back." She didn't wait to see if Justin followed her instructions. Placing both hands on Cade's chest, she surrounded him with her healing energy field. She could feel life within, but it was fading. Focusing on his heart, she channeled an electrical charge into the tissue.

His body arced off the ground, flopping back down with a thud. But his heart remained silent.

Resetting her hands, she struck him again. Nothing. Clutching his shirt, she gave him a hard shake. "Cade, don't you dare die on me."

But he didn't answer her.

Ignoring the tears that spilled over her cheeks, she blocked out everything but her connection to the life she sensed within him. Her energy flowed through her, driven by the elemental emotion that bound them together. Her own heart pounded like it wanted to leap out of her chest into his.

The next charge nearly levitated his entire body. But as he thumped back to the ground, an answering thump-thump started in his chest.

A sob choked her as she collapsed against him, cradling him in her arms. Her healing energy wrapped around him like a cocoon, binding him to her. She sent it flowing into his bloodstream, touching all the places she'd damaged, mending the trauma she'd caused. She pressed her ear against his tunic, listening to the steady metronome of his heart.

"Aurora?" His voice, the most beautiful sound in the universe.

She lifted her head, gazing into his green eyes. "I'm here."

He frowned, confusion evident in the lines of his face. "You okay?"

A strangled laugh broke through her lips. She couldn't help it. The question was absurd. She'd just killed him and brought him back from the dead and he was worried about *her?*

"Yeah. I'm good." She caressed his cheek, her fingers trembling. "How do you feel?"

His gaze swept down his body. He looked surprised to find himself lying down, surrounded by her energy field. "Like I touched a livewire." He turned his head to where Justin crouched on his other side. "What happened?"

Justin met her gaze. She didn't see any blame, just a question.

She cleared her throat. "You got electrocuted."

Cade's gaze swung back to her. "*Electrocuted?*"

She flinched, but didn't look away. "I didn't realize it was salt water." Her hand drifted to rest over his heart. "I'm so sorry."

Understanding finally dawned, clearing his gaze. "*Oh.*"

"Kreestol had me pinned. It was the only way I could think to—"

His hand settled over hers. "It's okay. You got away?"

"Yes."

"Kreestol?"

"She's—" She paused. She had no idea what had happened to Kreestol. Or the Sovereign.

She glanced over her shoulder at the river. And stared.

The bodies of the dead Setarips and guards still bobbed in the gentle current. But Kreestol and the Sovereign were gone.

Seventy-Nine

The Admiral's pulse had become erratic. Each change from the steady thrum made Nat cringe. How much longer could he hold out?

She glanced down the smoke-filled corridor. Cade had said Aurora's friends were sending a shuttle. But no one had contacted her.

A creak and a shudder passed through the ship, reminding her that the Admiral wasn't the only one in danger. She had *Gypsy.* And her collar was gone. She could get off the ship before it hit the atmosphere—if she had to.

She shoved the thought away and adjusted the strip of cloth she'd torn from the hem of her tunic. It covered her nose and mouth, blocking out some of the smoke, but her eyes had turned into leaky faucets.

Aurora's comband pinged, making her jump. She opened the channel. "Cade?"

An unfamiliar woman's voice came over the line. "No, this is Mya. We're approaching the starboard airlock. Can you open it from your side?"

She swallowed. She'd have to leave the Admiral. "Yes."

"Good. We'll be in position in a couple minutes."

"I'll meet you there." She shoved the rag into her pocket before slipping her fingers over the Admiral's wrist and checking his pulse again. Was it weaker? Or was her fear making it seem that way? She gave his hand a gentle squeeze. "Hang on. Help's almost here."

Saying a silent prayer that he wouldn't die in her absence, she retraced her path along the corridor to the main stairwell. The clanging from the galley grew louder as she descended. Her conscience pricked her, but she bypassed that deck to reach the cargo hold. The cook would have to wait.

A flashing indicator over the door confirmed the airlock was engaged. Luck was with her. She'd only stacked a few crates in front of it. Survival instinct and foolish hope had convinced her to keep a narrow corridor cleared to the two external airlocks. She'd just never truly believed she'd use them.

After moving the crates to the side, she tapped the command to cycle the outer door and moved to the airlock porthole so she could see into the chamber. But she was unprepared for the dark form that emerged through the open hatch.

The interior lights revealed deep green skin streaked with twisting lines, and fierce yellow eyes that burned right through her. *Kraed.* She'd heard stories, seen pictures, but never come face-to-face with one.

Two women, one dark haired, the other blonde, appeared beside the imposing figure.

The dark-haired woman stepped forward and spoke into her comband. "Are you the navigator?"

She recognized the woman's voice. "Yes. I'm Nat. You're Aurora's friend? From the ship that...glitters?" It seemed inane to ask, but the sight of the Kraed had put her on her guard.

"Yes. The *Starhawke.* Aurora's ship. This is Jonarel and Reynolds." She gestured to the blonde woman and the Kraed.

Aurora *owned* that ship? Just when she thought she had her bearings in this bizarre roundabout. She kept her gaze on the Kraed, the one Mya called Jonarel, as she keyed in the unlock command to open the inner door.

He was through the gap before it seemed wide enough to fit his bulk, looming over her like a panther about to pounce. "Where is he?"

His deep voice raised goosebumps on her flesh. She pointed. "Engine room corridor. Two decks up."

Without waiting for clarification, he disappeared down the gap in the crates before she could blink.

Mya's hand on her arm startled her.

"We need to go."

She gave herself a mental shake. *Focus, Orlov.* "Follow me."

The ship groaned like a wounded beast as they made their way to the demolished corridor. The Kraed had already moved the debris, the smoke from the explosion swirling around his large body. His muscles bulged as he lifted the beam pinning the Admiral to the deck.

Nat's jaw dropped. That beam had to weigh—

The Kraed set the beam down on the deck with a thud that vibrated through her boots.

Mya brushed past her, kneeling beside the Admiral and grasping his wrist. "Erratic pulse." Her gaze swept over him. "External and internal burns. Broken bones."

The ship shuddered as the grip of the planet's gravity tightened.

Mya glanced up, her expression tight as she turned to the Kraed. "How long do we have?"

His expression matched hers. "A few minutes."

Mya nodded, her gaze returning to the Admiral. She placed her hands on his chest, her breathing slowing, her body growing still.

Nat glanced at the Kraed. "Aren't you going to move him? He needs a doctor."

"I *am* a doctor." Mya murmured, her focus remaining on the Admiral.

But she wasn't acting like one. She hadn't brought a med kit and she wasn't doing anything to help him. "Then why aren't you treating him?" She stepped forward, prepared to move the Admiral herself if she had to, but the blonde woman wrapped a restraining hand on her arm.

"She *is* treating him." Her grip felt like iron, the look in her eyes giving no room for debate. But she cocked her head and frowned at the deck. "What's that sound?"

The banging had started up again. "The cook's below. Locked in the gall—"

Once again, the Kraed was in motion before she finished talking, leaping down the debris-strewn corridor with the grace of a cat.

The blonde woman—Reynolds, Mya had said—tugged on her arm. "Come on."

Nat resisted, unwilling to leave the Admiral when she wasn't convinced Mya was doing anything to help him.

Reynolds tugged harder. "Mya will save him. *Trust me*."

Trust. Not one of her strengths. Especially with strangers who weren't acting the way she expected. But she couldn't abandon the cook, either. He was here because of her, too.

She followed Reynolds down the ladder and along the corridor in the direction of the incessant banging. The Kraed stood outside the galley, a weapon pointed at the control panel. His eerie yellow gaze focused on her. "Anyone else onboard?"

"No. Just him."

He gave a curt nod and fired. The panel flew apart in a spray of sparks. He grasped the handle and pulled, his muscles straining the fabric of his tunic as the door ground open. The cook's hand appeared through the narrow opening. The Kraed forced the door wider.

The cook pushed his way out, like a baby exiting the womb, then reared back when he caught sight of the monster waiting outside. "*Whaaa–*"

The Kraed dropped his arms to his sides and stepped to the far wall. "We are here to help."

The cook backed against the opposite wall, his hands splayed on the smooth surface. When he met Nat's gaze, his eyes looked like two large ink spots on his pale skin.

Another shudder made the deck shift under her feet.

Reynolds placed a hand under each of their elbows, turning them toward the stairwell. "Let's go."

Nat reached the ladder first, but when she grabbed onto one of the upper rungs, the Kraed stopped her with a hand on her shoulder.

"You have a shuttle?" he asked her.

"Yes."

He gestured to the cook. "Take him and go to the planet's surface. We will contact you."

"But the Admir–"

"We will get him out. You go. *Now.*"

Nat glared at the Kraed. She wasn't about to take orders from this arrogant male. She'd brought the Admiral onboard. She'd make damn sure he made it off again.

The cook didn't share her reluctance. He practically fell onto the ladder in his eagerness to reach the cargo hold, climbing down while Nat squared off against the Kraed.

He glared right back, as immovable as a mountain.

Reynolds rested a hand on Nat's arm. "The longer you stand here, the more danger we're *all* in."

"Then let me hel—"

The Kraed growled, a menacing sound that made the hairs on her nape stand up. But she refused to budge, even though the look in his eyes told her he'd drag her to the cargo hold if necessary.

The deck shifted under her feet, like a boat going over the crest of a wave. A metallic groan and a crash from the cargo hold followed.

"We have to go!" the cook yelled at her.

The echoes of destruction from the cargo hold tipped the scales. *Gypsy* was down there, too. If she didn't want her shuttle to be part of the wreckage, she needed to disconnect from the ship before the mechanical systems failed.

She leveled a look at the Kraed before swinging onto the ladder. "I'll see you soon."

Climbing to the cargo hold took longer with the ship shimmying and bucking as the planet's gravity dragged it down. She was pretty sure Reynolds was on the ladder, following her, but she didn't bother to check. When she reached the bottom she spotted the cook scrambling over the fallen crates, making his way to the airlock outside *Gypsy*'s hatch. The overhead emergency lights glinted off the collar around his neck.

As soon as she reached him, she fished the key out of the inner pocket in her duster.

He lifted his hands to block her as she reached for his collar. "What are you doing?"

"Removing your collar."

"Wait! That's dangerous."

"So is leaving it on. It will self-destruct after the ship crashes."

His pupils widened. "It will? But won't the—"

She didn't have time to argue with him. "Don't worry." She pulled the neckline of her tunic down, revealing her bare skin. "I already removed mine. I have the key." She held it up.

The fear didn't leave his eyes, but he held still as she placed her hands around his collar. As soon as she pulled it free, his breath whooshed out like a freight whistle.

He rubbed his neck, his gaze on the collar in her hand. "I really hate that thing."

She set it on a nearby crate and turned to the control panel for the airlock. "Pretty soon it will be in pieces."

They stepped into the airlock and through *Gypsy*'s back hatch. The cook followed her into the cockpit, dropping into the co-pilot's seat while she prepped *Gypsy*'s engines.

The controls trembled in her hands. Taking off while the ship was in freefall would be a challenge. She cleared the pre-flight system checks and sent the command for the grappling arm to move them away from the ship.

It obeyed the command, but at a tenth of its normal speed.

She avoided looking out the viewport as they minced along. The planet was *way* too close. And she couldn't engage *Gypsy*'s shields until the ship let go.

Each second lasted an eternity as the shuttle trembled from the push-pull of the planet's grip and the clutch of the grappling arm. She calculated and recalculated their trajectory, adjusting as the ship plummeted.

"What's taking so long?"

She glanced at the cook. He was breathing like he'd run a marathon. "We channeled all the ship's power to the engines and shields when we did the burn. All the other systems are drained. I'll see if I can rerou–"

A jolt threw her against her restraints. Metal screamed and the running lights flickered. Bracing a hand on the console, she checked the readouts. The arm had descended, but the clamps hadn't released.

She resent the command. Nothing happened. She sent it again. And pounded on the console. "Let go of us you piece of junk!"

And then it did.

She engaged the shields and fired the engines, the abrupt change throwing her back into her seat. The ship's underbelly rolled toward them.

The cook yelled, but Nat ignored him. Battling with the controls took all her concentration as she fought to keep *Gypsy* from colliding with the ship and turning into a fireball. A near miss from the portside wing brought her heart into her throat. She swallowed as the ship swept past them.

But her maneuvers had altered their trajectory, putting them in the wrong position for reentry. The planet rushed up to grab them, the shields flashing a warning. She pushed the shuttle's nose into the correct alignment for their descent, her arms shaking from the effort of keeping the shuttle on course.

The shields held. Breathing got a little easier as they continued through the upper atmosphere. When they reached the lower atmosphere, she banked hard and pulled up *Gypsy*'s scanners.

"What are you doing?" The cook stared at her in confusion.

"Helping a friend."

She'd abandoned the ship. But that didn't mean she'd left the fight.

Eighty

The explosion had burned eighty percent of the Admiral's body and caused second-degree burns of his trachea and smoke damage to his lungs. The support beam had broken his pubic bone and one femur, although those were minor issues compared to the trauma to the muscles surrounding the area. When they'd been crushed, they'd released large amounts of potassium and myoglobin into his bloodstream that were triggering his erratic heartbeat and the onset of kidney failure.

But he was alive.

Mya surrounded him with a healing energy field, muting the pain receptors in his brain to ease his suffering. His nervous system responded like a firefly, blinking off and on.

The breaks and burns could wait. The most pressing concern was getting his bloodstream cleared of the toxic buildup to protect his heart and kidneys. Unfortunately, she had to divide her attention between treating the Admiral and continually clearing the gunk fighting to get into her own eyes and lungs. If Aurora were here, she could surround them in her shield to block out the smoke in the corridor. Mya didn't have that option.

His heartbeat thumped in a rhythm that threatened to trigger cardiac arrest. She focused on creating a barrier to the delicate electrical signals of his heart, and the rhythm smoothed out.

Pooling her energy, she poured it into the Admiral's bloodstream, isolating and surrounding the toxic substances before shifting to the damaged cells of the kidneys, working to create a solid whole from the chaos. She was fighting against time, struggling to repair the damage quicker than his body was collapsing. Almost—

"Mya?"

She jerked at the sound of Jonarel's voice, losing her concentration. When had he returned?

He crouched beside her, his features indistinct in the gloom. "We must go."

Go? She'd only just started. She shook her head. "He's not stable."

"We are out of time."

That's when she noticed the floor was shaking. No, *everything* was shaking. She glanced at the Admiral. Her energy field still surrounded him, but the loss of focus had allowed the toxins to start leaking back into his system. And moving him while his pelvis was still broken might—

The floor lurched, throwing her sideways. Jonarel caught her, wrapping his arms around her shoulders to prevent her from hitting the bulkhead or the deck.

She reached her hands toward the Admiral's chest. "I need to maintain contact."

Jonarel eased his grip, but didn't let go entirely.

She reengaged the field before meeting Jonarel's gaze. "What do we do?"

"Do not move." He shifted behind her, slipping his arms around her waist and under the Admiral's torso and knees, caging her between them. "I will carry you."

She held still, focusing on keeping the Admiral's broken bones cushioned with healing energy as Jonarel stood, taking both the Admiral and Mya with him. He pivoted, pulling her off her feet as he strode down the corridor.

The display of strength stunned her. But she grimaced when they reached the stairwell. How would they—

Jonarel didn't even pause. He placed a foot on the rungs, shifted the Admiral slightly, and guided her onto the ladder as he grasped the side rails.

"Rest your feet on mine and hold onto him."

She swallowed. It felt like stepping off a ledge, but she did as he instructed.

Jonarel took his feet off the rungs. She shrieked as they shot down like a bullet train. The landing, however, was as gentle as the lift on the *Starhawke.*

At least until the ship shuddered like it was caught in an earthquake.

Jonarel staggered but stayed upright. The scrape of something sharp against metal indicated he was using the claws in his feet to gain purchase on the deck. The emergency lights flickered as another violent tremor rocked the ship, followed by a thud and a cry of pain.

"Reynolds?" Jonarel swung in the direction of the sound, taking Mya and the Admiral with him.

"I'm okay," came the weak response. The security officer stumbled out of the darkness, cradling her left wrist. "The grappling arm for the shuttle didn't want to disengage, but I got it working. They're on their way."

The ship pitched again. Jonarel didn't let her go. Instead, he fought his way over the fallen crates to the airlock and into the *Starhawke's* shuttle, hauling Mya and the Admiral like they were a couple of pillows.

Reynolds moved to the controls for the collapsible med platform and lowered it into place. Jonarel settled the Admiral gently on top before releasing his hold on Mya and hurrying to the cockpit.

The shuttle was shaking almost as much as the ship had been. Mya braced her feet apart to keep from falling to the deck.

"What can I do?" Reynolds stood by the Admiral's head, her face lined with worry.

"Strap him in. And keep me from falling. I need to concentrate and I won't be paying attention to my surroundings."

"Got it."

Reynolds reached for the straps as Mya focused on the Admiral.

She'd lost most of the ground she'd gained. His heart and kidneys were both struggling. Ignoring the shaking of the floor, the rattle of loose items, and Reynolds's movements behind her, Mya concentrated on the Admiral's bloodstream. She dove in like a swimmer, flowing through his system as if it was her own.

Everywhere she turned cells were breaking down, connections slipping away. She shored up one area and another collapsed. She worked faster, her body and mind humming with energy, calling to the life force that drifted in the choppy waters, always just out of reach.

She felt pressure around her torso and registered vaguely that Reynolds had tethered her to the table and was supporting her from behind. The Admiral's body trembled under her fingers, shaken by the same forces that threatened to knock her feet out from under her.

But all that was background noise. The energy was all that mattered. Surrounded by its soothing touch, she called the cells back into their proper alignment. Isolating. Mending. Healing. Bringing balance. The body remembered. All it needed was guidance.

The Admiral wouldn't die on her watch.

Eighty-One

"You have to go." Cade's eyes glowed like green fire. "Don't let them get away."

Aurora stared at him. She couldn't *leave*. Not after what she'd just put him through. "I can't g—"

"You *have* to." Even in his weakened state, Cade managed to sound stern. "Stop them. End this."

Aurora's heart hammered in her chest. He meant what he said. He wanted her to go. To finish what they'd started.

Leaving him went against every instinct she had. But he was right. This was her chance to stop the Sovereign's reign of terror. To free the Suulh. Too much was at stake.

She glanced at Justin.

He nodded. "We're good here."

She drew in a slow breath, steadying her racing pulse. "Okay." Clasping Cade's hand in hers, she brushed a kiss across his lips. "See you soon."

Letting go took a supreme effort, but she forced herself to do it. With another quick glance at Justin, she took off across the river, splashing through the water and sprinting into the trees on the other side.

Her feet found a rhythm as she raced across the uneven ground. Tracking her quarry was easy. She could sense Kreestol like a dog could scent a rabbit. The closer she got, the stronger the vibration. And she *was* getting closer.

She leapt over a downed tree and raced through the undergrowth, her shield knocking obstacles out of her way. When she broke into a small clearing, she spotted three guards, Kreestol, and the Sovereign climbing over the summit of a low hill.

They must have heard her crashing through the trees, because two of the guards turned and fired. The blasts struck her shield as she tore up the incline, the field absorbing the energy like a wildfire devouring dry leaves. The guards kept firing, her shield lighting up with firework bursts, but she didn't slow down. Dropping her shoulder, she plowed into them with her shield, adding an energy surge to the assault. They flew out of her path, crashing into the underbrush.

She raced past, cresting the rise and continuing down the opposite side. Sunlight glinted off the sleek lines of the Sovereign's transport seventy meters ahead. Kreestol and the Sovereign were halfway there, but the Sovereign was limping, leaning on Kreestol and the remaining guard for support as they hurried to the ship. Apparently Aurora's blow to the Sovereign's leg had done significant damage.

Kreestol glanced over her shoulder. Her face contorted in a snarl as she released the Sovereign and planted herself like a tree, her shield swirling around her body. But it was a pale shadow of how it had looked earlier. And the anger on her face didn't match the powerful emotion Aurora sensed underneath. *Fear.*

Bracing against the agony that would follow, Aurora flung a blast of energy at Kreestol's shield, breaking through the flimsy barrier and striking her squarely in the chest. Pain exploded in Aurora's heart and lungs, making her stagger. But she'd succeeded in knocking Kreestol flat on her back, clearing a path to the Sovereign.

Struggling against the pain, Aurora leapt forward as the guard let go of the Sovereign and opened fire, lighting up her shield. The flares at such close range blinded her, but she didn't need to see. She could track the guard's terror like internal radar.

Gathering her strength, she thrust her shield forward. The distance weakened the impact, but it still struck the guard and the Sovereign with enough force to knock the weapon from the guard's hands and send the Sovereign crashing to the ground.

Aurora lunged for the Sovereign, but the guard tackled her before she could make contact. She landed with a grunt, batting away the blade the guard shoved at her throat. An energy burst sent the guard sprawling.

The Sovereign was crouched on hands and one knee a few meters away, struggling to stand.

Weapons fire from the direction of the Sovereign's ship lit up her shield again, but Aurora ignored it. Shoving to her feet, she stumbled the short distance and grabbed the back of the Sovereign's cloak.

The Sovereign screeched, a primal sound of rage unmasked by the vocal manipulation device. The cloak's hood fell back as the Sovereign twisted in Aurora's grip, revealing the face underneath.

Aurora's fingers went numb, the cloth sliding from her grip. *No. Impossible.* She recognized that face. She'd seen it a thousand times.

The hatred in the Sovereign's ice blue eyes pierced her like daggers. "Hello, old friend."

This time the voice sounded familiar. But colder than she'd ever imagined possible.

"*Reanne?*"

Reanne Beck's smile chilled her to the bone.

A guttural sound that wasn't even a word pushed up from her throat, but she didn't get any farther. A powerful blow caught her off guard, knocking her away from Reanne and slamming her into the dirt.

In her shock, she'd dropped her shield.

Kreestol's livid face was millimeters from her own. "*Don't touch her*!" she shrieked, clawing at Aurora's throat.

Instinct summoned her shield, preventing Kreestol from doing any damage, but Aurora couldn't get her muscles to move to defend herself. *This wasn't....she can't be...I just...*

The assault ended as abruptly as it had begun. Kreestol vanished like a genie in a bottle, leaving Aurora gazing at the treetops and sky.

She stared at the infinite blue, drawing in sips of air as the world spun around her.

Maybe she was dreaming. An elaborate, insane nightmare.

She turned her head in slow motion. *No. Not a dream.* There was the Sovereign's ship. And more guards at the open hatch, helping Reanne, Kreestol, and the three injured guards stumble up the gangway.

That galvanized Aurora into action. She rolled into a defensive crouch, but her body hadn't caught up with her mind. She staggered, tripping over her own feet as she stood. By the time she'd covered half the distance, the hatch had sealed and the ship had lifted off with barely a whisper.

Aurora halted in the center of the clearing. Reality slammed into her like a boulder and she dropped to her knees, staring at the ship as it glided over the trees and out of sight.

She couldn't move. Could barely even breathe.

How could the Sovereign possibly be...Reanne?

Eighty-Two

The dark shape of the Sovereign's ship rose above the treetops, stopping Cade and Justin in their tracks as it streaked across the sky.

They'd been following Aurora's trail for the past five minutes, making slow progress across the uneven ground. Tracking her hadn't been hard. She'd left a clear path of broken branches in her wake.

Cade leaned on Justin for support, his body reminding him with each step that he'd recently shaken hands with death.

"Do you think the Sovereign's onboard?" Justin asked, his gaze on the sky.

"I hope not." The Sovereign had a lot to answer for. And Cade planned to be the one asking the questions.

"Do you think Aurora's onboard?"

Cade's heart stuttered. That possibility hadn't occurred to him. It did now. But he couldn't contact her. Nat still had her comband.

Which left him with one option. He opened a channel to *Gladiator*. "Ellis to Drew."

The channel hummed, the sounds of battle booming over the connection. "...coming around our flank. Can't talk right now."

"The Sovereign's transport is headed your way."

A string of colorful curses followed. "Tell the *Starhawke* yo—" A series of loud bangs drowned her out. "*Get that warship off our tail!*" A muffled shout from Williams joined the cacophony in the background. "Gotta go," Drew said before the connection cut out.

He exchanged a worried look with Justin. The fight above wasn't going their way, either.

His comband pinged with an incoming signal. From Aurora's comband.

He opened the channel. "Nat?"

"Yeah. Was that the Sovereign's ship I just saw take off?"

Take off? Cade glanced at the sky. How could she know that? She should be on the *Starhawke* by now, or at the very least on the *Starhawke's* shuttle. How could she see what was happening on the planet? No way would Clarek or Emoto allow her on the bridge.

"Yes. Where are you?"

"In my shuttle."

"Her shuttle?" Justin murmured, looking as confused as Cade.

"Is the Admiral with you?" Cade asked.

"No. He's with Mya. And the other two. I hope."

"You *hope?*"

"They ordered me off Tnaryt's ship. They were going to get the Admiral out in their shuttle."

The tension in his shoulders eased a fraction. The *Starhawke's* shuttle was one of the safest places to be right now, especially if Mya Forrest was onboard. "Are you close by?"

"I'm approaching the landing area where I left you."

Thank you, stellar light. "Can you locate the spot where the Sovereign's transport lifted off?"

"Sure. Why?"

His throat tightened. "I don't know if Aurora's on that ship."

A beat of silence passed before Nat replied. "I'll find her."

Eighty-Three

"Kelly, get us around those warships! Gonzo, fire all weapons!"

Celia did her best to ignore Emoto's barked orders, but she was a security officer, not a communications expert. She itched to have her fingers on the weapons controls.

A small transport had appeared minutes earlier from the planet's surface and docked with the departing cruiser. The three remaining warships had created a moving wall, deflecting the *Starhawke*'s and *Gladiator*'s attempts to break through and disable the larger vessel.

Emoto glanced at her, concern in his eyes. "What about our shuttle?"

She hadn't heard from Mya or Clarek since they'd docked with the Setarip ship. "Nothing yet. I'm still trying."

"Keep at it." His expression grim, he returned his attention to the battle.

She listened to the open channel and watched the visual feed for any sign of movement. The Setarip ship was an orange ball in the distance, steadily breaking apart in the planet's atmosphere, the *Starhawke*'s sensors recording its gradual incineration. If the shuttle had disengaged successfully, they'd be appearing from that direction. If it hadn't—

The *Starhawke* shuddered as several blasts hit the shields full force.

Gonzo sent a barrage of return fire, striking one of the warships with pinpoint precision. An explosion bloomed on its port side. "One down," he called from tactical.

The ship listed toward one of its companions. The other warship was forced to adjust course to prevent a collision, opening a line of sight to the distant cruiser.

"Firing!" Beams lanced out, striking the other ship's shields, but not hard enough to punch through.

Static on the comm drew Celia's focus away from the screen. "*Mya?*" More static. "Mya? Clarek? Do you copy?"

A few syllables came through that sounded like Clarek's deep baritone, but the static broke it into unintelligible noise.

She spun to face the tactical console. "Star, can you clean up the channel?"

The Nirunoc's projected image vanished from Gonzo's left and reappeared next to the comm console. "The planet's atmosphere is interfering with the transmission."

"But it's the shuttle, right? Are they okay?"

Star's image froze as she established a connection to the shuttle using the Nirunoc equivalent of telepathy. Her lips didn't move as she spoke. "Engine functions and structural integrity within acceptable parameters." She blinked, her gaze focusing on Celia. "Jonarel, Mya, Reynolds and Admiral Schreiber are onboard."

Celia exhaled through pursed lips. They'd made it. Her gaze flipped to the bridgescreen. But the Teeli cruiser was getting away.

The crippled warship created a drifting obstacle while another swung back on a parallel line with the *Starhawke*, looking like it was preparing for a suicide collision.

"Kelly, get us a clear path," Emoto demanded.

"Workin' on it."

"*Gladiator*'s in trouble." Gonzo's voice had lost its professional detachment. He sent a new image to the bridgescreen. showing the smaller craft caught in the sights of the third warship. "Shields at fifteen percent."

Emoto stared at the image for a breath. *Gladiator* was to the aft. The Teeli ship was ahead.

Celia could read the decision in his body language before he spoke.

"Bring us about. All weapons fire on the warship." Emoto's gaze met hers.

Their quarry was going to get away.

Eighty-Four

Aurora stared at the sky long after the ship was out of sight.

Any moment now she'd wake up. That was the only logical explanation, the only one her mind was willing to accept. Just like the visions of her dad and Mya, this had to be a long, terrible dream. The other possibility, that Reanne Beck was...was...

She couldn't even finish the thought. She'd known Reanne longer than she'd known any of her friends except Mya. Longer than she'd known Cade. Or Jonarel. Or Kire.

Reanne had been a self-centered teenager and an irritating roommate, but they'd been close once. At least, until her manipulative behavior and envy had driven a wedge between them. But the slow death of their friendship didn't come close to explaining the raging inferno of hatred she'd seen in Reanne's eyes. Reanne wanted her to suffer. And she had no idea why.

The drone of an engine pulled her focus to the left. Nat's shuttle appeared above the break in the trees, its shadow sweeping over the clearing as it banked and descended, setting down near the spot recently occupied by the Sover—*Reanne*'s—ship.

Nat exited through the shuttle's back hatch and hurried over as Aurora rose to her feet. The bulge beneath the collar of Nat's tunic was gone, but her face and clothing were covered in ash. Her lips tilted up in an expression that was almost a smile. But it turned into a frown as her gaze swept Aurora from head to toe. "Are you okay?"

Such a simple question. And impossible to answer.

Cade's voice boomed out of the comband attached to Nat's forearm. "Did you find her?"

Nat lifted her arm. "Yes. She's here." Although the look of concern in her eyes remained.

"Is she alone?"

"Yes."

"Let me talk to her."

Without a word, Nat removed the comband and held it out.

Aurora stared at it. *Her* comband. The one she'd been wearing in the bar a lifetime ago.

Taking it from Nat's hand, she settled it on her arm. So familiar. So strange. Images flashed behind her eyes. Kreestol pinning her underwater. Cade lying like a corpse. Reanne...

Her arm shook, so she clasped her other hand on her wrist to control the tremors. But that didn't help with the constriction in her throat.

"Aurora? Are you there?" Cade sounded winded.

She had to clear her throat twice before any words could make it past her lips. "Yes?"

"What happened to the Sovereign?"

Aurora lifted her gaze to the sky. "She's...gone."

"*She*?" The shuffle of footsteps in the background halted. "You saw the Sovereign's face?"

Oh, yes. The image was burned into her brain like a brand.

"Aurora?"

Apparently, she hadn't said anything out loud. "We'll talk later." Much later. Right now breathing was a challenge.

Cade's silence mirrored her own. "Okay." A few more beats passed. "Are you...hurt?"

She closed her eyes. Was she hurt? "No." Hurt didn't even begin to scratch the surface of the pain burrowing through her like a nest of termites.

More silence. "Justin and I will be there soon."

Aurora closed the channel, her arms dropping to her sides like lead weights.

"You recognized the Sovereign, didn't you?"

She tipped her head toward Nat, whose gaze was focused on her like a tractor beam. No point in denying it. "Yes."

"Who is she? Someone from the Fleet?"

"No." Reanne had never shown any interest in joining the Fleet. Now Aurora understood why.

Nat folded her arms. "Is she someone the Admiral knows?"

"Yes." Someone they *all* knew. Someone—wait. "Did you say *Admiral?*"

"It's what Cade called him."

"Oh."

Nat's eyes narrowed. "I had no idea you were so well connected."

The comment triggered a hysterical laugh that Aurora choked down. Nat had no idea just how well connected she was. On both sides of the equation. "There's a lot about me you don't know."

Nat's gaze didn't waver. "And a lot I intend to find out."

Eighty-Five

Cade's comband chimed with an incoming message from *Gladiator* as he and Justin climbed a low rise. He opened the channel. "Drew?"

"The battle's over. But the Sovereign got away."

Cade gritted his teeth. Not the word he'd hoped to get. "What about the Admiral?"

"Reynolds is on her way to the *Starhawke* with Jonarel and Dr. Forrest. They're taking the Admiral to the med bay, but Reynolds thinks he'll be okay. Dr. Forrest saved his life."

Cade said a silent word of gratitude. Mya had come through for them once again. He'd be sure to thank her when he made it onto the *Starhawke*. "How about you and Williams?"

"Nothing serious. Williams can patch us up. Are you and Justin okay?"

Cade shot Justin a look before responding. He wasn't prepared to tell anyone about what had happened at the river. Not until after he'd talked to Aurora. "We're fine. Eager to get back to the ship."

"*Gladiator* will need some TLC before we can leave the system."

He'd expected that. "Start assessing the damage and let me know how much time you need for repairs."

"Will do."

Justin shifted his grip on Cade's waist as they continued up the hill. "Glad they made it through okay."

"Me, too." He hadn't lost a team member in several years. He intended to keep that streak going.

They crested the rise and Cade got his first glimpse of Aurora, standing with Nat beside Nat's shuttle. Aurora glanced in his direction but didn't move, even though he was leaning on Justin for support as they made their way down the hill.

That wasn't like Aurora. Normally she would have run to his side to help.

The worry that had woven through his stomach during their comm discussion sprouted another tendril, wrapping around his lungs like a python. Something was *very* wrong.

The breeze shifted as he and Justin approached, carrying the unpleasant odor of Nat's shuttle in their direction. He stopped within arm's reach of Aurora. She was pretty fragrant, too—not that he cared. But maybe she'd kept her distance because she thought he'd object?

Except she wouldn't meet his gaze.

"The Admiral's on his way to the *Starhawke*."

Aurora didn't react to the news, but he got Nat's full attention.

"He's going to be okay?"

"Yes. Mya's a talented doctor."

"Must be." The speculation in Nat's eyes told him she'd have questions later. But for now, she seemed inclined to let it drop. She looked him over from head to toe. "You're a little worse for wear since I last saw you. Need me to pull out *Gypsy*'s med kit?"

"I'm good for now." Not entirely true. His heart was still acting like a spastic rabbit in a cage. But he wasn't about to tell Nat that Aurora had taken him down. Not when Aurora was acting like a stranger.

Nat glanced behind him. "What about Tnaryt? And the females?"

He'd forgotten all about them. "Tnaryt's dead. The Sovereign's Setarip minions killed him."

Nat's eyes widened. "His own clutch ki—"

"No, these were Ecilam." The most lethal faction in his experience. "They killed at least one of the females, too." They'd passed her body as they'd made their way down to the river. "We encountered two others after we left you. They should be regaining consciousness soon."

Nat folded her arms over her chest. "Are we going back to fetch them?"

Cade shook his head. "Tnaryt picked this planet. I don't mind leaving the females as permanent residents." The planet had plenty of resources to survive. They were getting off easy, considering they'd imprisoned and tortured Aurora and the Admiral, and had planned to trade Aurora's life for a ship.

As if she'd heard her name, Aurora turned her head in his direction, but kept her gaze averted. "What about the Sovereign?" She spoke in a monotone. No inflection. "Did sh— did the ship—get away?"

"Unfortunately."

She nodded absently, like she'd expected the answer.

What's wrong, Rory? Was she in shock? Had the confrontation with Kreestol finally caught up with her? Or was it the accident at the river? Was she overwhelmed with guilt? If so, he'd put a stop to that as soon as he got a chance to speak to her alone. "Are you ready to return to the *Starhawke*?"

Another nod, but he wasn't even sure she was hearing him. He turned to Nat. "Can you give us a lift?"

"Sure. If you don't mind the odor." She lifted her eyebrows in silent question.

"It's not so bad." And he'd gladly sit in a garbage dump if it meant he had Aurora by his side.

"Oh, it's awful. But we're used to it."

Aurora wrinkled her nose, the only indication she was following the conversation.

Cade sat between her and Justin in the cargo area while Nat settled into the pilot's seat. A short man with a round face and greying curly hair peered back at them—the cook Aurora had mentioned—but he didn't seem inclined to strike up a conversation.

That was fine. Cade had plenty on his mind already. He slipped his fingers through Aurora's, cradling her hand in both of his. She didn't seem to notice. She remained silent and unresponsive the entire trip. Her behavior was making him jumpy as a frog.

Nat glanced over her shoulder as she guided the shuttle to where the *Starhawke* and *Gladiator* waited in orbit above the planet. "Which ship are we docking with?"

"Aurora's ship." He pointed to the *Starhawke*. He'd contacted Emoto before they'd lifted off to let him know Aurora was safe. If Emoto had been surprised he was the one making the call and not Aurora, he hadn't let on. He'd given Cade instructions for docking in one of the *Starhawke*'s shuttle bays.

"Head for the port side shuttle bay," he told Nat as they approached the ship.

She craned her neck, staring out the viewport as the ship towered over them. This time he heard her murmured comment. "One surprise after another."

More than she'd ever know.

When the shuttle touched down Cade unfastened his harness and stood. Aurora didn't move, so he unfastened hers and tugged gently on her hand to coax her to her feet.

The back hatch settled onto the deck with a thud. A second later, a dark form filled the wide opening. *Clarek*.

Without so much as a glance at Cade, he strode into the shuttle and hauled Aurora into his arms. Since Cade still had a hold on her hand, he was tugged along.

The Kraed bent his head and murmured something to her, but she didn't react. He might as well have been talking to a statue. He finally clued in to the problem, leaning back so he could see her expression.

She didn't look at him, just stared past his shoulder into the bay, although she might not have been seeing that, either.

Clarek's gaze darted to Cade, equal parts apprehension and accusation in his yellow eyes.

Cade lifted his shoulders in a shrug. He was as confused and concerned as the Kraed.

Clarek rested his palm against Aurora's cheek. "Aurora?"

"Yeah?" She still didn't look at him.

"Are you all right?"

"Fine." Her standard response. The one that usually indicated she was anything but.

Clarek shot another look at Cade before releasing her. "Mya is in the med bay with the Admiral. She is eager to see you."

Aurora nodded, taking a step forward like a wind-up toy that had been turned loose, pulling Cade with her.

Emoto stood in the shuttle bay, waiting for them. He moved into Aurora's path as she headed for the lift.

She stopped, but didn't meet his gaze, either.

He didn't move to hug her as Clarek had. The look on his face indicated he'd picked up on her strange behavior.

Instead, he rested a hand on her shoulder. "We've missed you, Roe."

She nodded in that not-quite-all-there way. "Me, too."

Emoto's gaze shifted to Clarek, who stood behind Cade like a breathing shadow.

"I told her Mya is waiting in the med bay," Clarek said.

"She's still working with the Admiral, so there's no rush." Emoto paused, as if waiting for Aurora to comment.

She didn't.

His thin brows drew together and his gaze moved to Cade. "Why don't you escort Aurora to her cabin so she can get cleaned up. I'll let Mya know she needs a little time to...unwind." His expression was as tight as his voice.

Clarek growled a warning, but Cade was happy to comply. Getting Aurora alone in her cabin would give him an opportunity to find out what had triggered her catatonic state.

Emoto lifted a hand to stop Clarek from following them as Cade led Aurora to the lift. She didn't offer any resistance, stopping when he stopped, walking when he walked.

When the lift reached the command deck, he guided her down the curving path to her cabin. The door parted soundlessly as they approached. He drew her through the main room and into the bathroom that adjoined her sleeping nook. "You're home."

She didn't answer, that same vacant look in her eyes. Not moving. Not reacting, her gaze on something he couldn't see. *What had happened after she'd left the river?*

The stench from her clothes intensified now that they were in a smaller space. At least he could do something about that. He carefully removed the filthy garments and the coil of wire she'd used as a hair tie, tossing the clothes in the sanitizer. Chances were good she'd never want to wear any of them again, but she could make that decision later.

His gaze traveled over her bare skin, looking for any sign of trauma that might have caused her odd behavior. But he couldn't find a single mark or blemish. If she'd suffered a physical attack while chasing down the Sovereign, she'd already healed herself.

He stripped off his own soiled clothing, dumping it in the sanitizer with hers before tugging her under the warm shower spray. As soon as the water touched her hair, she let out a gusty sigh, her eyes closing and her head falling back. But she continued to stand like a statue as the water sluiced over her body, making no move to scrub the grime from her skin and hair.

Knots twisted in his stomach. It was like she'd disconnected from her body, her mind off in a distant sphere he couldn't reach.

But if her body was all he had to work with, he'd start there. With infinite care, he slid his fingers through the tangles and knots of her hair, separating the golden strands, lathering and rinsing them until they glided over his hands like silk. He moved on to her skin, stripping away the accumulated grime, the citrusy scent of the soap she loved replacing the musky stench.

He was kneeling in front of her, running the soap along her calf and ankle, when she finally spoke.

"Don't."

He glanced up. The expression on her face kicked him in the ribs. No more vacant stare. Instead, she looked...haunted. There was no other word for it. Like the monsters of her worst nightmares were standing just behind him, waiting to drag her into the darkness.

He stood, reaching to cradle her face in his hands. "I'm here."

She avoided his touch, sidestepping out of the spray and onto the wood floor, her eyes grey. Barren. "Don't," she repeated, grabbing a towel from the rack and wrapping it around herself like a suit of armor.

When he moved to follow her, she thrust out a hand to stop him. "Don't. Just, don't."

He stood like she'd nailed him to the floor.

She backed to the archway, the dead look never leaving her eyes. "I'm sorry." She disappeared around the corner.

He forced himself to let her go.

Eighty-Six

Mya sensed Aurora before the doors to the med bay parted. The touch was achingly familiar, yet muffled, as though Aurora was caught in a thick fog.

She appeared in the doorway, dressed in a navy tunic and leggings that contrasted with her pale skin. Her hair was damp, the long strands pulled back in a haphazard braid.

She halted several meters away, her gaze slowly lifting to meet Mya's. The green that normally sparkled with vibrancy was flat and dull, lifeless. It was like staring at a corpse. "Hello, Mya."

That look knocked the air out of Mya's lungs. "Hello, Sahzade." Kire had alerted her to Aurora's strange behavior in the cargo bay, but seeing it firsthand raised the hair on the nape of her neck.

She longed to wrap Aurora in a healing embrace, but that dead look stopped her. Instead, she visually checked her from head to toe for any signs of injury. Nothing. Whatever trauma she'd endured hadn't impacted her physically.

Guilt burrowed under Mya's skin. She'd been on her way, so close to reaching her. She'd felt her need, her struggle. But she'd chosen to save the Admiral instead. It had seemed like the right decision at the time. Now, she wasn't so sure.

Aurora took a step toward the med platform where the Admiral rested. She moved with all the grace of a tin soldier. "How is he?"

"Healing. I've repaired most of the physical damage but I'm keeping him under heavy sedation while his body adjusts. He needs time to process the trauma he's been through."

Aurora's gaze remained on the Admiral. "What happened to him?"

"He was caught in an engine room explosion and got trapped under a downed support beam."

"How did he get here?"

"Jonarel, Reynolds and I took a shuttle to the ship." She cleared her throat. Might as well admit her failure. "Originally we were heading down to help you, but—"

"I'm glad you saved him."

The words should have comforted her. They didn't. "I'm sorry, Sahzade. I should have been there for you."

Aurora made a non-committal sound. The dead expression on her face remained unchanged, like she'd unplugged from her emotions. What a chilling thought. As an empath, Aurora lived in emotions.

"Can you tell me what happened while you were on the planet?" *And why you've turned into a zombie?*

Aurora's lips thinned, the first sign of an emotional reaction. "I met my aunt."

A stone dropped into Mya's stomach, the image Aurora had shown her of the blonde woman flashing before her eyes. "That was Libra's *sister?*"

Aurora nodded.

"But...but..." She couldn't seem to get the words out. *Libra had a sister? Why hadn't she told them?* "Do you think Libra knows? About your aunt?"

"She must. Kreestol blames my mom for abandoning her."

Kreestol. The Suulh name rang bells in the recesses of her memory. Questions popped up faster than she could process them. "Why was she there? Because of you?"

"In a way." Something dark flickered in Aurora's eyes as she met Mya's gaze. "She's the Sovereign's bodyguard."

"A bodyguard?" That certainly fit with what they'd seen at Citadel. And unlike the Suulh training on the beach, Aurora's aunt would have the ability to shield, though she wouldn't be as strong. "Is the Sovereign the other cloaked figure?"

"Ye—"Aurora frowned, a spark of life returning to her eyes. "How did you know she was cloaked?"

"We followed them here."

"You *saw* her? On the Suulh homeworld?"

The horror on Aurora's face wasn't an improvement over the blank stare. "Yes, although I didn't know who they were at the time." And she was still missing some pieces. "Why would your aunt serve as a bodyguard for the person who's imprisoning the Suulh?"

"She's been manipulated. Lied to. And she doesn't know about the cages. Or the Necri."

"My grandmother does."

Aurora's lips parted in surprise. "You saw your *grandmother?*"

"I didn't just see her. I talked to her."

Aurora blinked rapidly a few times. "What did she say?"

Mya's shoulders crept up toward her ears. "She was terrified the Teeli would capture me. She ordered me off the island."

"And you left her?"

"I didn't have a choice. We had to track the ship."
But the ache in her chest argued the point.

Aurora chewed on her lower lip. "Your grandmother.
She wasn't...caged, was she?"

"No. None of them were. But the island was heavily
guarded."

"So they were still prisoners?"

"Yes." Her grandmother had made that clear.
"Although most of them don't seem to know it. They
seem...happy."

"Happy." Aurora echoed, her gaze turning inward.
She was holding something back. Something that was eating
her from the inside out.

"What about this Sovereign? You said *she*. Do you
know who she is?"

The corners of Aurora's mouth tilted up, but it
wasn't a smile. It looked more like a silent scream. "An old
friend."

Mya frowned. "Old friend?"

Aurora returned her gaze to the Admiral. "Yes. And
she's devoted her entire life to destroying me."

A chill chased up Mya's spine as a horrible
premonition scratched at the back of her mind, demanding
to be let in. "Who is she?" she whispered.

Aurora's lips parted, but no words came out. Instead,
an image flashed into Mya's mind, as clear as if she'd
projected it into the room. A dark cloak with the hood
thrown back. A woman with straight brown hair streaked
with a shock of white at the crown. And ice-blue eyes so
filled with hatred they glowed.

Mya's breath hissed through her teeth. "*Oh...Sahzade.*"
It wasn't possible. Logic wouldn't allow her to accept it. And

yet, the image was undeniable. She'd seen that face too many times to doubt. *"How?"*

"I don't know." Aurora swallowed audibly, her fingers clutching the med platform like she was holding onto the lip of a volcano.

Mya made it around the med platform in two strides. She gathered Aurora close and engaged her energy field, wrapping them in its healing cocoon.

Aurora curled against her shoulder, the same way she used to as a child whenever Libra had scolded her for some misdeed. She didn't make a sound, but moisture soaked through the fabric of Mya's tunic.

"I'm here, Sahzade," she murmured, stroking her hand over Aurora's back. But the tension she found there didn't ease. Instead, it spread, taking up residence between her own shoulder blades. *Reanne Beck. How could one of the cloaked figures on the Suulh homeworld possibly have been Reanne Beck?*

Eighty-Seven

Aurora leaned into the comfort Mya provided, though it barely scratched the surface of the walls of guilt and regret closing in on her from all sides.

Reanne *hated* her. Why, she didn't know, but with Reanne, the list of possibilities was endless. Her mind was a complicated maze Aurora had never figured out. Eventually, she'd given up.

Now her failure hung like an anchor around her neck.

She pulled out of Mya's embrace, swiping her hands across her wet cheeks. Tears were a luxury she couldn't afford, especially since she had only herself to blame. "I'm the reason," she murmured, more to herself than Mya. "This is my fault. All of it."

"What do you mean your fault?" Mya folded her arms over her chest. "The reason for what?"

"For this." She gestured to the Admiral. "For the Suulh. The cages. The attacks. Gaia. Burrow. Everything. I'm the lynchpin. My connection to Reanne is responsible for everything that's happened."

"How can you say that? We don't even know how Reanne got involved with the Teeli in the first place."

"Doesn't matter. Reanne's in charge. And she made it very clear that I'm her target."

Mya's eyes widened. "You *talked* to her?"

"Yes. Before I knew who she was." And before she'd realized her own culpability. Back when she'd believed she was on the side of the right.

"What did she say?"

"She wanted to punish me. Cage me."

Mya paled. "She wanted to turn you into a Necri?"

Aurora paused. Had she? "I don't think so." Reanne had mentioned making the manacles a permanent condition of her captivity. That didn't sound like she planned to let Aurora out of whatever cage she'd devised. "Or maybe that's her end game. Mostly, she wants me to suffer."

"Why?"

Aurora spread her hands. "Your guess is as good as mine. But her hatred is driving her actions. She targeted Gaia because she could make sure I was sent there. Then she followed us to Burrow. Now here. She's hunting me. *Just* me. And she won't stop until she takes me down."

Mya stared at her, her arms dropping to her sides as she leaned against the med platform. "So...what do we do?"

"I don't know." She glanced at the Admiral. She could really use his advice right now. But he was in no condition to counsel her. She met Mya's gaze. "Any suggestions?"

Eighty-Eight

Nat would never take cleanliness for granted again.

She lifted her hands to her face and breathed in. A faint citrus scent reached her without a trace of the stench that had followed her like a shadow for the past year.

She ran her hands over the soft fabric of the tunic and leggings she wore. Her own clothes were still being sanitized, but the *Starhawke's* security officer, a strikingly beautiful woman named Cardiff, had brought her a set of clean clothes to wear in the interim. She'd had to roll up the cuffs on the leggings and tunic, since Cardiff was half a head taller than she was, but she was incredibly grateful for the loan. Clean clothes were a luxury she hadn't experienced in a long time. And an actual *shower...*

Her breath flowed out on a sigh as she gazed at her reflection in the mirror. Same dark hair, same brown eyes, but for the first time in what felt like decades, she was coming back into focus.

Her stomach rumbled, reminding her she hadn't eaten in a while. But food could wait. Now that she wasn't a walking stink bomb, she wanted to track down the Admiral and make sure he was okay.

It might take some effort, though. This ship was unlike anything she'd ever seen. Locating the med bay might require a bit of ingenuity. She'd been too busy fighting for her life to pay much attention to the unusual ship during the battle, but flying *Gypsy* into the shuttle bay had been a surreal experience. The ship had floated in the blanket of stars like an ice sculpture, all graceful curves and vague outlines.

She brushed her slippered foot over the planked flooring of the deck, something fitting a tropical island, not a starship. The walls, too, were out of place, the contoured wood surface making the cabin feel like the hollowed-out interior of a massive tree. It went against every expectation. Why would anyone create a ship that looked like it belonged in a forest, not out in space?

Yet another mystery to add to the long list regarding Aurora, her ship, and her strange crew. If she went exploring, maybe she'd get some answers.

She padded over to the door, but it didn't open. She looked for a control panel, but didn't see one.

"May I help you with something?"

The woman's voice made her jump, the sound coming from everywhere and nowhere, like the entire cabin was lined with speakers.

"Uh...yeah. I want to go to the med bay. To check on the Admiral."

"One moment, please."

The voice didn't sound like Cardiff, or any of the other crewmembers she'd met. Did Aurora have another security officer who monitored the guest cabins?

While she waited, she surreptitiously searched the area for cameras, but didn't spot any. However, that didn't mean anything. The design of the ship could hide a plethora of secrets.

The voice returned, again seeming to come from everywhere. "Follow the corridor to the lift. Lieutenant Cardiff will meet you there and take you to the med bay."

"Um...okay." The doors parted, a soft light glowing to her left. She headed in that direction.

Cardiff stood outside the open doors of the lift, waiting for her. "Feeling better?" she asked as they stepped inside.

"Much better. Thanks for the loan." She gestured to the clothes.

"You're welcome." The lift started up. "We should have your things back to you before the next cycle. Star's having to make some adjustments for the... challenge...they posed. I'm not sure if she'll be able to mend the torn tunic or not."

"That's okay." She'd be replacing those clothes as soon as she had money in her pocket. "Please thank Star for me." She hadn't met anyone with that name. Maybe she was their maintenance and cleaning person? Whoever she was, she did a great job. The ship was spotless.

The lift halted, the doors opening to reveal the glassed-in entry of the med bay. She spotted Aurora talking to Mya at the back of the room. The Admiral lay on a nearby med platform.

Nat followed Cardiff into the room.

"But I don't—" Aurora stopped mid-sentence, glancing over her shoulder.

The look on her face brought Nat to a halt. "I'm sorry. Are we interrupting?" She backed up a step. "I just wanted to check on the Admiral."

Aurora exchanged a look with Mya before focusing on Nat. "It's okay. Come on in."

Aurora sounded more like herself and less like an automaton, but Nat still hesitated. It felt like she'd interrupted something important. But when Aurora and Mya stepped away from each other, it became clear the two women weren't going to continue their conversation.

Nat joined Aurora by the med platform. The Admiral didn't react to their presence, so he was either unconscious or asleep. At least the monitor showed a steady heartbeat. And the burns on his skin looked a lot less severe than she remembered. She glanced at Mya. "How is he?"

She smiled, although it looked forced. "Recovering. He'll be fine in a few days."

A few days? Nat realized her mouth was hanging open. She snapped it shut. An injury like this usually took weeks or even months to heal. What exactly had Mya been doing to the Admiral while the rest of them were below decks?

Nat's gaze shifted between Mya and Aurora. They both struck her as unusual in a way she couldn't quite define. They were certainly more than what they claimed. This ship was proof of that.

Right now, they wore identical expressions of professional detachment. *Fleet Face*, her former captain Mirko had called it. Which didn't bode well if you were a smuggler. Or a thief.

But Nat had been in the trenches with Aurora. She was hoping that counted for something. So far, the crew had treated her like a guest, not a criminal. "What's our next move?"

Aurora blinked slowly, as if pondering the question. "I'm not sure." She glanced at Cardiff. "What's our status?"

"We came through relatively unscathed. Clarek's in the engine room running diagnostics. Ellis's ship took a lot more damage, including to the jump drive. Drew indicated it would be a few hours before they could leave the system."

Aurora focused on Nat. "What about *Gypsy?* Do you need help with repairs?"

She shook her head. She'd run diagnostics before leaving the shuttle in the bay. While *Gypsy* would benefit from a complete hose down to get rid of the smell, structurally she was sound. "She's good to go."

"Then where would you like us to take you?"

Now it was Nat's turn to blink. Aurora was going to let her go? No recriminations? No punishment for taking her hostage? No payback for the abuse she'd suffered at Tnaryt's hands?

All three women looked at her expectantly, no hidden agendas written on their faces. Nat's heart began to pound. She was going to be back in control of her life. The concept was exhilarating...and terrifying. "That's a good question."

She wasn't eager to return to Gallows Edge, even though it was a logical choice. She could find work there, sign on with a freighter or any other ship that needed a pilot. But there were too many dark corners and dead ends. And way too many bad memories...

In a nanosecond her mind leapt back in time. To the day she'd lost her freedom to Tnaryt. To sand dunes stretching out to the horizon. To a ship buried and forgotten. And to an enemy turned friend who'd entrusted her with his life.

The answer to Aurora's question was suddenly crystal clear.

"Troi. I want to go to Troi."

Eighty-Nine

Cade had been flattened by a herd of elephants. At least, that's how he felt. His body ached from the tip of his nose to the bottom of his big toe, but that was nothing compared to the pain in his heart. Both literally and figuratively.

Aurora had shocked him at the river, but when she'd rejected his efforts to comfort her, she'd made him bleed.

He hadn't followed her out of the bathroom. He'd learned years ago the futility of prolonging a confrontation when she called a halt. He would have only pushed her further down her path. Instead, he'd quickly finished his shower while listening to the sounds of her getting dressed in the other room. He'd hoped by the time he came out she'd have calmed down so they could talk about whatever was troubling her. No such luck. The cabin had been empty.

Walking over to the wardrobe, he pulled out a set of clothes. They'd been sharing her cabin since they'd left Azaana, but her behavior made him wonder if his privileges were about to be revoked. He wouldn't allow that to happen without a fight.

"Star, where's Aurora?"

Star's voice filled the room. "In the med bay."

That was good news at least. If anyone could bring Aurora out of the funk she'd fallen into, it would be Mya.

It also meant he couldn't make a trip to the med bay to have Mya check out the extent of the damage Aurora had caused. He needed Mya's healing talents to clear the aches and flutters in his chest. But he needed her help with Aurora even more. His trip to the med bay would have to wait.

In the meantime, he needed a distraction from his own thoughts or he'd go insane. "Where's my team?"

"Working on repairs to *Gladiator*, although Dr. Williams is on his way to see you."

"Oh." He should have expected a visit from Tam. "Will you let him in when he gets here?"

"Of course."

He didn't bother pulling on a tunic, since he'd have to take it off when Tam arrived. Instead, he walked into the front room and sank down on the couch. He groaned as the softness embraced him. After lying on *Gladiator*'s utilitarian cots, he'd forgotten what real comfort felt like.

He must have closed his eyes and drifted off, because the next thing he knew, Tam was standing beside him, running a bio scanner over his chest. He started to sit up but Tam stopped him.

"Relax. Your body needs the rest."

Cade let his head fall back against the cushions but watched the movement of the scanner. "What's the verdict?"

Tam's brows lifted. "Verdict? You're lucky you didn't have both feet in the water. Otherwise, I'd be conducting a post mortem." He crouched on the floor and inspected Cade's feet. The energy had entered and exited there, leaving some nasty burns. He pulled out an injector and pressed it against Cade's leg. A sharp pinch was followed by a soothing coolness. He repeated the process on the other leg. "That should help with the pain, at least until you get down to see Mya." His gaze searched Cade's. "Is there a reason you're not there now?"

"Aurora. She needs some time with Mya. Alone."

"I see." He set the scanner on the coffee table. "Justin said Aurora was acting a little odd. How is she?"

Cade shrugged, a sigh escaping his lips. "Freaked out. Closed down. Avoiding me like the plague. And I don't know why."

"That last part's understandable, considering. Guilt's a powerful motivator."

"She didn't mean to hurt me."

Tam's expression softened. "Of course she didn't. But intentionally or not, she did. And she knows it."

And now she was beating herself up for it. Talk about a no-win scenario. Cade stood, grabbing the shirt he'd tossed on the couch earlier. "Am I cleared to work on the ship?" It seemed like as good a distraction as any. And it would give him a chance to check in with Gonzo and Reynolds. He wanted to find out what had happened during the *Starhawke*'s trip to Teeli space.

"If you can handle the walk down, you're cleared to *supervise* the work. But no physical labor until Mya's given you the okay."

As tired as he was, he didn't argue. Williams filled him in on the repair plan while they took the lift down to the cargo deck.

Gladiator was connected to the *Starhawke* via a short airbridge attached to the airlock on *Gladiator*'s port side. Voices drifted out to them as they stepped through the open hatch.

"—dressed in this skintight outfit."

"And Cade didn't—"

The conversation between Drew and Gonzo halted as Gonzo spotted Cade. "Hey, buddy!" He made his way over and slapped Cade on the back. "Nice ship you got here."

Cade put a hand on the bulkhead to keep from hitting the floor. He was a lot weaker than he'd thought. "Thanks."

"Bet Weezel's hurting after seeing this baby lifted. Drew was filling me in on the moves Captain Hawke put on him."

A few more drops of blood leaked out of Cade's heart. "Yeah. She was...terrific."

The mirth left Gonzo's face. "Is something wrong? She's not hurt, is she?"

That was the question of the hour. "I'm not—"

"Cade?" Justin appeared in the corridor from the cockpit. "Aurora just contacted me. She wants the two of us to head to the conference room."

"Did she say why?"

Justin shook his head.

"Then let's go find out."

Ninety

Mya couldn't stop thinking about the look in Aurora's eyes when she'd walked into the med bay.

Aurora was strong. Resilient. A survivor in every sense of the word. If she got knocked down, she found a way back onto her feet. Always.

But not today. Today, she'd been beaten by Reanne Beck. Ironically, in failing to capture Aurora, Reanne had done something far worse. She'd taken her spirit.

Aurora had called a meeting with Cade, Jonarel, Kire, Justin and Mya to discuss their next steps. But as Mya walked into the conference room, the scene looked more like the start of a boxing match than a meeting.

Jonarel and Kire stood on one side of the carved wood table, close to the door Mya had come through, their arms folded and shoulders hunched as they talked in low tones. They kept glancing at Cade and Justin, who stood in a similar position on the opposite side of the room.

Mya's steps faltered when she spotted Cade. His energy field was a wreck. Damaged tissue showed throughout his body, concentrated at his heart and down his legs. The pattern of injury was consistent with electrocution, though she saw evidence of internal healing, too. Had Aurora done that? If so, when? And why hadn't Cade come to the med bay to get treated as soon as he'd arrived onboard?

When this meeting was over, she'd march him down there herself if she had to. And get some answers.

Both Cade and Jonarel turned their attention to her, their faces a matched set of hope and concern.

"Aurora is not with you?" Jonarel asked, his golden gaze troubled.

She hadn't noticed Aurora wasn't in the room. She was usually the first one to arrive. "No. She left the med—"

The conference room doors parted as Aurora entered. Normally when she walked into a room, the tension level dropped. She had a calming effect on people, which was one of the traits that made her such an excellent leader. But this time, the air coiled like a spring.

"Please be seated." Her voice was back to the robotic quality it had had when she'd arrived at the med bay.

To Mya's surprise, neither Jonarel nor Cade moved closer to Aurora. Instead, they sat across from each other with Kire and Justin beside them. Mya claimed the seat to Aurora's right, but Aurora remained standing, gripping the back of her chair and staring at a spot on the table half a meter in front of her.

"Thank you all for coming. I called you here because I've learned the identity of the person responsible for the attack on Gaia and Burrow."

Murmurs rose from both sides of the table.

Her gaze shifted, meeting Mya's. "And from what Mya discovered while visiting the Suulh homeworld, this person is also in charge of the Teeli fleet and at least two factions of the Setarips."

Aurora's chest rose and fell with her rapid breathing, her gaze boring into Mya. Her throat worked, like her words were struggling to break free.

Mya rested a hand on Aurora's, creating an energetic connection that eased the tension a fraction.

Aurora's voice grew stronger. "The Setarips and Suulh know this person as the Sovereign. But we know her as Reanne Beck."

Sharp inhales were followed by an explosion of male voices.

"What the hell—"

"No. That cannot—"

"*Reanne?* How could—"

"Oh, Roe—"

Aurora lifted her free hand, her voice carrying over the din. "It's true. I confronted her while I was on the planet."

Cade smacked his palm on the table. "That was *Reanne* under the cloak?" Fire burned in the syllables of her name. "You're absolutely sure?"

Aurora turned her head slightly in his direction, though her gaze remained on Mya. "Yes. I caught her after I left you. There's no doubt. It's her."

"*Reanne*." Jonarel's low growl made a promise of retribution. "How did she escape?"

Aurora still didn't look away from Mya. It was as though she needed that visual connection to keep herself upright. "I got...distracted."

Pulverized was a better word for what she saw in Aurora's eyes. And while Aurora's body had returned safely to the *Starhawke*, her spirit was clearly still in pieces on the planet's surface.

"But how can it be Reanne?" Kire asked. "How could she get power over the Teeli fleet? For that matter, how did she even come in contact with the Teeli in the first place? And the Setarips?"

Mya broke eye contact with Aurora and glanced at Kire. "I have a theory on that." It was a radical idea, one she wouldn't have considered if she hadn't spent hours observing the Teeli and Suulh on the homeworld. But it fit with the image of Reanne Aurora had seared into her mind.

She turned back to Aurora. "Did Reanne ever tell you how she got the white streak in her hair?"

Aurora's brows drew down. "She was born with it."

"She also never knew her father, correct?"

Aurora's frown deepened. "What are you getting at?"

"Do the math. She's three years younger than you. The first Teeli envoys arrived on Earth when you were two." She rested her elbows on the table. "What if her father's a Teeli?"

Aurora blanched, all the blood draining out of her face like she'd been bitten by the galaxy's biggest leech. She tightened her grip on the back of the chair.

"Half-Teeli?" Justin looked between Mya and Aurora. "Is that even genetically possible?"

"The Teeli are humanoid. Sexual relations are certainly possible. We don't know much about their internal physiology, and we certainly don't know anything about their genetic code. Whether a Human-Teeli pairing could produce a child is unknown. It's unlikely, but it would explain Reanne's connection to the Teeli."

"And if her father was part of the initial envoy, he would be a person of great standing in the Teeli hierarchy," Kire said. "Someone in control of vast resources."

Cade held up a hand. "But even if your speculation is correct, how did Reanne get herself into a position of power? Why would the Teeli take orders from her?"

Mya had a theory on that, too. "The same way she's gotten everything else in her life. Manipulation."

"Manipulation?"

Mya nodded. "I've never met anyone who can manipulate others the way Reanne Beck can. I learned to avoid her early on because I never felt like myself around her. Aurora's the only one who seems immune to her influence."

Aurora's brows lifted. "Immune?"

"Uh-huh. Your behavior never changed, even when the two of you were roommates and spending so much time together. But the rest of us always acted differently when she was around." Mya's gaze settled on Cade.

He sat up straighter. "Are you implying Reanne manipulated me?"

"I'm not implying anything. You and Aurora were getting along fine until Reanne returned from her study abroad program. That's when you started fighting."

Cade's shoulders tensed, his fingers gripping the tabletop as he stared at Aurora. "Is that true?"

She flinched, refusing to meet his gaze. "We had our first fight a couple hours after I introduced you to her."

He frowned. "I remember the fight. But—" He broke off, his eyes widening. "She said it like a joke. Now that she'd returned, that you'd dump me and spend time with her instead. But I got angry with you, not her." A muscle in his jaw twitched. "For some reason her comment made sense at the time."

"She affected Jonarel, too," Kire said. "He wasn't a fan of you two dating, but he didn't get aggressive until Reanne came into the picture."

Jonarel growled. "That is ridi—"

"Is it?" Kire challenged. "She was the one you were talking to the night you decided to go pummel Cade. Are you saying she *wasn't* feeding your anger?"

He glowered, clearly unable to give an answer.

Justin spoke up. "So you're saying Reanne has the ability to alter people's behavior? How?"

Mya spread her hands. "I don't know. If I'm right that she's half-Teeli, that might be part of it. The Teeli have certainly done a masterful job of manipulating the Suulh."

"Is that what you found out? At the homeworld?" Cade asked.

"Pretty much. The Suulh haven't been destroyed, but they're under the control of the Teeli without even realizing it. We saw Reanne there, though we didn't know it at the time."

Cade cleared his throat. "So how does her obsession with Aurora fit into all this?"

Aurora stared at the wall, her expression bleak. "She hates me."

"Hates you? Why? You used to be friends."

Aurora shrugged, the gesture so at odds with the tension in every line of her body.

Cade sank against the back of his chair like his spine had gone liquid. "She's insane."

No one denied it.

Jonarel rose from his chair, his biceps flexing. "Then we will destroy her."

Mya's throat tightened at the finality in his voice.

Kire stood, too. "I understand the impulse, but even if that's the course we wanted to take, she's not exactly easy to get to. She has the force of the Teeli fleet and untold Setarips behind her. We only have the *Starhawke*."

Jonarel's golden eyes glowed. "We have much more than that. We will—"

"No." The word was soft from Aurora's lips, but it cut Jonarel off like a knife. "Right now, the most important thing is getting Cade's team and the Admiral back to Earth. *They* can work on tracking down Reanne. Find out how much she's infiltrated the Council and the Fleet."

"And what will *we* do?" Jonarel's claws peeked out from the pads of his fingers.

"We will go to Stoneycroft." She faced Mya, her gaze as flat as a still pond. "Our parents deserve to know the truth."

Ninety-One

After the conference room cleared out, Aurora remained by the viewport, staring at the planet hovering in the distance.

Cade watched her closely. During the discussion, she'd reminded him of a tightrope walker, refusing to look down for fear she'd fall. Now, she resembled a turtle drawing into her shell.

He wanted to hold her, comfort her. But her body language told him such a move would not be welcome. "Aurora?"

She turned away from the viewport, finally meeting his gaze. "Yes?"

The lack of emotion in her eyes tore at his heart. He trembled from the effort of keeping his feet planted. "How can I help you?"

The muscles of her jaw flexed. "You can go, too."

He stared at her. "*Go?* Why?"

Her lower lip trembled. Not much, but it belied the flat look in her eyes. "You aren't safe with me."

"Safe?" He took a step forward. "What are you talking about?"

She took a step back, her breathing growing uneven. "I stopped your heart."

Oh. He'd been wondering when they were going to get to that. Right now, apparently. "By accident. Wrong place, wrong time." He took another step but halted when she backed up. "You also got my heart beating again." Right now, it was beating furiously.

"I could have killed you."

"But you didn't." According to Justin, she'd gotten his heart going again in less than a minute. So technically, he hadn't died. Sort of. "It wasn't your fault. Rivers are usually fresh water. You had no way of knowing this one would conduct an electrical charge."

"Doesn't matter."

"Of course it does." He spread his hands, palms up. "You weren't trying to kill anyone."

"But I *did*." The flatness disappeared, but the heartbreaking look that replaced it wasn't an improvement. "You could be dead! Because of *me*!"

Take it slow, Ellis. He'd known she was upset, but her reaction seemed extreme. What could he say to soothe her? How could he absolve her when she was determined to punish herself? "I don't blame you."

"*I* blame me." She backed toward the door. "You should, too."

He followed her. "I don't want to."

She held her palms out like a traffic cop. "I'm dangerous."

"No, you're not."

"Yes, I am. I've been fooling myself. Believing my ability was a gift. A challenge at times, but still a gift. It's not. It's a curse. One that brings destruction to everyone around me."

He threw his hands up. "How can you say that? Your abilities have saved countless lives. Including mine!"

"What about Reanne?" she fired back. "What do you think she'll do if she learns we're together? Assuming she doesn't know already. Do you honestly believe she won't target you to get to me?"

She had him there. It was exactly the kind of vindictive move Reanne would make.

"She might even decide to kill you just to torture me. I can't allow that to happen."

That got his ruff up. "Can't allow?" He took a step closer. "You can't control what Reanne does or doesn't do."

"Maybe not, but being with me puts you in unnecessary danger."

He couldn't believe what he was hearing. "I have a news flash for you. Danger has been part of my job ever since I left the Academy. Reanne or no Reanne, my life's continually on the line. Nothing's changed."

"But that's your job. You've chosen it. If you stay with me, you're in danger for no reason."

"No reason?" Heat surged into his face. "Are you insane? Being with you is all the reason I need." He reached for her, but she jerked back like his arm was a viper.

"Don't touch me!"

The words didn't stop him. The terror in her voice did. "Aurora...please. We can—"

"No." She backed until the doors parted soundlessly behind her. She stepped across the threshold. "As soon as your repairs are finished, I want you off my ship."

Ninety-Two

The soft lights in the med bay cast a glow over the still form lying on the med platform near the back wall.

Aurora approached silently. No reason to disturb the Admiral when he needed rest.

She watched the gentle rise and fall of his chest. His cheeks were pale, half-moons shadowing his eyes, but his skin looked healthy again, the burns fading away. His body was healing. In another day or two he'd be back on his feet.

And that counted for a lot.

She caught the scent of lavender, one of the essential oils Mya favored for patients recovering from trauma. She breathed it in, allowing the familiar aroma to flow over her, too.

She needed the comfort it provided, now more than ever. She'd spent the past twenty-eight hours in a self-imposed exile from the rest of the crew. The confrontation with Cade stabbed her with every breath, but she'd done what she had to do. His life was in danger as long as he was with her. He knew it even if he didn't agree with her decision. The only way to keep him safe was to put as much distance between them as possible.

The Admiral let out a sigh, as if he agreed with her.

Her gaze drifted over his familiar features. She'd known him half her life and yet, hadn't really known him at all. Their relationship while she'd been a cadet and an officer didn't jibe with how she saw him now. Back then, he'd been a paragon, an authority figure she'd respected and trusted, albeit one who'd lied to her with the best of intentions.

But on Tnaryt's ship, their circumstances had changed the dynamic. They'd become equals—friends—in a way she'd never expected. Which begged the question—where did they go from here?

His eyes fluttered open, a small frown appearing as he met her gaze. He drew in a breath that set off a hacking cough.

She fetched a glass of water and helped him sit up so he could sip it.

"Thank you." His voice scraped like sandpaper. He relaxed against the pillows with a sigh. "Is it...really that...bad?"

"Is what bad?"

"Whatever's on your mind."

She should have known he wouldn't miss a beat. Even after nearly dying in an explosion. But she didn't want to worry him while he was recovering. She dredged up the hint of a smile. "Everything's fine."

"Fine, huh?" He lifted a brow. "Now I *know* it's bad."

So much for concealing the truth.

"I can take a guess. I talked to Cade yesterday while he was getting treated by Mya."

Oh. "What did he tell you?"

"That you met your aunt. And confronted the Sovereign."

A chill swept over her skin. "And did he tell you—"

"About Reanne? Yes." He grimaced. "I should have figured it out months ago."

That brought her up short. "Why?" She certainly hadn't.

His lips set in a grim line. "After Gaia, Knox and I had suspicions that she might be involved somehow, but no evidence to back it up. I thought she was a pawn, being coerced into following someone else's plan. I never considered the possibility that she was the ringleader."

"Neither did I."

"Of course not. You were friends."

He meant to comfort her, but the words cut like a blade.

"I was surprised you weren't here while Cade was getting checked out."

She stared at the monitor, studying the numbers as if they held the key to the universe. She didn't want to talk about Cade.

"Aurora? Did something happen between you two?"

Yes. A river of things, actually. The memory of Cade lying on the bank, deathly still, ate at her from the inside out. She folded her arms over her chest. "We're on course to Troi to drop Nat off."

"And you're avoiding the question."

She visually traced the lines in the planks of wood under her boots. "I killed him."

The Admiral was silent for a moment. "The damage to his heart? You did that?"

She nodded.

"He was in range when you used your energy field?"

The vise around her chest squeezed, pressing the air from her lungs. "I was fighting off Kreestol. My aunt. I had to use my energy to drive her back. But the river was...the water was saline. I didn't know."

"And Cade was in the river."

"Just barely. One foot. But it was enough."

The Admiral's hand rested on her arm.

She leapt back like he'd jabbed her with a red-hot poker.

His brows drew together. "It's not your fault."

He sounded just like Cade. She shook her head. "Or course it is. If you fire a weapon and kill someone unintentionally, it's still your fault."

"You're not a weapon."

"That's exactly what I am." She curled her fingers into fists, her nails digging into her palms. "And Reanne Beck seems to be the only one who understands that."

Ninety-Three

Nat stood at the wide windows of the *Starhawke's* observation lounge, gazing at the planet below.

Troi.

Her heartbeat fluttered. The last time she'd had this view, she'd been racing full throttle toward the planet's atmosphere, fleeing Tnaryt's cruiser. A crash landing in the dunes later, and she and *Gypsy* had ended up becoming residents on that cruiser. At least until the Sovereign had taken it from Tnaryt, leaving Nat and the six Setarips adrift in the wreck they'd called home for more months than she cared to remember.

She drew in a deep breath, releasing it slowly. How different her situation was now. Aurora and her crew had risked their lives to free her, and then spent the journey here helping her get *Gypsy* in top form. Jonarel Clarek, the Kraed she'd faced off against when they'd first met, had proven to be an incredibly skilled engineer. He'd made a few modifications to *Gypsy's* systems that would improve the shuttle's engine efficiency and speed. He'd also boosted the shield strength, something he'd deemed necessary after noting that the shuttle seemed to see more action than most.

He was right. And considering her line of work, that fact wasn't likely to change any time soon.

"So, this is where it all started for you."

She glanced over her shoulder.

Aurora walked up the gentle incline to the windows, each step seeming to take more effort than the last. Some of the life had gone out of her eyes, too.

"Uh-huh." She hadn't volunteered any details or explanations for her choice, and Aurora hadn't pushed, accepting her decision to return without question.

A small worry line appeared between Aurora's brows. "Will you be able to find work here?"

"Sure." That was the plan, anyway. She also had a contingency in place if work proved scarce. She'd opened the crates Tnaryt had insisted she pack in the shuttle when they'd left the ship, and discovered enough food to last her for a month or more, plus an assortment of items he'd collected from the captives she'd brought up. Clothing predominated, but also credit squares and a stockpile of weapons, some of which would bring a fair price.

And she'd need that money. She had a ship to uncover. And a new enterprise to launch.

Aurora gazed out at the planet. "And the cook is going with you?"

"Marlin? Yeah." She'd approached him a couple days ago, offering him a position as co-pilot on shuttle runs. "He doesn't have any family or anything else to go back to." Which was one of the main reasons she'd chosen to take him to Tnaryt's ship in the first place. "I owe him a debt. And I could use his help. Hauling freight is hard work." Although if things turned out as she planned, she'd need his skills with cooking food and repairing plumbing more than his ability to haul crates.

Aurora nodded. "That's...good. Although I think the Admiral was hoping you'd come back to Earth with us."

"I know." She'd visited the Admiral several times, keeping him company in the med bay while he was recovering. During their conversation yesterday, he'd made her a job offer, working as his personal pilot. She'd turned him down. "If he was the ex-Fleet engineer I thought he was,

I might have been tempted. But I can't imagine working for a Fleet admiral."

Aurora studied her. "Because he's an admiral? Or because he's the head of the Fleet?"

Nat shrugged. "Both. I'm not used to following rules and regulations. I'd hate having to toe the line. It's not my style."

Aurora's gaze shifted back to the planet. "It's not the life for everyone."

"Including you?"

Aurora looked at her out of the corner of her eye. "Meaning what?"

Nat swept her hand to encompass the entire room. "You left the Fleet to captain this ship, didn't you?"

The muscles in Aurora's jaw flexed like she was biting her tongue. "Yes, I did."

"Then there must be something this ship offered you that the Fleet didn't."

Aurora was silent for a long moment, her gaze on the stars, although Nat doubted she was seeing them. "I believed this ship would give me freedom."

She didn't look very free at the moment. "Did it?"

"I have more choices now." The words said *yes,* but her tone said *no.* The weight of responsibility was written in the tense line of her shoulders, the tightness around her mouth and eyes.

"Do you regret your decision to leave the Fleet?" Nat wasn't sure what prompted the question. Curiosity, maybe. But it felt like something deeper.

Aurora's lips turned down. "No. But I regret...other things."

Nat's chest tightened. Aurora looked...lost. Defeated. The polar opposite of the beacon of hope she'd been on

Tnaryt's ship. What had pulled a shadow over her like a death shroud?

The Admiral had evaded Nat's questions, and no one else on the ship had seemed inclined to talk about Aurora, either, including Mya and Cade. He wasn't even onboard anymore. His ship, *Gladiator*, had followed them here and hung in orbit to the *Starhawke*'s stern.

But the crew's code of silence hadn't concealed the looks of concern on their faces every time Aurora put in an appearance.

"Can you change those things? The ones you regret? Set them right?"

Aurora finally met her gaze. Nat immediately wished she hadn't. The darkness swallowed her whole.

"You can't stop a supernova. All you can do is get out of its way."

Ninety-Four

"You look like the dark side of the moon."

Cade grunted as Justin dropped into the co-pilot's seat. The description was apt. His heart certainly felt like a crater.

Aurora wouldn't talk to him. She'd cut him out of her life with the precision of a surgeon wielding a scalpel. Cardiff had delivered his belongings to *Gladiator* while Mya had been treating his injuries in the med bay. Gonzo and Drew had given him sympathetic looks when he'd stepped onboard, which had only made the pain burrow deeper.

His visit to the med bay had given him the opportunity to talk to both Mya and the Admiral. Mya had been tight-lipped about Aurora, but she'd hinted that Aurora was making emotion-driven decisions. She'd counseled him to be patient.

Following her advice was a challenge. He hadn't seen Aurora since their showdown in the conference room more than a week ago. She'd rebuffed him when he'd contacted her during the layover at Troi, redirecting any questions to Emoto. And she'd ignored the personal messages he'd sent during the trip to Earth.

He expected more of the same when they reached Sol Station, which is why he'd be heading over to the *Starhawke* as soon as they docked. The Admiral's presence on her ship gave him a good excuse to put in an appearance.

The Admiral had been shocked by the news about Reanne, but had taken it in stride. And at least it gave them a focus going forward. No more chasing a ghost they couldn't see.

Cade had also repeated his conversation with the troll who'd taken up residence in the Admiral's front office. The Admiral had agreed the man had most likely been planted there by Reanne. Unfortunately, they didn't have any evidence of her involvement in the events at Gaia, and didn't know who on the Council they could trust even if they did.

The Admiral certainly wouldn't be arriving at HQ alone. Cade's unit would be serving as personal bodyguards for the foreseeable future, just in case. The Admiral was prepared to inform Admiral Payne that he'd called the *Starhawke* off the binary star research mission to assist him with a classified Fleet mission. That would put Aurora and her crew in the clear as far as the Council was concerned. And get everyone paid.

Now if he could only get Aurora to listen to—

"Three minutes."

Cade glanced at Justin. "What?"

"Three minutes. That's how long you've been sitting there glowering in silence."

Cade grunted.

"Buddy, you have to let go. If you're not careful, your behavior will get in the way of the job we have to do."

"I won't let that happen."

"Oh, no? So you've completed the analysis of which Council members each of us will be investigating when we reach Earth?"

Cade swore. He'd forgotten all about that.

"Like I said, you gotta let it go." Justin stood, resting a hand on Cade's shoulder. "This isn't the end. She'll get over it. Give her time."

Cade blew out a breath as Justin disappeared down the corridor. How could giving her time be the right move when being apart felt so wrong?

A chime sounded, indicating they were nearing the end of the interstellar jump. Cade returned his attention to the controls, transitioning the ship smoothly from interstellar engines to main engines. Earth showed as a pale blue dot in the distance, but a much larger object appeared in his field of view as the *Starhawke* sailed past on his starboard side, the starfield reflecting off her hull like a scattering of diamonds on black velvet.

Stay with me, Rory.

But she couldn't hear his silent plea. And wouldn't have listened if she had.

The *Starhawke* pulled away, like a swan gliding effortlessly past a madly paddling duck.

He opened a comm channel to Sol Station. "This is Fleet Commander Cade Ellis aboard *Gladiator*, requesting permission to dock." He didn't have any papers for his ship, a standard requirement for all incoming vessels, but he transmitted his Fleet credentials, which would guarantee him a docking berth, anyway. The Admiral would see to that.

"Acknowledged, Commander. You may proceed to dock C3."

"Roger that. Can you also tell me where the *Starhawke* will be berthed?"

"Her navigator informed us your crews were meeting up on the station, so we're slotted them in the same terminal, C6."

"Thank you."

By the time *Gladiator* reached the station, the *Starhawke* sat at the end of the terminal, the airlock bridge already in place. Cade guided *Gladiator* to C3, aligning the airlock with the docking port. The ship gave a little shake, like a dog twitching off a fly, when the docking clamps engaged, holding the ship in place. "Docking complete," he announced over the shipboard comm. "All crew to the airlock."

The display indicated Drew was powering down the engines. Cade left the cockpit as soon as the navigation system finished its shutdown sequence, his focus on getting off the ship as quickly as possible. This might be his last chance to change Aurora's mind.

Justin, Reynolds, Gonzo and Williams were waiting by the open airlock, a line of rolling packs containing their belongings beside them.

"Bella's almost ready," Justin said. "Do you want to go ahead, or—"

"We'll wait." He might be a heartbroken idiot, but he was still the team leader. That took priority. He glanced at Reynolds. "Everything secure?"

She gave a curt nod. "*Gladiator*'s locked down until we return."

"Any idea when that might be?" Gonzo asked.

"The Admiral indicated we'd be investigating planetside for at least a week," Cade replied. "Unless we run into unexpected complications." Like discovering Reanne's claws had sunk deeper into the Council leadership than they'd anticipated.

Drew's footsteps clicked along the deck. She appeared behind Justin. "All set."

The terminal bustled with activity, the wide corridors filled with an assortment of civilian passengers and uniformed Fleet officers. Cade spotted the Admiral standing along the wall across from their dock, talking to Emoto and

Kelly. Aurora and the rest of her crew were conspicuously absent.

He wove his way through the throng, stopping in front of Emoto. "Where's Aurora?"

"On the *Starhawke*." The look in Emoto's eyes added a silent *avoiding you*.

Heat seared Cade's chest. He shot a look at Justin. "I'll be back."

"We'll wait here," Justin called out as Cade stalked off.

He wouldn't let her get away with this. They'd been through too much, come too far, for her to treat him this way. She was hurting. And afraid. He got that. But shutting him out wasn't the answer.

The entrance to C6 was closed. He stepped in front of the scanner. His Fleet ID should allow him to—

The doors opened, revealing the cylindrical bridge that connected to the *Starhawke*'s hull. He covered the distance in long strides. The ship's exterior was smooth as glass, with no visible sign of an entry point. He placed a hand on the surface as Aurora had taught him to do.

Nothing happened.

"Let me in, Star."

No change.

The Nirunoc had to be listening. Knew he was here. She just wasn't responding.

He smacked the surface with his palm as the heat rose from his chest to his throat. "Dammit, Star, *let me in!*"

Silence. He closed his hand into a fist and lifted his arm.

A door materialized out of the smooth surface, parting to reveal a female figure. But it wasn't Aurora. It was Cardiff.

"Ellis."

He dropped his arm to his side. "Cardiff." He took a step to move past her, but she blocked his path.

"I can't let you onboard."

His spine stiffened. "Why not?"

"You know why."

He pointed over her shoulder. "She's wrong."

Her brows lifted a fraction. "Perhaps. But it's still her decision to make."

"You're taking her side?" He glared at her. "I thought you believed we were good for each other."

Her gaze gentled, but her stance didn't. "I do. Most of the time. But Aurora's on shaky ground. If you push, she might fall. I won't allow that to happen."

Of all the crazy, mixed-up—

He exhaled, his gaze sweeping up in the direction of the *Starhawke*'s bridge. Aurora was up there. Hiding. From him.

The heat drained out of his body, leaving him cold. Numb. He met Cardiff's gaze. "You'll watch out for her? Keep her from doing anything stupid?" *Stupider.*

"You know I will."

For now, that would have to be enough.

Ninety-Five

Someone had turned down the volume on her life.

As Aurora stepped through the front entrance into Stoneycroft's central room, the scent of pine filled the air, accompanied by holiday music and a profusion of colored lights. Her gaze swept to the staircase, where miniature wreaths had been tied along the railing, each with a festive red bow and tiny ornaments. She and Mya used to race down those stairs on Christmas morning, making a beeline for the enormous tree and the mountain of homemade presents under the thick branches.

She was aware of it all, her senses registering the sights, sounds and smells of home, but she couldn't generate an emotional response.

Her mom stood in the kitchen, talking to Gryphon, who was bent over the stovetop. The aroma of roasting garlic drifted toward the doorway, mingling with the pine.

"—not sure if we'll have time to—" Her mom turned as Mya shut the door behind them with a soft click. Her eyes widened and her lips parted. "Aurora?" She blinked, like she expected Aurora and Mya to disappear like a mirage.

"Hi, Mom."

"Aurora!" Her mom's paralysis broke. She rushed over, engulfing Aurora in a hug that didn't end. "I can't believe you're here."

Aurora went through the motions on autopilot, waiting for her mom to release her.

Her mom wiped her hands across her eyes, leaving streaks of moisture at the corners. She glanced at Gryphon, who had wrapped his arm around Mya's shoulders. "Did you know they were coming?"

He shook his head, his habitual smile conspicuously absent. "Not this time."

The antique grandfather clock at the base of the staircase ticked out the seconds as her mom glanced around the small group. No one was smiling. Her jaw tightened. "This isn't a holiday visit, is it?"

"No."

Her weary sigh spoke volumes. "I'll go get Marina."

Gryphon poured mugs of coffee and tea as they all gathered in the central room, Aurora and Mya on one couch, Aurora's mom, Marina, and Gryphon on the other.

Her mom sat forward, resting her elbows on her knees and interlacing her fingers. "What's happened?"

Her mom's attitude was completely different this time. No evading. No defensiveness. But her skin was drawn tight over her high cheekbones, her blue-grey eyes shadowed with apprehension.

Aurora cleared her throat. "When you fled the Suulh homeworld, you believed it was destroyed. That everyone was killed. Correct?"

Her mom flinched, but didn't look away. "Yes. Although when you were here last time you said—"

"I know." Her gaze flicked to Marina and Gryphon. "And we were right. The Suulh weren't wiped out."

Marina sucked in a breath. "You know this for sure?"

Aurora glanced at Mya.

She straightened. "Yes. I saw the homeworld. And I talked to the Suulh."

The air stilled, the plunk of water in the nearby fountain and the ticking of the clock the only sounds.

Aurora's mom stared at Mya. "You *went* there? You *saw* them?" Her fingers dug into her knees, denting the fabric of her pants. She turned to Marina and Gryphon. "You—"

"We gave them the coordinates," Gryphon said.

Her mom's jaw worked, but she didn't hurl accusations. Or condemnations. Her shoulders slumped and her head dipped. She returned her attention to Mya. "What did you find?"

"The planet is heavily guarded. And the Suulh are being manipulated, fed lies that keep them subjugated. But they're alive. I also met—" She paused, her gaze shifting to Marina. "Breaa. Your mother."

Marina's breath caught and she swayed like she was on a ship. Gryphon's arm came around her, supporting her. "You...you...she..." The words wouldn't come.

Mya slid off the couch, kneeling at Marina's feet and clasping her hands. "I talked to her."

Tears fell like raindrops down Marina's cheeks. "*She's alive?*"

"Yes." Mya brushed the tears away with her thumb. "She is. And now she knows you are, too."

The raindrops turned into a flood. Marina clutched Mya in an awkward hug. Gryphon wrapped his free arm around Mya, encircling them both. The light from the Christmas tree reflected off the dampness on his cheeks.

Aurora's gaze slid to her mom.

Her throat was working, too, but her eyes were dry as she met Aurora's gaze. "Were you there?"

"No." She didn't have to lie. "Mya took the *Starhawke.* I stayed behind."

Her mom's lower lip trembled and her chin dipped a fraction. "Thank you."

Don't thank me, yet. "But..."

Her mom's spine went rigid. "But what?"

"I met one of the Suulh, too." One with the same eyes. Same chin. And a heart full of rage. "Your sister, Kreestol."

Her mom's mouth sagged open, a strangled sound working its way out of her throat. She looked like she'd just seen a ghost. In a way, she had.

Marina jerked away from Mya and Gryphon, her face pale. "You saw *Kreestol?*"

"Yes."

"*Stellar light.*"

Her mom was still processing the news. "Kreestol," she murmured, her lips barely moving. "My baby sister's alive." She took a breath, her eyes narrowing on Aurora. "Where did you see her?"

That was too hard to explain. "She found me."

"How?"

"It's a long story. But it ends with her trying to kill me. She believes she's the rightful Sahzade."

"*What!?*" The word shot out of her mom's throat with the force of a bullet.

Aurora took the hit. The truth hurt. "She hates you, too. She blames you for abandoning her."

Her mom's eyes widened, showing white around the iris. "But—" Her neck swiveled in slow motion to Marina and Gryphon. "But I...we..." She started to shake like she was caught in an earthquake. "You said—"

"She was with your parents," Gryphon said. "We couldn't reach her. Or them. Only you."

The trembling intensified. "We left her *behind?* When she was still *alive?*"

Aurora sensed her mom's pain as though it was coming to her from a great distance. Muffled. Obscured.

"We didn't have a choice, Sahzade," Marina said, resting a hand on her mom's knee. "*We* barely made it off the planet. Your safety was our priority."

Aurora barely managed to stop a very inappropriate snort. How many times had she heard a version of those words over the last few months? Now Marina was parroting them to her mom. "Kreestol's being manipulated, used as a pawn."

Her mom's gaze snapped to hers. "A pawn? By whom?"

"The Teeli. And Reanne Beck."

Her mom's face twisted in confusion. "*Reanne Beck?* What does she have to do with—"

"She's in charge of the Teeli and Setarip forces we've encountered. She's the one who's been trying to capture me."

"*Capture* you?" Her mom looked like she was waiting for the punch line. "How could Reanne be—"

"I don't understand the history, but everything that's happened—Gaia, Burrow, the Suulh—it's all been because of Reanne. And me."

Her mom shook her head. "No. That's ridiculous. Reanne's not—"

"*Yes*, she is. I saw her. Faced her. Kreestol is acting as her bodyguard. She's controlling the Teeli fleet. And she's hunting me, using the Suulh, Setarips and the Teeli to do it."

Her mom's hand went to her throat. "Why? You were friends."

Friends. The word propelled Aurora to her feet. She paced beside the couch. "I don't know. And to be honest, I don't care. The cause doesn't matter. Only the result." She paused, turning to Mya. "Tell them what you saw."

Mya drew in a slow breath as all attention shifted to her. "The Teeli have taken control of the homeworld, but the Suulh don't see it that way. They've been convinced that the Setarips are the real threat, and the Teeli are protecting them. The Suulh with limited energy abilities work to provide food and resources for the Teeli until they've produced teenage children. At that point, the adults are taken away from their families and sent to work as servants and menial laborers in the cities."

A shadow fell over Gryphon's face. "Why would the Suulh put up with that?"

"They don't know. They've been told a story that the adults go to a place called Citadel, where they work beside the Teeli and other Suulh to defeat the Setarips."

Marina perched at the edge of the couch. "Is that where you saw my mother? In one of the cities?"

"No. She and the rest of the powerful Suulh are being kept on a heavily guarded island. The Suulh who live there are strong. And they're being encouraged to develop their abilities. They're even trying to figure out a way to combine their energies to create a shield."

Aurora's mom sucked in a breath. "Why?"

"To turn them into more powerful Necri, I assume. Breaa knew about the Suulh we rescued on Gaia. Knew their names. Some of them had lived on the island."

"And the Suulh don't realize what's happening?" Marina asked.

"No. Only your mother. The rest trust the Teeli implicitly."

"What about—" Aurora's mom had to clear her throat a couple times before continuing. "What about my parents?

Did you see them?" Her gaze shifted to Aurora. "Either of you?"

"No. I only saw Kreestol."

Mya shook her head. "I didn't see them, either."

Her mom let out a shuddering breath as her eyes closed. "I'd hoped—" A single tear tracked down her cheek. "Maybe it's better if—" Her eyes snapped open. "Where's Reanne now?"

"I don't know." A dull ache throbbed at the base of Aurora's skull as she replayed the last few moments of her encounter with Reanne. "In Teeli space, I'd imagine. Or back on her carrier. Wherever that is."

"Her carrier?"

"The one that attacked us at Burrow."

"Oh."

Aurora stopped pacing, the burst of energy spent. She sank down next to Mya. "The Admiral knows about her now. She can't go back to the Council or the Rescue Corps. Those lines have been closed."

"That's something." Her mom's brow furrowed. "How much does he know about the Suulh? Does he suspect—"

"He's been aware of Mya's and my abilities since shortly after we joined the Academy."

Her mom exchanged startled glances with Marina and Gryphon. "He has?"

Aurora nodded. "He and Knox, both. He's been managing our careers to keep us away from the Teeli. Keep us safe." The bitterness tied to those words had faded while she was on Tnaryt's ship. She didn't agree with his decision, but she understood it.

"How could he know?"

"He's a resourceful man. And he'll do whatever he can to help us."

Her mom frowned. "Help us with what?" Her eyes widened. "You're not going after Reanne, are you?"

"No." She didn't have to. "But she'll be coming for me. And everyone I care about. Including you."

Her mom stared at her, unmoving, the grey-blue of her eyes coalescing into tempered steel. "I'm not afraid of Reanne Beck."

You should be. Reanne was a bona fide psycho. "She's not the main problem. Kreestol and the other Suulh are."

Her mom blinked. "What? Why?"

"Because I can't hurt them without hurting myself." She swept her arms out to her sides. "The stronger they are, the worse the effect. To stop Kreestol, I nearly debilitated myself. If Reanne can convince them to attack me, like she did with Kreestol, I'll be vulnerable. And so will you."

Her mom exchanged a long look with Marina.

"You have to tell her." Marina's voice was gentle but firm.

"But—"

"You *have* to. If you want to help her, to protect her from Reanne and the Suulh, she needs to know."

Aurora's stomach churned. Her mom had *another* secret? Were the blows ever going to end? "What do I have to know?"

Her mom refused to look at her, focusing on Marina. "She'll *hate* me."

Her mom's plea didn't soften Marina's resolve. "*Tell* her."

The churning turned into rapids. "Mom? Tell me."

Her mom turned like a mannequin, stiff and disjointed. When she met Aurora's gaze, the look in her eyes reminded Aurora of someone preparing to skydive without a parachute.

"Your ability to feel the pain of others isn't part of being the Sahzade."

Not what she'd expected. "But it's our tracking system, isn't it? How we know our people are in trouble?"

Her mom shook her head. "As Sahzade, we sense when our people are hurting or afraid. That's true. It's like a type of echolocation, allowing us to follow the signal. But unlike you, I don't *feel* their pain. Not the way you do." Her mom's voice quivered. "That particular gift came from your dad."

"My dad?" It had never occurred to her that *any* part of her abilities might have come from him. After all he was just..human. "How could I get that from him?"

"He's a powerful intuitive and empath. I suspect that's why he's able to see my energy field. And why he's always understood exactly what I'm feeling."

"So I got that from—" She halted as her mom's words registered. Her heart pounded like a base drum in her chest, steadily working its way into her throat. "You said *he's*. Present tense."

Her mom's eyes misted, her face crumbling into a mask of misery. "Yes, I did. Your dad's alive."

Ninety-Six

Here it comes. Mya clutched the edge of the couch cushion in both hands. She'd been dreading this moment since Aurora was two years old.

"He's *alive?*" Aurora went from seated to standing over Libra between one breath and the next. "What do you mean he's *alive?*"

Libra flinched, caught in the shadow of Aurora's fury. Her gaze darted to Mya's parents.

"*Don't look at Marina!*" Aurora roared, the words echoing off the domed ceiling. "Look at *me*, Mom. *I'm* the one you need to keep your eyes on." Her fingers gripped her hipbones like she was fighting the urge to wrap her hands around her mom's neck.

Libra's eyes widened. "I-I'm s-sorry. I—"

"You're *sorry?* You've kept me from my dad my *entire life* and that's what—"

"I didn't keep you from him! I was protecting—"

Aurora's hand slashed the air like a knife. "Don't say it." Her voice dropped to a deadly whisper. "Don't you *dare* say you were protecting me."

Libra's mouth opened, but no words came out.

Mya's mom spoke up. "She wasn't only protecting you, Sahzade."

Aurora redirected her ire. "Don't start with me, Marina! You've known all this time. You could have said some—"

"We had our reasons!"

"So do I! Was my dad some kind of monster? Did he threaten my life?"

"Never! Brendan's a good man."

"A good man." Aurora's lip curled away from her teeth in a snarl. "Then what *reason* is there for telling me he's dead?"

"Your brother." The words were out of Mya's mouth before she'd realized she was going to say them.

They dropped like a bomb. Her parents and Libra stared at her in shock. Had they expected to keep that particular fact a secret?

Aurora pivoted in slow motion, like a character in a horror film who's just figured out the terrifying monster is behind her. "*My brother?*"

Mya rose on wobbly legs. She'd started this. She'd see it through. Aurora deserved to know the truth. All of the truth. "You have an older brother. Micah."

Now Aurora looked ready to topple over.

Mya reached out a hand to steady her.

She didn't resist. "I have a *brother?*"

"Yes. You were almost two when he and your dad left."

Libra fidgeted like she was sitting on an anthill. "Mya, I don't—"

Mya cut her off with a look.

"They left?" Aurora echoed, ignoring her mom. "Why?"

"To keep you both hidden from the Teeli."

"The Teeli?" Two spots of color bloomed in Aurora's cheeks. "They left because of the *Teeli?*"

Mya nodded.

Aurora craned her neck around, her gaze locking onto her mom. "What happened?"

Libra looked a little green, but she answered the question. "The Teeli tracked us to Fleet space. Made contact with Earth. You were so young. Your abilities so strong. I was afraid the Teeli–" She swallowed, her chest rising and falling with her rapid breathing. "Micah wasn't like you. He didn't have your abilities. He was more human than Suulh. I knew he'd be safe with your dad. But when he left–"

Aurora held up her hand. It shook like a leaf. "How old was he? When my dad took him?"

Libra's gaze darted between Mya and Aurora. "Three. A year-and-a-half older than you." She tilted her head, an odd mixture of fear and hope on her face. "Do you remember him?"

Aurora didn't act like she'd heard the question. Her gaze drifted to the staircase, slowly tracing the curve of the bannister and gliding along the open floor to the front entry. "Micah." Her voice was barely a whisper. "Yes, I remember."

Mya's breath caught as Aurora's gaze met hers. Fire and brimstone burned in the green depths.

"*You* weren't My-a. *He* was."

Ninety-Seven

The tendrils of Aurora's dream settled over her like a cloud, obscuring the present and transporting her to the past.

Her dad standing by the front door, clasping My-a's hand.

Not Mya. *My-a.*

It hadn't been a dream. It had been a memory. She just hadn't known what she was seeing—the night her dad had taken her brother and walked out of her life.

Now, the image was crystal clear. As was the little boy with dark blonde hair who called her Ror. And loved her with all his heart.

My-a. The closest her child self had come to pronouncing *Micah.*

An arrow pierced her flesh, shooting pain through her limbs and creating a hole that bled tears. She had a *brother.* A brother she'd *loved.* A brother she'd mourned, unknowing, for twenty-five years.

And the four people in this room had let her. Encouraged her. Convinced her to forget the brother she'd cherished.

The fire stoked in Aurora's core, the heat melting her self-control.

Mya paled, but didn't shy away. "You were heartbroken when he left. Inconsolable. I tried to soothe you—we all did—but—"

"It didn't work."

"No. You'd scream his name for hours, sobbing yourself to sleep. I moved into your room, stayed with you,

comforted you as much as I could. And over time, you
started to associate me with the name My-a."

"And you let me." She spit the words out like razor
blades.

Mya—*no. Lelindia*—took a step back. "It was the only
way to—"

"Deceive me?"

"Heal you."

Aurora snorted. "Thanks for that." She turned on her
mom. "Where are they?"

Her mom's hands fluttered in her lap. "They're in H-
Hawaii."

Her mouth dropped open. "*Hawaii?*' She was *such* an
idiot. All this time she'd believed her mom avoided traveling
to the tropics because she couldn't handle the heat. But that
hadn't been the reason at all. "*Where* in Hawaii?"

"Oahu. They work at the university."

Flames licked up her ribcage. "You've *talked* to
them?"

"No! I just...well, your dad and I...we—"

"Does Micah know?"

Her mom frowned. "Know what?"

"That he has a *sister!*'

Aurora's screech flattened her mom against the
back of the couch, her hand on her heart. "I-I...don't. No. I
don't think so."

"You don't *think* so. What about my dad? Does he
even care that I'm *alive?*'

Her mom's chin came up as her brows snapped
down. "Your dad loves you. He's always wanted to know how
you're doing."

"But not enough to be part of my *life*." If he *really*
loved her, he wouldn't have stayed away. "I'm not a child

anymore. I've been out in the world a long time, Mom. Out in *space!* He should have—"

"He couldn't!"

"Why not?"

"Because I told him not to!"

Ice froze Aurora's feet to the floor. The chill spread through her bones as it crept up her legs and torso. She shuddered. "*You told him not—*"

"I had to." Her mom faded into the couch like a wraith, her voice barely a whisper. "If you knew he was alive—"

"I would have had a *father!*" The inferno roared, consuming her. Moisture glazed her eyes, making it impossible to see. She had to get away. Had to go. Had to—

She was outside without any idea how she'd gotten there. Her feet pounded along the driveway, taking her to a well-worn dirt path. The crunch of gravel gave way to the thud of packed earth. The glow from the house dimmed as the trees surrounded her, but she didn't need light. She'd traveled this path a thousand times. She knocked branches out of her way with her shield, the warmth of the energy enveloping the firestorm within, turning her into a miniature volcano.

A massive redwood loomed in front of her, its multi-jointed arms reaching to the sky. Her breath rasped as she collapsed at its feet, a scream tearing from her throat as she pounded her fists in the dirt and raised her face to the stars. Her shield exploded, slamming into the silent sentinel and sending bark flying like spearheads in all directions.

Aurora collapsed on her side, curling into a tight ball with her arms wrapped around her knees. *Too much. Toomuchtoomuchtoomuch...*

The world faded away as she fell into a black hole.

Ninety-Eight

The chill of the damp earth woke her. She brushed the leaves and dirt from her cheek and sat up. Without her energy field to insulate her, the December chill cut through her shirt like it was tissue paper.

She crossed her arms over her chest, too weary to generate a field. Getting her feet under her, she stumbled forward, retracing her steps along the path until the glow of the driveway lamps guided her to the front door. She climbed the flagstone steps, her boots like anvils on her feet. The wooden door opened soundlessly, closing with a soft click as she stepped inside the darkened room.

A lamp shone from the table beside the couch.

Mya was waiting for her. She put down the book she'd been reading and rose, walking with hesitant steps to where Aurora stood, watching her.

Mya's gaze swept over her. "You went to the tree, didn't you?"

"Yes." The giant redwood had been her friend, her secret companion since she was a child. Its solid presence had always brought her comfort. Now it bore her battle scars.

"Aurora, I—" Mya spread her hands in a helpless gesture. "I'm sorry."

Aurora stared at her. *Sorry.* Such a small word for the years of deception, the loss, the betrayal. But what more was there to say? Nothing. Except to ask the one question she had left.

"Are there more secrets?"

Mya pulled her shoulders back, her gaze steady. "None that I know. Whether our parents are still holding some cards, well..." She gestured to the gallery above that connected the two family wings. "Only they can answer that."

Mya's emotions were as steady as her gaze. She was telling the truth. Or at least the truth as she knew it to be. "So where does that leave us?"

"That's up to you." Mya folded her hands in front of her. "I love you, Sahzade. That may be difficult for you to believe right now, but it's the truth. And I want to help you. If you'll let me."

"How?"

"Go with you to see your dad, for one. I think he could help you with your reaction to the Suulh, perhaps teach you to control your empathic response so it's not so debilitating."

"Why would he help me? He doesn't even know me."

"Of course he does! And he loves you. More than you know."

"How can you say that? You haven't seen him since we were children."

"Actually, that's not true. He came to your Academy graduation ceremony."

A tremor passed along Aurora's spine. "He did?"

"Yes. Libra doesn't know. He didn't tell her. But he told my parents. He wanted to see you. To see the woman you'd become."

Her heart thumped. "He was there?" She'd been so close. And hadn't even realized it. "Did you see him?"

"Briefly. From a distance. He was watching us when we were taking group pictures."

Her dad had come to her graduation? He'd watched her. Seen her. Cared enough to be there, even if he couldn't let her know.

Her throat tightened. She had a father. A father who *cared.* "Do you really think he could help me?" The thought generated a tiny glow of hope. Not much, but it was something.

"Yes. His empathic abilities are incredible. Possibly stronger than yours."

And if she went to see her dad, she could see Micah, too. Maybe. "What about Micah? Is he empathic?" That would give them something in common.

Mya's gaze softened. "I don't think so. He never showed signs of any abilities. He just enhanced yours."

Aurora frowned. "What do you mean?"

"It's part of the reason your mom was determined to separate you when the Teeli reached Earth." Mya sighed. "You were already so strong. Even your mom was amazed how much power you wielded, especially since Micah didn't have any energy abilities. But when the two of you were together." Mya made a swirling motion with her hands. "It was like Micah amplified everything about you—your shielding, your energy, even your emotions—and made them ten times more intense."

"Like the way you and I boosted your healing effect with the Suulh?"

Mya shook her head. "Uh-uh. We had to consciously merge our fields to make that happen. I channeled your energy to enhance mine. Your connection with Micah was different. He didn't have an energy field, but if he was near you, and especially when he touched you, your abilities went off the charts."

Her skin tingled. What Mya was saying was— "But why did my mom want to separate us if Micah made me stronger? Wasn't I safer with him around?"

"Except you were already drawing attention. Your parents had trouble explaining some of the incidents that had already occurred while you and Micah were out in public. All it would have taken was for a news post to reach the Teeli about the unusual occurrences—"

"And they would have caught us." She dropped her chin to her chest and squeezed her eyes shut. "As long as we were together, we were in danger."

"Yes. That's why your parents separated. Why Micah lived with your dad and you stayed here with us."

The logic was inescapable. And it cut through her like a sword. Her connection to her brother had driven them apart. If only the Teeli hadn't—

She shut down that train of thought before it gathered steam. In fact, judging by the shaking in her limbs, she needed to halt all the thought trains for a while.

She drew in air, filling her lungs and exhaling just as slowly. Lifting her head, she met Mya's gaze. "I'm going to bed."

A crease appeared between Mya's brows. "Okay." She raised a hand as if to rest it on Aurora's arm, but let it fall. "We can talk more in the morning."

"Morning," Aurora echoed, her feet already taking her toward the staircase. She climbed the steps, forcing her mind to remain blank, muscle memory carrying her to her childhood room. Not even bothering to change clothes, she slipped off her boots and collapsed on the bed, face first.

Ninety-Nine

Mya bolted upright like she'd been prodded with a poker. She blinked, trying to make sense of the shapes and shadows around her. Her conscious mind wasn't keeping up. What was going on? She was in bed. Was she even awake? Or was she still asleep?

She stared into the darkness as her surroundings steadily resolved into the familiar images of her childhood room. But the feeling of unreality didn't fade.

She looked around, but nothing seemed out of place. Her door and window were still closed. No sounds broke the stillness, no lights lit the interior other than the pale moon's glow. There was no indication whatsoever of why she'd woken so abruptly.

Slowly lowering her body to the mattress, she pressed her cheek into her pillow and sighed. Maybe she was still dreaming. It had been a stressful evening. If she closed her eyes, maybe she'd wake—

She snapped upright again. No. She wasn't dreaming. Something was wrong. Something important. And she needed to find out what.

Slipping out of bed, she grabbed her robe, pulling it on as she opened her door and stepped into the corridor. She paused, listening for any sounds that might clue her in to what she was sensing.

She tied the sash on her robe as she moved along the corridor to the gallery and the stairway beyond. Down one flight and up another, then following another corridor to reach her destination.

The hinges didn't make a sound as she pushed the solid wood door open and stepped inside. The moonlight painted fairy script on the frosted windows across the way, creating a pale glow on the fluffy cream blanket draped across the bed. Aurora's bed.

She hesitated, listening intently, but the room didn't give up any secrets. Drawing a breath to steady the flutter of her pulse, she crept across the floor. But even before she switched on the bedside lamp, she knew what she would find.

The bed was empty.

She surveyed the room. No sign of Aurora's pack. She walked to the closet and opened the door. Nothing there, either.

Fighting down panic, she allowed her gaze to sweep the room once more. This time, she spotted an envelope on top of the desk, anchored by a piece of polished rose quartz in the shape of a heart.

A name was written on the front. *Lelindia.*

Her given name. The one Aurora never used.

Mya's hand shook as she picked up the envelope and turned it over, pulling out a single sheet of paper. She sank onto the edge of the bed, the paper clutched in her hand. It only contained one line of text, written in Aurora's curving script.

Until I return, the ship is yours.

Aurora was gone.

Captain's Log

Aurora's Journey

Aurora really took a hit in this story. And she let me
know it. She had me bawling by the time she came apart at
the end.

When I started this book, I didn't intend to make her
suffer page after page after page. In fact, the revelation of
the Sovereign's identity was originally the only blow I
planned to deliver.

But the story that unfolded as I followed Aurora
into the wilds made it clear that she was surrounded by lies
and half-truths, and it was finally time for many of those to
come to light.

Unfortunately for Aurora, that meant she had to
deal with them, one after the other.

Walking that road with her has been a challenge
and a privilege. And it means this particular book doesn't end
with the warm fuzzies of the previous two. More the feel of
The Empire Strikes Back or *The Wrath of Khan* than *Star
Wars.* Sometimes we have to hit rock bottom before we can
pick ourselves up.

But if I've learned one thing about Aurora Hawke,
it's that she will always find a way back to her path, even
when she's lost in the darkness. Never fear. Her journey has
just begun.

From Sanctuary to Citadel

In the original version of this story, I'd envisioned
the Teeli telling the Suulh that their elders were taken to an

island sanctuary, not a citadel. A place where the older Suulh relaxed and were cared for by the Teeli after working hard to grow food.

But that idea didn't fit very well when I tried to explain why the thirty-something parents would willingly abandon their teenage children. Leaving the village to go lounge around on a tropical island for the rest of their lives while their children stayed behind and worked wasn't noble. Or sympathetic. Which is why Sanctuary became Citadel, and Faahn's story of what happened when the Suulh went there became a tale of personal sacrifice for the greater good.

Faahn was much happier, and so was I.

The evolution of Nat

Nat turned out to be one of those happy accidents I hadn't anticipated. In fact, the first version of the character she eventually became wasn't anything like her. The character was male, a vile egomaniac who ended up being killed off by Tnaryt shortly after Aurora was brought onboard.

But it didn't work. I felt like I was bending and molding my main characters to fit with him, which made no sense. Clearly, I didn't like him, since I'd killed him within a couple chapters of introducing him.

I went back to the drawing board. First, I transferred a lot of his personality traits to Weezel, since I still wanted Aurora to have to deal with that dynamic. Then I asked some tough questions about who I wanted Aurora to interact with on Tnaryt's ship. My first idea was to get Drew onboard with her, and I even wrote a few scenes that way. That caused complications, too, but it gave me insight into what I wanted. The character had to be female, and she needed to be, if not heroic, at least sympathetic. Someone Aurora could form an uneasy alliance with.

Nat came into focus pretty quickly after that. And the more I wrote about her, the more fascinated I became. She wasn't anything like the other major characters in my series. She thought of herself first, others second, but at the same time, when push came to shove, she tended to do the right thing, even when it cost her.

I liked her so much by the end of this book that I wrote a short story prequel, ROGUE, that explains how she ended up on Tnaryt's ship. Check out my website for info on how to obtain your copy.

Enjoy the journey!
Audrey

P.S. - I always write to music, and I select a different piece of music for each story, one that feeds the mood I need to get the words flowing. If you'd like to experience this story the way I did, listen to the soundtrack for *Avengers: The Age of Ultron* while you read.

Audrey Sharpe grew up believing in the Force and dreaming of becoming captain of the Enterprise. She's still working out the logistics of moving objects with her mind, but writing science fiction provides a pretty good alternative. When she's not off exploring the galaxy with Aurora and her crew, she lives in the Sonoran Desert, where she has an excellent view of the stars.

For more information about Audrey and the Starhawke universe, visit her website and join the crew!

AudreySharpe.com